A
Plain
Love
Song

Other books by Kelly Irvin

THE BLISS CREEK AMISH

To Love and to Cherish
▶ http://bit.ly/ToLoveandtoCherish

A Heart Made New
▶ http://bit.ly/HeartMadeNew

Love's Journey Home
▶ http://bit.ly/LovesJourneyHome

THE NEW HOPE AMISH

Love Still Stands
▶ http://bit.ly/LoveStillStands

Love Redeemed
▶ http://bit.ly/LoveRedeemed

A
Plain
Love
Song

KELLY IRVIN

HARVEST HOUSE PUBLISHERS
EUGENE, OREGON

Cover by Garborg Design Works, Savage, Minnesota

Cover photos © Chris Garborg; Iakov Kalinin, geargodz / Bigstock

A PLAIN LOVE SONG

Copyright © 2014 by Kelly Irvin
Published by Harvest House Publishers
Eugene, Oregon 97402
www.harvesthousepublishers.com

Library of Congress Cataloging-in-Publication Data
Irvin, Kelly.
A plain love song / Kelly Irvin.
      pages cm. — (The New Hope Amish ; book 3)
   ISBN 978-0-7369-5498-3 (pbk.)
   ISBN 978-0-7369-5499-0 (eBook)
   1. Amish—Fiction. 2. Life change events—Fiction. 3. Musicians—Fiction I. Title.
   PS3609.R82P55 2014
   813'.6—dc23

                                                                2013043582

Printed in the United States of America

              14 15 16 17 18 19 20 21 22 / LB-JH / 10 9 8 7 6 5 4 3 2 1

To Tim, Erin, and Nicholas
Love always

Shout for joy to the Lord, all the earth,
burst into jubilant song with music
make music to the Lord with the harp,
with the harp and the sound of singing,
with trumpets and the blast of the ram's horn—
shout for joy before the Lord, the king.
Let the sea resound and everything in it,
the world, and all who live in it.
Let the rivers clap their hands,
let the mountains sing together for joy;
let them sing before the Lord,
for he comes to judge the earth.
He will judge the world in righteousness
and the peoples with equity.

Psalm 98:4-9

The Original New Hope Families

Luke & Leah
Shirack
William
Joseph
Esther & Martha
(twins)
Jebediah
Hazel

Thomas & Emma
Brennaman
Eli
Rebecca
Caleb
Lilah
Mary & Lillie Shirack
(Emma's sisters)

Benjamin & Irene
Knepp
Hiram
Daniel
Adah
Melinda
Abram
Joanna
Jonathan

Elijah & Bethel
Christner
John

Silas & Katie
Christner
Jesse
Simon
Martin
Phoebe
Elam
Hannah
Lydia
Sarah
Ida Weaver
(Katie's sister)

Tobias & Edna
Daugherty
Jacob
Michael
Ephraim
Nathaniel
Margaret
Isabel

Aaron & Mary
Troyer
Matthew
Molly
Reuben
Abraham & Alexander
(twins)
Ella
Laura

Peter & Cynthia
Daugherty
Rufus
Enos
Deborah
Rachel
John
Mark
Phillip
Ruth
Naomi

Chapter 1

Not having a pencil and paper handy made writing a song a challenge for Adah Knepp.

But then she liked a challenge.

Adah belted out the lyrics, the *bob-bob* of the horse's head along with the *clip-clop* of his hooves keeping time on the highway. The squeaking of the buggy wheels joined in. Her voice carried on the warm June wind across the wheat fields of Missouri. Sparrows preening on the power lines that ran along the road served as her only audience. They probably thought she'd gone crazy, talking to herself.

She closed her eyes for a second, listening to her own words. They weren't quite right. They didn't sound like the songs she heard on the radio while she cleaned the Harts' house. Not like Carrie Underwood or Taylor Swift with their sweet voices. She sounded flat. Of course, she didn't have the benefit of steel guitars, fiddles, keyboards, and drums. She stomped one black sneaker and then the other against the floorboard, picking up the beat. "Love like sun-kissed apples..." She shook her head. *Nee, nee.* "Love like a baby's sweet kisses..."

No, that wasn't it either. Still mulling over the words, she turned into the open gate adorned with a huge wrought iron *H* and onto the sunflower-lined dirt road that led to the Hart farm. She would clean the house lickety-split and use the rest of the afternoon to work on her song before she went home. That way she wouldn't be late and *Mudder* wouldn't have cause to complain. *Stop mooning around, Adah, and get to work. Those dishes won't wash themselves.*

Which, of course, they wouldn't. Having six brothers and sisters, Adah surely wished they would. How about that for a fanciful notion?

She could write her song, cook, clean, and still be ready to take a ride after dark if Matthew Troyer should happen to shine his flashlight in her window. *Gott* was good.

A horse whinnied, an uncertain, unhappy sound that carried on a breeze that kept the day from being stifling hot. A man answered in a soft, coaxing singsong. The voice reminded Adah of the announcer on the radio the Harts kept tuned to a country music station. It was husky like sandpaper, yet smooth and warm like *kaffi* made with an extra dollop of milk and three pinches of sugar.

"Come on, steady, come on, you're okay, I promise. It's fine, it's okay, it's fine," the voice sang in a steady patter of sweet nothings.

Drawn by the velvety words, Adah hopped from the buggy and approached the fence. The voice belonged to a tall, lean man with a shock of black hair, ruffled and sweat-soaked under the rim of a dirty straw cowboy hat. He held a blanket in one hand while he used his other hand to hold the lead rope attached to a tawny Palomino with a long dark mane and tail. The man wore a T-shirt and tattered jeans faded to a blue-white. The sun glinted on the huge silver buckle on a belt that hugged his narrow hips.

"Come on, come on, girl," he crooned as he crept closer to the horse. "It won't hurt you, I promise. Remember this blanket? We played with it yesterday. You remember."

At that moment he looked across the corral and their gazes met. "Hey there, Amish girl."

He said *Amish girl* as if it were her full name. As if he'd been waiting for her. As if he were glad to see her. It made her smile. "I'm Adah."

Letting the lead rope out, he sidled away from the horse without turning his back on it. The horse pranced and arched her long neck as if she knew she no longer had the man's complete attention. "I know. Adah the Amish girl. The house cleaner."

Mrs. Hart called her the maid, a word that didn't bother Adah in the least. She did honest work and what she earned helped her family pay for the things they needed, things they couldn't grow or make.

"That's me."

For some reason she couldn't string words together in a simple sentence. She edged toward the buggy. She shouldn't have stopped. She should've gone right up to the house. *Mind yourself with these* Englischers. Mudder's voice echoed in her ears. *You clean their houses. That's all.*

"I'm Jackson Hart."

Adah figured as much. He was the spitting image of his father. She'd started working at the Harts' after Jackson left for the spring semester of college so she hadn't met him, but she recognized him from the dozens of photos that lined the walls of the Hart living room and the room they referred to as the study. The study where she lingered over her dusting so she could run her fingers over the ivory keys of a grand piano. On the wall were photos of family members posing with horses and steers and trophies and ribbons.

Jackson glanced at the horse and then back at Adah. "You ever seen someone break a horse to a saddle?"

"My *daed*—my father—does it."

"Maybe he should come do this one. This filly's a stinker."

"She's willful." That's what her daed said about Adah. He said she was worse than a wild horse when it came to being stubborn. Her mudder said she inherited that from Daed. Either way, she'd made more than her share of trips to the woodshed as a little girl. "She doesn't want to give up her wild ways."

Like Adah had been doing since starting her *rumspringa*. She'd been avoiding baptism for two years now.

"My brother says he can't be ridden. The family we bought her from waited too long to break her, but I think she can be taught to be a lady. Today is her day to learn who's boss." Jackson grinned, his teeth white against the dark stubble on his chin. The bottom teeth were a little crooked, but they took nothing away from the blinding effect. "That would be me. I'm gonna turn her into a rodeo horse."

Adah had seen the rodeo when her family went to the county fair to visit the exhibits. They didn't have money to buy tickets, but she'd peeked into the arena. Riding a bucking horse or bull or lassoing a bawling calf for sport didn't make much sense to her.

"I'd better get in the house." The words came out in a stutter. Why, she had no idea. She heaved a breath and tried again. "There are floors to be mopped."

"Mom went to the grocery store. Then she's stopping by the house in town." Somehow he made this information sound like an invitation to stay. "You've got all the time in the world."

"This house is big. Takes me all day."

"Yeah, but it's not like we're pigs or anything—well, except Rae-Anne, but she's at the house in town most of the time. I'm pretty good at picking up after myself and so is Jeff."

RaeAnne stayed at the farm sometimes and it always meant more work for Adah. Jeff, the other brother, kept his room neat and tidy, but she still had to vacuum, dust, take out the trash, and generally straighten up after him. She didn't mind. That was what they paid her to do. "You're never here, so I don't know."

"I'm here now."

No doubt about that. Adah couldn't take her gaze from him, as much as she didn't know why. She should get in the buggy. She didn't move.

Still grinning as if he liked having an audience, Jackson edged toward the horse, who snorted and tossed her head.

"Come on, girl. It's time. You know me. I'd never steer you wrong. You can trust me. It's just a blanket. You've seen this blanket before, remember?" He held it up. "It's nice. Soft. Warm. It's light. You won't even feel it on your back. I promise."

A chill ran up Adah's arms despite the June heat. Jackson spoke to the horse, not her. Still, she took a step back.

With a gentle flick of his wrist, he settled the blanket on the Palomino's back. The animal responded with a high, angry whinny. She sidestepped, snorted, and shook her head.

A second later, she reared and bucked, hooves flailing.

Still hanging on to the lead rope, Jackson stumbled back. "It's okay. It's okay, sweetheart, we're doing fine."

The words seemed overly optimistic. The Palomino came down and then reared again, bucking and shrieking.

Jackson moved, but not fast enough. The horse's front hooves connected with his chest.

Jackson crumpled to the ground.

Chapter 2

Adah raced to the corral gate and fought with the latch. Her shaking fingers wouldn't make it work. She fumbled with it, her gaze on Jackson. He sprawled on the ground. Not moving. She had to help him. Heart clanging against her ribs, she tugged on the gate.

Come on. Come on.

The Palomino snorted, reared, and bucked. Her front hooves came down on Jackson's leg. He rolled, came up on his hands and knees, and tried to crawl forward.

Her panting loud in her ears, Adah forced her fingers to navigate the latch. The gate swung open. She squeezed through and pushed it shut behind her.

Not taking her gaze from the horse with its frothing mouth and wild eyes, she scurried across the expanse to the man on the ground. "Can you get up?"

"Get out of here. Get out!" Jackson tried to lift himself up on his knees and then sank back, his face contorted in pain. "Get out."

And let him get trampled again? "Let me help you up."

The horse stampeded in a circle along the fence, its mane flying. She whinnied, tossed her head, and stormed toward Adah.

Adah froze for a split second. *Think. Think. Think.*

The Palomino was a gorgeous creature. God's creature. But God had put humans in charge—at least that's what her daed always said about

15

their livestock. She grabbed her apron and flapped it hard. "Haw, haw, get, yahaw, get!" She stomped her feet. "Go on, get along. Get along."

The horse veered left and raced away. She began to circle the fence as if seeking a way to escape. Adah darted toward Jackson and knelt next to him. Blood soaked one shoulder of his torn T-shirt. A gash ran along his collarbone. It was already beginning to darken in a long, deep, purple bruise. He clutched at his pant leg just above the boot, his breathing harsh. "Well, that was just stupid."

"You've not seen a horse react that way before?" She had, but Daed had never been hurt breaking a horse. He said it was his voice. Horses trusted him. "She doesn't know you. You just got here."

"I spent two days getting her used to the blanket. She walked all over it yesterday." Jackson gasped, a vein pulsing in his temple. "Do we really have to argue about this now? Help me up."

He held out his hand. She hesitated for a tiny second. His dark blue eyes sparkled and widened. "I don't have cooties. I promise."

"I know. I know." She took his hand. His fingers were long, his skin hard and callused. She'd never touched a man other than her family and Matthew. "I just...You need to go to the hospital."

"Nope. Help me up."

He weighed a good thirty pounds more than she did, but Adah let him lean into her as he struggled to his feet. His left leg buckled. He gasped as they nearly went down together. Inhaling his scent of sweat, cigarette smoke, and aftershave that reminded her of the woods, she braced her legs and stiffened her back. His arm went around her neck. His warm, ragged breath touched her cheek as he fought to stand up right. Together, they shambled toward the gate.

Adah glanced back. The horse pranced and snorted, its hooves digging the now torn blanket into the ground. "Come on, hurry." She tightened her grip around Jackson's waist and urged him toward the gate. "We're almost there."

A groan escaped his gritted teeth.

"Is it your shoulder or your leg?"

"Both."

She shoved the gate open just enough to let them squeeze through. Once on the other side, Jackson slid to the ground while she fastened the latch, turned, and sagged against it.

"Haw, get, yahaw?" Jackson chuckled and then coughed. "An angry filly is throwing a fit and you come storming in and flap your apron at her?"

"You're welcome."

"You're crazy, girl. I would've gotten myself out of there."

"On your hands and knees?" Adah should've left him on his own. "And then that horse would've kicked you two or three more times in the backside for good measure."

Jackson leaned over and spat blood on the ground.

"Maybe you're right." His face turned white under the beginnings of a summer tan. Teeth gritted, he inhaled and then exhaled. His dirty, blood-spattered hand went to his head. "Lost my hat. I don't suppose you want to go back in there and get it for me."

Adah tossed a quick glance at the corral. The hat was as flat as her chicken fried steak. No loss. It appeared old and dirty and sweaty. Besides, Jackson looked better without it. His thick black curls were damp with sweat and dust, but he had a nice head of hair. She gave herself a mental shake. No thinking about a strange man's hair. What had gotten into her? No wonder the *Ordnung* called for hats for all men and prayer *kapps* for women. "Forget it. It's a goner."

"It's not like I don't have half a dozen more in the house." Jackson shifted and stuck a hand on the fence as if to pull himself up. He didn't make much progress. "Help me get up. I need to get into the house."

"You need to go to the hospital. You're coughing up blood."

"Ain't the first time I've been kicked by a horse and won't be the last, I reckon." He coughed and spat more blood. "I bit my tongue, that's all. A cold soda pop, a cigarette, and a couple of aspirin and I'm good."

He had a strange way of doctoring himself. "Cigarettes will kill you if the horse doesn't. Is your father here?"

"He's out baling hay. I left my cell phone on the porch with my coffee cup. I need it and a cigarette bad."

"Stay. I'll get the phone for you." The cigarettes he could get under his own steam.

"Stay? What do I look like, a dog?"

Jackson Hart looked like he'd been beaten to a pulp by a guy twice his size and he was still full of vinegar, as Daed would say. "Just hush. I'll be back." Marveling at how quickly she'd learned to talk back to this Englisch man with his silver buckle and torn blue jeans, she turned and ran.

Better to put some distance between her and that silver buckle.

Chapter 3

Tired to the bone, Adah trudged from the barn to her house, the calico momma cat who lived there following her, surely hoping for scraps. Not tonight. Not even the thought of her mudder's fried chicken could make Adah lift her feet any faster. It had been a long day and she was late. Likely there wasn't much of that chicken left. It couldn't be helped. By the time Mr. Hart came in from the field and carted Jackson off to the New Hope medical center emergency room, Adah had been far behind in her work cleaning the house. She'd scrubbed it from top to bottom, concentrating on the kitchen first, where it looked as if Mrs. Hart had been making bread, such was the flour flung in all directions and the dough dried and caked on the counter. Floors had to be mopped, toilets cleaned, and furniture dusted. No one had returned by the time she finished, so she locked the front door as she'd been instructed in the past, pocketed the key that had been entrusted to her on her very first visit, and hurried home.

Momma cat meowed. Adah stooped to scratch her behind the ears. The cat rubbed up against her shoes and meowed again, a mournful yowl. "You must've had a bad day too." Adah patted her back. The cat's purr revved. "You should be taking care of your babies. You'd better run home to them."

"Where have you been?"

Adah jumped, straightened, and slapped her hand to her chest.

19

Momma cat bolted across the yard. Adah had been so deep in thought, she hadn't even noticed Daed sitting in a folding lawn chair on the front porch. It said nothing good if he'd decided to wait out front for her return. She sucked in a breath and steadied herself. "At the Harts'. There was an accident—"

"We'll get to that in a minute." He rose and stomped over to the steps, a sheaf of papers clutched in one hand. Adah's heart contracted in a painful one-two punch. Her throat closed. She wiped her damp palms on her apron. Daed knew. He knew. He shook the papers at her. "What are these?"

"What are what?" She stalled for time as she climbed the steps. She wanted to whirl and flee the way Momma cat had. Flee where? She couldn't hide in the barn forever. Her whole world existed right here on this farm, in this small community of Plain folks. "Where did you get those?"

"Your mudder found them in your room."

In a box Adah kept under her bed. She had nothing that was hers alone. The thought pressed on her. Even though she didn't have to share her room with her sisters, she still had no space to call her own. "It's nothing, just scribblings. Little poems to pass the time."

"Ben." The screen door creaked and Mudder stuck her head through the opening. "Might be better if we talk inside."

Mudder, with her soft voice and ready smile, had a way about her. A way of soothing Daed that fascinated Adah. As cantankerous as he might be sometimes, his rough edges smoothed whenever Irene Knepp walked into the room. Adah loved that about her mother.

"Fine." Daed clomped through the door. "Get in here."

Adah followed them both into the front room where Daed towered over her, his face stony and unreadable. They stood for a few seconds. No one spoke. Daed dropped the papers on the oak table wedged between two hickory rocking chairs. He crossed his arms over his broad chest and directed a frown at Mudder. "Tell her."

"I was looking to see what old dresses you might have outgrown. Figured I could take them down for Melinda." Mudder wiped her hands on a dishtowel, her thin fingers gripping it until the knuckles were white. Adah knew how she hated being in the middle. It seemed she always landed there. "I found a few things."

She nodded toward the table. Next to the papers lay the iPod. Adah closed her eyes. Her stomach rocked in waves of nausea. She smoothed her apron with sweaty palms. "I know—"

"I know you've chosen to dig your heels in and run around for over two years now." Daed's scowl deepened, his blue eyes full of angry flame. "I ain't said much. Not my place. But this"—his big, callused hand swept an arch over the table—"this I won't abide by. I don't abide by having this junk in my house. You know better."

"Daed—"

"And this stuff you call scribblings. Looks like songs to me. Songs about things you shouldn't be talking about, even thinking about. I brought you up right." He gathered steam as he went, his deep voice bordering on a bellow, stunning Adah into taking a half-step back. He never raised his voice. Never. "I've told your mudder more than once that you've taken this too far. Now you've proven me right."

"We only want to know our *dochder* hasn't lost her way." Mudder inched toward Adah. Her voice remained soft, but if she didn't stop wringing the towel it would be ripped into two pieces soon. "These words you've written here…they're…worrisome."

"They're just poems. I've always written poems." Adah tried to match Mudder's tone. She swallowed against the knot in her throat, determined to keep her voice even. No tears. No fear. "You know how I like to put words on paper. That's all it is. Poems."

Daed snatched up the top paper and smoothed the wrinkles he'd inflicted earlier. "What are these notes, then? They look like chords. Music. That's what it looks like to me. I've seen sheet music." He fixed his stern gaze on her. "I'm not stupid, dochder. I was young once too."

Hard to believe. Time had carved harsh lines around his mouth and eyes. White lines like scars from years of hard work in the sun. Silver and gray bolted in thick lines through his long beard. Lines, too, that bore witness to tragedy that went back before Adah's time. She ducked her head. Here she was giving them more grief. "It's just for…for fun, that's all. It doesn't mean anything."

"You've heard Luke and Silas talk about the slippery slope? Writing *Englisch* songs about love and such nonsense…" Daed crumpled the papers and shook them in her face. The corner of one sheet caught her on the chin. She flinched and jerked back. He lowered his hand, something like sorrow enveloping his rock-hard features. "This is that slope. Right here. It's time, girl. Time you put away foolishness. You should be studying for the baptism classes. The confession of faith. I don't see you working on that."

Adah swallowed, caught in his furious gaze. She'd never seen him so angry. Not even when he caught her sneaking from the house in jeans and a T-shirt on her very first foray into the Englisch world the night after her sixteenth birthday. Then he'd shoved his hat down on his head, turned his back on her, and walked away, his disappointment radiating in the stiff set of his shoulders. "I go to the classes. I listen. I do the reading. I try. It's just—"

"It's just what?" Daed growled. "It's not fun? Life isn't fun and it's time you learned that."

"What your daed means to say is we know it's been hard for you since we moved here." Mudder tossed the towel over her shoulder and turned on the pole lamp, her back to them both. She hated this. She hated to see discord between father and daughter. "I thought it would be better after the Masts moved in up the road with Mavis and Janice and the Planks in the other direction. Diana and Lizzy seem nice. I thought you'd make new friends…friends more like you."

Mudder turned. The soft glow of the gas light softened the lines on her face. "Spend more time with your own kind and you'll be more content. That's what he means."

Adah held her gaze. Mavis and Janice were nice. So were Diana and Lizzie. And she enjoyed working alongside them at the frolics. She'd seen them plenty of times at the Englisch parties too, looking so different without their kapps and aprons. She couldn't tell Mudder that. These girls were doing their own experimenting so it didn't matter if she sought them out. They were in the same boat. "I—"

"What is that on your apron?" Daed dropped the crumpled paper onto the table and leaned forward, his lips contorted in a deep frown. "That looks like...is that blood?"

"It is. That's what I started to tell you before." Adah grasped at this new topic, this opportunity to turn the spotlight away from her future and baptism and all it represented. "There was an accident. That's why I was late. Jackson Hart was breaking a horse in the corral and the horse trampled him. He was hurt, so I had to help him."

Daed's bushy gray eyebrows rose and fell. "You had to help him? You were there with him—just you two? What were you doing at the corral? You're supposed to be in the house, cleaning."

"I drove by and saw him working the horse. I stopped for a second. It happened so fast—"

"What did you do?"

"The horse kicked him. I ran in and helped him get out of the corral—that's all." She faltered. "Then I ran up to the porch and got his cell phone."

"You used the telephone?"

"No, he wasn't passed out or anything. He called."

"You helped him out of the corral. How?"

"Ben." Her mudder's voice held a note of entreaty. "You would have her stand aside and not help a hurt man in need because of propriety?"

Daed tugged at his beard. If he didn't stop, he would rip it from his chin. "Nee. I wouldn't. Still, I thought the boy was away studying."

"He's home for the summer." The image of Jackson's face and the smile he wore despite his injuries flashed in her mind. He wasn't a boy. She struggled to keep her face neutral. "He'll be working with his dad."

"And you'll be working in the house." Daed massaged his neck with one hand, a weary look on his face. "You're not to be alone in the house with him. If Mrs. Hart isn't there, you best come on home and clean the house another time. If that doesn't suit her, you can find a new house to clean."

"I'll tell her."

"Mind that you keep to yourself. Do your work. Get yourself home. On time."

Mrs. Hart wouldn't like this new rule. She went to town all the time, to shop, to visit, to get her hair fixed up and her fingernails painted. It couldn't be helped. Adah didn't want Daed to forbid her to go. She liked the Hart house the best of the three houses she cleaned. Because of the piano and the music playing on the radio and the books, lots of books, everywhere. She felt as if Daed's gaze bored into her forehead. She only wanted to snatch up her papers and run up the stairs. He could have the iPod. She would hear the music in her head anyway. "I'll talk to Mrs. Hart. I'll tell her. I'm sure she won't mind."

She liked having her house clean and Plain girls did it a lot more cheaply than most. She'd agree. Leastways, Adah hoped so.

"See that you do." Daed gathered up the papers and the iPod in one swoop of his big hands. "These go in the trash."

"Nee—" Adah started forward.

Mudder put her hand on Adah's arm. "Finish washing the dishes and wipe down the counters. The little ones are already in bed. I saved you a plate."

Mudder always saved her a plate. No matter what, she watched out for Adah. But this was one thing with which she couldn't help her daughter. Adah knew that. She nodded. Mudder's grip tightened and then her hand fell away. "Go on."

"Concentrate on the baptism classes." Steel grated in Daed's voice. "It's time."

Adah tried not to look back, but she couldn't help herself. Daed dropped the iPod on the floor and crushed it under his thick-soled, dirty work boot, the sound of plastic breaking loud in the silent, country evening. He crushed the papers in his hands until they were a tight ball. Mudder crouched and swept the shattered pieces of electronics into her apron. She rose and together they walked out the front door. They were headed to the barrels out by the corral where Daed burned trash and grass clippings and such.

Adah bowed her head and trudged into the kitchen. No point in looking back. What was gone was gone. They were right. She needed to look forward. Her throat ached with tears she refused to shed. No Plain woman cried over a few words on a piece of paper. It was pure silliness.

Pure foolishness.
Time to put this foolishness aside.
Foolishness aside.
Couldn't erase these feelings if she tried.
The words whirled in her head. Her fingers itched.
She couldn't help it. She felt another song coming on.

Chapter 4

Matthew Troyer tossed the last pitchfork of hay onto the platform from where he stood in the wagon and yelled for his daed to crank the pulley. He must've heard because the ropes creaked and groaned and the wooden platform began its ascent toward the barn loft. A quick glance upward told him Rueben stood at the edge of the loft, ready to take the load. He looked as beat as Matthew felt. Abraham and Alexander had been released earlier to fix a downed fence that was allowing the hogs to escape their pen. The twins were probably at the house already, chomping at the bit to eat supper. Matthew wiped at his face with the back of his sleeve and it came away drenched. The smell of his sweat mingled with the nicer scent of fresh cut hay. The sun flashed through the open door, its placement in the western sky telling him they were way past suppertime.

Daed had heard something in town about thunderstorms tonight and he wanted the hay in before it was drenched and had to dry again. So they'd worked long past the usual hour. Matthew didn't mind, truth be told. It had been a good day. A decent haul. The wheat looked good and so did the corn. If the weather held they should have a good crop later this month, early July at the latest. The work they did today made time for other chores tomorrow. A farmer's life. His life. He smiled to himself, liking the sound of those words rattling around in his head. His and Adah's life if he had his way.

He was getting ahead of himself as usual. Baptism classes were underway. He hoped to be baptized at the end of September. Then more courting. He liked the courting part when it involved Adah. A lot. The road ahead might be long, but there was joy in the journey. Praise Gott for that blessing.

"That's it. Time to call it a day." Daed strode around the wagon, looking as chipper as he had at dawn. Matthew wiped the telltale smile off his face before Daed asked him what he was grinning about. Daed was sharp that way. "Your mudder's squawking about having a good meal dry out because we don't know when to stop what we're doing and leave it for tomorrow."

"Because *you* don't know when to stop!" Matthew smiled to let Daed know he was joshing him. "She knows Rueben and I are ready to eat at the drop of a hat. I could eat an entire hog by myself right now."

"You earned your keep today." Daed clapped Matthew on the back with a hand big enough to palm a volleyball into the farm down the road. Now that they were caught up on the work, he wasn't quite so cranky. "'Course you do most days."

A rush of pleasure flowed through Matthew. Daed didn't hand out compliments much. That made this rare occasion all the more pleasing and unexpected. He ducked his head so Daed couldn't see the red that surely crept across his face. "I best unhitch the horses and get them fed and watered."

"Let Rueben do that." Daed shoved back the brim of his sweat-soaked straw hat, revealing a white band above his farmer's tan and just below a gray hairline. "Walk up to the house with me. Got something I want to talk to you about."

Surprise mingled with a generous dose of trepidation—had he forgotten a chore or left some remnant of his ongoing rumspringa in a place where it drew Daed's attention to its overt clash with their ways? His stomach clenched, taking with it the hunger that had made him ravenous only a minute earlier. His heart cranked up in his chest, he waited while Daed gave Rueben some last instructions and then fell in step next to him as they trudged up the dirt and gravel road that led to the house.

Daed didn't say anything at first. The only sound was the crunch of the gravel under their boots and the wind rustling leaves on the tree branches that provided a bit of shade now and again. Daed cleared his throat. "Your mudder and I have been talking."

"*Jah.*"

"We've been blessed since moving to New Hope from Bliss Creek. This farm...it's more than enough for our needs."

"It is."

Where was this going? Matthew knew better than to ask. Daed would get to where he was going in his own way and at his own speed. Which couldn't really be called speed. His *groossmammi* got to the point faster and she was nearing seventy.

"You're of age now." Daed did a two-step around a gray and white kitten who had strayed from its momma and planted itself in the middle of the road, where it seemed intent on giving itself a bath with a tiny pink tongue. "Won't be long before you'll be making some decisions about what you'll do next."

So that was it. Matthew hid his smile. Daed's judicious choice of words meant he was trying not to meddle, trying not to ask. It wasn't done. Rumspringa lasted however long it lasted. Young folks in this community were expected to make the decision to be baptized without prodding by their elders. That's how the bishop would know it was genuine. That regret wouldn't surface later, coupled with a desire to change the outcome.

Matthew's had gone on long enough. He had started his baptism classes and he meant to finish them and be baptized in September. Gott willing, Adah would too. She'd seemed reluctant to start the classes and her attendance was spotty, but she'd come around. Gott willing.

Daed's long strides slowed. "I've decided it's best to give you the forty acres west of the creek."

Matthew stopped walking. His mouth dropped open but he couldn't seem to shut it. Daed took a few more steps, apparently not realizing at first that Matthew no longer strode at his side. He slowed, stopped, and turned. "Well? I thought you wanted to eat a whole hog. A man could starve to death waiting on you."

"Are you sure you want to carve up the land in parcels like that?"

"Just two parcels. When it's Rueben's time, we'll see. He may decide he wants to ply a trade in town to earn his keep. The twins will share my piece when I'm gone."

Which, Gott willing, would be a long time from now.

Matthew pulled his hat down on his forehead, hoping to cover the tumult on his face. "I wasn't expecting this."

"You're a farmer. I have no doubt of that. I see it in your work every day." Daed's sunburned face turned a darker shade of red. "It gives me…it pleases me that Gott has provided for us in a way that allows this to happen."

Daed always gave all the glory to Gott. Always. Matthew nodded. "Me too."

Daed resumed walking. Matthew stood rooted to the ground, his mind racing, thinking of the lay of the land, how it might be cultivated, where they—he and Adah, Gott willing—would build the house.

Daed glanced back, his expression perturbed now. "Are you coming? If we're any later, your mudder will feed our supper to the hogs sure as the sun sets in the west."

"I'm coming."

"There's something else." Daed shoved his hat back on his head, giving Matthew a clear view of his expression. It could be described as surly at best. Whatever was coming didn't please him as much as the earlier discussion. "You remember the Gringriches?"

"I do." The ones who moved to Walnut Creek when the other Bliss Creek families decided to move to Missouri. Why, Matthew couldn't imagine. They hadn't been in Bliss Creek long when they decided to uproot and move again. Land was scarce up north and what did become available was much more expensive than in Missouri.

"The move to Walnut Creek didn't work out for them."

What was Daed getting at? More than one family had struck out in new directions only to find land too expensive, the Englisch rules too onerous, and farming no longer sustainable. Their way of life felt threatened more often than not. "It's a shame, but I'm sure Gott has a plan for them."

"Apparently that plan involves them staying with us for a spell."

"Oh." Now Matthew understood Daed's concern. They were squeezed into the house as it was. The Englischers who built it must've had few *kinner*. Bedrooms were scarce. They planned to add more rooms in the fall after the crops were in. "Molly won't mind sharing."

"They've got four daughters."

And no sons. Part of Enoch Gringrich's problem, no doubt. "We'll make it work."

"Jah, we will. Your mudder has her heart set on having Clara here. She's missed her friendship something fierce."

Matthew slowed again. First Daed announced the gift of the land. Then he proceeded to announce that six more people would be living in their house. Was he prodding Matthew to move quickly to marry Adah? To free up space for visitors?

Surely not. Daed wouldn't do that.

"We need to start on a *dawdi haus*."

Another statement out of the blue. "You're still young." Matthew blurted his response without thinking of how it sounded. "I mean, if you've decided—"

"Nee, don't be daft, son. I'm not ready for the rocking chair." Daed guffawed for a full thirty seconds. He wiped at his face with the back of his shirt sleeve, his expression somber once again. "Your *Aenti* Josie sent me a letter. My daed and mudder have become…feeble. She's doing her best to care for them, but Daed has become stubborn as an old mule. Mudder thinks he'll do better with us. Josie agrees."

Groossdaadi being stubborn Matthew could imagine, but feeble? The man didn't have a weak or lazy bone in his body. Matthew didn't realize how much he'd missed having his grandfather around until this very moment. He missed hunting and fishing with him. Missed his stories. Missed his cackling laughter when he teased Molly and the little ones. Having him and Groossmammi here would be a gift from God.

It didn't matter how crowded the house seemed. The more the merrier. "When are they coming?"

"The Gringriches get here next week. I'll head to Bliss Creek to fetch Mudder and Daed while you have the framing frolic for the dawdi haus."

"Before we finish it?"

"You and the other men can get it done. I'm just one set of hands. You'll have many more. Enoch is a good carpenter. He'll help."

"What about the code enforcement guy? He's been giving Michael a hard time over the house he's building for him and Phoebe."

"I'll stop in and talk to him while we're in town buying the supplies tomorrow. I have drawings we've always used. It's a small addition. Front room, bedroom, small kitchen, bathroom. That's it. Surely they can't find much fault with that."

The Englisch inspectors seemed to find fault with everything, whether it was the quality of the lumber, the number of smoke alarms, or the type of cement used for the foundation. He would want blueprints, not the simple plans they'd always used. "We'll work it out."

"It's in Gott's hands."

Matthew looked at the two-story house with its fresh coat of white paint. It would burst at the seams with eight more people. Good people. Family and friends. His heart lifted at the thought. "It'll be nice to have Groossdaadi and Groossmammi here. And the Gringriches are fun. They like a good game of volleyball, as I recall. Mudder will be happy to have all those extra hands for canning and sewing frolics."

Daed's expression eased a little. "They do and she will. But one thing I'd like you to keep to yourself. The other kinner don't need to know."

"Jah."

"Groossdaadi hasn't been himself for a while."

Groossdaadi? With his sharp blue eyes and tongue quick with a joke or a reprimand, both delivered in the same crusty voice edged with barely suppressed laughter. Nee. "Hasn't been himself?"

"He's a little hazy about who is who."

He'd been quick as a freshly sharpened ax the last time Matthew saw him. "Did he get doctored?"

"He refuses to go. Says he's fit as a man half his age." Daed sniffed his disapproval. "He tries to do too much. Then he can barely get out of bed in the morning. Josie says he has good spells and bad spells and she never knows which one it'll be. It's hard for her. Wears on her heart, I reckon. She says he may decide to take off down the road and try to go home. You'll have to keep an eye on him. We all will."

"I won't mind. It'll be good to have him around."

"I've got a hankering for some deep-fried catfish." The lines etched around Daed's mouth eased. He'd said his piece. Their talk had ended as they always did. Suddenly. Done was done. "After supper, I'm walking down to the river to check our lines."

Matthew considered the change of subject. An invitation lurked in the words. Despite his desire to race over to Adah's house and tell her his news—their news—about the land, Matthew felt a spurt of joy. With the company coming, he and his father would have little opportunity for this anytime soon. The news would wait one more day. "Fish sounds real good. I know Mudder would be happy to fry it up for us tomorrow."

"If we get any. River's down."

Didn't matter. The joy was in the company and the quiet time when no words were needed.

Even as they discussed the weather and the pros and cons of line fishing versus pole fishing, Matthew's mind raced. He managed a sedate walk next to Daed all the way to the house, up the steps, and into the kitchen where he washed his hands and face, all the while thinking of sharing his news with Adah. Tomorrow night, he would slip out after dark and shine his flashlight in her window. No doubt she would be as thrilled as he about the land. Now she would see that only the baptism classes stood in their way. She had been slow to embrace the idea that this was the summer. They needed to take the classes now. She'd found excuses to put it off. Now she would see. The crush of people at his house meant it was time for him to get his own place. Their own place.

His place with Adah.

Adah, with her fair skin and blue eyes and her sweet voice. She would give up the music to be his wife. He was sure of that. Every Plain woman wanted to be a *fraa*. This Plain woman seemed to want to be his fraa. At least he thought she did. Adah was a mystery to him. He sat down at the table between Rueben and the twins, his sisters across from them, bowed his head, and prayed.

Gott, let Adah be the one.

Chapter 5

Adah leaned her head against the wooden frame of the window, longing for a hint of a breeze to freshen the stifling air in her bedroom. The June night lay like a thick shawl on her shoulders. Her neck ached and her head throbbed. She'd spent the day cleaning the Stevens' house, with their three preschoolers and two dogs and four cats. The place smelled of litter box and the furniture was covered with cat hair.

Not that any of that mattered. The harder she worked with her body, the more time her mind had to form words into songs. She couldn't make it stop. The physical work didn't engage her mind. What was she supposed to do about that?

> *The tears that sear my face can't erase these feelings*
> *My heart hurts every time I think about the days ahead*
> *It's foolishness I know, but I can't erase the words you said*
> *When I told you I had to go. It's foolishness I know...*

Mudder hadn't just taken her stash of songs, she'd taken the pencil and the notebook. Her writing utensils. It didn't matter. The words wouldn't go away until she wrote them down. Tonight, she would sleep and tomorrow would be another day. When she went into town to clean the Johnsons' house, she'd stop at the Five and Dime, where nothing cost a nickel or a dime, and buy a new supply of paper and pencils. She'd go to the library in the afternoon, sit in the lovely, air-conditioned reading room, and write her song. *If* Molly Troyer wasn't working. Matthew's sister was sweet and kind—everyone loved her—but she wouldn't understand about the songs. She might tell Matthew.

Adah should tell Matthew. She shouldn't be hiding things from the man courting her. Tomorrow. She'd think about it tomorrow. She snatched her nightgown from the hook on the wall and laid it on the bed. Tomorrow was another day. This one had been long. Time to put it in the past, dust off her hands, and look forward to a better day.

A light flashed and danced on the wall behind the bed. It dipped and bobbed. She closed her eyes, opened them, sighed, and went to the window. Matthew stood, long legs apart, dusty work boots planted, looking up at her window, the flashlight tilted in her direction. He flapped his straw hat in a wide *come-on-down* motion, giving her a full view of the thick wheat-colored hair on top of his head. She waved back and withdrew from the window.

Weariness weighted her entire body. Still, she couldn't leave him standing down there. Matthew deserved better. He'd been nothing but a good friend for as long as she could remember. And he had the nicest smile this side of the Mississippi. His kaffi-brown eyes warmed her with every good-natured grin full of even, white teeth. He doled out those smiles with great generosity, one of his best qualities.

Adah slipped from her room and tiptoed down the stairs, not because she was sneaking—her parents couldn't help but know about Matthew—but because she knew how tired they were. They would be up before dawn. They needed their sleep. She pushed through the front door and trotted down the steps. Matthew twirled the flashlight, making its beam dance and bob in her eyes. She shielded them. "Hey, stop it!"

"Nice way to greet a man you haven't seen in three days."

"Sorry. It's been a long week."

Matthew tucked the flashlight on the floor of the two-seater and offered her his hand. "Too long to enjoy a ride? A short ride?" He must've seen the hesitation in her face. "It's been three days since we talked and it's a full moon. It'll be pretty down by the pond. And I have news I want to tell you. Good news."

She swallowed the weary protest that rose inside her. Matthew always made her feel better, no matter what her day had been like. He had a way about him. "No, not too long for that."

Adah took the hand he offered. Goosebumps ran up her arm and prickled the back of her neck just as they always did on those occasions when Matthew touched her. She examined that thought with care. Was it Matthew specifically? Or the fact that any man took her hand? Nee. It was Matthew. Why? She looked into his face, with his ready smile, warm brown eyes, and high cheekbones. Tufts of hair stuck out under the brim of his hat. A good, honest, face. One she'd known her whole life. He made her feel…content.

Not the feeling from which love songs came.

Or was it?

She climbed into the open-air two-seater and settled back. Matthew loped around to his side and hopped in. His familiar scent of man, hard work, and soap enveloped her. A few minutes later they were out on the back road that led to the pond and then onto his family's property. Adah felt better already. The night had cooled after the sun set and the air whooshed by her as the horse trotted down the road. It was indeed a nice night for a ride. The full moon caused the trees to cast long shadows on the road. The stars twinkled and seemed to hang down unusually close, as if they followed the buggy, looking over Adah's shoulder, lighting her way. She felt almost festive.

"You said it has been a long week." Matthew broke the silence first. "You cleaned at the Harts' and the Stewarts', right?"

The festive feeling drained away, like water running from a bucket with a hole in it. "Jah."

"Anything in particular happen?"

She shook her head and then realized he had his gaze on the road. "Nee." No need to tell him about Jackson Hart getting stomped by a horse. Jackson with the country-crooner voice and silver buckle. About the songs, that was another matter. "In particular, Daed was upset with me. Mudder found the iPod and showed it to him."

Matthew clucked and snapped the reins. "Ouch."

"He crushed it with his boot and threw it in the fire barrel."

"Sorry." Matthew glanced her way, but his expression revealed nothing. He'd been with her when she bought the slim, small music player and slipped the buds in her ears. He'd told her not to keep it in the house. She hadn't heeded his advice, but he would never rub her nose in it. "I know how you like to listen to it."

"Don't be sorry. I shouldn't have had it in the house. I knew better. It was just easier. For when…" For when she wanted to listen to it while she made her scribblings after her family went to bed. "It was just easier."

Matthew switched on the battery-operated radio he had strapped to the front of the buggy. He fiddled with the knobs and after a few seconds the crackling noises dissolved into guitars, keyboards, and drums melding into a beautiful old song about a faraway place with a pretty name: Amarillo. "There you go, George Crooked."

"That's George Strait, silly." She laughed, touched by how hard Matthew tried. It had been apparent to Adah all along that he didn't care much about country music. Or music in general. He bought the radio for her at a secondhand store, knowing one day he would have to sell it back to the store. Before his baptism. And hers. "Next you'll be telling me they're playing a Johnny Dollar song."

"No, it's Johnny Check." His impish grin widened. "Or is it Johnny Penny?"

They both laughed, drowning out the music for several seconds. Adah wiped tears from the corner of her eyes, feeling better. Matthew had that way about him. He wouldn't know a Johnny Cash song if he heard it, but he tried for her sake. He made her feel better about herself. He didn't see her as the black sheep, the way others did. He never looked at her with that perplexed look her mudder and daed sometimes had. But then he didn't know everything. He only knew she liked music and he wanted to please her. It shouldn't always be about her. She leaned close to him and turned the radio down. "How was your day?"

"It was fine. It looks like the wheat and the corn will be bumper crops. Daed is real happy." The good humor in Matthew's voice didn't fade. Aaron Troyer could be as cranky as Adah's father. He was a hard worker and expected his oldest son to match him stride for stride. Adah understood that. She simply couldn't understand why the two men couldn't smile more. Sing while they worked. Enjoy the sunrise before picking up the shovel.

"Is he as grumpy as ever?"

"He's not grumpy. He's the same old Daed he's always been. He works hard and expects the rest of us to do the same. If he's short with me sometimes it's because I'm at fault." Matthew halted the buggy on the banks of the pond. Frogs croaked in a chorus that threatened to drown out the crickets. A dragonfly buzzed Adah's ear. She leaned in to Matthew to hear his voice. It always softened when he talked about his daed. "He had some news to tell me yesterday. My grandparents are coming to live with us And the Gringriches too. For a while."

"All of them? At once?" The news sank in. Elizabeth, Abigail, Loretta, and Jenna Gringrich would be living in Matthew's house. Ages nineteen, eighteen, sixteen, and fourteen. A strange feeling like envy or jealousy or fear slithered through her. She didn't like that feeling. It made her feel mean-spirited. Hospitality and generosity of spirit went hand in hand. The Gringriches must be in need. The community would meet that need. "What happened?"

"My grandparents need looking after and Aenti Josie isn't up to it, I guess."

"Not that. The Gringriches."

Matthew shrugged. "They need a new start."

"Didn't they just make a fresh start in Walnut Creek?"

"Didn't work out, I guess."

"Your house will burst at the seams with eight more people." And he would see Elizabeth with her dimples and green eyes every day—morning, noon, and night. "Where will you put them all?"

"We'll start building the dawdi haus next week. We're having a frame raising. Luke has okayed it. Daed hired a driver to take him to fetch the grandparents."

"Do you have the permits?" Adah had listened to the men hash and rehash the issues they were having with the New Hope building codes while she served the sandwiches after the prayer service on Sunday. Michael Daugherty had had to start over on the foundation of the home he hoped to share with Phoebe after they deemed the cement not up to code. Whatever that meant.

"Yep. We had to get blueprints, but we did it."

"What did Luke say about that?"

"You know Luke. He says we need to meet them halfway. Seems like we've been doing that since we moved here, but it isn't our way to make a big stink about anything."

He chuckled, a sound that never failed to make her smile too. "What's so funny?"

"Reminds me of the sheriff giving us a big stink over not having a contract to carry off the waste from the outhouses at the school. I thought he would faint when he realized we use the waste to fertilize our crops. A big stink. Get it?"

"You're so silly." Leave it to Matthew to try to lighten the conversation. "Why don't we just do what they ask?"

"We've used human waste on our fields for generations and no one has ever objected. Besides, we don't sign contracts with Englischers."

"We've never had septic tanks or leach beds for the laundry and bathwater either."

"Luke is trying to placate them. Give in on some things so they'll give in on others."

"I don't think Englisch laws work that way. They apply to everyone all the time. No exceptions." The world around them continued to encroach on their way of life. The sound of the iPod crunching under Daed's heel echoed in her head again. "And now Emma and Katie have to have a permit and go through inspections to sell their jams and jellies at the food stand on the highway."

"They can't even have the food stand on the highway anymore. They had to back it up a ways. The sheriff said people slowing down to gawk at us might cause an accident. The sales have gotten so slow, they've decided to look for a place in town where we can sell the goods. Open a store."

Adah thought of the accident just outside of Bliss Creek that had killed Luke and Emma Shirack's parents. The sheriff might have a point, but she didn't voice the thought aloud. "Who would run it?

The men all have farms to think about. Simon already has his black-smith place and William runs the leather goods store."

"The women. Emma and my mudder have asked permission to share the duties with the other women in the community. Thomas, Luke, and Silas have agreed to it. The women will take turns working...if they can find the store space and get it at a price we can afford."

The women working in their own store. Another step toward the world. How could they not see her music the same way? "I can't believe Luke agreed to that. Will Leah work in the store?"

"Nee. Leah can't...you know Leah."

"She's better."

"Praise Gott."

"Praise Gott." She tried to praise Him in all things. If she could only have the answer she wanted on just this one other thing. It didn't work that way. She squelched a sigh. No whining. "What did my daed say? Will my mudder work too? She never mentioned it."

"He said your mudder best wait until Jonathan is a little older." Matthew moved closer. "From the look on his face, I imagine he was thinking of the baby they lost. Ruth was her name, right?"

"Jah. Mudder calls her Ruthie sometimes." She used to call her that when she got ready to walk down to the cemetery outside Bliss Creek. Not anymore. "She says Jonathan is the last one she'll have. I think she's a little sad about that."

They fell into step, side by side, following a well-worn path along the bank that suggested others had done the same. The pungent smell of grass and mud, of earth, filled the air. She inhaled and felt the strain of the day seep away. Matthew slid his hand through the crook in her arm. His gaze held hers for a second and then he looked up at the thick black night sky carpeted with those sparkling stars that welcomed them to God's great outdoors. "She has grandchildren to think of with Hiram and Daniel married. It won't be long before she'll have more." He glanced at her again, then away. "Beautiful night, isn't it?"

"Beautiful." Struck by the strange, hoarse emotion in his voice, she cast around for something light to talk about. "How's Molly?"

"She's fine. She's got her nose stuck in a book even more now that she's working at the library. I think she should take over teaching at the school, she's so learned."

"You make that sound like a bad thing." Matthew had no use for book learning. Adah hadn't been sad to leave school either, but she liked books because they were full of words. Beautiful words strung together in beautiful sentences that created beautiful pictures in her mind. She knew what drew Molly to them. The same thing that drew her to them. "As long as she earns her keep and still helps around in the house, why do you care?"

"She'll never find a husband that way."

"She's only a year older than us."

"Exactly."

"What are you saying? Are you in a big hurry to get married?"

"I guess I am." Matthew halted, forcing her to do the same. "That's why I thought we should talk…one of the reasons…I mean I wanted to talk to you."

Adah's heart skipped in an uneven, stumbling rhythm. They couldn't have this talk unless he knew everything about her. It wouldn't be fair. He had to know who she really was. The part of her she hadn't shared with him. Or anyone. "I wanted to talk to you too."

"Do you want to sit down?" He pointed the flashlight at a flat rock a few feet from the shoreline. "Looks dry."

"I'd rather keep walking."

He nodded. "You first, then."

"Nee, you first." She needed time to gather her thoughts, to make her argument, to let him know she'd stop if that was what he wanted. Even if it broke her heart. Better than breaking the heart of a man who'd done nothing to deserve it.

"We've been courting a while now."

"We have."

His hand slid down and gripped her wrist. His fingers were so long they wrapped around her thin bones in a complete circle and then some. "We haven't really talked about what we're doing."

"Nee."

"We've spent a lot of time together. We've had fun in the last two years."

"We have."

His grip tightened ever so slightly. "But you never say anything about…what you feel…if you do feel…for me."

Adah stopped. Her heart pounded in a *rat-a-tat-tat* so loud she thought he might hear it. This was it. This was everything.

"I care for you. I've been thinking about what's next and I realized I never asked you if you were thinking the same thing. Daed gave me some more news yesterday. He told me he's giving me forty acres for my own." Matthew paused as if waiting. He touched her cheek with one finger, letting it trail down her jawline. "Forty acres I can farm for myself. Where I can build a house for my family."

The feel of his finger on her skin captivated Adah, making it hard to breathe. It reminded her of fingers plucking the strings on a guitar, each note clear and beautiful. She shivered despite the June heat. Swallowing, she opened her mouth. Nothing came out.

Matthew's gaze shifted to the moon overhead. "I need to know. Do you care for me?"

"I do." Her voice quivered. She didn't sound sure, not even to herself. "I think…I mean…I do."

"*Gut.* I think." He started walking again, this time without touching her.

"Matthew." She scurried to keep up. "Wait."

"We've known each other for a long time, but you never seem to let me get closer." He had his head down as if he studied the path in front of them. "I don't know what you're thinking about anything. You joke around, but you don't tell me anything important to you."

"We have fun together." All those singings. The late-night gatherings at the abandoned shed on the Daughertys' property. The rides in Doo Doolittle's car. The movies at New Hope's only movie theater. Three music concerts in two years, all in Springfield. All their shared secrets.

Matthew had done these things for her.

Child's play that would—must—end soon.

"We do, I'll give you that. You laugh at my jokes when no one else does." He slowed his pace but still didn't look at her. "You're fun to be around. But there's more than that. I feel more than that for you. I want to know what you feel."

"What are you looking for?" Adah knew what was coming. She wanted to stall it. She wasn't ready for it. She couldn't settle down, not yet. She still had an itch to scratch, a hankering, an ache where her contentment should be. "What do you want?"

"I want to be a farmer like my daed. I want a fraa. I want to get married and have kinner like my folks did." His voice cracked a little on the last word. "I want what my mudder and daed have. Don't you?"

She thought of the way Daed looked at Mudder when she leaned over to set a plate of food in front of him. After all these years. After all they'd been through. After the baby who died. And all that came after. Adah wanted that. Someday. "I do."

"With me?"

She did. Just not yet. But if she waited too long, Matthew would find someone else. He wouldn't have to look far. Elizabeth Gringrich would be sitting at his supper table every night. "Jah, I do. I'm just not sure I'm ready yet."

"I guess that's my answer."

He turned. Not thinking, she grabbed his arm. He jerked away and whirled to face her. "I know you like me. You don't want to grow up. But it's time you do."

"I do like you." She didn't want what they had to change. "I just don't know what the hurry is."

"The hurry? We've been courting since we were sixteen." He shook his head, his face forlorn. "My parents' house will be overflowing soon. I need to get out on my own. I think that's what my daed was trying to tell me without sticking his nose in our business. It's time."

"I know. I know."

"It's the next step after baptism, isn't it?" He sounded truly bewildered. "Isn't that one of the reasons you agreed to take the classes this year?"

"I decided to take the classes because…" How could she explain to someone who'd been her friend before they began courting, for years, that she took the classes because she feared the deepening chasm between what she saw the other girls wanting and what she wanted? She'd hoped the classes would help her find her way back. "Because I needed to know more. I needed to be reminded of our beliefs."

"Like you'd forgotten them? I want to be baptized in September because I choose our faith and our beliefs." He took a long breath, stopped, and faced her, forcing Adah to halt as well. "I also want to be baptized so I can get married. To you."

Adah breathed the cool night air, trying to think. *Ready or not, here I come.* The words of the old game rang in her ears. Ready or not. She should be ready. She couldn't put into words the invisible ropes that seemed to hold her back. She cared for Matthew. She might even love him. She wasn't sure. She loved her family. She loved her community. She loved God, but she couldn't understand why He allowed some things to happen. Like letting baby Ruth die in a fire. Ruth had come and gone long before Adah lived and breathed, yet she still felt her sister's absence like an odd, glancing blow that came out of nowhere when she least expected it.

If Ruth hadn't died, she'd have a big sister. She wouldn't be the oldest daughter, the one expected to take care of the home and know just what to do.

Mudder said God had a plan. Adah's job was to do her best and be a good girl. She tried, she really did, but she didn't see a plan anywhere in sight that let her be who she was. A girl who loved to write and sing and make music.

That was selfish of her. Her parents weren't asking her to do anything they hadn't done themselves. So why couldn't she say the words? She was afraid. Afraid of missing something. That was silly. She would miss everything if she didn't tell Matthew what he wanted to hear.

"Let's just get through the classes and see where we go from there."

"I know where I want to go." Matthew's voice died to a husky, rough whisper. "And I want to go there with you. I love you."

The words hung in the air between them. Thoughts and words flitted around in Adah's head. *Say something. Say something.*

Her throat ached.

Matthew drew a sharp breath. "I guess that's my answer."

"Give me time."

"You've had time."

She'd never heard Matthew speak with such authority. He sounded...like Daed. She had that to which she could look forward. Moving from Daed's house to her husband's house.

"I know, I just don't see what the hurry is."

"If you don't love me, I understand. It's not something you can make happen." He squeezed her hand, his fingers tight around hers, and let go. "You still have time. All summer. But I won't wait forever."

Chapter 6

Adah rummaged in her canvas bag for her new spiral notebook with a black cover and selected a nicely sharpened pencil with a full pink eraser. She loved a new point on her pencils and a good eraser too. She'd found a perfect spot in the library's reading room. A table for two near the nonfiction section. A feeling as close to contentment as she could find these days rolled over her. She could leave all the upheaval in her heart outside on the sidewalk. Matthew's declaration, his challenge, his ultimatum. *I love you.* The words flitting around in her head like butterflies trying to take flight, but caught by an ever-tightening net. The airy, quiet room and the nearby overflowing bookshelves calmed her. She breathed in the smell of old paper and dust, the scents soothing.

The blank page of her notebook stared up at Adah. She should be reading the Confession of Faith articles for Sunday's baptism class. Instead, she closed her eyes and waited, letting all the tension and uncertainty of the past few days seep away. Hurting Matthew. Knowing from now on he could simply move on and pass the time with Elizabeth Gringrich. Elizabeth was nice. And she'd had her eye on Matthew at school, even though then they'd been too young to go to the singings or court.

Why dig up all these old memories? Matthew loved her. He'd said so. And she hadn't returned the favor. Sighing, she put the mishmash of feelings aside and tried to concentrate. Where were those words that had been knocking around in her head while she scrubbed Mrs.

Martin's kitchen, beat the dirt out of her rugs on the clothesline, and cleaned three toilets in record time so she could come here instead of going straight home to more house cleaning?

The words hummed and her pencil began to move.

> *The tears that wet my face can't erase these feelings.*
> *My heart hurts every time I think about the days ahead.*
> *It's foolishness I know, but I can't erase the words you said*
> *When I told you I had to go. It's foolishness I know.*
>
> *I have one foot in my world, one foot in yours.*
> *Everyone around me wants to shut the door*
> *And separate me from you and yours.*
> *It's foolishness I know, but I can't think about the days ahead.*
> *It's foolishness I know to think of the words you said.*
>
> *Please say them once more. Tell me you won't let them shut*
> *　　the door.*
> *We'll be together again. Tell me it's no sin.*
> *Tell me we'll be together again.*
>
> *It's foolishness to think I can set this aside.*
> *The door is standing open so wide,*
> *I can see forever in your eyes.*
> *I can fall into you and drown in the rushing tide*
> *Of feelings I couldn't stop if I tried.*

Rough. Still, having a few words on the page opened up the channels and gave her something to work with. She had the ingredients. Now to stir them until they were smooth and satiny like bread dough kneaded and risen and kneaded again.

"Studying for baptism class?"

Startled, Adah looked up as she let her hand slide over the page. She'd been so engrossed in the words she hadn't heard Molly approach. Curiosity written all over her round face, Molly peered through dark-rimmed glasses over Adah's shoulder. Adah closed the notebook.

"Nee. I was jotting down some thoughts. And I want to write a letter to Abigail Gless in Bliss Creek." She spoke the truth. Her to-do list included writing such a letter. "You remember her. She moved there right before we moved to New Hope. Her daed married Helen Crouch—"

"I remember her." Molly squeezed into a chair on the other side of the table and plopped down a large paper sack in front of her. "I didn't know you were friends."

"I talked to her some." Adah shoved her notebook in her canvas bag. "I should probably get home. Mudder has a bunch of sewing she wants me to finish today while she cans another round of tomatoes. She's stewing them and making sauce. We have a big crop already this year. Emma, Leah, and Katie are helping. How's your garden doing?"

Her mouth ran over and she knew it, but she couldn't figure out how to stop. Molly would tell Matthew she'd seen Adah at the library. She'd never lied to Matthew about anything. He knew about her love for music. She hadn't told him about the songs. A lie of omission. Still, nothing said she couldn't write a poem. A person was allowed to let her imagination run wild in poems. It was make-believe. Fiction. It didn't mean a thing. She'd penned a poem about love and it didn't involve Matthew. Why couldn't it be about Matthew? He worked hard. He loved his faith and family. He was kind and strong and pleasing to the eye. He never raised his voice and he never criticized her. So why didn't she write about him?

"What's wrong?" Molly tilted her head to one side. She looked like a wise owl with her black-rimmed glasses, big brown eyes, and small, turned-up nose. "You look sad."

"Nee. Just tired." Another lie. Her cheeks burned. When had it become impossible for her to talk to someone like Molly? The girl never had a bad thing to say about anyone. She loved her brother, though, and wouldn't want to see him hurt.

Adah didn't want to see him hurt either. "I mean I'm…I'm just try-ing to figure some things out."

"I always bring an extra sandwich in my lunch." Molly held up the bag. "I'll share if you'll keep me company. Sometimes it's easier to think on a full stomach."

Given Molly's round figure, she must do quite a bit of thinking. Adah stifled a smile at the thought. Matthew once told her she could do with a little more meat on her bones. No matter how much she ate, she remained scrawny. Probably from the constant somersaults and back-flips her mind did on the trampoline in her head. "That would be nice."

"There's a picnic table in the back under a big sycamore. With any luck there'll be a little breeze so we don't melt." Molly popped out of the chair. "It's just peanut butter and jam, but Mudder's strawberry preserves from last summer are really good."

Adah followed after her, not trying to squeeze a word in. Molly led the way to the picnic table, which indeed enjoyed a lovely shaded spot in a patch of grass and a small garden of sunflowers, yellow belles, and other blooming flowers that someone obviously had been weeding. Molly doled out a sandwich heaped with so much jam it ran out and filled the crevices of the plastic wrap, followed by a bag of chips and a bag of oatmeal-raisin cookies. And an apple.

"Do you always pack two lunches?"

"I'm always hopeful I'll find someone to share with." She smiled as she unwrapped her sandwich, a twin of Adah's. "It's more fun that way."

"What if you don't find someone?"

"I have a nice afternoon snack or I give it to that old man who sits on the bench in front of the hardware store all the time."

Molly really was a sweet person. Why hadn't she been snapped up by a man? Adah considered. Matthew's sister was only a year older than her. She still had plenty of time. On the other hand, most of the men in the New Hope District from Molly's circle of friends had already married. At the moment, she didn't look too concerned about her future. She looked completely captivated by the sandwich. Adah took her own bite and almost moaned. Delicious. They chewed in companionable silence. Molly pulled a thermos from the seemingly bottomless pit of the paper bag and filled the plastic lid with tea. "This we'll have to share. I forgot to bring an extra cup."

"I don't mind."

"*Gut.*" Molly laid her sandwich on the plastic wrap and wiped her mouth with her napkin. "Were you writing a song?"

The straightforward question caught Adah off guard. "Sort of. Until you put the words to music it's really just a poem."

Molly wrinkled her nose. "It looked like English. It's not a hymn, is it?"

"Nee."

"What's it about then?"

Adah wished she knew. If she couldn't explain it to herself how could she explain it to a simple, plainspoken woman like Molly. "It's about…feelings…and trying to figure them out."

"Feelings for my brother?"

Not so simple, but definitely plainspoken. Her appetite gone, Adah pinched off a piece of the thick homemade bread and rolled it around between her thumb and forefinger until it formed a ball. "My feelings are all mixed up, I guess. That's what the poem is about. Being mixed up."

"My mudder says the grass is always greener on the other side of the fence."

"Mine too." Adah popped the bread in her mouth, chewed, and swallowed, giving herself time to think. She needed to move the conversation away from her, somehow. "Do you think you'll get married?"

"If it's Gott's will."

The standard answer. It should be enough for Adah. "How does a person know if it's Gott's will?"

"I wish I knew." A sudden sadness heaped itself on Molly's face. She leaned forward, her voice dropping to a whisper. "I've been patient. I've waited. I don't understand why I'm the only one who hasn't found a special friend. I got baptized over a year ago. And here I sit."

"I'm sorry."

"I didn't mean it that way." Molly's hands flew to cheeks that stained red. "I'm enjoying eating lunch with you."

"I knew what you meant."

"I shouldn't complain. It's wrong. I've been blessed. I love working here and helping Mudder around the house and taking care of the kinner."

"But you want your own house and your own kinner."

"I do. Is that selfish?"

"It's natural."

"It's what every Plain girl wants, isn't it?"

Adah struggled to keep her face neutral. Every Plain girl except her, it seemed. She did want to be a fraa; she wanted kinner. But she also wanted to make music. Which was more important?

Family, of course. "Jah, it's what we all want."

They finished their sandwiches and chips in silence. Molly dumped her apple and her cookie into the bag and brushed crumbs from her hands. "I think I'd rather have ice cream for dessert. What do you say?" Her tone sounded determinedly cheerful. "Come with me to the soda shop at the drugstore. They have a scoop on a waffle cone for a dollar."

"Jah, we can drown our sorrows together." If she didn't allow herself to write, she might as well console herself with an ice cream cone. "Or smother them in ice cream, in this case. My treat since you brought the sandwiches."

"That's what I don't understand." Molly tossed the rest of the tea in the grass and screwed the lid back on the thermos. "What sorrow do you have? Matthew never looks at anyone but you."

"I really don't think we should talk about this."

"I would never tell Matthew anything. That's a promise." Her tone crisp, even bordering on sharp, Molly paused, her forehead wrinkled as she stared at Adah. She stood and picked up the bag. "You know why? I would never do anything to hurt my brother. Can you say the same?"

"I haven't hurt him." Again, not true. She strode after Molly. "I haven't done anything."

Molly stopped and Adah nearly ran into her. "Why does Matthew seem so sad when he looks at you? I know my *bruder* well. It's something about you."

"It's between him and me."

For a plump woman with short legs, Molly covered a lot of ground quickly. Adah was relieved when she stopped at the corner to wait for a line of cars to pass. "Even with everything he's had on his plate, with the building of the dawdi haus and Enoch and Clara moving in with us, Matthew's been studying for the classes. He intends to be baptized in September with Groossmammi and Groosdaadi looking on."

"I know. He told me."

"Were you listening?"

"I just said he told—"

"Did you hear what he was really saying? Matthew wants you to be his fraa." Her voice softened and trailed off to a whisper Adah had to strain to hear. "He needs someone he can count on."

"What is it? What's wrong?"

Molly took off the second the light changed. Adah scampered after her. The other woman didn't look left or right as she made a beeline for the drugstore. "Molly!"

Finally, she halted at the door. "You have a man who loves you and wants you for his fraa. You take that for granted. Not everyone gets that."

"I don't take it for granted." The sadness in Molly's face made Adah squeeze her arm even as her own heart contracted. "You will find someone—"

"God's will. God's plan." No bitterness tinged the words, but sadness hung from them, like the moss in the trees. "I'll make the best of it. I always do. I try to, anyway."

The door opened and Richard Bontrager strode out, a white paper bag in one hand and a waffle cone piled high with two—no, three—scoops of ice cream in the other.

"Adah!" He let the door slam behind him, apparently oblivious to Molly who, although a good foot shorter than the towering man, stood in his direct line of sight. "I was just thinking about seeing you at the frame raising. When are you coming to a singing again?"

Adah couldn't imagine going to the singings, knowing Matthew wouldn't be driving her home afterward. "Soon. Next time, we'll—I'll be there. If I can."

"Hi, Richard," Molly interjected, her voice unusually high. "That's a lot of ice cream. You must be hungry."

She didn't sound at all like herself. Her face flushed a deep, unbecoming red that spread in splotches to her neck. She clutched her wrinkled paper bag to her chest with one hand and shoved her glasses up the bridge of her nose with the other. Richard nodded at her, but his gaze swiveled back to Adah. "I like a good ice cream cone now and again. Is that where you're heading—to the soda shop?"

Adah jerked her attention from Molly's face to Richard. Richard didn't have a clue. Knowing he'd gotten himself tangled up with Phoebe last spring when everyone knew she was in love with Michael Daugherty proved it. Why were men so dense when it came to women? "It was Molly's idea. We're drowning our...we're having dessert."

"I see." Richard licked his ice cream, which had already begun to drip on his hand. "I'd like to go back in there with you, where it's nice and cool, but I'd best get myself back to the farm. Edna's waiting for her medicine and I promised to pick it up while I was in town getting the horse shod."

"I imagine they keep you pretty busy between the two farms." Adah searched for something to say that would bring attention to Molly. "It's like Molly here, she works at the library, but she still does a lot of work at home."

"Like you do, I reckon." Richard shifted his cone to the hand that held the bag and proceeded to remove his straw hat, revealing a head of rumpled brown hair. He wiped his forehead on the back of his sleeve. "I mean, you clean houses and then go home and clean some more."

So he'd been keeping track of her life. "We all do our share." What else could she say? "All in a day's work."

"All in a day's work." He settled the hat back on his head and grinned, showing off a set of white teeth against his dark farmer's tan. "Speaking of which, I'd better get back to mine. Enjoy your ice cream. Don't be strangers."

"We won't—I mean we will—I mean we'll enjoy the ice cream." If it were possible, Molly's face reddened even more. She pulled at the strings of her kapp, looking miserable. "But we won't be strangers."

Richard smiled at Molly directly for the first time. If she were a scoop of ice cream, she would've melted onto the sidewalk right there and then. "That reminds me. Can you stop by the house on your way to town in the morning?"

"Jah, jah, of course." Molly's face brightened. Her fingers stopped fiddling. "I'd be happy to come by."

"Edna has some books from the library that need returning and she's been feeling poorly. It would save her the trip. I figure since you're headed that way anyway..."

If Adah's parents hadn't brought her up right, she would've aimed a swift kick at the man's shins. Could he not see the way Molly's face crumpled and how hard she tried to smile as if she'd known all along he intended for her to do Edna Daugherty a favor? She'd never thought of him as being cruel so he must be oblivious. Like most men were, it seemed.

"It's no problem." Molly opened the door, her head down. "I'll come by right after breakfast."

"*Gut. Danki.*" He strode off without a backward glance. "See you."

He didn't say it, but that was directed at Adah. Maybe he meant to include Molly, but it didn't seem that way. Adah scurried into the drugstore after Molly, who'd ducked into the cosmetic aisle and seemed to be studying a vast array of lipstick tubes as if she were in desperate need of one. As if she'd ever worn lipstick in her life. Adah squeezed in next to her. "What are you doing?"

The woman turned. Her eyes were bright with tears behind her glasses. "That's why I'll never marry. Men don't even know I exist unless it's to take care of some chore for them."

Adah couldn't stand the forlorn look on the other woman's face. She wrapped her in a quick but firm hug. "Isn't that what we all learn to do so we can be good fraas?"

Molly hiccupped a laugh and slapped her hand to her mouth as if to muffle it. She sighed and let her hand drop. "Why don't men notice me? I know we're not supposed to stand out, we're supposed to be humble—but at this rate I'll spend the rest of my life alone. As alone as I can be, living at home, which I'll probably do forever. I know I'm supposed to be happy with God's plan—"

"Molly, Molly, stop! Stop. It's okay. I know all about trying to be content with God's plan. Believe me. You don't have to explain." Adah touched a tube of red lipstick, marveling at how much it cost and how little use it had. "Do you like Richard? Is he the one who found someone else?"

Sniffing, Molly shook her head, her gaze on something called blemish concealer as if it were the most interesting item in the entire store. "Nee, it was someone else, but that was a long time ago. I've…been interested…liked…or thought I might…like…Richard for a while."

"It's okay to say it. It doesn't hurt anything."

"It's not something you talk about, especially if the man doesn't even pay you any more mind than he would a stray kitten or a squirrel. Less. It's like I'm invisible. I'm the invisible girl."

Maybe she needed to do something to make him sit up and take notice. Moving on to the hair products that ran the gamut from hairspray to mousse to gels that Adah had no idea what to do with, she pondered what would make Richard sit up and take notice of Molly without being too forward. Something a good Plain girl could do.

Together, they left behind the rows of eyeliners, mascara, eye shadow, and lipsticks for the good stuff—the ice cream at the soda shop. Adah studied the problem as they walked. How could she help Richard notice Molly? It would make Molly happy, and, in turn, make Matthew happy.

Maybe it would be the first step on a long road toward making up for hurting him.

She waited until they ordered their cones—rocky road for Molly and plain chocolate for herself—to venture into new territory. "When you stop by the Daughertys', take a plate of your double fudge brownies with walnuts and make sure you tell Edna you made them for Richard. They're his favorite."

"How do you know—"

"I saw him eating them at a frolic the other day and he told me so."

"Why would I—"

"Just do it."

Molly accepted her cone from the clerk behind the counter. She started to dig money from her bag, but Adah shooed her aside and handed him two crisp dollar bills and enough change to cover the tax. Molly licked her cone, her eyes narrowed as if trying to decide if it were the right flavor. "Are you matchmaking?"

Adah feigned great interest in her own cone. "Me? Never. Courting is private."

She turned and made a beeline for the door so Molly couldn't read the glee in her face. *But sometimes you have to give love a little push.*

Chapter 7

Adah sneezed so loudly the sound reverberated around her in the Harts' cavernous living room. The room had a high ceiling, thick, tan carpet so soft it made her feel as if she walked on air, and half a dozen pieces of mammoth leather furniture. Even with all that furniture, it seemed empty because of its size. It didn't have the coziness of the study, but maybe that's because it didn't have the piano and the books she so loved. Dozens of windows allowed sunlight to spill across the room, highlighting particles of dust that hung suspended in the air around her. Sniffing, Adah turned the knob on the stereo radio so the song, a beautiful ballad about three crosses, enveloped her, and went back to wiping down the endless knickknacks on the enormous stone fireplace mantel.

Bronze horses in all sizes and shapes covered the varnished wood. Rearing on their hind legs, with riders, riderless, large and small. They made for tedious work on her part, but she liked them. The sculptor had taken great care with the details of the muscle, sinew, and the hair of the manes and tails. She hummed as she worked. A new song came on, this one about a girl mad at her boyfriend for cheating on her so she beat up his car.

The humming died in Adah's throat. She scurried across the room and flipped the dial to another station. She drew the line at some country songs, a lot of them, truth be told. About drinking, cheating,

57

fighting, and…other things. Guilt made the muscles in her neck and shoulders feel tight. Truth be told, she felt like the cheater. She hadn't done anything wrong, but her situation with Matthew was never far from her mind. He wanted her for his fraa. He wanted to move from courting to marriage. That was what Plain couples did.

So why did the thought make her chest tighten and her hands sweat? She scrubbed her face with the back of her sleeve. Even the frigid air-conditioned air whipped by the whirring blades of the ceiling fan didn't seem to cool her.

One of her favorite songs began. Determined not to think about the problem with Matthew, she sang along, letting her soprano soar and mingle with the singer's baritone. The writer of this song was a kindred spirit. Adah knew she was hard to love because she didn't follow the rules. She tried, but she fell short. Over and over. The songwriter must've felt the same way, but at least he knew the woman in his life loved him anyway.

Matthew said he loved her. The thought shook her. She sang louder to drown it out.

"You have an incredible voice."

So did the person who spoke. Husky. Unmistakable. Red heat searing the skin of her neck and cheeks, Adah whirled to find Jackson standing in the doorway, leaning on one crutch, his left leg in a cast that ended below the knee. In his other hand he held a beautiful guitar, its honey-colored wood burnished to a lovely sheen. A white bandage peeked from the V of his black T-shirt and the bruise around it had darkened to an angry green and purple. Adah didn't know where to look first, so she glued her gaze to the intricate designs stitched into the soft brown leather of the cowboy boot on his right foot. Something about his bare left foot made him seem…young.

"I'm serious. You have a beautiful voice—what my music teacher calls a natural vibrato." He shook his head, his mouth hanging open for a beat. "Don't stop. Go on, keep singing."

She had no idea what a vibrato was, but she wanted to know. She wanted to know everything his music teacher had taught him. She wanted a music teacher. *Stop it!* Her job was to clean the house and Jackson was getting in her way. "What are you doing here?"

"I live here." The force of his gaze didn't lessen. "Thought you knew that."

Before she could answer, a dog hobbled into the room, circled Jackson, and halted in front of him, as if standing guard. He was a medium-sized dog with a white face, black ears, and a patch of black over one eye. He also had a limp. "This here is Captain. Captain, this is Amish Girl. Captain! Slow down, there's a good boy, take it easy." Jackson spoke to the dog much the same way he'd spoken to the horse in the corral. "He's laid up like me."

Englisch folks had interesting names for their pets. "Why Captain?"

"It's short for Captain Jack—you know, the pirate. Patch on his eye, wooden leg." He grinned. "My sister named him. She gets a kick out of calling the dog Jack, you know—like me, Jack, short for Jackson."

Englischers also had a strange sense of humor. "He seems pretty spry to me. What happened to his leg?"

"My dad accidently ran into him with the truck. He's a border collie, a working dog, so he tended to herd everything. He can't work no more so he went off to school with me. He's pretty psyched to be home, though. Living in an apartment with city boys ain't his thing. Mine neither, come to think of it."

Captain sidled up to Adah and sniffed. She held out her hand. He sniffed again, woofed, and circled back to Jackson, dragging one back leg.

"You passed inspection."

"That's good. I'm cleaning in here so you'd both better not have dirt on your feet. Don't be tracking up my carpet."

"We wiped our feet, didn't we, Cap?"

Captain woofed again and laid down at Jackson's feet, plopped his head on his paws, and fixed Adah with a quizzical stare.

Adah returned the look. Captain had intelligent eyes and a snout that made him look as if he had a perpetual grin. Dog and owner...they looked a lot alike. She balled up the dust cloth and smoothed it out.

Work, she needed to work. She grabbed another bronze horse, this one heftier than the others, and gave it a quick swipe with the cloth. "Your mother said you went in to town with your brother."

"I did. He dropped me off and headed out to mend a fence that the cattle busted down last night."

"I see."

"So you won't sing for me?"

Back to the subject she'd rather avoid. Jackson was turning out to be as stubborn as a heat rash in summer. Sort of like herself. "I don't sing for an audience. Just to keep myself company while I work."

"That's a shame. A waste. Maybe you'll sing for me later, when you get to know me."

Would she get to know him? Nee. She couldn't. She focused on dusting, ignoring the sudden trembling of her hands.

Jackson hobbled into the room and laid the guitar on one end of the chocolate brown sectional sofa. Captain popped up and followed, circling the sofa and settling in front. With a grunt, Jackson lowered himself next to the instrument, tossed the crutch aside, and propped his leg on the rustic pine coffee table—the one she'd just cleaned. He wiggled his toes. He had big toes. Big feet, really. "You aren't even going to ask how I'm doing?"

Her first time back at the house after the accident, Adah had learned from Mrs. Hart that Jackson had suffered a broken ankle. The cut on his chest had required nine stitches, he had half a dozen broken ribs, and the bruises had been many and colorful, but he would live, as his mother put it. "From the looks of you, you're doing fine."

"Nice."

She did sound sharper than she intended. "I mean, you seem to be mending quickly."

"It's irritating my dad that I'm not helping out more." He waved his hand over the cast. "But truthfully, it's been good. It's giving me time to work on my music and finish some songs I started while I was at school. I figure things happen for a reason. Anyway, I thought I'd sit here and work on a song I just started."

He wrote songs. Not just the lyrics like she did, but the notes too.

The melody. It took every ounce of her willpower not to ask questions. How did he make the words match the music? Did the words come first or the music? Did the words whirl around in his head the way they did in hers?

Daed's words beat a rhythm in her head. She wasn't to be alone with Jackson. She breathed and tried to smooth her expression. *Maid, house cleaner, nothing more.* "Where's your mother?"

"I think she went for a ride. She likes to exercise her horse herself." He pulled a nub of a pencil sporting an oversized pink eraser from behind his ears. His skin reddened under the dark stubble on his chin but his gaze stayed on the paper in front of him. "She told me what your dad said."

Heat blistered Adah's skin. She felt as if she'd been dipped in boiling water. Why would Mrs. Hart share this conversation with Jackson? She'd looked surprised at Adah's explanation that she would have to come back another time if Mrs. Hart wasn't there when she came to clean. "She did?"

"You helped me out when I was in a fix. I appreciated it. I thought we got off to a good start. Now your father thinks I'm dangerous or something?" Jackson seemed to have a great interest in the notebook in front of him. "What did you tell him about me? All I did was get kicked around by a horse. That may make me an idiot, but it don't make me dangerous."

"It's not that. It's we're…he's…we…we're traditional." Was that the right word? She searched her vocabulary for a word an Englisch man would understand. "You're not married. I'm not married. It's not considered…proper."

"I may have some rough edges, but I don't take advantage of women." Now his gaze met hers. Some emotion she couldn't pinpoint danced in his eyes. He leaned back and tugged a pick from his jeans pocket, then picked up the guitar and began to pluck one note at a time, slowly and carefully. Each note sounded hopeful. Hopeful that another might follow. "My parents brought me up right. I try real hard to be a gentleman when it comes to the ladies."

He did seem to have good manners. Still, she'd promised Daed.

"Then why are you sitting here if you know I'm not supposed to be alone in the house with you?"

"Good point." A red the color of beets seeped across his face and crept up to his hairline under hair so tousled it looked as if he'd forgotten to comb it. "Sorry. I was stuck on a verse that isn't coming out right. I thought a change of scenery would help." He plucked another single note. "Back at school, I found that really helped. I'd drive to a park or just drive around and the words would come. Now I can't drive so I'm stuck here."

"I'm supposed to feel sorry for you?" Adah slapped her hand to her mouth. The man was the son of her employer. No call for her to be rude. "I mean, I'm sorry you're stuck, but I have to clean the house, not babysit."

"Do I look like I need a babysitter? I just thought…you're good company. You're cleaning, I'm writing, what does it hurt?"

He'd spent all of an hour—most of that writhing in pain—with her. How would he know if she were good company? "I'm almost finished in here. It's fine. You can write in this room while I clean in the kitchen."

"Thank you, ma'am." A splash of sarcasm painted the courtesy. He strummed this time, a higher note, then a lower one. She wanted him to show her how to do that. He patted the guitar as if to say *good job*. "Would you mind turning down the radio?"

If she turned down the radio, he'd expect her to continue to make conversation. She would forget all about her job and watch him play the guitar. Maybe learn how to play herself. That was the last thing she needed to do. She had enough problems with Daed…and Matthew. Still, it was Jackson's house, and his parents were her employers. "I don't know, I—"

"It's hard to write lyrics for a song with the radio blaring, that's all. I can't hear them in my head. I promise I won't interfere with your cleaning."

He would write lyrics while she cleaned house. It seemed unfair. No, this was her life. The one she was born to live—if Daed and Mudder had any say in it. "Okay."

She flipped the radio off and began to dust around an enormous flat screen TV mounted on the wall. A long, low bookshelf below it contained rows of DVDs interspersed with photos in black and brown wood frames. Photos of Jackson and his brother and sister posing with steers and hogs and huge ribbons. She picked up the first one, a photo of a younger Jackson wearing a blue jacket with FUTURE FARMERS OF AMERICA embroidered in gold on the front. Grinning ear to ear, he held an enormous ribbon in one hand and his steer's harness with the other. Strange things these Englischers documented with photos.

> I've met my match.
> No matter what I do, I can't catch her.
> Every time I get close, she rears up and lets me have it.
> She doesn't give one bit.
> No matter what I do, even something completely new,
> she rears up and lets me have it.
> God knows, He sees how hard I try, but He knows I've met
>   my match.

Adah couldn't help herself. She settled the frame back in its place and turned so she could watch Jackson's right hand pluck the strings and the fingers of his other hand move up and down the frets, agile, quick, making music. Now and then he stopped, frowned, picked up his pencil, and made scratches on the paper he'd laid on the table. He was making music. Fascinated, Adah forgot to feign dusting. She stood, transfixed, as he created a song that she was the first to hear.

"It's rough, really rough." He looked up and presented her with an *aw-shucks* smile. "Sorry you have to hear it before it's finished."

"It's nice…pretty…"

"Naw, it's a mess. It needs a lot of work."

"How do you do it?" She had to know. Here sat another person who did what she longed to do. Write songs and play them. "Do you hear it in your head? Do you hear the words first or the notes?"

"Sometimes the melody comes first, sometimes it's the words, but they get all mixed together in my head. I never know what's gonna come out." He cocked his head, his expression puzzled. "Do you play?"

She shook her head. "I love the way it sounds, though. Sometimes

I hear the words in my head too. I can barely read notes, just what I've learned from looking at books in the library and the bookstore."

"You can't really learn music that way. You have to practice." He slid the strap over his head and held out the guitar. "I can teach you. With a voice like yours, you should learn. I taught my sister RaeAnne. She's no good because she doesn't practice, but that's not my fault."

"No. Thank you, but no." It was all she could do to back away. Every fiber of her being wanted to touch the instrument. "We don't play musical instruments."

"Seriously? Not at all? Why?" His eyebrows rose and his forehead wrinkled, giving him a quizzical look as if someone had asked him a question that stumped him. "That's just crazy talk."

Captain's head popped up and his ears flopped as if he heard something in his master's voice that concerned him. He growled low and soft and laid his head back on his paws. Jackson leaned down and patted his head, his hand sliding along the dog's back with a gentle, calming touch. Adah had to tear her gaze from his hand.

"We don't like to draw attention to ourselves. Playing an instrument would be like saying, *Hey, look at me. I'm special.*" That's the way Daed had explained it to her when she was a little girl and wanted to learn to tap dance like her Englisch friend Tammy. "We sing hymns at church, all together, and we sing at school every day. We have music, just not how you do."

Jackson frowned as if he was turning the information over in his head, studying it really hard. "A cappella?"

"Aca-what?"

"Singing without instruments. It's called a cappella. No wonder you have such a gorgeous voice. You've developed a good ear. You have to hit the notes with no musical accompaniment. Nice."

"I never thought about it. The hymns don't have high notes. They're slow, very slow, almost like chanting."

He plucked a few more notes, first low, then high. "I'm planning to play music for a living." He glanced at the door as if checking to see if anyone were there. "That's our secret, okay?"

A secret. Just like she had to keep her songwriting a secret from her parents, Jackson didn't want his parents to know he wanted to make music for a living. Why would they care? Was it against their religion too? "How do you do that? Make a living playing music around here?"

"You don't. Have you ever heard of Branson?" He lingered on the name as if it tasted sweet on his tongue. "Branson, Missouri?"

"I've heard of it." She tried to recall what she knew from listening to her Englisch friends talk at the parties she'd attended out in the open fields on farms far from her daed's. "People go there to see shows."

"Musical shows. Country music shows." His face shone with excitement as if he could see himself there already. "Soon as I can, I'm going there to audition. I want to try to play some shows."

He made it sound easy. That ugly snake of envy that had plagued Adah before slithered through her again, this time wrapping itself around her heart and squeezing. She wanted to go to Branson. She wanted to see the shows. She wanted to hear the music. She wanted to *play* the music. "When are you going? What do your parents think of this plan?"

"It'll all come to a head soon." His mouth turned down in a tight frown as he tapped his pencil against the paper in a one-two beat. "They don't know it, but I got so involved in making music in Columbia, I didn't really go to class much. I didn't do so hot on my finals. I was already on academic probation. I'm not planning to go back."

"You haven't told your parents?"

"Nope."

"What happens when they find out?"

"Things will blow up. They'll yell about the wasted money, but it wasn't their money. They'll get over it."

"Because it wasn't their money?"

"Part of it I raised by selling my 4H steers at auction each year. Part of it came from a trust fund my Gramps left me. They're not out a dime."

The Englisch kids were allowed to keep the money from the sale of livestock. Adah couldn't imagine. Her family needed the money to feed and clothe themselves and buy basic necessities. "It doesn't seem like it's about the money. They're your parents. Won't they want you at home with them?"

"I'm twenty-one. Sure, Pop wanted me to study agribusiness and come back here to farm with him, but my brother can do it. It's not my thing. Pop will get over it."

Then he wasn't like Daed. Her father wouldn't get over something like that. Not ever. Not because he was mean. He loved her and wanted her to give up worldly ways for the one true God. She clutched the dust cloth and breathed. Time to turn away from this temptation. That was all it was. A temptation.

"Sing with me." Jackson's voice tugged at her. She glanced back. His head was cocked, his gaze hopeful. "It's just a song. Songs give people pleasure. And they give people like us a way to express stuff we can't any other way. What's the harm in that?"

There was plenty of harm if it took her away from her family and her faith. A man like Jackson wouldn't understand that. "I can't."

"Come on, come on, you know you want to."

She did want to, in the worst way. She wanted to sing and play with Jackson so much it hurt. Her throat ached with the need.

"I can't. I have to work." She edged toward the door, caught her knee on the coffee table, stumbled, and dropped the dust cloth. The tips of her ears hot with embarrassment, she snatched up the cloth and made a final dash to the door like wild hogs were chasing her. "Goodbye."

Wild hogs didn't chase her. Jackson's voice calling her name did.

Chapter 8

Adah squeezed out the washcloth and hung it on a hook to dry. Mrs. Hart's kitchen looked spotless. Finally. Her back ached from slapping the mop back and forth over the tile so hard it was a wonder the handle didn't break. Better to put all that energy in something useful. The floor shone. Adah knew from experience this would last only a few hours—just until Mr. Hart traipsed into the kitchen looking for a diet Pepsi and tracked dirt and straw all over it. He didn't seem to understand the concept of wiping his boots on the braided rug sprawled across the doorway that led to the back porch. He wouldn't even notice the damage he'd done. Or care. She dried her hands, resigning herself to the inevitable annihilation of her work. She'd finished the bedrooms, vacuumed, and dusted the dining room and the study and scoured all three bathrooms. Everything. Time to go.

Instead her feet carried her down the carpeted hallway, her footsteps silent, to the living room. The whole time she'd been cleaning, she'd expected Jackson to show up and ask for some lemonade or reiterate his offer to teach her to play or ask her what she thought of his song or ask her to sing with him. Nothing.

Gut. That was *gut.*

She paused near the door, listening. The song fluttered in the air around her, Jackson's voice wandering up and down the low end of the scale in pursuit of the notes.

I've met my match.
No matter what I do, I can't catch her.
I get close, she rears up and lets me have it.
She doesn't give one bit.
No matter what I do, even something completely new,
she rears up and lets me have it.
God knows, He sees how hard I try,
but I guess He knows, I've met my match.

Adah leaned against the wall, clutching the dishtowel to her chest, listening. He was trying to write a song about breaking the horse. Leastways, that was what it sounded like to her. She liked the rhyming and the rhythm of it. It was just a beginning, but he had a piece of something. She liked the chords he'd chosen.

His voice drifted away and died out. A scratching sound told her he was marking on the paper. She wanted to see what he was writing. Hear what he was thinking. Did the words flow into his head the way they did hers?

"Whatcha doing, Amish girl?"

He peeked around the corner. To her chagrin, she jumped and the heat on her face advertised the fact that she was blushing. "I finished cleaning. I'm heading out."

"Sure. You were listening to my song."

"I…it's nice. I like it."

"Good, 'cause it's about you."

"Is not," she sputtered. "It's about the horse, the corral, and breaking the horse."

"Sure, it's about that too." His grin broadened. "It's not finished yet. You'll see."

"I have to go."

"Promise me one thing and you can go."

"You can't keep me from—"

"Just promise me you'll let me play the whole song for you when I finish it."

"We'll see—"

"You're my first audience for this song. Besides Cap, of course, and I think he's tone-deaf. He sleeps through most of it. Don't you want to hear how it turns out?" He gave her that hangdog expression her brother gave her when he wanted the last piece of fried chicken—the one she'd already put on her plate. She always gave in. "Come on, Adah."

"You called me by my name."

"I know your name." He leaned against the opposite wall and rubbed at the spot above the V of his T-shirt where the stitches were. "Come on, I'll share my song with you and you can share yours with me."

"I don't have any songs."

"Sure you do. That's why you asked me if the words came first or the melody."

She struggled with how much to tell him. "So?"

"So, I'm gonna be a country singer someday, a star. With your voice, you could be too. We could be a duet like Conway Twitty and Loretta Lynn."

"You're daft." Her mind saw it, imagined it, even as she dismissed the possibility as an impossibility. "I'm the Amish girl who cleans your house. You don't know anything about me. And your parents will expect you to finish college and come work here on the farm. People usually end up doing what's expected of them."

Leastways that had been her experience. As much as the boys and girls she knew ran around when they came to their age of rumspringa, they almost always settled down and did the right thing. They wanted the Plain life. She wanted the Plain life.

Didn't she?

"Not always. They don't always." The showboat cowboy from the corral had disappeared. His blue eyes were dark, his expression pensive. "I'm not spending the rest of my life figuring out how many bushels of wheat we're getting to an acre and how much fertilizer is needed to increase the yield. You want to spend the rest of your life cleaning other people's houses?"

"I'll marry and clean my own house."

If she didn't mess it up.

"Stick with me and someone else will clean your house for you." He straightened and took a step toward her, leaving the crutch leaning against the wall. He balanced himself within reach. "You have a huge, beautiful voice. That's a gift. Not everyone gets that gift. You said yourself you like to write songs. We could write together. We could sing together."

She couldn't drag her gaze from his face. The cadence of his voice mesmerized her. He meant what he said. He was offering her the very thing she'd always wanted. Her dream stood before her in tattered blue jeans, a black T-shirt, and one cowboy boot. "Your song is nice." Her voice sounded breathless in her own ears. "You have a nice voice too."

"So let me play it for you when I finish it? And then we'll see what happens after that. Just don't run away from the idea."

"I don't know if I can—"

"What's going on here?" Mrs. Hart strode through the hallway, shedding a pair of riding gloves as she stalked toward them in brown leather boots that reached her knees. She wore her jeans tucked into the boots and a crisp white blouse with a button-down collar. Not one red hair on her head moved. "You'll not get the house spotless standing there chatting with this ne'er-do-well."

Mrs. Hart talked like that, like she'd learned English from an old novel. Adah forced a smile. "I'm finished. I was just letting your son know that I'm leaving."

Mrs. Hart shook one long, slim finger with a nail painted a deep red at Adah. "Not just yet. The tiles in the guest bathroom look a little scummy. Take another pass at them, will you? And then stop by the kitchen and I'll pay you."

The tiles in the guest bathroom were perfectly clean. The bathroom hadn't looked as if it had been used since the last time Adah scoured it. "Yes, ma'am."

She squeezed past Mrs. Hart and darted toward the hall that led to the bathroom.

"Adah."

Adah turned back at the command in her employer's high pitched voice. "Yes, ma'am."

"You said your father doesn't want you working in the house when I'm not around."

"Yes, ma'am."

"It takes two to tango."

Adah had never danced, let alone done the tango. "Ma'am?"

Mrs. Hart fixed her with a hard stare. "You do your work, you get paid, you hustle home. That way no one gets into trouble."

Jackson shifted on his crutch. The paper in his hand fluttered to the floor. "Mom, nothing's going on here. I was just talking to her about—"

"Hush now. I know how you are with girls." Mrs. Hart picked up the paper. She didn't even look at it before she crumpled it in a ball. "I don't want any lip from you. You may be twenty-one years old, but I can still take a hickory stick to your behind. By the way, you stink like cigarettes. I catch you smoking in my house, I'll tan your hide."

Adah doubted that, but she understood Mrs. Hart's point. Clearly. "I'll take care of the bathroom."

"Double check the toilet as well."

"Mom—"

Mrs. Hart stalked away.

"Adah—"

"No." Adah didn't look at Jackson. Her place had been made clear.

"Come on, Adah. Don't let her spoil things."

There was nothing to spoil. Mrs. Hart was right. Adah headed to the bathroom. A toilet awaited her attention.

Chapter 9

Once inside the Harts' guest bathroom, which was bigger than her own bedroom, Adah shut the door and leaned against it, breathing in and out until an unexpected, unworthy anger mingled with embarrassment subsided. She had no need or right to be angry. Mrs. Hart was right and this home belonged to her and Mr. Hart. Adah simply cleaned. Nothing more. Mrs. Hart had reminded her of her place. Adah inhaled again and knelt to remove the cleansers from the cabinets that ran underneath the long marble counter fitted with two deep sinks and brass faucets. The aroma of spearmint and eucalyptus hand soap calmed her. Cleaning calmed her.

She glanced in the gold-framed rectangular mirror that covered the entire wall over the sinks. Ugly, cherry red blotches darkened her cheeks and neck. Her prayer kapp had slid to one side and tendrils of hair escaped her once neat bun. She didn't look like a good Plain girl. She looked guilty. Her hand went to her kapp, fumbling to straighten it. Her fingers shook. She smoothed the hair and closed her eyes against the self portrait in front of her. *I'm sorry, Gott. Sorry. I don't know why I can't seem to do better.*

A sharp rap at the door broke the silence. She jumped, her heart slamming against her rib cage. Surely Jackson wouldn't follow her into the bathroom. Unless he was bent on getting her fired. She needed this job or she would quit.

No, she wouldn't. Not when she had the chance to see Jackson play the guitar, see how it was done, hear how it was done. Sing songs with him.

The door swung open. RaeAnne Hart stuck her head in, her long, shiny black hair hanging down in a rippling curtain that partially hid her face. "Hey, Adah. Mom said you were in here."

Adah tried to arrange her face in neutral lines. Jackson's sister didn't know her. RaeAnne wouldn't be able to read the turmoil that raged in her. More embarrassment cascaded over her like a steamy waterfall. Matthew had told her once he could read every emotion on her face. He liked that about her. She couldn't hide her feelings. An honest face, he'd said. He didn't like it so much the night he told her he loved her and she hadn't returned the favor. What he'd read on her face had hurt him, something she never wanted to do again. "Did you need in? I can wait outside."

"Nope. Stay put." Her flip-flops slapping on the slick black and white tiles, RaeAnne sashayed in skintight jean shorts over to the toilet, flipped the lid down, and plopped on it. She snapped her gum a couple of times and studied Adah with sharp blue eyes that were bright against her fair skin and dark hair. She and Jackson could be twins, if she were a whole lot taller, heavier, and a little bit older. "I want to talk to you."

In the months that Adah had cleaned for the Harts she'd run into RaeAnne a sum total of three or four times. Jackson's only sister spent a lot of time riding horses or staying in town where she attended high school. Adah had seen her around town and at a couple of the concerts she and Matthew had attended, but never close enough to exchange hellos. They lived in different worlds, after all. When RaeAnne stayed at the farm, she made a huge mess of her room and didn't seem to know the purpose of a dirty clothes hamper, choosing instead to drop her clothes wherever she stood when she undressed. "Did I need to work on your room some more?"

"No, dude. It's so perfect it gives me the willies. Who knew there was carpet under all those clothes? Problem is when you put them in the hamper like that, Mom expects me to actually wash them."

That made sense to Adah, who'd been doing laundry since she was tall enough to fill the wash machine with water and run the clothes through the wringer to the tub of rinse water. All RaeAnne would have to do would be drop the clothes into a machine, add soap, and turn a knob. That didn't actually amount to work in Adah's way of thinking. "Is that what you wanted to talk to me about?"

"Nope." RaeAnne snapped her gum some more, plucked at the hem of her purple T-shirt, which read REAL WOMEN DRIVE PICK-UPS, and fixed Adah with a sharp stare. "Jack has a girlfriend."

"What?"

"My brother has a girlfriend."

"That's good, I mean, I guess." Adah picked up a sponge and the bottle of glass cleaner. Why would RaeAnne tell her this? All Adah wanted to do was finish cleaning the bathroom, collect her payment, and get home. She didn't want Daed sitting on the porch waiting for her when she arrived. "But it's none of my concern."

"That's the thing. Dani Jo is a friend of mine. She's had a crush on Jackson for like forever, you know?" RaeAnne leaned back and crossed her arms over her flat chest. She sounded much aggrieved. "They hung out over the Christmas break and he's been texting her and talking to her on Facebook and all that while he was at school. She was all excited for him to get back to New Hope and now he's home and he hasn't called her once in two weeks."

And all that. All things Adah didn't do. Couldn't do. She'd watched the kids at the concerts, whipping out their phones, their thumbs flying, expressions intent. Half the time they were on the phone and missing the performance. "Okay."

"He's totally ignoring her." RaeAnne's voice caught. She ducked her head. "When she messages him, he doesn't answer."

"Why are you telling me this? Why aren't you talking to your brother about it?"

"After you helped him out when he had his little accident in the corral, he pestered Mom with questions about you at the supper table. He even asked me about you, like I know anything about you guys. I told him to get a life. He's been mooning around the house ever since."

"He has a broken ankle."

"His fingers aren't broken. I'm telling you, he stopped texting her the day he met you."

"Maybe he thinks he can't court her because he can't drive right now."

"Dani Jo can drive. Leastways she can when her parents unground her for that fender bender she had on the way to the movies Friday night."

"Did you ask him about it?"

"I did. He said the time away at school kind of like changed his thinking on things. He says Dani Jo's too immature for him. That's totally bogus, if you ask me." RaeAnne raked her hand through her hair. It fell in a perfect wave on her shoulders. "She's eighteen and she has a job at the Dairy Queen and she's on the honor roll at school. She'll be the head cheerleader in the fall. She does it all. What more could he ask for? Dani Jo's been my best friend like forever. She's perfect for him."

Adah struggled to find a response. She hadn't asked RaeAnne for any of this information. During her rumspringa, she'd had plenty of opportunity to see firsthand the life of Englisch teenagers in New Hope. She didn't covet what they had. Okay, if she were honest with herself, she did covet, a little, some things, like the freedom to decide for herself. Not about clothes or makeup or schooling or the Friday night football game and the funny little outfits the girls wore when they jumped up and down and did cartwheels on the sidelines. She'd sat in the buggy with Matthew one night and watched it all from the parking lot. It had been fun, but it hadn't stirred a feeling of want in her. Or need.

Her rumspringa had been...research. Peeking at another life to see if it were the right life or the better life for her. Would she be more content with that other life? No, she was content in the Plain world...for the most part. It was the music. That was what she coveted. The music. She didn't need to know about Jackson Hart's social life. Or lack thereof. It didn't matter. Couldn't be allowed to matter. "I'm sure Dani Jo is very nice, but maybe your brother spent some time with her and realized she isn't the right one for him. It happens."

"It sounds to me like he met somebody else."

Adah waved the sponge in RaeAnne's direction. "I need to finish cleaning. I have to get home. My mother expects me to help with supper."

RaeAnne didn't budge. "Are you interested in Jack?"

"We don't do that." A true statement. But not the whole truth. "It's not our way."

"Do what? Hang out with boys?"

Adah's community had been living near New Hope for three years now. Some of the folks there still didn't have a clue about the Plain life and what it entailed. "Your brother is…he's a nice man, but we keep to ourselves. We don't mix with Englisch folks when it comes to"—she sought words the girl would understand—"hanging out."

"You might want to tell Jack that."

"Why? Did he say something to you?"

"He didn't have to. He's got this hangdog look on his face and he's writing love songs about you."

"He's not…it's not like that." Or was it?

RaeAnne stood. "I know my brother. I don't know why, but a lot of girls think his scraggly hair and five o'clock shadow and those big blue eyes make him cute. Dani Jo has had a crush on him since we were in grade school. I keep telling her he's not worth it, but she really likes him and I don't want to see her hurt."

"You need to tell your brother that."

"He goes through girls like I go through new purses." RaeAnne's tone bordered on disgust. "And right now, he has his eye on you."

"Why?" Adah pointed at her apron and long skirt. "What would he see in a girl like me?"

"All I know is men have barf for brains when it comes to women." RaeAnne brushed past Adah and slapped her hand on the doorknob. "All I can figure is Jack likes a challenge."

She opened the door and looked back. "And girl, you would be the ultimate challenge."

Chapter 10

Matthew slammed the hammer against the nail with a quick *pop, pop, pop*. He pulled another one dangling from his lip, positioned it, and pounded it in. The swing of the hammer against nail felt good. He could do this all day. Had been doing it all day. The frame of the small dawdi haus had gone up in a few hours. Helping hands made a difference. He didn't even mind the brilliant sun broiling a spot between his shoulders or the sweat rolling down his forehead and collecting in his eyebrows. Hard work felt good. It felt clean. It smelled clean, like woodchips and sawdust. It felt a long way from the conversation he'd had with Adah he'd been playing over and over in his head for two weeks now. The arrival of the Gringriches had kept him occupied along with the start of the harvest. An off-week for services meant they didn't see each other on Sunday either. He could've shone a flashlight in her window, but what for? So she could tell him she wasn't in any hurry to spend her life with him?

He dropped the hammer, leaned back on his haunches, and lifted his hat so he could wipe away the sweat with his sleeve. The beehive of activity around him soothed him. This community could be counted on.

Unlike Adah.

"I brought you a lemonade." A voice as light and sweet as angel food cake caused him to swivel. Elizabeth Gringrich sauntered across the yard, a plastic yellow tumbler so filled with liquid and ice the contents sloshed over the side as she walked. She smiled and slipped an errant curl of blonde hair back under her kapp with her free hand. "You look baked."

"Broiled more like it." Matthew stood, took her offering, and gulped a long swallow. It was icy and sweet and sour all at the same time. Like life. He took his time, inhaling her scent of vanilla and soap, as he set the glass on a plank propped up between two sawhorses and wiped at his mouth with his sleeve. "Danki."

Elizabeth had a bright, clean look about her that made him think of a late spring morning. All crisp and clear. A wide open smile with nothing to hide. No words milling around in her head, trying to get out. Simplicity.

He could do with some simplicity.

Elizabeth smiled. "I should be thanking you."

For what? Opening their home? One could expect no less. Even if it meant the girls had been sleeping three to a bed and the little ones were enjoying sleeping bags and pretending to camp out every night. "No need."

"Your family's hospitality is much appreciated."

"Our doors are always open to friends."

"Anybody with eyes can see you're crammed into the house. It's full to the rafters." She leaned against a stack of sheetrock as if she had all the time in the world for this conversation. "And your groossmammi and daadi aren't even here yet."

"It's fine."

"Do you always talk so much? I can barely keep up."

He chuckled and shoved his hat over his eyes so she wouldn't see his expression. He wasn't a big talker and he'd been in the habit of letting Adah fill the spaces in the conversation. An occasional joke seemed all she needed to keep her chattering. The girl never lacked for words. She had stories to tell, ideas to share, thoughts she couldn't seem to contain. It might bother some men, but he liked that about her. He couldn't wait for the next thing that would pop out of her mouth and send him over the edge, laughing. He rubbed his fingers over the rough stucco of the drywall to ground himself. "I'd better get busy. They'll be here by nightfall."

"With all this help, you'll be *done* by nightfall."

"Elizabeth!" The booming voice made them both turn. Enoch Gringrich strode around the corner of the frame that would be the small sitting room. Shaking his head so his thick gray beard bobbed, he held one hand up as if it pained him. "Elizabeth, run inside and tell your mudder I need tweezers. Caught a nasty splinter here."

Without a word, Elizabeth tossed Matthew a quick, dainty smile, lifted her long skirt, and scurried toward the house. Matthew turned back to his work.

"My dochder is a hard worker."

Surprised, Matthew paused and looked up at Enoch, who looked like a big wounded bear. He stood wringing his hand, the size of a platter, as if the splinter caused him more pain than his stoic expression would permit. "That's *gut*."

"She's a good girl."

Matthew saw no need to respond to such a statement. He'd known Elizabeth for many years, but only in small bursts as they visited back and forth. She seemed nice enough. Easy on the eyes. Uncomplicated.

"An innocent girl."

Matthew straightened. "You're blessed."

Enoch sniffed. "I am. Her mudder and I pray every day that she is a good fraa to a good man."

"Gott is good." What more could he say? Most likely, Daed had said something to this man. Or with all the moving about, Enoch felt he'd deprived his girl of her chance to forge a special friendship with a suitable man. "His plan will provide."

As if satisfied by the answer, Enoch swiveled and stomped toward the house.

What had that been all about? Matthew smacked another nail on the head, hammering the plank mercilessly. What had Daed told Enoch? What did Daed know?

"He knows."

Matthew missed the nail and hit his thumb. He dropped the

hammer and danced around, shaking his hand, and found his sister bearing down on him. A regular parade of people getting in the way of his work. "Molly! You can't be sneaking up on a man like that. Look what you made me do!"

"*Ach*, poor thing." Molly scooted between him and the sawhorse where he'd set the glass of lemonade. She scooped a piece of ice from it and held it out. "Here."

"That was my lemonade." He took the ice and rubbed it on his thumb. "Aren't you supposed to be fixing supper?"

"My hands are clean. There are twenty women in there. The kitchen is so packed, I couldn't move." Molly sipped his lemonade, an appreciative expression on her face. "Enoch knows."

"What?" Matthew turned his back on his sister. "Knows what?"

"I heard Mudder and Daed talking about Enoch and Clara's daughters. How Elizabeth is of marrying age. How she'd make a good wife for you. Daed says Enoch asked about you special. Daed told him you were having a hard row to hoe with your special friend."

"How would he know that?" Molly's love of stretching stories out so she could savor the effect annoyed him greatly. "Courting is private."

"Anyone with eyes can see. I saw her at the library the other day and she was writing love songs. In English." Molly sighed, her round face troubled. "She was nice to me and I like her, but I'm worried for you."

"Why? I'm a big boy."

"You're my bruder."

"Jah."

"She's far from the path. You have to see that. Daed does. Mudder does. Thomas does."

"Did you say something to Thomas?"

"Nee. Not my place to be talking to the deacon about anything. I'm telling you—"

"Everyone should mind their own business." Matthew picked up another piece of sheetrock and leaned it against the wood frame. "Carrying tales is a pitiful way to pass the time."

"Nee, it's not like that." Molly set the lemonade on the sawhorse and slid a little closer. "You can burrow your head in the sand all you want, but it doesn't change the fact that Adah is on a dangerous path and it's taking her away from you. You have to let her go. Otherwise, you'll be lost too."

Matthew studied his sister's face. He'd never seen her brown eyes so worried behind her thick-rimmed glasses. She was the calm one, the one who always thought the best of people. The one who always prayed that things would turn out but was willing to accept whatever came. Even being alone when all her friends had married.

"You're exaggerating. Everyone is." He set the hammer down and straightened. "She's a little lost, but she'll come around."

"Why isn't she here today?"

"She's cleaning houses, like always. She works hard."

"You might give some thought to what else she does at those houses. And with whom."

"If one of our sheep falters and gets lost, we have to bring her back into the fold."

Molly's face softened. "You're right about that. But maybe you're not the best person to try to do that. You should leave it to Thomas and Luke."

"This is what a rumspringa is for."

"I know, but sometimes what it does is lead a person to where she really wants to go. A place that might not include you."

"I'm not giving up on her. She'll find her way back."

Molly's answer was lost in a host of shouts and whoops. They both turned toward the road. A van pulled up into the yard and the doors flew open. Daed unfolded his long legs and hopped out. Groossdaadi's somber, unsmiling face appeared behind him.

Groossdaadi had arrived. He would understand. He'd know what to do. He had a vast store of knowledge and wisdom that never failed.

Matthew laid the hammer on the sawhorse and strode toward the van. Molly flew ahead of him, arms flapping as if she might take off like a bird in sheer excitement. "You made good time," she called out. "We didn't expect you until supper."

"We did. They were packed and ready to go right after breakfast." Daed brushed past Matthew. "Give me a hand with their bags."

"I just want to say hello real quick."

Daed headed for the back of the van without answering. Matthew turned to his grandfather. "It's good to see you. We've got the frame up and we're started on the walls. Your *haus* will be ready in no time."

Groossdaadi stared at him. "Who are you?"

Taken aback, Matthew wavered. "It's me, Matthew."

Groossmammi hopped from the van with all the agility of a young girl, ignoring the hand Molly held out for her. "I'm fine, girl, fine. No need to hover." She gave Molly a kiss on the cheek and then stuck her hand through the crook in Groossdaadi's arm and held on tight. "Joseph, it's Molly and Matthew. I do believe Matthew's grown since we saw him last year at Christmas."

"Nee." A wave of embarrassment rolled over Matthew. He was too old to still be growing. "It's the new straw hat. Makes me look taller."

"He's Aaron's oldest, you remember, right, Joseph?" Groossmammi elbowed her husband. "He caught that catfish that was longer than he was tall the summer he was ten years old."

Groossdaadi peered from behind wire-rimmed spectacles that perched just above the ridge in his nose. He cocked his head. "That was some mighty fine eating, that catfish." He leaned closer, head cocked. "That you, Matthew?"

"It's me."

"Hmmmph." Groossdaadi escaped Groossmammi's grasp and strode past Matthew, skinny legs pumping. His faded blue shirt and black pants hung on him as if he'd shrunk or Groossmammi had sewed them a size too big—something she would never do. "Then hitch up the buggy. You can take me home."

"You are home." Groossmammi waved a finger at Molly, who scurried after him. "We talked about this. Go on in. I'm right behind you." Groossmammi turned to Matthew. "He's a little peeved at the move, but he'll settle in. Like I told your daed, he's a stubborn old coot, but he'll get used to the idea."

Matthew bent to hug her. She felt like a bag of bones, all hard angles and points. "Welcome to your new home."

"No need to get fancy." She squeezed from his grip. "Point me in the direction of the kitchen and I'll get busy and help. Looks like you have a lot of mouths to feed."

"We have plenty of help. Molly will show you the room they made up for you—just until we get the haus ready." Matthew searched for a way to ask the question.

"Don't worry. He'll be fine once he's settled in. He's a little tired from the drive. A change in his routine sets him back a bit. Doctor says it's to be expected."

"He's been to the doctor?"

"He fell and hit his head Friday, so he didn't have a choice." If Groossmammi was tired, it didn't show. Her wrinkled cheeks were pink and her faded blue eyes bright with good cheer. "It's old age, pure and simple. Ain't nothing pretty about it, but we'll get by."

Matthew watched as she fairly skipped up the front porch steps. Spry as ever. It seemed old age picked on some more than others. Daed trudged by, bags in both hands. "You gonna help or stand there watching?"

"He didn't recognize me."

Daed dumped the suitcase on the porch and reached for the screen door. "When I got there yesterday, he called me Levi."

"Who's Levi?"

"I have no idea."

Chapter 11

Adah scooped the steaming stewed tomatoes from the large pot with a long ladle and poured the contents into the Mason jar, careful not to spill a drop of it on her bare hand. She wiped at her sweating face with the back of her sleeve. The billowing steam coming from the pans on the propane stove enveloped the entire kitchen. The pungent aromas of fresh tomatoes, dill, onion, and oregano made her mouth water.

Three rows of six jars each already sat on the prep table, their lids popping in a merry tune that sang in her ears. They sang of contentment, prosperity, blessing, bountifulness. She hummed along in a tune that had no need of lyrics. The chatter ping-ponging among Matthew's mother and his Grandma Frannie, Emma, Katie, Mudder, and Clara and Elizabeth Gringrich, who were seated around the prep table, provided the harmony as they cleaned and chopped cucumbers and onions, the knives rapping on wood, the percussion in this canning frolic.

"You're sure quiet over there." Emma's voice wafted over the steady give and take of the other women. "Whatever are you thinking about, Adah? A boy, maybe?"

Not a boy anymore. A man. Men. Two men. A cowboy and a Plain man. Cowboy hat. Straw hat. Work boots. Cowboy boots. There was a song in there somewhere. Jackson had walked into her life like a cowboy right out of a country western song. Matthew had always been in her life, like a farmer working the fields year after year, certain he would reap what he sowed.

Adah kept her back to the other women so they couldn't see the heat rising on her face. At least she could blame the steaming tomatoes for it. She'd been able to avoid Jackson for a couple of weeks now. He was off at doctor's appointments or out with his father. Hopefully tomorrow would be the same. She hoped. Really. She would clean the house and that was it. In the meantime, she expected to see Matthew here, but so far their paths hadn't crossed. He worked with the other men in the dawdi haus, finishing out the interior rooms, laying the linoleum in the kitchen, and painting.

"Adah? You really are daydreaming, aren't you?"

She started, realizing Emma was waiting for a response. "Nee. I was thinking about the books Molly likes to read sometimes. Westerns."

"Cowboys," Emma giggled, a funny sound coming from the mother of three and stepmother to two more. "The cowboys around here are fun with their hats and boots and Western shirts."

"And those big buckles," added Katie, sounding more like a teenager than a grandma. "They do like to show off, don't they?"

Big buckles. Show-off. Jackson didn't strike Adah as a show-off, more as someone at ease with who he was and what he wanted. The heat deepened on her face, spreading to her neck. She could never be at ease, because what she wanted was something she shouldn't want. Thankful she had her back to the other women, she wiped her hands on a dishtowel and threw it on the counter. "I'm going to see what's taking the twins and Rebecca so long to dig up those beets. They should be back from the garden by now."

"I'll go." Elizabeth rose from the table. "You have your hands full here."

"Nee. I'll go. Don't worry about it."

"It may take both of you to get them in here. They probably decided they'd rather pick strawberries. None of them likes beets much. 'Course, what one says, they all repeat." Emma bent over and smoothed the hair of baby Jeremiah, sleeping in a basket at her feet.

"Knowing little Mary, she probably took a detour to the barn to see the new batch of kittens."

Emma's younger twin sister, little Mary, so known to distinguish her from Matthew's mother, Mary Troyer, had become known as the instigator of many an escapade on which her twin Lillie never failed to follow. Older stepsister Rebecca's influence helped some, but Emma despaired of taming their unduly stubborn streak. While no one offered the excuse, Adah often wondered if it had to do with losing their parents at such a tender age. They were sweet yet wayward girls. "I'll get them back on track." She brushed past Elizabeth, who had a puzzled look on her heat-flushed face. "They know me. They'll do as I ask."

The implication being they didn't know Elizabeth.

"Make them pick the beets. Don't you do it," Emma directed. "They can't be allowed to shirk their assigned duties."

"Don't you worry. I have no problem with that." Adah liked digging around in the fresh-smelling dirt in the garden, but today her job was at the stove. Still, the cooler air outdoors—if July air could be called cool—would be nice after the stifling, damp heat of the kitchen. "I know how it is. I used to be just as wayward."

"Used to be." Mudder and the others cackled with laughter. "You're a reformed soul now, are you?"

"I'm a grown woman." Adah trotted to the door, trying not to catch her mother's gaze. "I've given up childish play."

She hadn't written a single word since her encounter with the various members of the Hart family. She wanted to be good. She didn't want to stray. Yet the words pressed inside her head, longing to be released. Words with notes attached. Now that Jackson had opened her eyes to the possibilities of writing music to go with the lyrics, she couldn't stop hearing the tunes in her head. When she lay down at night, when she awoke in the morning. Why was writing music—playing music—wrong? How wrong could it be? The rest of the world did it. They couldn't all be sinners.

Such thoughts for a Plain woman. She did her best to stifle them. Time to set aside childish play. Time to grow up. The Ordnung was the

Ordnung. One didn't question why. The point was to give oneself up. To put God first. No others before Him. No idols. The women's laughter followed her as she fled out the door and down the back steps, her thoughts chasing her like a pack of snarling, hungry coyotes.

Mary's garden had flourished despite the endless days of one hundred degree weather—with the help of a few soaking rainstorms scattered across the last few months. To Adah's surprise, the twins hunkered down next to Rebecca at the far end, a nice pile of beets next to them, dirt still clinging to their roots. Like her, the girls were trying to be good, it seemed.

"Girls, that's probably enough for today," she called, shielding her eyes from the sun with her hand. "We have a bunch of pickles and green beans to do first."

"Does that mean we have to go inside?" Lillie's face puckered in a frown matched by the one on little Mary's face. "It's too hot in there."

"I'd like some lemonade," Rebecca offered. "Wouldn't you? Let's take these in and get a nice, cool glass of lemonade."

"You need to clean the beets and get them ready to pickle," Adah added. "They're waiting for you. One of you needs to bring another box of empty jars up from the cellar too. It won't take all three of you."

"I'll do it." Rebecca popped to her feet, brushing dirt from her apron. "Meet you inside, girls."

Lillie frowned. Little Mary pulled another beet and plunked it down on the pile. Neither responded to Rebecca's cheery statement.

"Let them have their fun." Richard Bontrager strolled across the yard toward her, his broad shoulders silhouetted against the fierce sun. "Can't you see they're having a ball getting dirt on their faces and under their fingernails?"

They didn't look particularly content to Adah. "What are you doing here?"

"Helping finish out the dawdi haus." He glanced at the house and then back at Adah. Something about his expression told her there was more to it. "I thought I'd fill a cooler with lemonade. The water's about all gone. The men are thirsty."

She started to turn. "I'll get it for—"

"Nee, I wanted to…I mean I need to wash up anyway."

Adah studied his sweaty, sunburned face. No way Richard came up to the house to wash up. The men didn't do that. They might stick their face in the horses' water trough to cool off now and again, but they didn't care if they were dirty and sweaty. No sense cleaning up until the end of the day. "What are you really doing here?"

"Getting lemonade."

"Did you come to see someone?" The memory of Molly's longing face floated in Adah's mind. Had Molly taken her advice and made the brownies to take out to Edna's when she picked up the library books? "You did, didn't you?"

"How do you know I didn't come to see you?" He flashed her a smile. "How come you didn't make it to the last baptism class? I thought I'd see you there."

She ignored his question. "I don't live here so you had no cause to think I would be here. It's Molly, isn't it? You wanted to see her."

A dull red crept up his neck, deepening his tan. "She brought brownies to the house a while back when she came to pick up some books to return for Edna." He hesitated, his gaze falling to his feet. He shifted his weight from one foot to the other. "She told Edna…well…anyway, I thought I'd thank her for the brownies."

"That's real polite of you." Plain folks didn't abide much by fancy thank yous, but it didn't hurt to let a person know a kindness was appreciated. In this case, Richard had played right into her plan. Unfortunately, Molly had to work at the library today. "Molly's at work. I bet she has her hands full helping with all the extra company and the grandparents here."

"That's why I'm here. I'll be helping out for the next month or so, maybe longer. Tobias said he could spare me."

Good. He'd see Molly on a regular basis. "That's *gut*."

They were both silent for a few minutes. "I guess I should—"

"I should—"

They both stopped, waiting for the other to finish the sentence.

"Are you and Matthew courting?" Richard's face darkened to the color of the pile of beets on the ground next to Mary and Lillie. "Still,

I mean. I know you were, but lately, I hadn't seen y'all together, and, well, I just wondered…"

Adah opened her mouth and shut it. She wasn't sure how to answer that question—not truthfully, anyway. "Courting is private."

"I know it's an awkward question, not one I should be asking." He traced a line in the dirt with his dusty work boot, looking like a little boy with his head ducked. "But I got myself into trouble once before and I don't want to do it again. So I figure it makes more sense just to flat out ask and save everyone a lot of embarrassment."

Adah had heard about those problems, seen them firsthand with her brother Daniel's friend Michael and his special friend, Phoebe, now his fraa. She had enough man troubles already. "If you're asking about me, my heart is taken."

Those words were the flat-out truth. Two men had a hold of her heart and between the two of them, they might tear it apart.

"A day late and a dollar short…again." Richard's woebegone expression squeezed Adah's heart. He sighed. "I guess God's plan is for me to be a bachelor."

"Nee. You must be blind as a bat." Men were so thickheaded sometimes—most of the time. "Don't you know why Molly brought those double fudge brownies with walnuts for you?"

His forehead wrinkled under the broad flat brim of his straw hat. He cocked his head. His dumbfounded expression would be funny were it not so painful. "Molly?"

"Jah, Molly." Adah wanted to stamp her foot. Matchmaking was frowned upon, but Plain women could be forced to it in a pinch when men wore blinders. "You think she bakes brownies for everyone?"

"Molly," he said again, his face more contemplative. "Huh. She's nice. I never thought of her like—"

"Well, you should. She's sweet and kind and a good cook and a hard worker and smart—and did I say kind? She's so kind she makes two lunches every day so that she'll have one to share with someone—anyone who crosses her path. And she's—"

"Whoa, whoa. She's like you, you mean—"

"Nee, nee, she's a much better person than I am!"

"She really makes two lunches every day?"

"She really does."

"What's going on here?"

A chill brushed Adah's neck. Her heart froze. Richard's gaze went over her shoulder. To his credit, his expression didn't change. "I was just telling Adah here that your sister Molly makes a mighty fine brownie."

His voice was calm, collected, his expression genial. The embarrassment that had Adah in its grip receded. She faced Matthew. "You must be as thirsty as Richard is. I'll fill the cooler with lemonade if you'll cart it to the haus."

"In a minute." Matthew's cool gaze spun over her to Richard and then back. "I'd like a word, if I might."

"With me?"

"Jah."

Richard eased toward the back porch steps. "I'll get the lemonade."

Matthew leaned on the nearest post, but his stance still seemed tense. He was wound tighter than a barbed wire fence. "I spoke with Thomas."

No *hello*. No *how are you*. No *I miss you*. Matthew had never been one for sweet nothings, but he'd always made her feel as if he cared for her comfort and well-being. Right now, nothing about his attitude indicated he thought more of her than he did the two girls digging in the garden on the other side of the fence. Adah could be just as cool. "About what?"

"He said he'll let you make up the lessons you've missed. Do the reading. Talk with him separately until you're caught up if you decide to be baptized this fall."

Irritation—no, anger—whipped through her at his attitude. "Why would you do that—talk to Thomas on my behalf? Baptism is a decision I must make. No one can make it for me."

"Because I care…you're a…this is…" His jaw pulsed as he gritted his teeth. His Adam's apple bobbed. "I'm worried for you."

"My spiritual well-being?" A curious look on her face, Lillie got to her feet and stuffed a few more beets in the basket. Adah fought to bring her voice down so only Matthew could hear her. "I'm fine. Don't worry."

"You'll take the baptism classes then?" His voice softened and something crept into his expression. It looked like hope. "With me?"

"Is this about baptism or about us?"

"Both, I reckon."

Adah became aware that the twins had stopped any pretense of digging in the garden. They both stared, unabashed curiosity on their faces. "Girls, that's plenty. Take those inside and wash them off." Gripping the nearest fence post with both hands, Adah waited until they traipsed by, taking their sweet time. She turned to Matthew. "How can you think about this right now with all the work you have to do? With your grandparents being here and the harvest and a full house with the Gringriches?"

She wanted to say *with Elizabeth*. But she didn't. She wouldn't blame him if he chose another. She'd pushed him away. And her mind daily thought of another. Matthew could never know about Jackson. Never.

"For those exact reasons, I find I have no place to go that isn't already full." His voice roughened. "I rode those acres Daed plans to give me. There are lots of shade trees and a pond. I found a spot...a good place to build a house for my family. With lots of room for kinner."

His tone begged her to see it with him. Adah could see it. Clearly. The muscles in her neck and shoulders clenched. She rubbed her hands over the rough wood of the post, focusing on the grooves under her fingers. "I'll talk to Thomas."

"Pray about it."

"I will."

"What is it? What is it that's holding you back?" Matthew pushed away from the fence and faced her. Hurt mixed with confusion etched his face. "I don't understand."

"I'm sorry. I can't explain it. I'm so sorry."

"Is it about the music?"

"Who told you about the music?" How could he know? No one

knew except Jackson. And Molly. Maybe Molly had said something after that day at the library. "It's nothing. I'm not doing anything wrong."

"I didn't say you were." He looked confused. "You know I've always let you have your way on the music. I went to the concerts with you. I bought the radio for the buggy. It's your rumspringa."

"I know, I know, I just thought you meant…something else."

"There's something else? Something besides the concerts and writing the songs?"

"Nee, there's nothing." She held his gaze and his dark eyes studied her. They seemed to see right through her. He looked tired. So tired. "How about you? How are you?"

"Fine." He bit out the word as if he were angry, angry at having to answer that question so often.

"Your grandfather seems good."

Matthew's gaze faltered. His eyes were liquid with emotion. Adah wanted to take his hand, to hug him tight. She didn't dare and that made her sad. She cared about Matthew. She should be able to touch him.

He cleared his throat. "He'll be better when we finish the house. Right now, he doesn't have his own place to go."

"I'm sure he misses familiar ground."

"He keeps asking where his bedroom is." His face reddened. He swiped at his nose with the back of his sleeve. "And whatnot. He'll settle in. Groossmammi is fine so he'll be fine as long as he has her around to remind him where he is."

The urge to hug him overwhelmed her. She willed her arms to stay at her side. He might consider her touch untoward and Richard would be back any minute with the lemonade. "They'll settle in."

"Jah."

She searched for words that would give him some measure of comfort equal to a hug. "We've put a notice in the *Budget* for a card shower for them."

"I heard."

"They know a lot of folks in Lancaster County and up in Indiana.

Your mudder said the word has already spread. They've received many cards already."

Matthew took a step closer. His gaze intensified. "One of the many good things about our community. I've grown to appreciate it more in recent weeks. I want to commit to it." His hand covered hers on the fencepost for a fleeting moment and then withdrew. "Don't you? With me. I need you to want it too."

The admission that he needed her left Adah's lungs flat. The enormity of his willingness to bare his thoughts and fears to her...this was a gift. He didn't want to face the future alone and he'd chosen her to share in it. Tears floated close to the surface. She breathed, forcing them back. "Matthew..."

"I'm sorry. I didn't mean to put my burdens on you." His hands dropped to his side and then clenched into fists. "It's not fair. You have to make this decision about baptism on your own. I know that."

"Matthew—"

"I need to get back to work."

He stalked away, head bent against the blazing sun, arms swinging.

She wanted to call him back, but she couldn't. He was right. She had to figure this out on her own. She had to find her way to him.

But first she had to find her way to God.

That meant going to the baptism classes.

And staying away from Jackson Hart.

Chapter 12

Adah managed to clean the Harts' kitchen, guest bathroom, and formal dining room before she ran into Jackson. She caught the spicy scent of his aftershave mixed with the *schtinkich* of cigarette smoke before he spoke. He smelled different from the sweat and dirt smell she associated with Plain men. They smelled of hard work. Dust cloth clutched in her hand, she debated. Maybe if she didn't turn around, he'd give up and leave the room. She gave the ceramic fruit bowl in the dish hutch a final wipe, waiting.

Sharp notes plucked with fine precision filled the air. Crystal clear, running up and down the scale. Running up and down her spine. "Amish girl." Jackson sang the words. "I've missed you."

The familiar *woof woof* that followed told her Captain accompanied his master. The plaintive note in his bark suggested he might also have missed her. Both of them were full of hooey. They didn't know each other well enough to miss each other. So why did she feel the same way? She'd been on edge from the second she entered the front door. Wondering if he was here. Wondering if she would see him. Wondering if he would play for her. Now that he was here, her stomach did backflips. She had to deny the feelings. She was stronger than they were.

Determined to try, she picked up the glass cleaner, sprayed the windows on the hutch doors, and began to wipe with greater vigor. *Work. Work. Work.*

I've met my match
I knew it when I saw her standing in that dirt patch
Her hands fumbling with the gate latch.
No matter what I do, I can't catch her.
I get close, she rears up and lets me have it.
She doesn't give a bit, no matter what I do,
Even if I try something completely new
She rears up and lets me have it.

God knows, He sees how hard I try
But I guess he knows I've met my match.

She's like a wild horse waiting to be tamed.
She needs a soft voice, a gentle touch.
No rush.
I got time. I'm gonna give her all my time.
All my touches 'cause there's no rush.
I'll take it real slow because
I've met my match.
No matter what I do, I can't catch her.
I get close, she rears up and lets me have it.

I've met my match.
But so has she.
I'm like a wild horse waiting to be tamed.
I need a soft voice and a gentle touch.
This ain't no wrestling match.
It's a love match.

We'll take it real slow
Because we've both met our match.
Two wild horses waiting to be tamed.
It's a love match. It's a love match. It's a love match.
Between her and me.
Between you and me.

She closed her eyes, gritted her teeth, and blew out air, trying to even out her breathing. *Don't do it. Don't do it.* She turned. "The lyrics need some work, but I like the melody."

"Feedback noted." Jackson leaned back in his seat on the couch and patted the guitar. Instead of the usual cowboy hat, he wore a red St. Louis Cardinals baseball cap with the bill turned to the back, but his usual uniform of faded jeans and T-shirt hadn't changed. "Writing about unrequited love is hard. There are so many songs out there about it already that it's hard to have an original thought, let alone original lyrics."

Not so unrequited. Adah slapped her hand to her mouth and then realized she hadn't said the words aloud. Her feelings were such a mish-mash, torn between what her head demanded she do and what her heart shouted. She chewed her lip, trying to keep staggering emotion from pouring out from her and onto this man who stood not five feet from her, looking so warm and so certain he could give her what she wanted and needed. She'd only known Jackson for a month. She'd known Matthew her entire life. Matthew was a nice fire in the fireplace, Jackson, a raging inferno that threatened to burn every living thing in its path. Including her. "I have to clean."

"Mom got called out to the horse barn. Something's wrong with her horse. The one she's planning to ride in the barrel racing competition at the rodeo in Springfield next week. She's in a tizzy." He leaned the guitar against the couch. "RaeAnne went swimming with her friends in town. Jeff's working with Dad."

"RaeAnne went swimming with her friend Dani Jo, your girlfriend?" He dated a high school girl, a cheerleader. Adah had been reminding herself of this fact for weeks now. "You should've gone with them."

"She's not my girlfriend." His eyebrows rose over wary eyes. "Who told you that?"

His denial rang truthful, but RaeAnne made it sound like Jackson chased a lot of girls. "It's none of my business, anyway."

"RaeAnne told you, didn't she? She's always meddling in my business. Takes after Mom. You heard wrong."

"It doesn't matter." Adah couldn't let it matter. "Why would I need to know all the comings and goings of your family?"

"Look, Dani Jo is a good kid who got the wrong idea."

Because he'd led her on? "You did nothing to make her think you were interested?"

"I was nice to her. She's a sweet girl, but she's just a kid."

A kid who was Adah's age. "Like me?"

"What are you, eighteen?"

"Yes."

"You may be the same age as Dani Jo, but you're light-years older." He pulled a stick of gum from his pocket and began to unwrap it, his gaze glued to the paper as if it required his complete concentration. "I don't know what it is, exactly. I've tried to figure it out. You're raised different. You seem older. Something about you is different from any girl I've ever met."

He hadn't met many Plain girls, then. She was no different from Molly or Phoebe or Ellie or Diana or Jolene. They all worked hard. The difference was none of her friends were standing in the living room of an Englisch family's house, about to do the wrong thing with an Englisch man—as far as she knew. Did they have the same temptations? She'd always been afraid to ask. What if it was just her? "I need to finish in here. I'm almost done. My mudder is expecting me home to help with supper."

He folded the stick of gum twice and stuck it in his mouth. Chewing, he studied her with an expression that reminded her of her brothers on venison stew night. "We're alone. I can give you what you want."

She took a step back and found herself wedged against the hutch. "I have work to—"

"I'm talking about the guitar." He touched the neck with two fingers. "I can teach you to play."

He could give her what she wanted. Something she had no right to want. Something she didn't need, truth be told. If she didn't stop chewing on her lip, she would have a hole in it.

"We're not supposed to be alone while I'm working." The protest must've sounded as feeble to him as it did to her. He picked up the guitar and held it out. It was a beautiful instrument. She swallowed and dropped the dust cloth on the table. "I can't."

"You know you want to try it. Just for a few minutes."

She did want to, in the worst way. She swallowed hard against the lump in her throat. This was what rumspringa was about. Trying things out and making a decision. She closed her eyes and opened them. Jackson still stood there, guitar in hand, Captain lolling at his feet. "Just for a minute. I have work to do."

"Sure, sure." Jackson nodded toward a chair. "Have a seat."

He laid the guitar in her lap, leaned the crutch against the floor, and pulled a chair up close, the instrument the only thing between them. "Relax. Hold it like you would a baby, firm, but gentle." He patted the body of the guitar as a father would the head of a child. "Don't hold it with your hands; support it with your body."

It felt awkward in her hands. "Like this?"

"Try crossing your legs so it sits a little higher. Good." He grinned at her. She couldn't help herself. She grinned back. His smile widened. "This is fun, right? Okay, now, left hand on the neck, thumb under it." He pushed her fingers into position toward the top of the neck. "Make your hand like a claw. You use the tips of your fingers. They should be in the middle of the frets."

"I can't reach. My hands aren't big enough." She wiggled her hand, trying to get it right. "Or the guitar is too big for me."

"No, it's fine. It's fine. It just takes practice."

Adah glanced from her fingers, stretched and awkward, to Jackson's. "That's easy for you to say. You have long fingers. Mine are short."

"Lots of women play the guitar. Now look at your right hand. You're holding the pick wrong."

How many ways could there be to hold a little piece of plastic?

Jackson held out his hand. "Like you're doing a karate chop."

"A what?"

"Like this!" He demonstrated and then bent his index finger and held the pick between his finger and thumb. "Stay loose. Relax. Rest your other fingers on the guitar. You want to be able to pick up and down."

Her head felt like it might explode. "I don't know—"

"It'll feel awkward at first, but you'll adjust. Strum a couple of times to see how it sounds."

Adah took a breath and strummed the way she'd seen musicians do. The notes rippled around her, sweet, melodic, the thrill of it a second wave through her body. She closed her eyes, then opened them, not wanting to miss a second of this lesson. *I'm playing a guitar. I'm making music.*

How could this be wrong? *God, how can this be wrong?*

"Beautiful. Awesome." Jackson pumped his fist and hooted. "Okay, now pluck each string, one at a time, starting at the bottom. Hear the notes? Bottom to top, high E, A, D, G, B, low E."

"Jah, yes, I do." She couldn't help herself. She laughed. A light burst through the clouds, filling the air around her. A beautiful light. "I do."

"You're a natural." Jackson leaned forward and touched her cheek in a soft, quick caress, his fingers warm and sure. "I knew you would be."

Adah froze. She should return the guitar. She should clean. She clutched it harder. The pick fell to the floor. "I shouldn't...we shouldn't. I mean, this is wrong."

"I'm only teaching you to play the guitar. That's all."

Adah knew it was more. His expression told her so. His touch shouted it. The welling up of emotion inside her said it was much more. Their gazes held.

"I shouldn't have touched you. I'm sorry." He tried to look contrite, but didn't quite manage it. "It's hard, because you're...you probably don't know how pretty you are. I'm betting you don't have a clue, but I promise not to touch you again—not like that. Until you say it's okay."

She would never do that. "Okay."

"Okay." His somber gaze faded, replaced with that wide-open grin again. "Every good boy does fine."

"E-G-B-D-F?"

"That's right. You learned something in those books at the library. It's the first step to reading music. E-G-B-D-F. Those are the basic musical pitches. Pitch is the highness or lowness of the note. The notes go on a staff. If they sit on the line, they are E-G-B-D-F. Every good boy does fine." He laid a slim book on the table, open to a page with the title "How to Read Music." "If they sit between the lines, it's F-A-C-E. Face. Do you remember that? Face. This book will refresh your memory on the basics."

She tore her gaze from the book, wondering how she'd ever remember all this. She wasn't all that coordinated. And time flew by. She had houses to clean and vegetables to can and socks to darn and laundry to do and pies to bake.

And baptism classes to take.

"What about the strings? Which note is which?"

"Start here." He stood and limped behind her. His long fingers curled around hers, showing them where to go. "This finger on this fret. This finger here. Now pluck the bottom string."

Forcing herself to lean away from his warm breath smelling of Doublemint gum, Adah tried to concentrate. She plucked.

"That's an E."

"That's an E! I played a note. A note." She couldn't help herself. She laughed, her face inches from his. The pleasure in his eyes told her he enjoyed the moment almost as much as she did. "I played a note. Thank you for this."

"It's a start." His hand hovered near her shoulder and then withdrew. "You're a natural, Amish girl."

She blew out air, so acutely aware of his presence that she felt his blood pulse through her veins. She swallowed hard and shifted away some more, increasing the distance between them. Still she felt his physical presence warming her skin. She held out the pick. "I have to get back to work."

"I know. I know." He offered his palm and she dropped the pick there without touching him. "I don't want you to get in trouble."

"We can't do this."

"We just did. I've been thinking a lot about this. It's not a crime to love music or want to play an instrument." His wheedling tone reminded Adah of when her little sisters wanted cookies only minutes before supper. This wasn't about spoiling her supper. This was about the way she would live the rest of her life. And where. And with whom. Jackson leaned forward, his expression intent. "In the Bible they play music and dance and leap for joy, praising God."

Confusion whirled in Adah. She didn't know that much about the

Holy Bible. She'd listened to Luke and Silas's sermons. She attended prayer service faithfully, but she left the theology to her elders. Luke said musical instruments weren't allowed because playing them drew attention to a person. It made a person seem big on himself. Or herself. It took attention away from God. That's what Daed said too.

She could still try out things. Rumspringa allowed her to do that. She still had time to decide. Her question at this moment left all the other questions of faith in the dust: How could something that gave her so much joy be wrong? She glanced up to see Jackson watching her, waiting for her, waiting for an answer.

"We have rules. One of them is no musical instruments. The adults in the church met and they voted and they kept that rule because they believe it's the best way to make sure we don't get…too big for our britches. It's about God, not about us. We have rules. I don't know how else to explain it."

"That's an understatement. You got more rules than I can shake a stick at." He picked up his ball cap and slapped it down on his head. "Sometimes rules are made to be broken. Because they're wrong."

Adah smoothed her hand over the slick, burnished wood of the guitar. "If a rule turns out to be wrong, isn't it better to change the rule than to break it? In our community, the members of our district meet once a year and vote on changes to the Ordnung, our set of rules. The rest of the year we have to follow them. We have rules to bring us closer to God and farther away from worldly things that will come between us and Him."

"I can understand that, I think." Jackson cocked his head, his eyebrows drawn, mouth pursed as if thinking so hard hurt his head. "But music isn't one of those things. Music brings us closer to Him. At least it does me."

"Are you close to God?"

"Go to church every Sunday with my family."

"That's not the same thing."

"I know." He slid the ball cap around so the bill rested in the front. "I don't feel close to God at church. It's a bunch of mumbo-jumbo most of the time. A bunch of hot air. I feel close to God when I'm on my horse on the back forty with the wind blowing and the sun shining and

Captain is trotting along after me, his old snout grinning. That life is good because God is good."

Adah knew that feeling. She had it when she walked by the pond and saw fish jumping and a turtle sunning itself on a rock and a blue jay jabbering at her from a spruce, telling her to stay away from its nest on a low-hanging branch. But she also felt it when she sat on the bench between Mudder and Laura, little Jonathan on her lap, and sang those slow, low, long notes of a hymn from the *Ausbund*. Their kind of music. Worship music. Their voices rising in praise to the One who made all things possible. The One who planned out their lives for them and took them home on His time. Not theirs.

Shaken by the thought, she stood and thrust the beautiful instrument at him. "I need to clean."

"Take the book with you so you can study the chords. I know you don't have a guitar to practice on, but at least you can study the pictures." He laid the guitar on the table and pulled something from his jean pocket. "And this."

He held out an iPod. Adah stared at it, thinking of the one that had ended up crushed under the sole of her father's boot. "I can't."

"It's a gift." His face reddened. "I made you a playlist. Songs that you can think about and use as examples when you're trying to write your own songs. Rhythm, rhyme, how to make the lyrics join with the melody. They're the classics—they don't play them on the radio anymore. Patsy Cline, Loretta Lynn, Tammy Wynette, June Carter Cash, Tanya Tucker, Reba McIntyre. Women with real country voices, not the pop crud you hear now."

The slim device lay in the palm of his hands. He draped ear buds over it. "Consider me your teacher and this part of the lesson, if it makes you feel better. Not a gift, a loan of equipment for the lessons."

"You're my teacher?"

"Your music teacher."

She couldn't pull herself from his gaze, so intense, boring into her. "Okay." The word came out a whisper. She cleared her throat and let him lay the iPod on the palm of her hand. He wrapped her fingers around it and let his own hand drop. "Teacher."

Nothing more.

The ferocity of emotion crackling in the air between them caused her breath to catch in her throat.

"Student." He heaved a sigh. "Study hard. When can we get together for your next lesson?"

"What?"

"Lessons. You need lessons. The sooner you get started, the sooner we can move on to writing songs together."

"I can't—"

"How 'bout next Wednesday when you come to clean? They're switching out the cast for a brace on Monday, God willing. The doc says I can start driving again. If you finish a little early, I'll meet you out by the fishing pond. You'll still be home on time."

"You've given this a lot of thought." Why? She didn't dare ask why Jackson was so intent on getting her to do this. The possibilities scared her. "I don't know."

"Just think about it."

She nodded, but she stood in that same spot until he picked up the guitar, gave her a tiny salute, and turned away. At the door, he pivoted on the crutch. "Bring your lyrics. I can start putting them to music if you want."

Did she want? She did. God help her. "I don't know. They're not ready yet."

"They're ready. See you."

With Captain hobbling behind, he slipped out, a self-satisfied grin on his face that said he knew he was right.

His absence seemed to suck all the air and light from the room.

She held the iPod against her heart, wishing she had time to listen to it now. To hear what he heard. "Jackson, what are you doing to me?"

Her words echoed in the big room. No answer came. "What am I doing to myself?"

Chapter 13

The pungent aroma of frying catfish, dipped in flour and spices and dropped into oil heated on the open grill, wafted over Adah. Even after consuming a full plate of freshly caught and fried fish, coleslaw, potato salad, and more than her share of deviled eggs, she found her mouth watering. Mudder's idea of a fish fry had been a good one. After the prayer service they'd had a whole afternoon for visiting with family and friends. Tired, she sighed, stretched, and began to pick up the dirty dishes from one of the picnic tables placed along the banks of the creek that meandered through the Troyers' property. This spot, with its thick fringe of huge sycamores, elms, and poplars, fully loaded with shade-giving leaves, served as everyone's favorite gathering place.

She should've been rested and ready for her baptism class this morning. Instead, she'd almost nodded off after spending half the night listening to the songs on the iPod Jackson had given her. Memorizing the words without meaning to do so. Humming the melodies and imagining how she would play them on Jackson's guitar. Finally sleeping and dreaming of songs mingled with music filling the air over the pond on the Harts' property. Thomas had called on her twice in class and she hadn't added anything to the discussion, hadn't even known where to begin. At first Matthew had looked happy to see her there, but as the lesson progressed, he'd looked perplexed and confused and then stony. He hadn't spoken to her.

Not once.

She was too tired to figure it out. What she wanted. What she should do. They were two different things. She wanted to stretch out on the blankets with the napping babies. She wanted to cast a line in the river and stick her pole in the mud the way the older kinner were doing even though the men had caught more than enough catfish to feed most of the families in the district. She wanted to stick her feet in the mud and feel it ooze between her toes and think of nothing else.

She wanted to listen to the rumble of the men, deep in conversation at their tables, discussing crops and weather and who knows what else, the patter of their deep voices enough to allow her to grab on to a sense of security and comfort that seemed to be lost as she grew up.

She would slip away in a few minutes and snooze by the babies. A little bit of sleep and she'd be better. No one would notice.

"Leave those dirty dishes and come visit with us," Mudder called from the picnic table she shared with half a dozen other women. She patted a seat on the bench next to her. "Emma and Katie are telling us about the building they found for the store. Thomas and Silas already put the money down to buy it. They just have to clean it up and we can start carrying in the items we want to sell."

Elizabeth sat on the other side. Adah tried to bat away the feelings that washed over her every time she saw the woman. It wasn't her fault she lived in the same house as Matthew. Adah had no right to blame her for any of the problems between her and Matthew. They'd begun before her arrival. Still, she looked so calm and sure of herself. So content. What man wouldn't want such a woman as his fraa? "I was just going to stack the dishes—"

"They'll still be there in five minutes. Come on, Adah, sit a spell. Take a load off." Bethel Christner dunked a chunk of fish in the red sauce and held it up to her mouth, pausing as if admiring her work. "I have three quilts ready to sell the minute you open. And a dozen baby blankets."

Adah ignored the spot between her mudder and Elizabeth and slid instead into the corner seat across from Bethel. The older woman popped the fish in her mouth and chewed with an air of great satisfaction, swallowed, and then wiped at her mouth with a red checkered paper napkin. "I figure we can save the money toward medical expenses in the future."

Almost simultaneously the women at the table glanced toward the padded tops of Bethel's crutches leaning against the far end of the table. Getting Bethel down to the edge of the river on those crutches had been a chore. She refused to let Elijah carry her, calling the idea silly. The look on his face as he watched her slow, torturous descent had etched itself on Adah's memory. She wanted someone to look at her like that. So caring, so committed to making sure she didn't fall, didn't hurt herself. Would Jackson do that? Matthew would, no doubt, none at all.

At least he would've if she'd said yes that night at the pond. All she had to do was say four words. *I love you too.*

What about Jackson?

"We'd like to add on to the house—not just the dawdi haus, but more bedrooms." Mary Troyer shredded a piece of sourdough bread between her fingers, her expression absent. Dark circles around her eyes said she hadn't been sleeping well or had been working extra hard with all her company. "Aaron has a few pieces of furniture to sell. He'll make more once we get the harvest in."

"It's fun. Opening a new store is fun. It'll be good for us. We'll sell much more than we did at the roadside stand or at our farms. Being in town is good." Bethel selected another piece of fish from the platter sitting in the middle of the table, this time dousing it in tartar sauce. "My physical therapist used to tell me attitude is everything. I believed her. I still do, even though I didn't get the answer to my prayers that I wanted."

"You do just fine." Mudder patted the other woman's shoulder. "A fine family you're making with Elijah."

Bethel smiled, her free hand going to her big belly in a self-conscious gesture. "I'd hoped for a breather, really. John is a handful now that he's walking. Yesterday he pulled a sack of flour over and dumped it all over the floor. Then he decided it would be fun to play in it. By the time I cleaned it up and cleaned him up, the ham and cheese casserole had burned."

As if on cue, a high-pitched wail broke the peace of a Sunday afternoon in the great outdoors. "That would be my boy." Bethel reached for her crutches. "His is the loudest ruckus of any baby I've ever heard. It's as if he hears his name and has to get in on the conversation. He never sleeps more than an hour at naptime and wakes up at least once or twice during the night with a caterwauling that would wake the dead."

"Have you tried giving him a snack of bread and butter before bed?" Phoebe asked, as if she, mudder of a tiny one-month-old girl named Loralee, had a store of wisdom to draw on. "Maybe he wakes up hungry because he's such a big boy for his age."

"He eats like a horse," Bethel conceded. She winced and rubbed her belly again. "And this little one kicks like a horse."

"You sit, I'll get him." Adah popped up, waving Bethel back into her seat. "Rest. I'm young and I don't have a baby waking me in the middle of the night."

"I'm still young." Bethel pretended to be offended, but she grinned and sank back onto the bench. "But I'm no fool. I'll let you. I don't recall the last night I had a good night's sleep. Between carrying John and then having him and now carrying another…"

Adah didn't remember the last time she'd had a good night sleep either, but for completely different reasons.

"You love it," Katie Christner shook a finger at Bethel. "Don't tell us you don't."

"Every minute of every day." Bethel's smile grew wider. "I never forget how close I came to not having this. Who could want more than this? Gott is good!"

He was indeed. So why couldn't Adah be as content as all these women, her family and friends, seemed to be? She had no answer for that question, one she could never ask aloud. "I'd better get him before he wakes the others."

She strode toward the blankets they'd spread under the shade of the live oaks for the sleeping babies. Dry grass crackled under her bare feet, tickling her toes. A burr bit into her sole. She stopped, hopped on one foot, and picked it out, head bent, the hot sun beating on her back. She didn't want Mudder to see her face. Mudder had grandchildren now, with Hiram and Daniel's growing broods. And she still had a baby at home with little Jonathan. She never seemed tired. She always seemed thankful. She saw only the blessings, never the burden. Why couldn't Adah be content like Mudder and Bethel?

John's cries intensified and Adah hastened to the blanket. They didn't need all the babies awake. He'd rolled over on his tummy and scooted toward the edge of the blanket, his small face scrunched up in determination as he tried to plant himself on his short, fat feet. He looked so like Elijah with his blue eyes and tufts of blond hair sticking up all over his small head. Adah grinned and scooped him up. "What's the problem, little John? You're supposed to be sleeping and letting your mudder rest for a bit, don't you know that?" She held his warm body to her chest, inhaling the scent of baby. And something else. She held him away from her, shaking her head at his red, tear-stained face. "Phew. No wonder you're fussing. I'd fuss too if I smelled like that."

His wailing increased in intensity. "Hush, hush, you silly goose. You're fine. It's just a dirty diaper." She plunked him on the blanket on his back and reached for the bag of diapers and supplies left to one side for everyone's use. Emma's little one slept blithely on, as did Rachel's and Phoebe's and baby Jonathan, who looked like a miniature Daniel. Everyone with their babies. Something caught at Adah's throat. She swallowed against it and focused on the smelly bundle of joy in front of her. "You hush now before you wake your cousin Loralee. Your Aenti Phoebe wouldn't appreciate that."

John didn't seem to care. He flailed about, arms and legs flying in all directions, making it hard for her to remove the offending diaper. "Will you stop, you little floppy fish?" She grabbed his legs by the ankles and hung on. "What you need is a song."

The words came to her with little or no thought. A lullaby floating about, waiting to be released from her innermost thoughts and dreams.

Little one, if only you could see
What I see when you're sitting on my knee
Blue eyes so wide, staring back at me.

Baby, you are an empty slate yet to be filled
With the life God has willed.

John's thrashing body stilled. His crying stilled at the soft voice singing a song just for him, not the adults close by. He stared up at her with those big, wondering, bright eyes. Still singing, she removed the stinky diaper, wiped his bottom clean, and patted him dry.

Little one, if only you could see
What I see when you are sitting upon my knee
Blue eyes so wide staring back at me.

Humming, she paused to contemplate the rhyme. "Field, kneeled, reeled, wield…"

Summers of sun and work in the field
A back made strong by the tools you'll wield.
Winters of snow and venison stew
Days filled with all the work you must do.

The new diaper firmly in place, she pulled the baby's long shirt down and hoisted him to her lap. He'd ceased to cry, but she continued to sing. He seemed to like it and she did too. She let her voice meander about, quietly, not waking the other babies, but still exploring the song.

Only a few things are sure in this life.
There will be laughter and tears.
A mudder to quiet your fears.
A daed to teach you wrong and right.
To teach you about sin,
To learn from where you've been,
To look ahead at where you'll go,
To look always to God and you'll know
He'll be wherever you go.

He'll be wherever you go.
He'll be wherever you go.

Little one, if only you could see
What I see when you're sitting on my knee
Blue eyes so wide looking back at me.
God's love painted on your face.
God's love shining back at me.

He'll be wherever you go.
He'll be wherever you go.
He'll be wherever we go.
Wherever we go.
Wherever we go.

"I've often pictured you doing that."

The words dying on her lips, Adah looked up. Matthew towered over her, his broad shoulders blocking the sun behind him. He lugged an ice cream maker in his arms, a towel wrapped around the top to keep the rock salt in place.

Pictured her doing what? Kneeling on a blanket, giving a concert to a group of babies, most of whom slept? Adah scrambled to her feet and lifted John onto her hip. He wiggled, stuck his hand in his mouth, and began to babble as if continuing the song she'd begun. "Hey."

"Hey." Matthew shifted the ice cream maker and set it on the ground. He rubbed his arm as if he'd pulled a muscle. "We made the ice cream. I just went up to the house to pick it up."

Obviously.

"I was just changing John's diaper for Bethel."

Obviously.

"Well, I'd better get this situated. It's getting late." He stooped as if to pick up the ice cream maker. "And this'll start to melt pretty quick."

"Pictured me doing what?" She glanced around. No one paid them any mind. She had to ask. Did he like the song she'd made up on a whim? Did he like the sound of her voice? "What did you picture me doing?"

"Being a mudder." Matthew's voice turned husky. "Holding a baby."

His skin darkened under his deep tan. He ducked his head and looked around as if searching for someone. Or making sure no one heard his words but her. "My baby. Our baby."

Not singing. Holding a baby. Their baby. "I—"

"You'd be a good mudder, if you gave it half a chance. The ice cream is melting." He hoisted the machine and turned his back on her. Then he swiveled for a second. "There's nothing better than a mudder singing her baby to sleep at night."

Then he tromped away. John started to fuss again. Adah bounced him on her hip, only half paying attention. She began to sing again, this time in a mere whisper, almost like a prayer.

> *Show me. Tell me. Lead me. Fill me. Remake me. Mend me.*
> *Give me the strength to be the daughter you sketched in the*
>   *womb,*
> *The woman you want me to be in everything I do,*
> *From the time I was born until the trip to my tomb.*
> *Give me the strength to allow myself to be torn and broken.*
> *To cry out to you, Lord Father.*
> *To hear and believe the words you have spoken.*
> *To know you will heal every hurt.*
> *Until that moment when my flesh and sinew melt into dirt.*
>
> *Forgive me. Love me. Show me. Tell me. Lead me. Fill Me.*
>   *Remake me.*
> *Mend me. Forgive me. Show me. Tell me. Lead me.*
>
> *Remake me.*
>
> *Love me.*

꙳꙳꙳

Matthew dumped the ice cream maker on the picnic table farthest from the babble of the women. He turned his back on them and gazed out at the creek, wishing the breeze that washed over him held a hint of cool air. He wiped at his face with his sleeve. He needed a minute to compose himself. Every time he talked to Adah he fell deeper into the pit of misery and uncertainty. She'd been a mess at the baptism class. Half asleep, clueless about the topic, and distracted. He'd been determined to let her go, start over, look for a woman who wanted to be a fraa. Adah did not. He was certain of that. Then to see her singing over baby John. She looked so at home, so natural with a baby in her arms. She knew what to do and her soft, lilting voice sang with such warmth, any baby would be soothed.

Their baby.

The pain that thought brought nearly doubled him over. She didn't seem to want that life with him. She wanted something else. He had no idea what. But it wasn't him.

"Penny for your thoughts?"

Matthew dragged his gaze from the water lapping along the river bank. Elizabeth strolled toward him, her head cocked as if studying a problem that included him. He turned and swept the towel from the ice cream maker and began rearranging the rock salt. "Not worth that much."

She paused at the corner of the table, hands at her side. Something in her expression seemed amused. "I'm stretching my legs a bit. I ate too much. I need a walk."

"I know the feeling. I could use a nap myself." Heat rushed to his face. The tips of his ears burned. "I mean—"

"I know what you mean. It's so warm and the lapping of the water is like music." Now she grinned outright. She had a nice smile. "It's enough to make a person nod off in the middle of a sentence."

"I should get back up to the buggy for the other batch." He inched away from the table. "With this bunch, one flavor isn't enough."

"I could help you. I'm sure there are some bowls and napkins that need carting down here."

Aware of the throng of friends and family sprawled along the riverbanks, seemingly absorbed in conversation but always on the lookout for something, anything, amiss, Matthew hazarded a glance behind him. Luke, Thomas, and Silas sat on one side of a picnic table, Ben Knepp, Enoch Gringrich, and his daed on the other side. What would

Enoch think of Matthew taking his dochder for a walk in the middle of the summer afternoon, in front of God and everyone?

A simple walk, nothing more.

Before he could decide, Daed slid from the bench and meandered in their direction. "I'll help you bring down that other batch of ice cream."

His tone left no room for discussion. Elizabeth ducked her head and moved back to the circle of women, deep into the pros and cons of homemade soap as opposed to the store-bought powder Emma had tried the previous week.

"You tuckered out or something?" Daed set a serious pace on the path that cut through the Indian paintbrush and sunflowers mixed with high grass on either side. "I thought you'd be itching to pour choc-olate syrup over this stuff by now."

"I'm stuffed."

"You're never too full for ice cream."

"Nee."

Daed stomped onto the dirt road where buggies were parked in a long line. The horses had been tethered in the field where they could eat to their hearts' content. "I saw you talking to Adah."

For Daed to come right out and state this fact so baldly left Mat-thew wordless. He nodded.

"None of my business, I reckon." He turned his back on Matthew and tugged at the ice cream maker. "But I've prayed on it and I've talked to Luke about it."

"About me and Adah?"

"Jah."

"Why?"

"There's been a lot of talk."

"Talk. There's always talk. Folks don't have anything better to do, it seems."

"Your mudder and I have concerns."

"No reason."

"We're not sure Adah is...would make a good fraa."

"That's for me to decide."

"It is. But I've seen what can happen when two people are unevenly yoked."

Unevenly yoked. He'd never felt that with Adah. Not until the last few months. "It's wrong for people to talk and start rumors and such."

"Agreed." Daed shoved a bag of napkins Matthew's way. "But I'm your daed. I have a right to say this much: I can't rightly give property to a son who isn't smart enough to know when a woman won't make a good fraa. A woman who might leave the community because she likes Englisch music and cowboys more than she loves God."

Speechless, Matthew tried to breathe through the anger. His father would take back the land because he didn't find Adah suitable?

Matthew couldn't lash out at his father. Daed deserved respect. He had a right to his opinion. But to listen to a river of gossip that flowed through their small community was wrong. To punish Matthew on the say-so of a bunch of wagging tongues? He swallowed his anger and worked to keep his tone civil. "No one knows what's in Adah's heart. She's trying. She went to baptism class this morning."

"Unprepared."

Thomas had said something. He wouldn't, not to Daed. Elizabeth sat in the same class. Would she carry tales to Enoch and Clara? To Mudder? "So we should try to bring her back into the fold, shouldn't we? Aren't we called to do that?"

"Her parents are. Her bishop and her deacon are."

"But not the man who..." He couldn't say it aloud. Those words should only be spoken to Adah herself. "Shouldn't we all seek to save the lost?"

"Not if it means losing yourself."

"I won't."

"See to it that you don't."

Matthew tugged the ice cream from his father's grip. "I'll take this. You go on ahead."

Daed clumped toward the trail. He looked back. "I saw Elizabeth talking to you too."

"Jah."

"She's a good girl. Hard worker. Enoch says she's committed to baptism, works hard on her lessons." He tugged his hat down on his forehead, obscuring the expression in his eyes. "Kind of woman who makes a good fraa. A man could work the land with her, knowing she'd take care of the house and kinner, not wander off, writing Englisch music and such."

Matthew picked up the ice cream maker and stalked past Daed. He didn't have an answer to the unspoken question. Why couldn't he turn his attention to Elizabeth? He could try. But trying was something a man did with his head.

Not his heart.

He dumped the ice cream maker on the closest picnic table, turned his back on the clusters of folks waiting for the ice cream to be served, and stomped along the riverbank. He needed to put some distance between himself and these people. Most days, he loved the small, tight-knit feel of living in a place where everyone knew everyone, everyone cared. Some days, though, it felt like a tiny room with no windows and no door. Crowded, airless, and without means of escape.

He breathed the smell of mud and fish. A tepid breeze lifted the leaves on the tree branches just above his head, stirring air heated by a blazing sun that burned the back of his neck. The chatter of his friends and family faded as he put distance between them. Mud squished between his toes and tickled the arches of his feet. He closed his eyes for a second, trying to think of nothing else.

An explosive snore interrupted the chirping of sparrows and the steady squeak of crickets. Startled, Matthew looked around. Up ahead sat his grandpa, straw hat pulled down over his eyes, chin on chest, back propped against a rock, his fishing pole stuck straight up in the mud next to him. His hands were crossed over his flat belly and his skinny legs were crossed at the ankles. His boots sat beside him, socks neatly folded and laid over the laces. Chuckling, Matthew eased his way through the weeds and straggling grass until he could squat next to him.

Another deep snore caused his lips to open, flutter, and close. Matthew laughed outright. His response was met with another snore, louder than the last.

"Groossdaadi?" He lifted the brim of the hat with one finger and slid it back. "Wake up."

"Who's sleeping?" Groossdaadi's eyes opened. Not looking the least bit startled, he frowned. "I was just thinking about you."

Who did he think Matthew was? His son? His brother? Someone named Levi? "About me?"

"Jah, about that big catfish you caught when you were ten."

Groossdaadi was with him, even if only for a few minutes. Matthew would take it. Especially today. He looked out at the river, remembering. Forty-pounder. It had weighed almost as much as he did. It had taken him and Daed working together to bring it in. The memory of the taste of it, breaded in flour and spices, dropped into hot grease, and served with homemade red sauce with lots of horseradish and capers made his mouth water even now. "That was a good day."

"A good day." Groossdaadi straightened. His neck popped and he put his gnarled fingers to it and rubbed. "You have to appreciate those good days when you get them."

"Is this one of them?" Matthew settled down in the grass next to him, letting his long legs sprawl out so his feet were immersed in the lukewarm water. "For you, I mean."

"I know you're Matthew, my grandson, not somebody I reckon I should know but can't quite remember. I know we got fishing, family; we got ice cream. We got sunshine and a nice little breeze to break the heat. What more could a man want?"

A counting of blessings. "What more could a man want?" Matthew repeated. *I'm sorry Gott. Gott, I want a fraa and I want children, but Your will be done. On Your time. Your plan.*

"I reckon you're wanting a fraa about now. Your own place to farm."

Groossdaadi always could hit the nail on the head. Matthew nodded. "Jah."

"What's the hurry?"

"It's time. At least I think it is."

"Gott's time."

"I know. I know."

"That girl Elizabeth, she likes you."

Matthew avoided his grandfather's steely gaze. "How can you tell?"

"Ain't you learned nothing about girls? She follows you around with a plate of cookies from the time you come in from the fields to the time you turn in."

"She offers cookies to everyone."

"You aren't the sharpest tool in the shed, boy."

"Groossdaadi."

He cackled. "She ain't the one, then."

"The one what?"

"The one you been mooning over night and day."

"I'm not mooning—"

"Ain't nobody can figure this out but you. Some folks will try, but you can't listen to them."

"I know."

Groossdaadi thumped his chest with both hands. "You figure it out in here." He smacked his forehead. "Not up here."

"Jah."

"See that you don't forget it."

"How did you know Groossmammi was the one?"

"I just told you." Using Matthew's shoulder as a leaning post, he hauled himself to his feet, his knees popping and cracking. "My heart told me. I could no more choose another than I could cut off my feet and walk around on stumps. Your mudder was the only one for me. I got a hankering for some ice cream."

Matthew stared up at him. "You mean my groossmammi, she was the only one for you."

"Get a move on then, before all the ice cream is eaten or melted." He rubbed his back with one hand. "I'm getting too old to sit on the ground. Let's go. The way you love ice cream, Aaron, I figured you'd be first in line."

Groossdaadi was gone again. Still, his advice remained good. Matthew knew what his heart was telling him. What was Adah's heart telling her?

Chapter 14

Adah clucked the reins, urging Dusty to a steady trot. He snorted and whinnied his disapproval. The horse wanted to head home, she was sure of it, not in the opposite direction toward the pond on the Harts' property. She had equally mixed feelings about her destination. Jackson had been out with his father on Monday and today he had been nowhere in sight when she cleaned his family's house from top to bottom, moving quickly from room to room, dusting, sweeping, mopping, emptying trash cans, cleaning windows and mirrors. She'd been careful not to shirk any of the tasks. She didn't want her work to suffer because of what she was about to do.

Or not do.

She'd told herself as she cleaned that she would declare to Jackson how sorry she was, but it had been a mistake to accept the iPod and play his guitar. True, she'd listened to the playlist over and over. She lay in bed long into the night, letting the voices captivate her. Patsy Cline's "Blue," Loretta Lynn's "Coal Miner's Daughter," Dolly Parton's "Coat of Many Colors," and June Carter Cash's "Ring of Fire." Beautiful songs that resonated with her musically and in the lyrics. She found herself humming the tunes as she worked in the garden, mouthing the lyrics as she took laundry from the lines and whispering the words as she kneaded bread dough. More than once she'd caught Mudder staring at her, an alarmed look on her face. She said nothing, but her expression didn't bode well.

Jackson had given her songs by male singers too. Johnny Cash, Hank Williams, Garth Brooks, Toby Keith, Alan Jackson, and her favorite, George Strait. Listening to Johnny Cash and George Strait made her think of Matthew and his little jokes the last time he'd shone a flashlight in her window. It seemed ages ago. So much had happened since then. The Gringriches. His grandparents. Jackson.

Jackson.

He'd also included a duet. Johnny Cash and June Carter Cash singing "Jackson."

He had a sense of humor, Jackson did.

She couldn't help but like his brazen full-tilt way of going after the things he wanted. She'd been taught not to do that. Every day for as long as she could remember. Daed had resorted to the woodshed when necessary to tame her stubborn streak. That's what he called it. Jackson would call it *pluck* or *standing up for herself* or some such thing.

She shouldn't let Jackson come between her and life as a Plain woman. Or between her and Matthew. She would end it now. She only came because it would be impolite not to show up if Jackson was waiting for her.

Maybe he hadn't come. Maybe he realized this was all a silly flight of fancy. Maybe his daed had put him to work now that his ankle was almost healed. Maybe, maybe.

The buggy crested the hill and a huge silver monster of a pickup truck with shiny chrome and big tires came into view. It was parked next to the pond under the shade of a tall, sprawling sycamore, all the doors open. Music wafted on the air toward Adah, showering her in sweet notes. She pulled up on the reins and gathered her courage to her, like a shield she hoped would protect her from herself.

"Whoa, Dusty. Whoa." She hopped from the buggy, tied the reins around a tree, and strode to the truck, whispering to herself the instructions she'd given the horse. "Whoa, Adah, whoa. Stop. Just stop."

"You talking to yourself?" Jackson popped up from the bed of the truck, a cigarette dangling between his fingers. "Or did you bring company?"

She jumped and slapped her hand on her heart, pulse racing like a cat chasing a mouse. Or maybe she was the mouse being chased. "Don't you know cigarettes are bad for you?" She said the first words that came to her mind. "They'll kill you."

He took a drag from the cigarette and sent it sailing toward the lake with a snap of his thumb and forefinger. "What are you, my doctor?"

"I just don't understand why people do things that are bad for them."

"You came here, didn't you?"

She had no response for that. With a loud hoot, Jackson slapped his hat on his head and eased over the side of the truck. He landed on his good leg, only a trace of a grimace as he put his weight on the other one with his ankle now encased in a short black canvas brace. His now familiar scent of aftershave mixed with tobacco enveloped her. She breathed it in deep in spite of herself. Captain woofed, jumped from the truck, and proceeded to hobble in a circle around her, tail wagging all the while.

"Settle down, Cap, settle down before you scare her off."

Captain halted his spin and squatted next to Adah, but his tail continued to beat a pattern on the ground. Jackson looked as eager as his companion. If he'd had a tail to wag, it would have been a blur. "Did you like the music on the iPod?"

"I did."

"I knew you would."

"Especially the duet."

"I figured."

"You're funny."

"I like to make you smile, Amish girl. You have a beautiful smile."

Feeling as if she were all arms and legs and big feet and hands, Adah stood still, barely breathing. She wanted to break the gaze that held between them, but found she couldn't, so mesmerized was she by the man before her. He grinned, his smile like frosting on the cake. The silence reverberated between them. Jackson ducked his head first, his gaze shifting to the pond. "It's a beautiful day, Amish girl. Especially now that you're here. I wasn't sure you'd come."

"I didn't intend to come." She found the courage to look up. He wore a blue Western-style shirt with snap buttons and a collar. She'd never seen him in a real shirt before. Jeans as usual, even in this heat. His feet, however, were bare. Back to his face. It was safer. "But I couldn't stand the thought of you here waiting for me and me not showing up. It would be rude."

"And you're too nice to be rude?"

"I try to be nice."

"You are nice." He swiveled and pulled a guitar from the truck bed. It was different from the one she'd touched the previous week. The finish was blonder and the half circle near the center a darker brown. "That's why—one of the reasons why—I brought you this."

He offered it with a flourish. She backed up, her hand creeping up to her neck. "For me? Are you trying to give it to me?"

"So you can practice. It's my old guitar, the first one I ever owned. Grandpa Hart gave it to me when I was six years old. God rest his soul. He knew before my parents ever figured it out that I had the musical gene."

"Gene?"

"My Grandma Hart did some singing. She even sang backup for some bands at the Grand Ole Opry in Nashville way back when."

She'd read about Nashville. The birthplace of country music. "I can't take your guitar."

"Just borrow it." He held it out again. "So you can practice."

"I can't."

"Why not? As a loan, if a gift is too much."

"I can't because I can't take it home." She hated to say the words aloud. He wouldn't understand. The sound of the iPod being crushed under Daed's boot reverberated in her ears. What would he do with a guitar? Dismantle it? Bury it? "My parents won't let me have it in the house. If they see it, they'll have to throw it away."

"That's the craziest thing I've ever heard." He propped the guitar against the truck, its sheen glinting in the sun. "I don't get it. I don't get them and I don't get you for going along with it."

"I know you don't get it." Adah looked out at the water, shimmering in the brilliant afternoon sun. A dragonfly buzzed her ear. Crickets creaked and a bullfrog sounded his horn. A concert of a different kind. The kind that wouldn't get her in trouble. "I don't expect you to understand, but I came here to tell you I can't do this."

Jackson slapped his hat back on his head, his jaw set. "Why did you let me give you a lesson in the first place?"

"Because I love music and you won't understand this either, but we have something called…rumspringa, which means when we turn sixteen we have a time when we try things out and we decide if we want to be baptized. I'm still in my rumspringa. I haven't been baptized. Yet. That's the only reason I'm here today. The only reason I tried the guitar the other day. I'm allowed to do that."

"You're allowed to try things out?"

"Yes, so that I know for sure I want to join our faith and reject worldly ways for the rest of my life."

"And if you don't want it?"

"Then I leave my community and make my way in the Englisch world."

"Leave your family?"

"Yes. For good."

Jackson tugged a pack of gum from his shirt pocket and proceeded to unwrap a stick, his gaze fixed on the paper. "That's a no-win situation. It's not fair."

"It's not about fair. It's about living a godly life apart from the world."

He didn't look convinced, which didn't surprise Adah. She found it hard to understand too and she'd lived it her whole life. Jackson stuck the gum in his mouth and chewed hard. "So you have to choose between music and your family?"

"Not all music. We have music. In church and we sing songs while we work." She nodded toward the guitar. "Just not that kind of music, and not with instruments."

"My kind of music, you mean. You have to choose between me and your life."

"Yes."

"So choose me." He shifted so he stood tall, looming over her, his face close, a look on his face that Adah recognized. She'd seen it on Matthew's face. "Choose me."

She took another step back, yet the distance between them seemed to shrink. The air hummed with anticipation. "I hardly know you."

"It doesn't feel that way." He brushed past her—to her relief—and limped toward the pond, turned, and limped back. The hum grew. "We have a connection. You can't tell me you don't feel it."

"I don't feel it." Teetering on the brink of an abyss filled with uncertainty and the unknown, she did feel it. "I can't. I mustn't."

"There's a difference between can't and won't." His tone rasped with disappointment he made no attempt to hide. "Give yourself a chance. Give the music a chance. Give us a chance."

"There is no us."

"There could be." He grabbed the guitar and held it out, within her reach. "Even if you don't want something more with me, I know you want the music. It's written all over your face every time you get near me. At least take the chance with the music. You don't have to take the guitar home."

She stared at the guitar and then at Jackson. He nodded, his face full of something she couldn't decipher. "Please, take it."

"Am I a challenge to you?"

"What?"

"Your sister said you liked a challenge."

"RaeAnne was just mad about Dani Jo. She's a good friend."

"She's also your sister."

"Yeah, but we don't always get along. She shouldn't have stuck her nose in my business." He held out the guitar a second time. "I promise, you're not some girl I'm chasing because I can't have you."

Despite her best intentions, Adah accepted his offering. The songs crowded her, begging her to play them. The songs forced her hand, not him.

Leaving her no chance to change her mind, Jackson grabbed her arm and propelled her around the end of the truck. Without so much as a by-your-leave, he hoisted her onto the bed and scrambled up next to her. Captain turned in a circle twice and flopped down in the grass, his tongue lolling from the side of his mouth. Adah was certain the dog was grinning at her.

"Hey." The word sounded weak in her ears. "You can't just—"

"Hush up." He grabbed his other guitar and settled next to her, his long legs dangling over the side. "Here we go. Remember the notes? Remember what I told you?"

She did. She'd gone over the book he gave her a dozen or more times, wishing each time for a guitar on which she could practice. Her fingers might not be as nimble as her ear, but the next few minutes revealed to her that she did indeed have a knack for this. She could hear the song in her head and find the notes on the guitar. How or why, she didn't know.

"I told you, you're a natural." Grinning, Jackson pumped his fist. "You'll catch up to me in no time."

That seemed unlikely but the kind words buoyed her. They did simple chords and put them together in little songs like "Mary Had a Little Lamb" and "Farmer in the Dell." Jackson cheered when she got it right, laughed and cajoled when she didn't. Their voices mingled with the notes and made a music that was sweeter than any she'd ever heard.

"Good, good, you're doing great!" Jackson leaned forward, his legs kicking back and forth. "You're the next Loretta Lynn, I'm telling you."

"You're just saying that." She leaned into the guitar. It felt so perfect nestled on her lap, the wood warm in the sun, the strings tight against her fingers. "But thank you. I don't have any desire to be anyone else. Just me."

"Just you, Amish girl." He plucked a new tune, one she didn't recognize. "You're pretty wonderful, just you."

"Don't."

He held up a hand, pick clutched between thumb and forefinger. "Sorry, sorry. Just play. Try this."

She closed her eyes and listened to the notes, then strummed them herself.

"You're amazing."

She opened her eyes to see him grinning at her, his face suffused with delight and that other thing...that thing that scared her. "No, I'm not. I'm just me."

"Okay. Don't get that scared look like I'm the boogie man or something." Jackson played a few measures. "How about 'Jesus Loves the Little Children'?" You folks only do religious music. That's fine. This should be right down your alley."

With each trial and error, each do-over, each new run-through they sounded better. The song made her smile...until she thought of her little brothers and sisters. Jesus loved them. He loved the little children. Here she was, engaged in child's play when she should be home helping Mudder get supper.

"I have to go." She held out the pick. "It's way past time."

"We haven't gotten to the good stuff yet." Ignoring her outstretched hand, Jackson pulled a folded piece of paper from his shirt pocket. He smoothed it out and laid it on the tailgate next to his leg. "I finished a song. I want to play it for you." He ducked his head, his cheeks staining a deeper shade of red than warranted by the sun overhead. "It's kind of rough, but I think you'll like it. It's called 'The Plain Truth.'"

Before she could respond, he began to play, his voice softer, gentler than she'd ever heard it before. A sweet twang resonated in it that reminded her of the singers she heard on the country music station.

> It seems like our worlds don't touch, they don't meet.
> They're hot and cold, black and white, bitter and sweet.
> We're walking on opposite sides of a raging river, no bridge
>   between us.
>
> But the first time I saw you
> Looking all angelic in your apron and your bonnet,
> I saw that place where hot and cold meet, thunder rattles,
>   and lightning strikes

In a near fatal miss.
Where bitter and sweet entwine, lips pucker and smile, lead-
ing to that first kiss.
Where black and white collide, we see that nothing is so
simple.
Blinded by the light, I don't see the near miss, I see blue eyes
and lips and dimples.

You say our worlds don't touch, they can't meet.
They're like hot and cold, black and white, bitter and sweet.
We're walking on opposite sides of a raging river, no bridge
between us.
I say our roads met the first time I saw you.
I want you and you want me.
That's the plain truth
Lord, it's the plain truth
Coming down on you and me.

On Sunday morning you sit on a bench in a barn.
I'm planted in a pew in the Methodist church
Down on Main Street where the sweet sound
Of organ music invites in sinners and saints.
I'm a little of both, I admit, but
We've both been loving on Jesus our whole lives.
There is no river, there is no great divide.
All you have to do is admit it.

I want you and you want me.
That's the plain truth
Lord, it's the plain truth
Coming down on you and me.

I want to love you for the rest of my life
Someday, I want you to be my wife.
I want to share a spot in the cemetery when this life ends
I look into your blue eyes and hear eternity calling on the
wind.
Hear that sound? That's the sound of you and me and eternity.

I want you and you want me.
That's the plain truth
Lord, it's the plain truth
The plain truth coming down on me and you.

The music died away. She found she couldn't speak. Neither did he. Birds cackled overhead. A dog barked. Captain lifted his head, whined, and went back to his nap. Jackson plucked a note. Then another. Finally, still staring out at the pond, he smiled.

"It's just a song. Don't look so scared." He laid the guitar in its case and shut it. "It's way too long for the radio. I need to cut it down. Sometimes I do this sort of stream of consciousness thing to get the words down and then I start paring it back and paring it back until I get down to the nice, white, polished bone. You ever do that?"

"Sometimes." Her voice sounded breathless in her ears. "It's beautiful."

"Thank you."

"How can you think all those things?" Of all the questions milling around in her mind, that was the only one she could voice. Kisses and dimples and wife and babies and sinners and saints. All in one song. "We hardly know each other."

"I just wrote what I felt." He smoothed his hand over the leather case without looking at her. "Isn't that what you do?"

"Yes."

He looked up and met her gaze. "It's just a song."

So he'd said.

"I have to go."

He stuck his pick in his pocket as if to punctuate her statement. "We'll do this again."

He made it sound like a vow.

"I'll try."

"I knew we would be good together." He smiled, but his eyes held hers with a look so like a promise she couldn't bear to break the hold he had on her. "Your voice is its own instrument, Adah. Even if you never play the guitar, they can't take your voice from you."

A sob welled up in her with such force it nearly strangled her. Jackson understood her in a way no one ever had before. Not even Matthew. "I really should go." She choked out the words that were the opposite of everything the quickening of her heart told her. "I need to get home to my family."

"If you need to go, go. I understand about family stuff, but there's something I want to ask you first."

Considering his previous invitation had brought her here, Adah girded herself for this new temptation. "Whatever it is, I can't."

"At least hear me out."

That's what kept getting her in trouble. "I have to go."

"Meet me at the fairgrounds Monday night."

"What?"

"The stock show and rodeo is in town. Clayton Star and his band are playing at the fairgrounds after the rodeo. They're really good. I want you to hear them."

"I can't." It wouldn't be any different from any of the other concerts she'd attended. Only then she'd been with Matthew. She'd felt protected, as silly as that sounded. Being with her own kind made her feel as if no one was looking at her like a misfit or an outcast. An oddity.

"You've never been to a concert?"

"It's not that. I have been. I just don't know—"

"If you should go with me? You don't want to be seen with me?"

The only ones who might see her were friends also still in their rumspringa. Matthew wouldn't be there. The only reason he went was for her. "I don't want you to think there's more here than there is."

"There is more here, even if you don't want to admit it." He tilted his head, a sudden look of pain creasing his mouth. "Is there someone else?"

Heat curled around her face and made her ears hot. Her tongue felt tied in knots.

"There is." He leaned back and grabbed a black cowboy boot sitting behind her. "But that's okay. You wouldn't be here if you weren't interested."

"In the music. I came because of the music."

He pulled on a sock and yanked on his boot. Adah switched her gaze to the pond. A duck waddled from the edge of the water up the bank, a string of babies following behind her. A family. Adah belonged with family. She grasped the side of the truck and hoisted herself down.

"Don't run away." Jackson slid from the truck and stood, towering over her. "Wait! You said yourself you're on your running around or whatever you call it. Until you decide to commit, you're a free agent. You can do whatever you want. That's what you said."

Not wanting him to see her face, she kept her back to him. "I know what I said."

"Then come. For the music. It's a learning experience. Going to a concert after you've started to learn to play an instrument is different." Adah could feel his presence in every bone and muscle in her body. She should never have come. But she had and now Jackson had her captivated as surely as a hunter did his prey. "You watch their style, the way they play, the things they can do, and you learn from it. You want to do those things too. You'll see, you'll want to play like they do and sing like they do."

Adah gazed out at the pond, watching the wind make ripples in the water. The leaves rustled, making their own music as they danced. A mourning dove cooed. Bees buzzed over the sunflowers that turned and stretched toward the sun overhead. Music existed everywhere, but especially here, close to the earth. Her heart ached in rhythm with the water lapping against the earth. "This once. Just this once."

"Amen and hallelujah!" Jackson grabbed her around the waist, lifted her from the ground, and twirled her around, once, twice, and plopped her back on her own feet. "You won't regret it."

Staggering, trying to find her balance, Adah threw out her arms. Jackson laughed and grabbed them, steadying her. His grip was strong and warm. Nee. She couldn't depend on this man. She jerked from his touch. "I can't. I changed my mind."

"Too late." He tugged something from his back pocket. "Take this. Call me when you get close to the fairgrounds. I'll meet you at the gate by the back parking lot. The overflow lot."

He held a phone in his hand. He'd known all along she would say yes. Adah backed away from him. "I can't take that."

"It's a disposable phone. I bought minutes for it. When the minutes are gone, you can buy more or throw it away. I want to be able to find you at the fairgrounds. I don't want us to be searching for each other in a crowd. My number is programmed in it. If you need me for anything, call me."

If the way she felt had anything to do with it, Adah knew they'd been searching for each other for a long time. It couldn't be allowed to matter. "You won't notice a girl in an apron and prayer kapp driving a buggy?"

"If you're scared to come alone, bring a friend."

What friend could she bring who would understand about Jackson? The concert, yes, but Jackson, no. At times like this Adah wished for a big sister. Ruthie, who would be five years older than her. She would have experience. She would be done with rumspringa and baptized. She would have advice. She would've known what to do.

"I'm not scared." Adah took the phone. "I have to go."

"See you there."

Adah climbed into the buggy. The last time she looked back, Jackson had his guitar in his hands. He strummed, waved at her, and strummed again. Making music with her to the very last second before she disappeared from sight.

Chapter 15

Adah looked at herself in the tiny square of dusty mirror hanging from the wall in the Daughertys' old shed. Her pale image stared back at her. She used her sleeve to wipe the mirror clean. Despite the fact that she'd already looked around twice when she slipped into the old building, she glanced around a third time. No one saw. No one came out here since Tobias and Michael built the new shed closer to the barn and corral. She and her friends had been using this shed for their rumspringa meeting place for the last two years. No one ever seemed to notice their comings and goings at night—and early in the morning. Or they pretended not to notice.

Stop stalling. She smoothed her hair with a trembling, damp hand. The face looking back at her was unfamiliar, framed by her long, curly blonde hair no longer wrapped in a bun and covered with her kapp. She removed her apron. There, she drew the line. The dress was a nice deep blue. It would do. She'd worn Englisch clothes before, when she knew she'd be with Matthew. He never said much, but she saw him watching her, a curious expression on his face when she strode from the shed in jeans and a T-shirt. Like he didn't recognize her. He seemed to like what he saw, but what he saw wasn't the Adah he knew. She understood that.

Tonight was different. She would be with Jackson. She didn't know him, not like she did Matthew. Matthew could be trusted. Besides, she liked her dresses and they were what a woman should wear. Especially to pass the time with a man like Jackson. Especially in a place like the stock show and rodeo, which would be packed to the brim with Englisch men.

Her hand went to her hair again. Cover it. No. She'd worn it down before and nothing had happened. No bolt of lightning. No deep voice thundering from afar. It was harmless.

So why did it feel different this time? Because Jackson would see. He'd made it clear he already liked what he saw.

His smiling face hovered in her mind's eye. So did she. Heart hammering, she leaned forward, trying to catch her breath. *Gott, what am I doing?*

No answer.

Time to go. Her heart hiccupped. She'd never started out on her own. She'd always been with Matthew. It wouldn't be the same without him. Matthew served as more than a friend on these forays into the world. He was her buffer and protector. He made her feel safe. Why wasn't that enough? Why was she doing this to herself? To him? She sighed and picked up the phone from where she'd laid it on a crate that served as furniture in their little hideaway. She could still call this off.

Nee. Not with the joy of hearing live music within her reach. She tucked the phone into a denim bag and smoothed her hair one more time. Outside, she climbed into the buggy parked behind the shed and headed to New Hope, pushing Dusty to a steady clip.

Forty-five minutes later she pulled into the fairgrounds on the edge of town. A steady stream of trucks and cars clogged the entrances at both ends. Not a buggy in sight. No surprise there. Her hands felt slick on the reins. Dusty tossed his head and whinnied, a high, nervous sound. She knew the feeling. "Easy, boy, easy."

The back parking lot, Jackson had said. The overflow lot. She clucked and snapped the reins. A horn sounded. She jumped and nearly dropped them. Dusty swerved and jerked forward. A rusty red and white pickup truck, its paint faded, zipped past them, its muffler backfiring. Dusty whinnied. "Sorry! Sorry!" She fought to control him. "Easy, boy, come on, we're almost there."

She pulled off the main street and maneuvered onto the asphalt road behind a steady stream of pickup trucks of all sizes, shapes, and colors. Englisch farmers loved their trucks. The road looped around toward the exhibit hall and the long, flat tin buildings where animals were housed until they could be shown. Swarms of people walked along the road, men in cowboy hats and women in jeans with fancy rhinestones embroidered to the back pockets and cowboy boots in all colors. They all seemed to be eating something—caramel apples, funnel cakes, fried oreos, ice cream, cotton candy, or sausages on sticks. The smell of barbecue mingled with manure and dirt. The noise of people talking, engines rumbling, and tinny carnival music blaring assailed her. How would she ever find Jackson in this mess? Everyone in the county showed up for the stock show and rodeo in a town where it constituted the social event of the year. Everyone except her Plain neighbors and friends. The thought gouged her like an arrow between her shoulder blades.

A shrill ring made her jump. The phone. Of course, the phone. She wrapped the reins around one hand and rummaged with the other in her bag, still keeping her gaze on the road in front of her. A little boy dressed in blue jeans, a red Western shirt, boots, and a belt sporting a buckle the size of his hand meandered across the road leading a goat as if he didn't see the horse and buggy. Not like one of those big monster trucks. She jerked on the reins and swerved. The boy lifted his cowboy hat to her, revealing corn silk colored hair. Her hand found the ringing phone. She peered at the screen in the glare of the overhead street lights. Which button would stop the ringing and connect her to Jackson? There. "Hello?"

"You answered." Jackson's voice, big as life, in her ear. "I thought maybe you threw it away."

"Nee. No. I'm here."

"You came."

"I did, but I think maybe I made a mistake."

"No. No. You did good. I promise. Where are you?"

She looked around. "On the road by the exhibit hall."

"Good. That's good. You're doing great. Come on around on the loop and I'll meet you at the back parking lot. We can walk over to the arena together."

To Adah's relief, Jackson proved to be as good as his word. He leaned against the gate, the ever-present cigarette dangling from his lip. He straightened, tossed the cigarette to the ground, and squashed it under the heel of his boot. "Pull over here," he called, pointing to a grassy stretch along the fence. "You can tie up your horse here and he can have a little snack while he waits."

She did as he said. He followed along, giving directions as if she'd never parked a buggy in her life. "Okay, I think I have it."

"Let me help you down." He stood, arms outstretched in front of her, looking up. His mouth gaped open. "Wow."

"What?" She jerked back. "What's the matter?"

"Nothing. You look real nice."

Stunned by the frank appreciation in his eyes, Adah wavered, stuck between what she knew to be proper and how nice his compliment made her feel. Truth be told, he looked good too, even if she tried hard not to notice. She couldn't help but see that the forest green Western-style shirt with the white embroidery around the pockets and the mother-of-pearl snaps looked good on him, along with the jeans and the one black dress boot that matched his black brace. He'd even shaved recently. No five o'clock shadow. He looked like every cowboy she'd ever imagined when she listened to the country music radio station.

"I won't bite, I promise." He waved his fingers in a *come-on-down* gesture. "I promise to be the perfect gentleman. You don't ever have to worry about that. I promise to bring you right back here the minute you're ready to go home."

He hesitated a fraction of a second, looking from her to the buggy and back. "Although I'd feel a whole lot better if I were delivering you back to your house in my truck. I don't think driving these buggies at night is safe."

"I've been driving at night for a long time." His words snapped Adah from her heady reverie. She was quite capable of taking care of herself and she had no need of an Englisch ride. "I have headlights."

"Of course you do."

She let him take her hand and help her climb down even though she'd been getting out of buggies on her own most of her life. Something about the way he looked at her made her believe every word he said…and even the words he didn't say.

"This way." He put his hand on her elbow and guided her toward the gate and into the flow of people moving toward the rodeo arena. "I was late buying the tickets so the seats aren't great, but you'll be able to hear fine. Clayton Star's musicians are really outstanding. He has a good voice too. He's going places, for sure. He won't be doing the county rodeo circuit much longer."

"What will he be doing?" She had to lean close to hear his voice over the chatter of the crowd that pressed against them, carrying them along in a steady flow. "Going where?"

"Nashville, I reckon. That's the place to get the big break."

"Is that where you'll go, after Branson, I mean?"

"Yep. Leastways, I hope so."

Jackson handed two tickets to a man wearing an orange vest that read VOLUNTEER and they squeezed through an entrance packed with people flooding up a series of steps that opened into the arena. She hadn't thought of the tickets. She should pay him for hers. He shouldn't have to pay for her. She tried to tell him that, but the screaming of the crowd made it impossible to talk anymore. A cowboy whipped up and down, arm in the air, hat flying to the ground, as he clung to an enormous, irate horse. An announcer yelled words she didn't really understand. The rider landed on his backside, popped up, and ran, his hat flapping in one hand while two clowns teased the horse in the other direction.

Jackson grabbed her arm and gently propelled her up steep cement steps until he found a row with two seats on the end. "This is it," he leaned in and said directly in her ear. She could feel his breath on her cheek and smell the Doublemint gum he chewed. A shiver rippled up her neck. He put his hand on her back. "We'll be able to see everything from here."

"Where's the band?" She sat down and craned her neck, trying to see everything at once. She'd never seen such a rowdy, rambunctious crowd. They were screaming as another cowboy tried his luck with a different horse and had the same results. What exactly did winning look like in bronco riding? "I thought you said this was a concert."

"They have rodeo events first. The concert's always last. We missed the mutton busting—you would've liked that. And the kids trying to catch the pigs. But they haven't done the barrel racing yet. Something tells me you'll like seeing women ride horses fast." He shoved up his shirt sleeve far enough to reveal a watch on a silver band. "Got the bull riding after that. About an hour and then it's music city."

To Adah's surprise, the time flew by as Jackson explained the event, talking about the riders, the scoring, and who was favored to win and why. She did like the barrel riding, as silly as it seemed. The way the horses flew around the orange barrels without touching them. The way the women controlled the horses, riding low, staying on despite the twisting and turning. She also liked one night of being someone else long enough to enjoy a concert with someone who loved music as much as she did.

Finally, the bull riding. "How do you know who wins?"

"Simple. Whoever manages to stay on the longest."

A monumental task it seemed. One cowboy flipped off the saddle the second the gates opened on the chute. Another got thrown against the fence and limped away holding his arm after only three seconds.

"Why do they do this?" She had to shout to be heard over the crowd.

"Because it's an adrenaline rush. Because it's fun," Jackson shouted back. "And because that's how they make a living."

There had to be easier ways. "You did this?"

He shook his head. "Calf tie-down and team roping. I haven't done it for a few years, though. I miss it sometimes."

"Why?"

"I like competing. Makes you feel alive knowing everyone is watching and cheering for you."

He didn't feel alive now? She studied his face when he looked back at the competition on the field. He looked plenty alive to her. Smiling, clean shaven for once, eyes dancing. She felt alive at this moment, very alive. Being here felt alive.

Dangerous grounds. She inhaled and fixed her gaze on the competition, determined not to look at him again. The noise died down. The events ended. Some people filed out while others squeezed into the long flat rows of seats. People scurried around down on the field, setting up equipment, bringing in speakers. Soon a set of drums appeared, and then keyboards. Adah watched, fascinated, as the stage began to appear before her eyes,

"Why country music?"

Jackson's soft question brought her out of a wide-eyed attempt to see everything and tuck it away to turn over in her mind later, absorb, and think about when she was back in her world. Courtesy dictated she look at him, as much as she tried to avoid it. "What do you mean?"

"Why do you like country music so much?"

She switched her gaze to her hands folded primly in her lap and then out at the musical instruments arranged on stands, waiting to be brought to life by their owners. "The songs tell stories."

Like her poems did.

He nodded. "Yeah. Not like heavy metal, which is just a bunch of screaming."

"My brother Daniel liked to listen to what he called classic rock when he was running around." She smiled, thinking back to the time she'd caught him in the barn dancing around like a fool with his ear buds on when he was supposed to be mucking the stalls. "It was okay, but I couldn't understand the words or the words were the same over and over. No real story."

"Exactly. Where do you even hear music if you can't have it at home?"

"In stores and restaurants." She smiled. "In the houses I clean."

"Yeah, like my house. Lucky me."

"I don't believe in luck."

"What about fate?"

"No."

He sighed. "Me neither. That's why I know this is right."

"Jackson—"

"Hey, Jackson, long time no see!" A huge guy with a black Western shirt bursting at the seams over his enormous shoulders and biceps stopped in front of them, two rows down. He flopped his black cow-boy hat up and down, revealing a head of carrot-colored hair. "You're in town and you didn't even bother to give me a call, man? What's up with that, dude?"

Jackson's hand covered Adah's. It felt warm and a little damp. "Hey, Bert. What's up? I busted my ankle right after I got home from school. Haven't gotten out much."

"You're out now." Bert's gaze lingered on Adah. "And then some."

"Yeah, and then some." The short, slim girl standing in his shadow caught Adah's attention. Her voice radiated hostility. "Guess you lost your phone or something."

"Hey, Dani Jo." Jackson's tone didn't waver. "How ya been?"

Dani Jo tugged at the deep scooped neck of her pink shirt. It didn't do any good. "Like you care. I guess RaeAnne was right. You dumped me for your maid."

Chapter 16

It took Adah a few seconds to realize this was *the* Dani Jo. RaeAnne's friend. The one Jackson claimed he wasn't dating. Standing here at the rodeo arena with a date and a scowl on her face. Jackson's face went beet red. His jaw pulsed. Before he could explode, Adah jumped in. "I'm Adah. We're not dating."

"I guess not or you would've worn something a little nicer." Dani Jo bared even white teeth through thin lips covered with bright pink lipstick. "You must stink to high heaven, sweating in that get-up."

"I like her get-up just fine and she smells good," Jackson sounded like an old barn dog awakened in the middle of the night by a prowling wolf. "At least she doesn't flash it around like you do."

"You used to like what I flashed plenty."

Bert continued to look Adah up and down like a starving man contemplating a nicely grilled venison steak. He seemed oblivious to the sparks flying through the air between his date and Jackson. "Don't recall seeing you around, honey."

"I told you, she's one of those Amish girls." Dani Jo tossed curly black hair over her shoulder, covered only by skinny straps on a shirt that ended well above her navel. She wrapped the words in a blanket of disdain. "She cleans Jackson's house."

"She does a lot more than—"

"Jackson." Adah didn't need to be defended and she felt no shame for her hard, decent work. "Pleased to meet you, Bert, and you too, Dani Jo."

Bert's expression remained perplexed as his gaze jerked from Adah to Jackson and back. Dani Jo didn't give him time to ask another question. She wiggled closer in her short-shorts, slid her hand through the crook of his arm, and yanked. "You said you'd buy me a pop and a candy bar. Let's go before the music starts."

"Yeah, yeah." Bert shrugged. His massive shoulders threatened to tear the seams of his shirt. "Nice meeting you, Adah. Don't be a stranger, you two. There's a kegger at the Dawsons' later tonight. Come on out."

"Yeah, sure." Jackson's hand tightened on Adah's. "We'll see you there."

Not likely. Adah kept her mouth shut.

"The music is starting." Dani Jo's voice had a distinct whine now. "And I need a restroom."

"Yeah, yeah."

They disappeared into the flow of people moving to and from seats.

"That was awkward." Jackson heaved a sigh. "Sorry."

Adah yanked her hand from his. "No skin off my nose."

He snorted. "I can tell by the sour look on your face."

Adah couldn't help it. She laughed at the equally sour look on his. "It's not your fault, I reckon."

"You got that right. Let's start over. You want something to drink? A pop? Some lemonade?"

It was a long way to the concession stand and Adah didn't want to miss a thing. She didn't care about Bert and his lingering stare or Dani Jo's hostile tone. She'd come for the music and the band members were striding across the arena to the stage that had popped up in the middle in what seemed a matter of seconds.

"The music is starting."

And indeed it was. Loud and foot-tapping and all encompassing. Adah could think of nothing else. She lost herself in the guitar riffs and the drum solo and the way Clayton Star could take a note and make it last and last until her own lungs might burst. Jackson left and came back with root beer and popcorn. She hardly knew he was gone and barely tasted his offering.

The music ended long before she could sate her desire for more. The band did two encores and still the crowd clapped and chanted. Adah, to her own surprise, joined in. She wanted one more song, three or four more minutes before she had to go back to being Adah Knepp, Plain girl, who cleaned houses and liked it.

Finally, it ended. No more encores.

"Come on." Jackson threw their cups and popcorn containers in the nearest trash can. He dusted off his hands as he helped her navigate toward the exit. "I've got a surprise for you. This way. If we hurry we can catch Clay."

"Why would we do that?"

"Don't you want to meet him?"

The thought made her stomach do backflips. Meet a man who had just entertained five or six hundred people with music he wrote and performed? "I don't know. I mean, yes. Can you really do that?"

"He's originally from these parts. We jammed a few times when he was in Columbia for gigs." Jackson grinned, obviously pleased with the surprise on her face. "You think I'm just blowing smoke when I talk about being a musician. I work at it hard. I have been since high school. Even had a band of my own for a while."

While his parents thought he was in class, he made music instead.

He guided her through the back of the arena into a tunnel that ran underneath the seats overhead. The laughter and noise told her when they were close. The band members were hooting and hollering and carrying on, blowing off steam. A huge, hairy man who looked like a brown bear in a black, too-tight shirt tried to wave them off, but when Jackson insisted he call back on the radio, he grudgingly did just that. A few seconds later he silently waved them through.

A couple of the guys from the band brushed past them as they entered what looked like a dressing room, laughing and shoving each other like little kids. "Hey, Jack, go on in. Clay's just relaxing. We'll be right back."

Jackson waved and kept moving.

The room was stuffed to the brim with chairs, a couch, a table covered with makeup and brushes and all sorts of stuff Adah couldn't identify. It smelled of sweat, cigarettes, beer, and too much cologne. Along one wall sat a series of stands, each holding a beautiful guitar. Some acoustic, some electric. Also a banjo and something Jackson had told her was called a mandolin. She liked it. She liked them all. She almost veered that direction, but the man in the center of the room drew her toward him instead.

Clayton had removed his red Western-style shirt to reveal a white T-shirt. He lounged in an easy chair, a brown, long-neck bottle dangling from three fingers. A skinny blonde in tight jean shorts and a red, white, and blue tube top that made her look like a miniature flag sat on his knee. He grinned and waved them in. "Hey, Jack, good to see you. I wondered if you were out there. You shoulda come by before the show. I would've jammed with you on stage. You need to get some face time, bro."

"Next time." Jackson nodded toward Adah. "I had a date."

Clayton stood, dumping the girl to her feet. He towered over all of them. No wonder he looked so massive on stage. Up close, he was even bigger. "Aren't you a sweet thing?" He held out a hand. "I don't bite, ma'am, I promise."

He called her *ma'am*. Adah found her tongue twisted in three kinds of knots. She shook his hand so fast it might've been a hot poker.

"Adah has a hankering to be a country music singer. She writes her own songs." Jackson slung his arm around her shoulders in a casual motion that caught her by surprise. She stood rooted to the spot, not certain she still breathed. "She has a great voice and she's practically playing the guitar after one lesson. I keep telling her she's a natural."

"Really?" Clayton scratched at the reddish-blonde stubble on his chin. He dropped back into the chair and the flag girl, who didn't seem to mind that she hadn't been introduced, slipped back on his knee. Clayton rubbed her bare back with a hand bigger than a catcher's mitt. "As it happens, I got an opening. You looking to audition for backup singer?"

He directed the question to Adah. Her mouth opened. The words stuck in the back of her throat. "What?" The single syllable came out in a squeak. "Nee. No."

Did he mean right now? Did he want her to sing now? Her mouth had gone dry and her tongue stuck to the top of her mouth. She couldn't remember a single word to a single song she'd ever written. Eying the distance to the door, she considered making a dash for it. Jackson had no right to put her in this position. He knew she couldn't do this.

"Whoa, hang on now." Jackson rubbed her back in a motion exactly like the one Clayton employed with flag girl. His touch only intensified her anxiety. "From the look on her face, she's pretty starstruck at the moment. And she's way too good to be a backup singer. She needs her own band."

Clayton snorted and took a long draw from the bottle. He wiped his mouth with the back of his hand. "You always were full of yourself, buddy. You know the drill. Everyone has to start somewhere. She needs to get her foot in the door. That's why you brought her down here, isn't it?"

"Hey, man, I came by to tell you the show was great. Got my money's worth. I wanted my girl to hear some good music and see that it can happen. A local boy can make good." Jackson's hand slid down Adah's hair in a soft brushing motion. "How 'bout I send you a demo once we get one made? You can hear for yourself."

My girl? A demo? Jackson was making things up as he went along.

"I don't know if this local boy has made good just yet, but thanks for the vote of confidence." Clayton took another swig from the bottle. "Send me a CD. If she's as good as you say she is, I'll pass it around. What about you? You got one yet?"

"Working on it. Got a bunch of new songs."

"That's good, real good. Be sure to use a good studio. Get a decent product. That's the secret. I'm headed to Branson from here and then on to Nashville, with any luck. You've still got my email address though." He leaned down and set the bottle on the floor. Flag girl popped up and went to a nearby cooler. A second later, Clayton had a fresh beer in his hand. "Where are my manners? Have a seat, have a seat! Y'all want a drink or something? Corky and Sam went for another bottle of Crown, but we still got plenty of beer. The little lady might like a wine cooler. There's a bunch of food too, finger foods, mostly girlie stuff. Corky's picking up some barbecue for us."

Jackson must have felt the tension ripple through her body. His arm dropped and his hand wrapped around hers. "I have to get Adah back to her buggy, but maybe I'll circle back a little later. I know you're gonna do a rehash of tonight's show. You messed up on that last song before you did the encores, didn't you?"

"You noticed that? It's new and we're still working out the kinks." Clayton chuckled. The sound died away. "Did you say buggy?"

"See y'all in a while." Jackson's gaze went to the girl. "Nice meeting you, ma'am."

As if they'd actually met her. Adah let Jackson tug her back out into the tunnel. Otherwise she'd still be standing there, mouth open, trying not to stare at so many beautiful musical instruments all lined up and ready for picking.

"What was that all about?" She jerked her hand from his and scampered along the corridor, her feet fueled by fury. "Why would you do that to me?"

"Do what? Introduce you to someone who can help you with your career? Or get you in front of people?"

"Number one, you shouldn't be touching me. You promised." She couldn't outrun him even though he was handicapped by his bad ankle. The faster she walked, the faster he hobbled along. Feeling guilty at making him put a strain on his injured leg, she slowed. "And what career? You're just filling my head up with stuff that will never happen. Never."

"That's what you're mad about?" He grasped her arm at the elbow and swung her around. "You're mad because you want it and you're afraid you can't have it."

"I know I can't have it. There can't be a demo or a career." She jerked free of his touch. "Not without giving up everything that's important to me."

"You wouldn't have to give up me."

Like she had him. The way he looked at her, that was exactly what he was saying. If she touched his hand at this moment, the electricity would knock her into tomorrow. "I'm not your girl. You promised not to touch me and you broke that promise. How can I trust anything you say?"

"I know."

"You promised."

"I know." He kicked at a clod of dirt, messing up his shiny boot. "Boy howdy, do I know."

"Is it so awful?" She couldn't imagine what he saw in her with her long, faded blue dress and black sneakers. What with all the girls around them dressed in skintight blue jeans decorated with rhinestones on the back pockets, shiny boots, and tight tops with skinny straps and hems that ended above their belly buttons. "Just being friends?"

He ducked his head. It bothered her that she couldn't see his face under the brim of his hat. "Is it so bad, Jackson?"

"It's not bad at all." He looked her in the eye. "It's an honor to be called your friend."

"Why?" She stopped in the middle of the path that led to the overflow parking. "Why do you say that? I'm nothing special."

"Honey, you are all kinds of special. I don't know why you can't see that." He faced her, his eyes shining in the overhead street light. "When you sing, you sound like an angel."

"Nee, nee." She stumbled away, walking faster. "You can't do that. Don't compare me to anything close to God."

"I can't help myself."

Jackson caught up with her, snatched her arm a second time, and whirled her around. His kiss took her so utterly by surprise she nearly sank to the ground. He wrapped his arms around her waist and held her up, the kiss deepening until she was sure she would black out and he'd have to carry her to the buggy and drive her home. He tasted of tobacco and mint gum and the promise of more. He tasted like freedom. The thought only made the blood race faster from her heart to her head and back, blotting out any thought of what was right or wrong, good or bad. Finally, finally, he backed away, but his hands tightened around her hips, his gaze locked on her face.

Gasping for breath, Adah stared up at him. Her heart slammed against her ribcage. She could feel the blood pumping through her body. Every nerve quivered like a cloud of hummingbirds, their wings beating in agitation against a net. She waited, thinking he would say something. Still, he didn't speak. He simply looked at her, his expression daring her to respond. Anger burned through her, turning everything inside her to ashes. "You promised." Two words. They were all she could muster. "You promised."

"I know—"

"Goodbye, Jackson."

She turned and fled.

"Adah, wait."

"No, you spoiled it. You said you were a gentleman."

"I am, but I'm only human."

She untied the reins from the fence post with hands that seemed to be all thumbs. The reins dropped to the ground. She stooped, scooped them up, and scrambled into the buggy. Before she could get Dusty moving, Jackson hauled himself in on the other side and plopped down next to her.

"Get out."

"Not until you accept my apology."

"Get out."

"I'm sorry."

"You shouldn't have done that."

"I know, but you make a man crazy. The huffier you get, the more your eyes light up and the more your skin turns that pretty pink color." Jackson stared straight ahead. He breathed so hard, he sounded as if he'd been running. "You have beautiful lips. Did you know that? You're driving me nuts!"

"Why?"

"I don't know why. I don't know!"

He flung the words at her, the truth of them etched across his face.

Adah stared at the reins in her hands, unable to remember what to do with them. She'd been driving buggies since she was seven.

"I *am* sorry."

"I know." She didn't look at him, didn't dare, or she might do something horrible, like lean in to him for another kiss. "You have to get down."

"Let's go hang with the band."

"No."

"Go to Bert's party, then."

"No!"

"To the pond? We'll write a song."

"No."

"Then just sit here with me for a minute."

Considering the shaking of her body and the tears that clouded her vision, Adah figured she needed a minute to collect herself. It wasn't so she could spend another sixty seconds in Jackson's company. Not at all.

Neither of them spoke. Jackson tugged a cigarette from his pack and flicked open a silver lighter with a stallion etched on the cover. The acrid smell of butane and burning tobacco floated in the air, mingling with the earthy smells of hay and manure. She couldn't have found words if she tried. Monster trucks rumbled by, stirring up dust and hurling diesel fumes at them. The overflow parking cleared and the traffic dwindled. Fresh air blew in on a night breeze, finally cooling the dark and banishing the smells.

"I *am* sorry, Amish girl." His voice was so soft and hoarse she could barely hear him. "But if you could see yourself the way I see you, you'd understand."

"No, I wouldn't."

"I thought you folks were all about forgiveness."

"We are."

"Then how about spreading a little of it my way? Give a guy a break. Especially one who's falling in love with you."

"You're not helping your case."

"It's not a crime to love someone."

"There can't be anything between us."

The silence stretched. He sighed, the softest, saddest sound Adah had ever heard. "Meet me at the pond Wednesday after you finish cleaning? For another lesson?"

"How will that help your…our…situation?"

"Just because I'm a jerk doesn't mean you should give up your music."

"You're not a jerk."

"I'm glad you can see that. Come to the pond."

"We'll see."

He smacked his hand on the side of the buggy. Adah jumped. He sighed. "Sorry. That's what my mom says when she means no."

"I mean I'll see. I have to think. I can't think with you sitting next to me."

"Then I'll let you go." He climbed down. She breathed for the first time all evening, it seemed. He looked back. "For now."

She stopped breathing again. "You're not helping."

He flashed a grin, his teeth white against the growing darkness. "You kissed me back."

"Did not."

"You just keep telling yourself that."

His laugh followed her all the way home. Her first kiss and it had been with a man she barely knew instead of the man who'd been courting her for two years. Matthew didn't deserve this. Her heart ached with the shame of it and knowing she desperately wanted to kiss Jackson again. *Gott, what is wrong with me?* She pulled over long enough to fix her hair and pin her kapp to her head. Her apron was wrinkled from being stuffed in her bag, but it was better than nothing. At least she didn't have to stop at the shed to change her clothes. At least she hadn't gone that far.

The heady excitement of the music fled as she pulled back onto the road, chased away by the events in its aftermath. Dani Jo and her hostility. Bert and his eyes that seemed to peek under her dress. Clayton Star with his knowing smile and patronizing tone. The combination left her with a headache and the sure knowledge that she'd made a terrible mistake. She'd tried to have it all. It couldn't be done. One thing led to another. She'd raced toward the slippery slope full tilt, and found herself at the bottom on her behind, just as Daed had predicted.

She urged Dusty into a trot, anxious to get home and to bed. For a rumspringa night it was still early. She still had time to get a decent night's sleep and be up early to do chores around the house. Time to study the Confession of Faith articles. Time to prepare for baptism class. Time to get right with Gott.

Relief flowed through her. She could get her bearings again among her own people. Find herself. From now on she would concentrate on baptism classes. Give her parents what they wanted. What she needed.

Feeling a little better, she pulled onto the dirt road that led to her house and let Dusty lead the way. The breeze cooled her face. Earthy night smells, country smells of dirt and grass, calmed her. She breathed, her heart settling into its normal pace. If she could only forget the feel of Jackson's hand rubbing her back or his lips on hers. *Stop it. Gott, I'm sorry, so sorry. Forgive me.*

In the moonlight, something moved in front of the house. The beat of her heart stumbled over itself in a painful hiccup. Who would be outside this time of night? Surely not Daed waiting up for her. Her heartbeat took off in a dead run. He would see her face and know. She pulled up on the reins, trying to slow Dusty down, but the horse slogged on, anxious, no doubt, for his stall and rest.

A horse's head bobbed. It whinnied. A horse and buggy sat by the hitching post, battery operated lights luminous against the dark night.

A stream of light from a flashlight whooshed over her and then circled back. Adah squinted and slapped her palm to her forehead as if that would help her see who stood behind the flashlight's brilliance. She pulled back on the reins again and came to a stop by the other buggy.

"So there you are."

Matthew.

The headache came back full force.

"I was beginning to think you were ignoring my flashlight." His tone crackled, as brittle and dry as two-day old toast. "It never occurred to me you weren't home."

"Matthew, I was just…"

He turned the flashlight off, leaving his face in darkness. Without speaking, he climbed in the buggy, snapped the reins, and drove away.

Chapter 17

Matthew ignored the *clip-clop* of another set of horse's hooves. He pulled through the Knepps' gate and turned on to the road that led to the highway. Heat burned his face and neck despite the warm night breeze. What had he been thinking? He'd been thinking he would take Adah for a drive and give her a good talking to. He'd make her see. He'd prove his daed and Molly and all the others wrong. Groossdaadi was right. A person had to fight for the person he loved. Matthew had set out to fight for her. Instead, he'd only embarrassed himself. Why hadn't he seen it? Adah couldn't commit to him because there was someone else. Her cheeks were bright red and her hair looked done up in a hurry under her crooked kapp. The sight of him had sent guilt rising on her face plain as day. Who? His mind raced over the possibilities. Not that many existed. The New Hope district was too new, too small.

Richard Bontrager. He'd make a good candidate. The way he looked at Adah the day of the canning frolic, before he realized Matthew approached. But if Richard came courting, he would come in his own buggy, take her for a ride, and bring her home. What was she doing out gallivanting on country roads at night by herself? Who had she been meeting?

"Matthew, stop! Come on, stop!"

Adah's buggy pulled up next to his on the wrong side of the road.

"Are you crazy? You can't drive on that side." Matthew pulled toward the shoulder of the road. Much farther over and he'd be in the ditch. "What do you want?"

"Stop. At least give me a chance to explain."

"You don't owe me an explanation."

"Jah, I do. Please."

Matthew yanked the buggy over to the shoulder and came to a stop. Not because she asked him to do it, but because he knew better than to drive when he was so furious. He'd never felt this angry before in his life. Thanks to Adah Knepp.

Adah drew her buggy onto the shoulder a few yards ahead of him. She made no move to get down. Apparently she expected him to come to her, which of course he already had done once this evening.

He counted to ten. Then to twenty. Then to thirty. Finally, he jumped from his buggy and stalked toward hers. "If you have something to say, say it."

"Could you please get up here and sit? Please."

Words he would never say aloud bobbed in his head. He swatted them away. No point in standing here looking up at her like a little boy at the candy store, wanting something he couldn't have. He'd come to talk. Might as well talk. He did as she asked.

For a few minutes, she didn't speak and he saw no reason to be the one to initiate the conversation. Crickets sang. An owl hooted.

"I don't know what I'm doing." Her voice, laden with unshed tears, hurt his heart. His anger whooshed out, fizzled, and sank to the ground like a spent balloon. "I want to do the right thing, but if I do, I'm afraid I'll never be happy." She shook her head. Her prayer kapp slid some more. Her bun slipped. "Happy isn't the right word. Content. I want to be content."

She might as well have shot him through the heart with her daed's hunting rifle. Matthew swallowed against the pain of the inference that she could never be happy or content with him. "What do you want? What would it take for you to be happy?"

"I want to play my music." She peeked sideways at him. "But I also want my family and my friends and my community."

She didn't say it, but the way she looked at him gave Matthew a faint hope he might be included in this circle of people she wanted in her life. He stared at the carpet of sky thick with stars. He'd stared at them so many times with Adah at his side. Had she been content in his company or only feigning it? Why wasn't he enough for her?

What an arrogant thought. Didn't he want the woman he made his fraa to be happy and content with her lot? "Isn't it enough to have the music we sing while we work and while we play? Isn't it enough to sing praises to God? Even to sing praises during the prayer service?"

"If I weigh it all out when I'm alone or at the prayer service or doing the laundry at home, I think it's enough. It's when I get too close to all of it that I find myself drawn to the other music, the other life." She said the words fast as if it were a release to let it out. "Isn't that what the rumspringa is for? So we can see the other life and know that it's not for us? What if we find out it *is* what we want?"

She didn't have to specify what *it* was. He'd seen the shine in her eyes, the way her lips parted and her breathing quickened when they went to the concerts. She didn't drink the pop he brought her or hear him when he spoke to her, so entranced was she by the music. She also didn't look at him like that. "Do you really want to wear goop on your face and shiny shoes and strut across a stage and sing for strangers who ogle you and turn to you for pleasure instead of to God?"

"Nee. Nee, that's not what makes me happy. Besides, I don't want to be apart from my family."

Did she want to be apart from him? The question nearly burst from Matthew's lips, but he wrestled it back. This wasn't about him. It wasn't about them, even. It was about Adah's walk in faith.

"Stay away from it. Stop getting yourself so mixed up in all that muck." He cleared his throat, knowing that what he asked her to do would be painful for her, even if he didn't understand why. "Choose to do the right thing. That's part of growing up. It's not much fun, but it's what we're supposed to do."

She kept her gaze on her hands, tucked together in her lap. "I need to talk to Mudder and Daed."

"Jah, you do."

"I need to find a different job."

"You'll stop cleaning houses?"

"The Harts' house, for sure." She hesitated. "I don't know about the other two. But no more Harts."

He wanted to ask why the Harts in particular, but he didn't. It was enough that she had trusted him with this much. He would help her avoid the temptations—he could imagine what they were. He had seen the Harts in town. Jackson, Jeffery, and RaeAnne Hart were close to his age. Jeffery never spoke, but Jackson Hart sometimes said howdy as he passed by and once or twice their paths crossed at the harness and blacksmith shop Simon Christner had opened. Jackson seemed okay with his cowboy hats and boots. Flashy, though, driving around in that big diesel-guzzling silver truck spewing fumes in Matthew's face as he swerved around the buggy and sped up. In all likelihood, his family were good folks, but they led a different life, a worldly life that somehow snared Adah into wanting something she shouldn't.

Adah picked up the denim bag that lay on the seat between them. She rummaged in it for a second or two and then produced two flat rectangular objects which she held out to Matthew. He picked up the flashlight and turned it on. A telephone and an iPod. He snapped the light off. "I thought your daed got rid of your iPod." He took her offering, not sure what she wanted him to do with either item. "I didn't know you had a phone. When did you get it?"

"A friend gave them to me."

He waited for her to elaborate, but she didn't. She couldn't seem to look at him. "Why do you want me to have them?"

"Get rid of them for me. Please." She took a breath and let it out. "You have so much going on right now and I'm sorry I'm making it worse for you. The last thing you need is a friend acting silly when you have all these people in your house and you have to finish the dawdi haus and finish the harvest."

The word *friend* leaped up and bit him like a rattler. "You're not just a friend." He slapped his mouth shut. If she only wanted to be a friend, he should accept that. He should be her friend in her time of need. "I mean, don't apologize. I always have time to help. I want you to find your faith."

She wrapped her arms around her middle as if she were cold on a hot, humid night in July. "I just need a little time to get myself in order. I'm a mess." She made a sound that was half giggle, half sob, wet and unhappy. "As if you couldn't see that. Just do this one thing for me."

"I will."

"Get rid of that stuff for me."

Matthew tightened his grip until the edges of the phone bit into his skin. If these little boxes were coming between Adah and God, he would put as much space between her and them as he could. "See you at baptism class on Sunday?"

"I'll be there." She sounded certain of that. It gave Matthew hope. "See you then."

He wanted to do something more. He wanted to hug her. He wanted to wipe that stricken look off her face. Something told him he didn't have the power to do that. Not yet. He wouldn't give up. "See you then."

And as many times and as many places as it took to make her see what she had right in front of her nose.

He climbed down and went back to his buggy, her offerings tight in his hand. He contemplated throwing them in the ditch, but then someone might pick them up. Instead, he waved at her as he passed, then glanced back to make sure she turned her buggy around safely and headed home.

Despite an overwhelming weariness born not of any physical work, but more from upheaval in his head and his heart, Matthew headed down the dirt road that led to the pond where he liked to take Adah walking. The humid night air weighed heavy on him. He glanced at the phone and the iPod on the seat next to him. So small, yet so big to Adah. Why? Who had given her the phone? What was on the iPod? Songs. Just songs. Little snippets of a world they tried so hard to keep at arm's length. Why was that so difficult for Ada? He had no desire to be immersed in the flash and strut of that world. But he wasn't Adah. He drew to a stop close to the pond's edge and hopped down. He turned to pick up the phone.

It rang.

The sound halted him in his tracks.

The strident buzz broke the peaceful stillness of a country night. He breathed.

Answer it.

No.

Answer it.

Tell whoever it is not to call Adah anymore. Help her sever the connection. For himself? Or for her? Both.

Matthew pushed the button.

"Adah, Adah?" A hoarse, slurred voice filled his ear. "Don't hang up! Honey, I'm sorry. I shouldn't have kissed you and I shouldn't have teased you about it."

His ripped heart hammering in his chest, the words ringing in his ears, Matthew held the phone out, looking at the display. Numbers, no names.

"Adah? Adah! Are you there? Answer me, Amish girl!"

Fury and hurt mingled, their razor-edged wings striking his face and head. Hand shaking, he put the phone to his ear. "Stay away from Adah."

He slung the phone in a high arc that sent it spiraling over the pond's water, glittering in the moonlight until it disappeared in a satis-fyingly loud splash in the deepest, darkest center of it.

Without hesitation, he sent the iPod to the same watery grave.

He stood there for a long time, hoping for a peaceful silence restored. Instead, the man's voice battered him in a continuous loop, stealing the serenity he'd always found in this place, Adah at his side.

I shouldn't have kissed you. I shouldn't have kissed you. I shouldn't have kissed you.

Chapter 18

Adah kept her gaze on the pie crust as she lifted it from the floured cutting board and laid it across a pie pan filled with fresh sliced peaches, sugar, and cinnamon. She cut away the excess crust and began to pinch the edges, bringing together the bottom crust and the top in a nice fluted pattern. The everyday task, one she'd done hundreds of times, steadied her shaking fingers. She sighed and glanced at her mudder, who stooped to take a pan of peanut butter pecan cookies from the propane oven.

"Whatever it is, girl, spit it out." Mudder straightened and set the pan on potholders spread across the counter. "That's about the tenth time you've sighed in the last five minutes. You look like a raccoon with those big circles around your eyes, and you didn't touch your breakfast. Best get it over with, whatever it is. You'll feel better."

Adah picked up a knife and made small slits in the middle of the crust to allow steam to release. Her own steam needed release too. She cleared her throat. "I wanted to talk to you and Daed."

"Yet you waited until he headed to town to bring up the subject, whatever it is." Mudder scratched at her nose, leaving a smudge of flour on it. "That's not like you. Sometimes I think you like getting him riled up."

"Nee, I don't. That's why I thought maybe I'd talk to you first."

"A woman could grow old and die in the time it takes you to spill

161

the beans." Mudder chuckled and slipped another pan of cookies into the oven. "Have a cookie and tell me what's on your mind."

Adah picked up a cookie the size of Daed's palm and laid it on the napkin, ignoring the heat on her fingertips. The aroma of warm peanut butter curled around her, calming her. "I can't clean at the Harts anymore."

Mudder stopped washing the mixing bowl. She laid it on the counter still coated in soapy bubbles and faced Adah. "Do you want to tell me why?"

"Nee." Adah broke the cookie in half and crumbled up the bigger piece. The smell made her mouth water, but her stomach clenched at the thought of eating it or anything else. "I just think it's better if I don't."

"But you'll keep cleaning at the Stewarts and the Johnsons?"

"I could. I guess it depends. I'd need a new third house to clean."

Mudder moved to the prep table and pulled out a chair. She pointed at it. Adah sat and Mudder took the chair across from her. "You're my dochder. I'm your mudder. You can tell me the things that bother you." Her frown deepened and an emotion like anger flitted across her angular features. "If something happened...if one of the Harts did something, you can tell me."

"The things that happen during rumspringa aren't something to share with parents."

"If they're things you want to do or you want to happen, that's true. But rumspringa is not a time for someone to take advantage of a young girl not so familiar with the ways of the world."

"It's not like that." Adah's cheeks burned. She wanted to think it was from the heat of the oven and a July day already steaming with sultry humidity, but it wasn't. She could still feel Jackson's lips on hers. She could still feel his hands gripping her waist. Shame burned her face. "I'm not so innocent."

"Maybe not innocent, but true of heart. You look as if someone hurt you."

"It's not that kind of hurt." She struggled for words to explain something she didn't understand herself. "It's my fault. I did something I shouldn't have done."

Mudder sat back in her chair, one finger tapping restlessly on the table. Her frown deepened, creating grooved wrinkles across her forehead. "Maybe you should talk to Thomas."

"I will." She dreaded that conversation as much as she dreaded talking to Daed. Maybe more. "Tomorrow."

"You've always been my little independent girl." Mudder stopped tapping and began smoothing her red, dishwater-chapped hands across the rough varnished pine as if to remove the marks. "It will cause you pain in the life we choose to lead. You will suffer the consequences of your actions until you learn to control them and yourself. I understand that and I can't fix it, much as I would like to. But nothing you do will stop me or your daed from loving you."

The unadorned words cloaked Adah in a sense of security as surely as if Mudder had draped one of her handmade quilts over her shoulders. "I know."

"That said, you also have to know there are things you might do that would force us to no longer have contact with you. We love you, but we love our Lord God more. The decision is yours. It will always be yours."

"I know." The harsh reality of her mudder's frank statement chilled Adah to the bone in the midst of an oven-heated kitchen She mustered a whisper. "That's why I can't work at the Harts anymore."

"You're trying to do the right thing?" A bit of sweet relief crept into Mudder's voice. "Is that it?"

"I am."

"*Gut.* That's *gut.* It's best you let me talk to your daed about this first."

"He'll be angry."

"Jah, but not at you. Your daed is a papa bear when it comes to his girls."

"Because of Ruth."

"Because he loves you and wants to raise you right. Losing Ruth makes it harder for him to let go of the rest of his kinner." Mudder slid her hand across the table and patted Adah's. "Remember that when he acts all stern and grumpy."

"I will."

Mudder pushed back the chair, the legs scraping against the linoleum. She stood and looked down at Adah. "It's best you give up cleaning in the Englisch houses altogether. That's what Daed will say. He'll say better to remove the temptation all together. Emma and Katie need help in the new combination store. You could work for them."

Where Mudder's two best friends could keep an eye on her day in and day out at the new store with its Amish goods. Quilts, jams, pickles, fresh eggs, produce, furniture—whatever the folks in the district wanted or needed to sell, all in one place. She would never be alone with an Englisch boy again. Mudder had reaped much from the few words Adah had carefully selected. "You think they'll want me?"

"I'll talk to them. You'd best get that pie into the other oven." Mudder picked up the mixing bowl and doused it in the tub of rinse water. "Your daed will let the Englisch folks know. No need for you to go back to their houses."

Adah dragged herself from the table. While her heart had ached with shame only seconds ago, now it throbbed like an open wound. She wouldn't get one last chance to see Jackson or hear his voice or run her fingers down the ivory keys of the grand piano. Or pluck the guitar and sing, her voice mingling with his.

She would never hear the words of the next song he wrote.

"It's for the best."

Adah turned to see Mudder staring at her, a knowing look in her eyes. "It might not seem that way now, but it's for the best."

"How do you know?" The question burst from her mouth unbidden. "I mean—"

"I haven't always been old." Mudder chuckled, a rich, lovely note. "Neither has your daed. We had rumspringas too."

"I know."

"Nee, you don't. It's the folly of youth to think you're the first to ever experience something."

"You thought of being with someone besides Daed?"

"He did, not me."

"But he chose you."

"He chose me and never looked back, even when I made the worst mistake a fraa can make. He stood by me after I caused Ruthie's death and burned down our house. That's true love between a man and woman. Remember that."

Mudder rarely spoke of the accident that had taken her first baby's life. Now she turned her back to Adah and peeked into the oven at the cookies, telling Adah no more would be said of it.

Would Matthew do for her what Daed did for Mudder? His expression last night when he took the phone and the iPod without insisting she explain them said he would, but he didn't have all the facts. He could never know where they came from or why she gave them to him.

Matthew said he loved her, but could his love survive her betrayal?

Chapter 19

Heaving a last sigh, Adah slipped across the Brennamans' yard and squeezed onto the bench next to Lizzie Shrock. She glanced first at Thomas. If he was irritated at her late arrival he gave no sign. She smoothed the papers in her hand. At least she'd remembered to bring her homework. After a fitful night of strange dreams involving runaway horses and her father angry and shouting at her, she was surprised she'd arrived at all. She sneaked a glance at the men's benches on the other side. Matthew sat between Caleb and Richard. He'd left a big gap between himself and Richard, who looked at her, smiled, and nodded. She forced a return smile. Matthew's gaze remained fixed on Thomas. She waited for him to look her direction. He didn't. Not even for a second.

"We've been talking about Article Twelve. The State of Matrimony." Thomas fixed her with a rather mournful gaze. Why? What did he know? Or was it her guilty conscience? He cleared his throat. "Let's read through it first."

Thomas wet his thumb and shuffled through a pile of papers on the picnic table. A gust of wind spun two onto the ground. Matthew lunged for them. Adah took the opportunity to do the same. Their shoulders brushed. The skin over his collar turned scarlet. The color rose in a furious wave across his face and lost itself in the roots of his hair underneath his best black hat.

"What's the matter?" she whispered as she tried to take the paper from his hand. His grip tightened. "Why do you look like a snake coiled and about to spew venom?"

He shook his head, let go of the paper, rose, and went back to his seat without saying a word.

Thomas accepted her offering. He cleared his throat again. "I seem to have a frog in my throat this morning. Adah, why don't you read that first paragraph?"

Her cheeks burning, Adah cleared her throat. She should've known. Thomas saw all, knew all, heard all. He knew or thought he knew.

"'We confess that there is in the church of God an honorable state of matrimony, of two free, believing persons, in accordance with the manner after which God originally ordained the same in Paradise and instituted it Himself with Adam and Eve, and the Lord Christ did away and set aside all the abuses of marriage which had meanwhile crept in, and referred all to the original order and thus left it.'"

Adah's voice quivered and broke.

"That's good." Thomas saved her from herself. "Matthew, you take it from here."

He did know something. Adah sideswiped a glance at Matthew. His face darkened to the color of overripe tomatoes and a pulse beat in his clenched jaw. He sucked in air audibly.

"Matthew?"

He swallowed and began to read, his voice stiff, his jaw jutting.

"'In this manner the apostle Paul also taught and permitted matrimony in the church and left it free for everyone to be married, according to the original order, in the Lord, to whomsoever one may get to marry among their kindred or generation so the believers of the New Testament have likewise no other liberty than to marry among the chosen generation and spiritual kindred of Christ, namely, such and another, who have previously become united with the church as one heart and soul, have received one baptism, and stand in one communion, faith, doctrine, practice, before they may unite with one another by marriage. Such are then joined by God in His church according to the original order; and this is called, marrying in the Lord.'" Matthew's voice didn't waver. After he finished, he lowered the paper and looked directly at Adah. His face held a welter of emotions. She couldn't decipher most of them, but two stood out. Anger and hurt.

What did he know? She broke the chokehold his gaze had on her and stared at her hands clasped in her lap. Her fingers hurt.

"So, what does all that mean?"

No one spoke. Lizzie wiggled on her seat. She nudged Adah. Adah shook her head. She'd done the reading. Someone else's turn.

"Anyone? Or are you all sleeping this morning? I'd like to get in to the service before Silas starts the sermon. Wake up!"

"It means a man has to be right with God before he can be right with his fraa." Richard offered. "Seems like common sense to me."

"Me too," Elizabeth chimed in. She sat on the bench in front of Adah, so she couldn't see her face, but her tone said it all. *Everyone with a brain knows that.*

"And the woman has to be right with God or she has no business getting married." Matthew made the statement sound like an accusation.

Thomas nodded and pursed his thin lips. His beard bobbed. "What's good for the goose is good for the gander. Both must be believers. They must be baptized. They must take communion and be members of the body of Christ."

"They have to believe the same thing or there will be arguments and one will end up dragging the other one down." Matthew stared at the sun-scarred grass beneath his Sunday shoes. "Unequally yoked, that's what Luke called it."

"I'm glad to know you've been listening to Luke." Thomas smiled like a proud daed. "It seems like a simple thing, but a tiny seed of doubt or discontent or disagreement can grow into a huge division between a man and his fraa. It can destroy the unity of the family. God must be at the center of a marriage, at the center of a family, at the center of our community."

"What if somebody wants to put something else at the center?" Matthew's gaze darted in Adah's direction. "What if they make something more important than God?"

"There is nothing more important. To place something above God is to worship an idol." Thomas's expression grew serious, his voice deepened. "That is a terrible sin. The Bible says we shall have no idols before Him. We have to remove from our lives anything that comes between us and God."

"Does that mean we can't do things we enjoy?" The words sounded more defensive than Adah intended. She tried to rearrange her features. Just a question. Just trying to learn. So she'd know, if the issue came up somewhere down the road. "Does anything fun or enjoyable have to be discarded because it might come between us and God?"

"Scripture says God wants us to enjoy life. But remember, we're only passing through this life. What is important is eternal life. When that thing you enjoy in this life becomes more important to you than God's plan for you, that's when you have a problem."

Adah dropped her gaze to the ground under Thomas's steely perusal of her face.

"Any other thoughts, questions, discussion?"

No one spoke.

Thomas cleared his throat. "I'm feeling under the weather today. I'll close early. You can get settled in for the sermon before it starts for a change. Think about what we read. If you have questions, bring them next time."

Adah stood with the others and angled her way toward Matthew.

"Adah, a word."

Thomas's voice commanded, it didn't ask. He crooked a long finger toward the house, away from the other scholars straggling toward the barn. Matthew turned his back on her.

She ducked her head and followed the deacon. He stopped near the hitching rail. "I saw your mudder earlier when she brought the cookies up to the house. She said she thought you wanted to talk to me about something."

Adah kicked at the gravel in the road. A kitten stretched, trotted down the steps, and wound its long, skinny body around her shoes. She knelt and petted it, letting Thomas see the top of her prayer kapp.

"We have a service to get to." Despite the words, his tone held an infinite patience. She loved that about Thomas. He was like an *onkel* to every one of the men and women who went through his classes. "What did you want to talk about?"

She swallowed the hard lump in her throat and straightened. "I did something."

"Something you wished you hadn't done." He made it a statement. "Something you'd like to undo and can't."

"I didn't mean to do it. I didn't start out to do it, but it happened."

His gaze hardened. "Something sinful? Something you need to confess?"

"I'm not sure…I mean under these circumstances, I think so. Not under all circumstances, I guess, but as it happened, surely it was. It is."

"The fact that guilt is written all over your face leads me to believe it was. If it felt wrong, it was."

"Not intentionally."

"You've heard the saying the road to hell is paved with good intentions."

"Jah."

"Do you want to tell me what it was?"

"Nee." A white hot sheet of embarrassment wrapped itself around her. She couldn't look at Thomas. Her voice came out in a squeak. "I'd rather not."

"Then all I can tell you is to pray. Pray for forgiveness and for the strength to avoid this temptation, whatever it is. To do something once and ask forgiveness is acceptable, but to keep doing it when you know it's wrong, that's truly sinful."

"I know."

"Do you?"

"Jah."

"What is it that Matthew is so concerned about?"

"What?"

"What is the idol you're worshiping?"

"There is no idol."

"Are you sure about that?"

"I'm sure."

Thomas coughed. New guilt washed over her. He didn't feel well, yet here he stood, trying to help her. "I'm sorry."

"Don't tell me. Tell God." He pointed toward the sky, then let his hand drop so it rested on his chest, over his heart. "We all have holes inside us we're trying to fill. All of us. That's the nature of original sin. Nothing but God can fill that hole."

"I know."

"Get yourself to the service and don't miss any more classes." He coughed. "I'm right behind you. I need a glass of water and something for my throat."

She left him standing by the steps of his house and began what seemed like a long trek to the barn. The voices of her friends and family wafted from it in low, steady tones. Music to her ears.

"Adah."

She looked back. Thomas hadn't moved. "Music can't fill the hole. Neither can an Englisch boy."

Mudder had told him about the Harts. Adah tightened her fingers around the edges of her apron, trying to breathe evenly. "I know."

"See that you don't forget it."

"I won't."

"I don't want to have to raise this concern to Luke."

"You won't have to do that."

"*Gut.*"

She bowed her head and slipped through the barn door. She trusted Thomas. He was wise. So why did the hole inside her grow with each step?

Chapter 20

Matthew swallowed the last bite of his sandwich and pushed away from the picnic table. He hoped his parents didn't want to linger too long visiting with folks after the service. He used to like hanging around on Sunday afternoon, eating good cookies, visiting with friends, playing volleyball, waiting to catch a glimpse of Adah, exchanging a quick, secret grin with her. Those days were over. All night, the words spoken on that tiny telephone had swirled in his head, keeping him from sleeping. Now he had wool for brains and a headache to go with it. Time to get home. If Mudder and Daed weren't ready to go, he would walk. The walk would do him good. Maybe he could work off the anger that ate at his belly. He swiveled, threw his leg over the bench, and rose. Adah stood right behind him, a full platter of cookies in her hands, a determined look on her face. Matthew did a two-step and managed to avoid knocking both her and the platter to the ground. "Sorry, I didn't see you there."

She held on to the platter with both hands. "I guess not."

"No need to be snippy."

They simultaneously glanced both ways. Richard, deep in conversation with Jesse Christner about the pros and cons of free range chickens, waved at Adah but kept talking. Rueben looked half asleep over his ham and Swiss on sourdough bread. The twins were telling knock-knock jokes and laughing so loud it was a wonder they didn't wake their brother. Adah leaned toward Matthew, or maybe that was his imagination. Why would she try to get closer to him? "What's wrong? Last night you were—"

"Hush about last night." Aware of Richard and Simon's curious gazes, he ducked past Adah and strode away, not able to move quickly enough.

"I will not." He heard the plunk of the platter on the table. A second later, Adah scurried next to him, arms and tongue flapping. "Last night you wanted to help me, like you cared. Now you're acting like I have the plague."

She whispered the words, but still, he looked around. No one seemed to notice her tagging along at his side. "This isn't the time or the place. Go away."

"Nee."

"You would make a terrible fraa."

"That's a mean, awful thing to say." She lifted her chin and veered away from his path. "Fine."

He ducked his head and stomped down to the road where the buggies were parked. The horses raised their heads and went back to munching on the grass. He smoothed a hand over the sorrel, Daed's favorite horse. The most calm of their horses. The most likely to get his family safely to and from the service. The horse snorted and kept eating.

Running his hand through the horse's thick mane and along the haunches, Matthew breathed in and out, trying to stifle the anger that ran rampant through him. He'd been mean to Adah. Such behavior was no better than what she'd demonstrated to him. He needed to act like a good Plain man, even if she didn't know her place. He needed to try to help her as one Christian to another, one Plain person to another. Mortified to the very marrow of his bones, he whirled and marched back along the road.

Adah came at him from the other direction. Her face glowed scarlet and her arms swung as she kept a pace even he would be hard pressed to match. "I may be a harlot or some such thing, but at least I'm not mean." She slammed to a halt in the middle of the road. "I would never be mean to you."

"That depends on how you define mean," he fired back, advancing on her. He had twelve inches and thirty pounds on her. He had the advantage. The thought made him feel even meaner. "Letting someone believe you have feelings for them when you're really courting someone else, that's mean. It's not just mean, it's wrong."

She stumbled over loose rocks in the road and nearly fell. He reached for her. She recoiled from his touch and regained her balance on her own. "What are you talking about?"

He did an about-face and together they kept walking, side by side, a space the size of a wagon gaping between them.

"A man called you on the phone last night."

She gasped and her hand went to her mouth. He waited for her to explain. To apologize. To do something. The sun beat down on them and sweat slid from his hair and tickled his ears.

"What did he say?"

That's what she wanted to ask him? "What do you think he said?"

"I'm sorry."

"Yeah, he said he was sorry."

"I mean, I'm sorry, not him."

Sorry didn't begin to cover it. The image of Adah's face close to another man's...it made his stomach rock and his fists clench. He didn't know whether to vomit or punch a wall. Neither would be acceptable.

Forgive. He should forgive. How? What she had done was unforgivable.

Nothing is unforgivable.

The argument raged in his head as it had done ever since he heard those words. *I'm sorry I kissed you.* "Too late."

"It was Jackson Hart. He gave me the phone."

Jackson gave her the phone and something much, much more important. Her first kiss. He assumed it was her first kiss. Maybe Daed was right. Maybe Molly was right. He should never have given Adah his heart or his trust. He'd been blinded by his feelings for her. How could he have been so stupid? "He kissed you."

"How do you know that?"

"He called to say he was sorry for kissing you."

Adah's face blanched. Her hand went to her mouth and she swallowed as if she felt the same upheaval in her stomach he'd experienced when he heard those words. "You had a conversation with him?"

How could she sound so mad? As if he'd done something terribly wrong. Not her. "Nee. Not exactly."

"What did you say?"

"Are you afraid I upset him? So sorry. Too late."

"Nee, I mean, not like that, I mean—"

"You have to make your choice." He slowed his pace. "I told you before I wouldn't wait for you to be ready. Now I know you aren't waiting for me."

She stared up at him, her blue eyes huge and wet. "Yes, I am. I want us...I mean...I'm so sorry. I want things to be the way they used to be between us. The walks and the rides and the singings."

He wished it could be too. He wanted to somehow erase the voice in his head. *I'm sorry I kissed you.* "You don't sound sure."

"I'm not sure of anything."

"You should be sure by now, but you're not. What does that say?"

"It says I'm still finding my way."

"It's not like I haven't wanted to kiss you." Why tell her that? Why let her know how much her actions hurt him? The words tumbled out of their own accord, out of the onslaught of hurt. "Many times."

"Me too." Her voice was so small he could hardly be sure she'd said those words. "I mean, I've wanted it too."

But he hadn't kissed her. If he had, would things be different now? "You know why I didn't kiss you?"

She nodded. "You were waiting."

"Waiting for the right time." Silly him. "To do things the right way."

"I know. I'm sorry."

"Me too."

After everything that had happened, after everything she'd done, he still wanted to kiss her now, to make her forget Jackson Hart and music and guitars and iPods. It seemed incomprehensible, but it was true. He still wanted to kiss Adah. But he wouldn't. He wouldn't stoop to that level. He wouldn't become another Jackson Hart. An Englisch man who thought nothing of taking that special first kiss from a girl he barely knew. "You know what the worst thing is?"

"Another man kissed me."

Matthew kept his gaze on the road ahead of them, watching the swirls of dust kicked up by the breeze. "If I do kiss you…someday…" He forced himself to look at her, trying to gauge her reaction. "I won't be the first. I always thought I would be the first to kiss the woman who became my fraa."

"Me too. I wanted you to be the first." She swiped at her face with her sleeve. "I know. I don't know how this happened. I'm sorry."

Jackson Hart lured her, but she had gone willingly. Of that, there seemed little doubt. And Matthew had been cruel because her actions hurt him. That didn't make it right. "I'm sorry I was mean."

"You were provoked."

"That's no excuse."

She sighed. "But it's human."

"That it is."

Together they turned and began the trek back to the house. He drew a long breath, trying to ease an ache in his throat so profound he tried not to swallow for fear it would worsen. "You will make someone a good fraa." His voice sounded dry and brittle. "Someday."

"But not you?" Her voice quivered. "This can't be fixed?"

"I'll forgive you, but I don't know if I'll trust you again." It sounded *gesflitch*, said aloud, but it was the truth. His pride ached. "There's no way to get it back."

"If I could take it back, I would."

He wanted to lash out at her. What was it like? Did she enjoy it? Had they kissed more than once? He batted the questions down. No sense in creating more wounds that had to heal before they could begin again. "What was on the iPod?"

"Music. Just music."

"He plays music?"

"Jah."

A kindred spirit. "I don't."

"I don't expect you to play music."

Their chances—his and Adah's—of fixing this dwindled as he thought of the things she shared with this other man. A man who loved what she loved. Music. "So now you have to choose."

"There's no choosing."

"You have to choose. This life or a life with an Englisch man. It's not about me anymore. It's about your faith and your community. As for us, if you choose me, I have to figure out if I can trust you again." He jerked his head toward the buggies. "I need to get home and do my chores."

"Matthew, please." She scurried along beside him. "Wait."

"Go home and pray. You have your own work to do."

She stopped in the road, her hands pressed together as if already praying.

He hoped she did, but he feared instead she would go home and hide in her room with her pencil and paper and write a silly love song about how she'd hurt a man who loved her. A love-gone-wrong song. Because that was what Adah did.

He would need a woman he could rely on. That would be the sensible way to go, but it had never been his way. Adah's waywardness drew him to her. Her untamed spirit lifted his. He could admit that to himself, if not the world.

None of that could matter. What mattered was Adah's walk in faith.

He looked back at her, still standing in the road, her expression stricken. "Talk to Thomas. Come to class. Please."

"I'll try."

If it was the best she could do, he would have to accept that. He would ask God to forgive him for being so selfish. He wanted her to choose her faith because he wanted her to choose him.

Who needed greater forgiveness?

Chapter 21

Adah set a quart jar of bread and butter pickles on the shelf next to three more just like it. She adjusted each one so the hand-drawn labels were even. Emma had done a nice job with the labels, but it was the contents of the jars that drew the customers to the New Hope Combination Store. They seemed to love those pickles. Just as they loved Edna's peach jam and Mudder's chow-chow. The canned goods sold the best. That and the hand-sewn goods.

Humming, she picked up a feather duster and began to dust the row of wooden toys and handmade dolls. Funny the things the Englisch folks in New Hope would buy. It was a good thing too, a good source of income for the Plain families, still struggling to make ends meet on their farms, even after three years in their new home.

A tune worked its way into her brain. She flipped the feather duster in time to the melody. Words floated along on the notes. *Nee. Nee. No songs. Please, Gott, no songs.* Songs only caused her trouble. Great trouble. Trouble with Matthew. Trouble with the deacon. Trouble with God.

The work was easy. Too easy. It didn't occupy her mind or wear her out. It gave her too much time to think about things. Like Matthew, who hadn't spoken to her since that day after the prayer service. Or Jackson, whom she hadn't seen since she quit cleaning houses. One, then the other. Which one? She knew what was right. Why did she have such a hard time doing it? Trying to stifle the thoughts, she hummed louder.

"What song is that?"

Adah jumped. She'd forgotten Emma sat at the table working on the ledgers. She shut her mouth. The song didn't have a name. It didn't have words. It kept flitting around her head, waiting for her to write it, waiting for her to sing it and play it.

Not happening. She was through with all that. The tune reminded her of Clayton Star's music. A lot of country, a little bit of rock and roll. A touch of something else with the fiddle and the electric guitar playing a twosome that seemed mournful, yet playful.

She sighed and turned to Emma, who sat at the window, sun spilling in on her, making her fair skin fairer and her blond hair peeking from her prayer kapp blonder. "I don't know. It's just some notes to pass the time."

"You can hum. I don't mind." Emma dropped her pencil, leaned back in her chair, and stretched her arms over her head. "I didn't recognize the tune."

Emma wasn't much for music. Her job consisted of keeping track of every sale so that the families who had money coming to them received their fair share. Turned out the former schoolteacher had a penchant for addition and subtraction. Adah's worst subject.

If Emma only knew how different they were. "It's nothing. Just noise."

"You're bored, aren't you?" Emma picked up the pencil again and twirled it in her fingers. "It's pretty quiet around here sometimes, but things will pick up when it gets close to payday."

"Nee, not bored." Adah turned her back to the older woman. Emma saw and knew way too much. How much she shared with Thomas, Adah had no way of knowing. "There's plenty of work to do. I hum so it's not so quiet."

"I imagine the Englisch folks you worked for had radios and TVs playing and such."

Emma had no idea. "Sometimes."

"I never worked in an Englisch home or store. It must be kind of interesting."

"I liked it all right."

"But you decided to quit doing it."

"Yah, it was time."

A perplexed look on her face, Emma scratched her nose and then scribbled something on the ledger. "You like this better?"

"I'm used to working at my own speed and time." Cleaning houses, she set her own schedule and worked until she was done. Then she was free. Here at the store, she had regular hours. Sometimes they had lots of customers, some days, like today, only a few. "It was harder work, though, and it's not much fun cleaning the toilets of other folks."

Emma chuckled. "Nee, I imagine not."

The door opened and Leah tromped in, little Jebediah and Hazel toddling behind her like a parade. "Come on, come on." Leah shooed them in and shut the door behind her with a definitive bang. She carried a basket filled with embroidered napkins and placemats.

Emma stood and rushed to take it from her. "Oh, these are nice. The Englisch ladies will love them." She set the basket on the glass counter and ran her fingers over the French knots and daisy stitches that created a bright bouquet of sunflowers on the napkin lying on top. "You do have such a nice, fine stitch. I don't know how you have the patience."

Emma's sister-in-law grabbed Hazel's arm just in time to keep her from swiping a doll from the display case. "It soothes me, truth be told. The doctor says I need a hobby that soothes me. He calls it therapy."

She laughed and hugged Hazel to her chest. Emma smiled and nodded. "For me, it's baking bread. Something about kneading the dough. I liked to push it around a bit."

They exchanged smiles. Adah marveled at how much Leah had improved in the last year. She didn't try to hide the fact that she was seeing a therapist in Jefferson City. Mr. Lewis drove her all the way to the city once a week. Adah liked the woman for her forthrightness, even if she was a bit prickly and stern. She suffered an ailment most Plain woman couldn't imagine—depression after childbirth—but she soldiered on with her growing brood that now numbered six.

Leah's gaze fell on Adah. "I heard you were working here." Her smile disappeared, replaced with her bishop's wife frown. "Doing better, I hope."

"Doing well." Emma spoke before Adah could. She dropped the napkin back in the basket. "Would you like to help me price these?"

"Surely." Leah turned back to the counter. "If Adah will keep an eye on the babies."

"Of course." Adah breathed a sigh of relief. Emma knew just how to handle Leah. After all, she'd lived with her sister-in-law at one time. "Go on back. I'll keep them out of trouble."

The two women headed into the workroom where the items would be catalogued and the price tags attached. "Mudder, Mudder!" Hazel tried to toddle after them. "Mudder!"

Adah scooped her up. "No you don't, little one. Stay here with me. You two can be my helpers."

Jebediah plopped on his behind and stuck his hand in his mouth. Adah knelt next to him and placed a basket of blocks in front of the two children. "Shall we build something first? I can dust anytime and I'd rather play with you today."

Jebediah grabbed a block and flung it. It smacked Adah in the forehead and bounced away. "Hey! What did you do that for?" Laughing, she rubbed her forehead. "Build, don't throw."

He crowed and threw another block that ended up underneath a chair near the door. Hazel clutched a small piece in her chubby hands and began to chew on the corner.

"Nee." Adah tugged it from her hand. "We don't eat the blocks. We don't throw the blocks. We build with the blocks."

"You're no fun."

She froze at the sound of that voice. Her heart hammered in her throat. She shouldn't be so happy to hear it, but she was. She'd missed that voice.

"I wish you didn't mind getting your picture taken. I'd snap a few with my phone. You look so perfect with those little babies. You'll make a fine momma someday."

So engrossed in having fun with the kinner, she hadn't heard the door open and close, bringing into the store the one person she shouldn't be seeing. He sounded so much like Matthew complimenting her on her singing of a lullaby to baby John. The two men weren't so different. Different hats and different ways of getting around. But at the core, they wanted family to love. A mishmash of emotion roiled inside her.

Matthew wanted what was best for her.

Jackson liked her just the way she was.

She managed to raise her head. Taking a few steps forward, still with that slight limp, he towered over her. "I heard you were working here."

Breathless, Adah tried to scramble to her feet. For some reason she had two left ones and her fingers only had thumbs. She fumbled to straighten her kapp, sure her hair straggled out and her apron was dirty. He looked clean and neat in his white Western shirt tucked into his blue jeans and the ever-present silver buckle. Her gaze went to his face. To his mouth. The memory of the look on his face when he bent and his kiss engulfed her. She felt the soft touch of his lips on hers all over again. *Stop it. Stop it.* Her face burned. *Gott, forgive me.*

She gritted her teeth, breathed, and lifted her chin. "How did you know I was here?"

"Dani Jo's sister came in for some peach preserves. She told Dani Jo and Dani Jo told RaeAnne, who told me." His smile disappeared into a frown made of granite. "Her way of rubbing it in, I imagine. She still thinks Dani Jo has a chance."

Their grapevine worked much the same as the one in the Plain community. "So you had to come see for yourself."

"Don't get snippy with me." His voice dropped to a growl. "You're the one who didn't even say goodbye or give me one good reason why."

"I didn't work for you. I didn't have to tell you." Adah stopped, her hands on her hips, her face hot. She didn't want Emma and Leah—especially Leah—to come running out to see why she was yelling at a customer. "You know the reason I couldn't come back."

"I told you I was sorry. You didn't have to quit." He squeezed his hat in his big hands, flattening the brim. "I called you."

"I got rid of the phone. And the iPod."

"Why?"

"Why? How can you ask that?"

"I've listened." His volume grew equal to her own. Adah slapped a finger to her lips and nodded toward the back. He heaved a sigh and twisted his hat in his hands. "I've listened to you sing and heard you talk about how much you love music. Your face lights up when you talk about it. You and I are a team."

"You need to leave."

"I talked to Mac McMillan, Clay's manager."

"Jackson—"

"Hear me out. I sent him a disc I burned of you and me singing—"

"Where did you get a recording of me singing?"

"I made it on my phone, the last time we sang together, but you're missing the point—"

"You recorded me without telling me?"

"Let me finish, will you? Mac liked what he heard. He said to come on down to Branson. He'll work with us to make an audition CD and help us set up some auditions for the shows there." The hat flapped as he waved his hands. "This is big, really big."

A chance to sing in Branson. A dream always out of reach suddenly thrust in her face. She could stay here, dust wooden toys, and straighten shelves, or she could sing and make music.

She'd have to give up her family. And Matthew. "I can't."

"Come on, you know you want to do this. You'll regret it for the rest of your life if you don't!"

Hazel's round face squeezed. She began to fuss. Adah gathered her up. "Hush, you're scaring the baby."

"You are the most frustrating, irritating woman I've ever met." His volume dropped to a hissing whisper. "You can't tell me you don't want this."

Adah rocked Hazel on her hip, trying to soothe her. She'd never wanted anything more in her life. She shook her head. "No."

"Think about it. I'll pick you up in town so you don't have to try to get a ride or mess with a buggy." If he didn't stop pulling on the hat, it would be torn in two. "Don't let me down."

She searched his face, trying to understand the angst behind those words. If she went with him, was she committing to the music or to him? Or to both? She couldn't be sure which scared her more. "I can't go with you to Branson. Where would I stay?"

He looked puzzled and then he laughed, a hoarse chuckle. "I scared you away once. I won't do it again. My Aunt Charlene takes care of the cabin we own on Table Rock Lake. You come with me, that's where we'll stay. Aunt Charlene will take good care of you."

Adah jostled Hazel to her other hip. She kissed the toddler's silky curls and inhaled her baby scent. Even that couldn't calm the wild patter of her heart. "What about your parents?"

"They know I'm not going back to school."

"They know about Branson and they said it was okay?"

"I didn't say that. They know I withdrew from the university. They're fired up, they're so mad. If I tell them I'm going to Branson, Pops will self-combust and end up a heap of ashes on the ground."

"Your aunt won't tell him?"

"I imagine she will, but I'll already be there. What's he gonna do, come drag me home by my ear? I'm a grown man."

Hazel fussed. Adah loosened her grip and bounced her on her hip. "Shhh, you're fine, you're fine."

"You're thinking about it, aren't you?"

Jackson took a step toward her, one hand out as if he would touch her. The sheer desire of the moment wrapped itself around her chest and pressed, making it hard for her heart to beat. Blood pounded in her ears. What about Matthew? Matthew needed her.

Her throat ached. She swallowed and took a step back. "You have to leave."

"I'm going. Tomorrow." He slapped his hat on his head and backed toward the door without taking his gaze from her. "You're coming with me, aren't you?"

"Go, please."

"I'll park over at the bakery. If you don't show by five-thirty tomorrow, I'll know you're not coming."

A crash made her jump and the pungent smell of vinegar and dill and pickles wafted through the air. She whirled. Jebediah stood on bare feet in a puddle at the bottom of the display case, pickle juice soaking his pants and shirt. He looked up at her, a frown on his chubby face. "I want pickle."

He squatted, grabbed a spear, and waved it in the air.

"Nee, nee, little one." Fearful of glass shards, Adah plunged in his direction, plucked the pickle from his grasp, and scooped him up with her other arm. "You'll cut yourself!"

Jebediah squalled and flung himself about, trying to get down. "Pickle!"

"What was that?" Leah rushed into the room, Emma right behind her. She stopped short, her gaze darting from Jebediah to Adah to Jackson. "What happened? Who are you?"

"I believe he's the reason Adah doesn't clean houses anymore." Emma swept past Leah and took Jebediah from Adah's arms. She set him on top of the counter and began to pick sprigs of dill and slices of onion from his soaked pants. "If you're not planning to buy anything, Mr. Hart, it would be best if you moved along."

Jackson slapped his hat on his head. "Actually, I wanted a jar of those pickles. My daddy loves bread and butter pickles."

"Adah, you heard the man. Get him a jar of pickles." Emma wiped Jebediah's feet and handed him over to Leah, who scowled at Jackson before taking her child. "Then clean up that mess."

Adah scrambled to grab a jar from the shelf and scurried around the counter to ring it up on the old cash register Luke had rescued from an auction.

"I'll ring it up." Emma squeezed in next to her. "You'd better get a mop and a bucket of soapy water from the back. That juice is sticky."

Adah didn't dare look back until she reached the workroom door. Jackson had his head down as he peeled off dollar bills and lined them up on the counter. He picked up the jar and eased toward the door. At the last second, he looked her way.

And winked.

Chapter 22

Matthew settled into the rocking chair on the porch, the bowl of peach pie and homemade ice cream in one hand, a large serving spoon in the other. Molly and Elizabeth chattered inside, as they had been doing all evening. They sounded like a flock of blue jays. He wasn't sure why he still lingered. The chores were done. Daed and Mudder had gone to bed. Matthew could go on to bed himself or go check their fishing lines down at the river. Instead, here he sat, his shirt wet with sweat and his feet aching to get out of his dusty work boots. Why that made him feel out of sorts, he couldn't say. He should be happy sitting here with his dessert and a cool evening breeze. What more could a man want?

His own place. A place he built for his fraa. Matthew wiggled in the chair. In Gott's time. He had no right to question. His time would come. For now, he should enjoy the breeze and the best peach pie this side of the Mississippi. Leastways that's what Daed always said about Mudder's peach pie.

Having the Gringriches around had made evenings even more enjoyable, he had to admit. Enoch told a good story and his daughters, especially Elizabeth, loved to laugh and contradict the stories. Enoch's fraa was quieter, always rushing to the kitchen to refill the serving bowls, as if she had to make up for any extra work their presence may have caused. Supper had been followed by a rousing game of Scrabble.

Of course Elizabeth and Molly went head to head. Matthew was a terrible speller. Mudder and Daed had thrown in the towel early, going to bed right after Groossdaadi and Groossmammi. Enoch and Clara hadn't been far behind. That left the kinner, one by one, to call it a day until finally only Elizabeth, Molly, and Matthew remained. He should go to bed. But he didn't. Neither did Molly. She just gabbed on and on. Two girls with the gift of gab. They'd be up half the night.

"Nice evening."

He glanced up to see Elizabeth standing at the screen door.

"That it is." He took a big bite of the pie and let it sit on his tongue for a second. Sweet and tart at the same time. They were blessed to have fruit trees in their yard. He let the thought float away. Such an obvious statement. No need to make it. He couldn't think of a thing to say, so he ate.

Bringing with her the clean scent of dish soap, Elizabeth plopped into the chair next to him, a bowl containing a much daintier portion of ice cream and a sliver of pie in one hand. "Especially for early August." She smiled and stretched out long legs so her ankles peeked from under the hem of her lilac dress. "Molly will be out in a bit. She ran upstairs to look for a book she wants me to read."

"Jah, it's not too hot for August." He squirmed in the chair, feeling like he did the first time he went to a singing. Like a dog in the middle of a herd of cats. "September is just around the corner."

"Ice cream helps. Molly and the girls do crank a good batch of ice cream." Elizabeth took another bite, a rapturous look on her face. "Vanilla is still the best. Doesn't need a thing."

"It's nice having a moment of quiet." The words sounded different spoken aloud than they had in his head. "I mean—"

"I know what you mean." Her expression bland, Elizabeth stirred her melting ice cream. "I know it's been a hard adjustment for y'all. Having my whole family here. My daed says it won't be much longer. He's got his eye on a piece of property up yonder past the Tobias Daughertys."

"I like having you here fine." Matthew's face burned hot as if he'd bent too close to an open fire. "I mean, it's no problem. We all like the company."

"I'm headed to bed! I'm awful tired now. I'll leave the book on the table," Molly called from the living room, where apparently she was dawdling over the book and eavesdropping at the same time. "Have a nice visit."

Elizabeth giggled, the fair skin of her cheeks turning pink. Chagrinned, Matthew tried to smile. What was his sister up to now? If she were trying to make a match, she was barking up the wrong tree.

He had no intention of courting anyone. He couldn't. Adah might have kissed another man, but he couldn't untie the strings that bound them from one minute to the next. His heart couldn't do it. Elizabeth was nice. She never missed a baptism class and she joined in the discussions with good questions and observations about life. She was smart. And not hard on the eyes.

"I like it here too." She giggled again. "I mean I want my family to have a place to call home, but in the meantime, this has been nice."

"The more the merrier, right?"

"Right." She licked her spoon and went back to stirring, turning the ice cream into a pudding. "Walnut Creek wasn't home. Bliss Creek isn't home anymore. So New Hope must be it. That's what I figure."

"It grows on you."

"Like people do."

Matthew stole a glance in her direction. She smiled at him. Whatever she was trying to tell him, he wished she'd spit it out. He was no good at figuring out women, with their double talk and half talk. "I reckon."

"I reckon too." She giggled yet again.

Maybe he was comparing her to Adah—unfairly. Adah might say one thing and mean another, but that didn't mean all women did that. Did it? Matthew leaned back, content to let silence overtake them.

"There's someone coming."

"Hmm." He open his eyes, aware that he'd been close to dropping off. Embarrassed, he straightened in the chair and set his bowl on the table between them. "What?"

"A buggy's coming up the road." Elizabeth stood and went to the railing. "Looks like a girl."

He rose and stood next to her.

Adah drove the buggy that came toward them at a fast clip. That was Adah. Always in a hurry, except when it came to him and her. He crossed his arms over his chest as the peace of the evening drained away. "It's Adah."

"I should turn in. It's late and we have laundry day tomorrow." Laundry day had turned into a massive undertaking with the doubling of the house's occupants. "Good night."

Matthew doubted there would be anything good about Adah's visit, but he refrained from arguing. If by some miracle there were, he would be so grateful. He didn't need an earful tonight. He'd had enough.

Elizabeth nodded, her smile gone. She picked up their dirty dishes. He held the screen door for her, a nicety she acknowledged with a slight nod of her head as she slipped inside.

Forced to face the moment of truth, he stalked to the buggy. "Adah."

"Matthew."

Only two syllables, but she managed to make them sound accusing. Anger stirred in Matthew. He pushed it away. "I'm surprised to see you here."

"I imagine you are." Again with the unspoken accusations. Her gaze dropped. "I needed to talk to you and you haven't come by in a while."

She really thought he'd come looking for her after their last conversation? "I've been busy."

Her gaze dropped. She wrapped the reins around one hand, then unwrapped them. "I know. I know."

"What did you need to talk to me about?"

Her gaze went to the house. Something in her eyes made his gut clench. She looked so sad. "I guess I'm too late. It doesn't matter."

Did all women beat around the bush like this? "Too late for what."

"For us."

That two words could cause him such pain didn't surprise Matthew. He waited until he was able to unclench his fists and his jaw to ask a question that surely should be obvious to her. "Is there an us?"

"It doesn't look that way."

"You're not making any sense. You don't talk to me for days." He fought to keep his voice low. He didn't recognize the growl that came out of his mouth. "You don't show up for baptism class. What am I supposed to think?"

"You were the one who wouldn't talk to me. You yelled at me the last time I went to baptism class. You stopped shining your flashlight in my window."

"You kissed another man." Matthew hissed the words, aware of the open door and the woman inside. "And I have responsibilities here. Daed is thinking of taking back his offer of the land."

"What? Why?"

"Because he thinks I make poor choices when it comes to picking a fraa, for one."

Red splotches appeared on her cheeks and spread to her neck. She snapped the reins and clucked at the horse. "I'll get out of your way. It looks like you have courting to do."

"There's no courting going on here. I promise you that." He gripped the edge of the buggy as if he could hold it there and make her stay until they worked this out. "It surprises me that you care. Why did you come?"

Her expression crumpled and for a moment she looked like the little girl he knew back in Bliss Creek who loved to jump rope, fish, play volleyball, and swim in the creek, but had a terrible fear of snakes that kept her from the water's edge. She stared at the reins in her hands, her eyes wet with unshed tears.

"Adah? Talk now or I will walk away."

She shook her head. "I shouldn't have come."

"But you did. Say what you came to say."

"I needed...I don't know. Don't worry about it." She clucked and shook the reins. "I won't add to your responsibilities. You're better off with Elizabeth. She's a good girl."

"You're a good girl too. You can be, anyhow." She tried to be. No one knew better than he did how hard she tried. Why it wasn't in her nature, he didn't know. He spent so much time praying God would mold her to this life. Make it easier for her somehow. God didn't do easy—that Matthew had learned from the move to New Hope, the attitudes of the Englischers here, and even his groossdaadi's condition. They didn't have an expectation of easy, only that God would be there through the hard. "Talk to me."

As usual, she didn't obey. She drove away, the buggy wheels kicking up dust in his face.

She'd never been good at obeying. Surely, that was one of the things that drew him to her. Adah had a mind of her own and he never knew what she would do with it. She might not be a typical Plain woman, but he loved even that about her flawed character. Surely he was no more perfect that she. Or anyone else in their community.

It didn't matter. She'd taken that independent streak and ridden it away. She'd made up her mind to leave him.

"Adah!"

No answer. Not even a glance back. "Come on, Adah!"

Finally, when she disappeared from sight completely, he turned and stomped up the stairs. Elizabeth stood at the screen door, staring out at him, the surprise on her face telling him she'd been listening to the entire conversation.

Chapter 23

Adah set another plate in the drain, trying to ignore Melinda and Joanna, who were bickering over who would dry the dishes and who got the silverware. She didn't know what difference it made, but her little sisters were like that. They loved to squabble over every little thing. She would miss that, as silly as it seemed. The two of them going on and on. If anyone said one bad thing about either one of them, the other would spring to her sister's defense. She squeezed water from the washrag and wiped down the counter for the last time in this house. She looked around, memorizing the clean, neat kitchen and the way Melinda's kapp always sat askew on her curly blonde hair and the way Joanna's freckles covered her nose and cheeks after a day of picking strawberries.

She committed to memory the window over the sink where she could stand and listen to the birds chatter in the branches of the big elm in the backyard, making a kind of music that only she seemed to hear. They'd lived in this house three years, but it seemed like a lifetime. She touched the black cast iron skillet sitting on the top of the stove, waiting to be put to use frying bacon or sausage or her mudder's fine fried chicken. A knot stuck in her throat, making it impossible to swallow. She might never see this place again.

Matthew had made his decision. He'd moved on. He had Elizabeth. He wouldn't miss Adah in the least. Try as she might she couldn't stop picturing him sitting on the porch next to Elizabeth. The two of them laughing and talking, eating dessert. The picture, framed with pain and longing and jealousy, had burned in her mind. Every time she closed her eyes, she saw Elizabeth laughing at something Matthew had done or said. Matthew was like that. Funny. Sweet. Adah didn't deserve him. She'd kissed another man and now she had to live with the consequences.

Someplace else. Not here.

"You two stop that bickering." Mudder trotted into the kitchen, a huge laundry basket in her arms. "I could hear you all the way upstairs. I just got Jonathan back down. That cough kept him up half the night—me too. I won't have you waking him up again. Get along or I'll send you both to the woodshed when Daed comes home."

Joanna hung her head. Melinda busied herself drying a platter.

Mudder, not one to be impressed by a mere show of contrition, held out the basket. "Since you have so much energy to run your mouths on and on, I think you should sort the laundry and get the tubs ready—both of you."

Melinda slid the platter onto the shelf and dried her hands. "Sorry, Mudder."

Joanna took the basket. "We'll make the clothes so clean, you'll think you did them yourself."

They truly were two peas in a pod.

"Good. See that you do."

Mudder rubbed her hip, her forehead wrinkled. For the first time, Adah noticed the thin ribbons of silver in her dark hair. "You'd better hurry if you're getting a ride from Daniel. He stopped by to borrow something from your daed and said he'd give you a ride into the store. No laundry day for you."

Adah fought the urge to wrap her arms around Mudder's neck and hug her tight. She wouldn't mind doing laundry. She liked the smell of bleach and soap and she liked hanging the clothes on the line and feeling the breeze and sun on her face. Instead, she busied herself covering the cinnamon rolls they'd made before dawn, serving them hot, the frosting soft and the cinnamon and sugar gooey in the middle. Just the way Daed liked them.

"Adah, did you hear me?" Mudder grabbed a dishtowel with one hand and a wet plate with the other. "What's wrong with you, girl? You've been in never-never land this morning. Have you been staying up all night scribbling on those tablets again?"

"Nee." Not this time. Her brain had been blank her last night in her bedroom. No songs had come. The only words in her head had been *goodbye* and *sorry*. "I couldn't sleep, that's all."

"It's good to know you've given up that foolishness." Mudder slid the plate onto the stack in the cabinet and dropped the towel on the counter. "It's for the best."

Adah clenched the washrag tight in her hands, glad her mother couldn't see her face. She didn't dare answer for fear her plan would come spilling out. "Is it really foolishness?"

"Surely you know that by now. You finish your baptism classes, join your faith, and then become a fraa and then a mudder. That is the proper road, the one we all take."

Somehow Adah had missed a turn and ended up on a strange highway with no familiar landmarks. "But what if there isn't a husband here for me?"

"What's wrong?" Mudder's smile faded, replaced by the faint beginnings of disappointment and uncertainty. "Does this have something to do with that Hart boy?"

Adah's heart did a two-step stutter that made her chest hurt. She busied herself over the tub of dishes, not wanting her mother to see the flash of chagrin that surely colored her face. "What makes you bring him up?"

"Emma stopped by last night to pick up the tablecloths I embroidered for the store." Mudder rubbed an already dry platter so hard with the towel, it was a wonder it didn't break. "She mentioned his visit. She seemed to think you had some sort of spat with him. I told her that couldn't be. You had nothing to say to this boy. It must've been purely accidental. You haven't seen him in weeks and have no plans to do so."

Adah opened her mouth, then closed it. Nothing could be said that wouldn't amount to a lie. She couldn't lie to her mother's face. Nor could she tell her the truth. Mudder swiveled toward Adah, her eyebrows drawn up so far they almost met in the middle. "I told her, unless I miss the mark completely, I suspect you already have someone special. I told her I suspect we'll be hearing from Thomas about it in the fall."

Had someone special. *Had.* In the past. Adah gritted her teeth, the ache in her throat worse than when she had that terrible strep throat last winter. She couldn't tell Mudder. It would break her heart.

"I told her right, didn't I?" Mudder tugged a plate from Adah's hand, her gaze drilling Adah between the eyes. "You have nothing to talk to this Englisch boy about."

Her breakfast in her throat, kaffi burning her stomach, Adah swished the skillet back and forth in the soapy water, wishing the ground would open up and swallow her whole. "Mudder, I…"

Her stomach heaved. She whirled and dashed through the open back door and lost her breakfast in the petunias and impatiens planted along the steps.

"You're sick. Maybe you'd best stay home today." She felt Mudder's hand on her back, rubbing. "I thought you looked awful peaked."

"Nee." Adah gasped and wiped at her face with the back of her sleeve. If she stayed home, she'd lose her chance, her only chance. She found she desperately wanted that chance, as much as leaving her mudder hurt in every muscle and inch of tissue in her body. "I'm fine. Emma's expecting me."

Mudder handed her a dishtowel. Her face had lost the hard edges of a few minutes earlier. "It's natural to feel uncertain, to be a little scared. I know I was, but after your daed and I were married, we settled in. Matthew's a good man. You'll find your way."

What was she talking about? Heat curled around Adah's ears and scorched her cheeks. Her problem wasn't what happened after the wedding, it was whether to go there at all. She couldn't tell Mudder, standing there so expectant, so sure her dochder would do the right thing.

"It wasn't perfect. You know, with your daed. Especially after Ruth died in the fire. It took us a long time to get back on an even keel, but

Daed was patient with me. He wanted things back to normal, so we got them back to normal." Mudder touched Adah's forehead with the back of her hand like she used to do when Adah was small and had a fever. "We grieved, but we knew Ruth was with God. We had no right to be selfish and question God's will."

If Adah didn't know better, she'd think Mudder could read minds. She questioned God's will. She was selfish. She hadn't appreciated what she had in Matthew and now he'd found another, better woman to be his fraa. "You're human."

"We have faith." Mudder's somber expression deepened. "So must you. It's what is expected of you. If you're sure you're all right, go to work. I'll get your dirty clothes from your room. Don't keep Daniel waiting. It's bound to be busy at the store today, what with a lot of the Englisch folks getting their paychecks."

"Nee, nee, I'm fine. I'll get the clothes." Relieved to escape those knowing eyes unscathed, Adah scurried toward the door. She didn't want Mudder to find the note. Not yet. Not until tonight when she didn't return for supper. Her throat closed. The ache was unbearable, worse than any cold or sickness she'd ever endured. "He'll wait. I should've brought them down earlier."

"That's fine, but be quick about it."

Adah turned back. "Love you, Mudder."

Mudder couldn't look more surprised if Adah had suddenly turned into a goat in the middle of the kitchen. "What's gotten into you, dochder? You must be sick. I can fix some chamomile tea and get out the castor oil."

"I'm fine. I just…I'm fine."

Wiping at her eyes with her sleeve, praying Mudder hadn't seen the tears that threatened to betray her, Adah whirled and trotted through the living room. At the bottom, she paused, one hand on the banister, and closed her eyes. *Gott, I'm sorry. Forgive me for the pain I will cause Mudder and Daed. I'm so sorry.*

"Adah, hurry up!" Daniel held open the screen door. "You are forever daydreaming, girl. I don't have all day."

Another person she wouldn't see again. Bruder Daniel, a bigger joke teller than even Matthew, hot of temper, quicker to forgive. The best big brother a girl could ask to have. She ran up the stairs, dashed down the hallway, and scooped up the dresses she'd left on the bed in her haste to leave. She couldn't bring anything with her that didn't fit in her denim bag. It would raise suspicion and who knew what she would wear in that strange new world called Branson.

At the door she took one last look around. "Bye, room," she whispered, feeling silly.

Goodbye to all the memories and all the dreams and hopes and songs written in this room.

Goodbye to the only life she'd ever known.

Chapter 24

Trying not to sneeze in the billowing cloud of cloyingly sweet perfume that wafted from Mrs. Billingsly, Adah smoothed her customer's twenty dollar bill on top of a stack in the register and snapped the drawer shut. "Here's your change." She fumbled with the quarters. One dropped to the counter, wobbled across it, and fell to the floor where it proceeded to disappear under the display case. "I'm so sorry."

"Don't worry about it." Her huge gold hoop earrings swinging, Mrs. Billingsley accepted the alternate quarter Adah slid from the register, along with the rest of her change. She picked up her bag of homemade candles and a jar of honey, smiled at Adah, and padded away on flip-flops that made a *slap-slap* sound on the wooden floor. "Everyone has a bad day now and then. Tomorrow is a fresh start."

A fresh start. If this lady only knew what she was saying.

"Thank you. Have a nice afternoon." Adah's stomach rocked. *What are you doing? What are you doing?* "Enjoy the honey."

"Will do. You have a good evening too."

A good evening. An evening that would change her life forever. In the last eight hours she'd gone back and forth a thousand times. *Go. Stay. Stay. Go.* Seeing Matthew sitting on the porch with Elizabeth had changed everything. They looked so content sitting there side by side in their lawn chairs. The fact that Elizabeth had slipped in the house without saying hello told the story. She felt guilty. Matthew didn't seem to feel the same. Adah understood that. Matthew never did anything he didn't want to do and he never lied. If he said there was no courting, there was no courting.

But maybe there should be. She wasn't a good Plain woman and Matthew deserved a good fraa. Someone content to sit on the porch and eat ice cream on a summer night. Not gallivanting about to music shows at the rodeo or writing songs with an Englischer. Matthew would be better off without her.

She dropped to her knees and peered under the display case. The errant quarter lay near the center. She flattened herself to the floor and wiggled her arm under the case until she could reach it. Dust bloomed in her face.

She rolled up and sneezed. Served her right for being so clumsy. Shaking out her apron, she glanced at the battery-operated clock sitting on the window sill next to the table where Emma hunched over the ledgers, doing a final count for the day. "It's five o'clock. Shall I put up the closed sign?"

Emma rubbed her eyes and looked up. "Might as well. You've been dropping things and knocking things over all day. You best get home before you hurt yourself or a customer. You've been itching to close up for the last two hours."

"It's been slow today."

"Not that slow." Emma slapped the ledger shut with a definitive bang. "You act like you have ants crawling up your legs."

"Just feeling unsettled."

"Are you nervous about baptism? If you have any questions, you know Thomas will answer them. Don't be afraid to ask."

Why did everyone immediately assume this had to do with baptism? She only had two classes left, plus the makeup sessions. She would never take that final step. Never become truly Amish. Adah's stomach flopped. She put a hand to her mouth, afraid she would vomit. She couldn't ask Thomas about Branson. Nor could she ask Emma. They would tell her parents and they would intercede. If she were going, she had to go before baptism. While she was still in her rumspringa. Now or never.

Never was such a long time.

"Jackson Hart seemed like a nice man."

Adah halted, her hand on the sign hanging from the door, glad her back was to Emma.

"He is."

"I can imagine how charming he could be."

No, she couldn't. Adah forced herself to turn and move back to the counter, hoping her face didn't reveal her turmoil. "He's a nice man."

"So nice you had to stop working for his mother."

Adah ducked her head as she trudged back to the counter. "It's hard to explain."

That was an understatement.

"Before I married Thomas, I had another special friend." Emma turned the pencil end over end between long fingers. "A man I *thought* was special."

"You did?" Adah didn't remember that. Maybe she'd been too young. "What happened?"

Emma's expression said she'd gone far away to some other time and place. "He left."

"He turned Englisch?" Adah didn't want to be Englisch. She wanted to straddle two worlds, to have her cake and eat it, to have her music and her community. "He left the district?"

"Jah. But then he came back and tried to fit himself back into our life."

"What happened?"

"He couldn't do it. He'd changed and he'd made decisions that made it so he had to go back to his Englisch life." Emma's tone remained soft and calm. Whatever pain this had caused her had long since dissipated. "There were people he'd left behind to whom he had obligations."

"Were you hurt?"

"The first time, jah, but not the second time." She gathered up the ledger and stood, her chair making a harsh scraping sound on the wooden floor. She moved to the counter where she deposited the ledger on a shelf and then turned to look at Adah. "By then Thomas had made his feelings known. It seemed complicated at first, but then it wasn't at all."

"You didn't want the other man back?"

"Not under those circumstances."

"What circumstances?"

"His Englisch life was more important to him. It changed him." Emma's gaze seemed to seep under Adah's skin, searching her head and her heart. Adah feared what she might find. Emma was older and wiser and too knowing. "It changes a person so much that most can't come back."

Adah searched for another road to keep the conversation away from her own situation, her own thoughts, her own weaknesses. "Like your sister Catherine."

"Catherine has never wanted to come back. She made her choice and she's happy with it." Adah wanted to look away, but she couldn't. Emma's gaze held her prisoner. "If you start down that road, most likely you won't come back."

"What makes you think I'm going down any road?" She'd been so careful to not say or do anything. "What are you talking about?"

"I'm talking about Jackson Hart." Emma smacked the lever on the cash register, making the bell ring and the drawer open. "I should count the receipts for the day."

"Didn't you ever have dreams?"

Emma began withdrawing the bills, counting as she went through each denomination. She plopped down a small stack of tens and wrote the number on a piece of scratch paper. Then she turned to look at Adah square in the face. "I dreamed of becoming a fraa and a mudder. That was my dream."

Adah swallowed. She too wanted those things. "But nothing else?"

"What else is there?" Emma waved a hand toward the store. "It's fun doing this, working here, and having a little business, helping to pay the bills, but nothing gives me more pleasure than the look on Thomas's face when I set a bowl of his favorite beef stew in front of him with a big hunk of sourdough bread and he's so happy. Nothing makes me happier than to see my little ones eating the fry pies I made. You'll see, when you marry."

Cooking or making music. It didn't seem possible that she would get the same satisfaction from the former as she did the latter. How she wished she could. "I'll straighten things up, get ready for tomorrow."

Adah took her time with the straightening and sweeping, making sure everything was ready for the next day. She didn't want to leave Emma and the other women in a lurch. Yet that was exactly what she was doing. Mudder had relied on their kindness to get her this job. They didn't really need her. *Stop justifying.*

Still arguing with an inner voice that sounded a whole lot like Daed, Thomas, and Matthew rolled into one, she picked up her canvas bag, heavier today than normal. She hadn't been able to put much in it, not without drawing attention to it. A dress, a clean apron, her Sunday shoes, her nightgown. Most importantly it contained her savings from her cleaning jobs and the few weeks that she'd worked at the store. Her nest egg. "Goodbye, Emma."

The words *see you tomorrow* wouldn't roll off her tongue. *Don't add lying to deceiving and running away.*

"Don't you want a ride?" Emma didn't look up from her notations on the store inventory. "If you wait a few minutes, I can drop you by on my way home."

"Nee, I want to get a couple of things from the bakery." She swallowed against the lump in her throat. The voices grew louder, as if someone had turned up the amplifier for the electric guitars at the concerts she loved so much. *Liar. Liar. Liar.* "I'll get a ride from Molly. She's at the library today."

Gott, forgive me. One lie led to another. Daed's famous slippery slope. It couldn't be right if she had to lie about it. Thomas's voice boomed inside her head. *It's the only way.* Her voice, small and whinny, responded. Emma couldn't know, not until Adah was safely out of town. Daed would try to stop her. He *would* stop her. She wouldn't see him again. None of them. Not Mudder or Hiram or Abram or Melinda or Joanne or baby Jonathan. Or Daniel. Or Matthew.

Matthew. She'd left him standing in front of his house, dust blowing in his face. He didn't deserve that. Or this. He deserved better than her. He deserved a good Plain woman. She would pray he found that woman. Her getting out of the way would help.

Adah paused, hand on the doorknob. To never see her family again. She whirled, strode across the floor, and gave Emma a quick, tight hug.

Emma's eyes widened and her frown turned to a startled smile. "What was that for?"

"For being kind and for letting me work here." Adah clamped down on the emotion threatening to seep into her voice. "I know you didn't really need my help, but you let me work here because Mudder asked."

"Jah, because she asked, but also because we like having company when we work. Makes the day go faster." Emma tilted her head, her intent gaze inquiring. "Are you sure you don't want a ride? You look a little peaked."

"No, I'm fine. I'll catch a ride in a bit." She'd heard that lying got easier the more a person practiced. So far, she didn't find that to be true. She hated lying to a good and kind person such as Emma. She hated lying period. Her insides felt coated with something putrid and rotting, something that belonged buried in the ground. "I just need some fresh air."

"Then I'll see you tomorrow—no, I'm off tomorrow. Your mudder has her very first shift."

Adah didn't answer. She couldn't. Mudder had decided she was ready to leave Jonathan in Katie Christner's care and work a shift or two in the store. Would Mudder come to work or would she be distraught after she discovered the note Adah had left in her room? She couldn't go without leaving a note. It would be too cruel. It told Mudder not to worry, that she would be fine. She would write soon. But it didn't say where she was going.

Mudder would worry. Daed would be angry. As well he should be.

She could still change her mind. She could still tell Jackson she couldn't go. She couldn't simply not show up. No, she couldn't leave him sitting there, waiting for her. That would be as wrong as not leaving a note for Mudder.

Heart pounding, Adah scurried across the street and nearly ran the three blocks to the bakery. She slowed when Jackson's monster silver truck came into view. It sat idling in front of the bakery, the engine throbbing gently. Suddenly, her feet felt as heavy as a twenty-pound sack of baking russets. The canvas bag seemed to weigh twice that, the straps biting into her shoulder.

The window rolled down. Jackson leaned out, his ball cap pushed back on his head, a tentative grin on his face. Captain squeezed through the window and barked. "Hush, mutt, you'll scare her away." Jackson grabbed the dog's collar and pulled him back. The dog's head disappeared and the barking turned to a soft *woof-woof.* "You came."

Adah glanced around. Not a soul she knew traipsed on the sidewalk between the truck and bakery. No buggy passed by on the street. No one to take note or stop to ask what she was doing.

"I don't know if I can do this." The words came out a whisper, as if someone might hear and know how Adah had let everyone down. Matthew. Mudder. Daed. Now Jackson.

"Sure you can. Get in the truck and we'll talk. Just talk. Okay?" He waved a hand toward her, his tone the same one he used to cajole the horse in the corral that first day they met. "Get in and we'll talk pros and cons."

"I don't know."

Jackson popped his door open and strode around to the other side. "Your chariot awaits." He pulled the door open. "It's only natural you'd feel a little jittery. This is a big step. It's huge. The biggest. But it's gonna be fine, you'll see. Just get in and we'll talk."

She closed her eyes and drew a long breath. Now or never.

She crawled in and he shut the door behind her, the sound like one she'd never heard before. Capturing her or setting her free. She couldn't be sure. She shivered, goose bumps prickling up and down her arms in the cold air blasting from the air conditioning vents. It smelled like pine tree, tobacco, and wet dog in the truck cab. Cup holders held a pile of multicolored picks and a tall cup beaded with condensation. Captain plopped his front paws on the back of the seat and panted in her ear. Add doggy breath to the smells.

A country song she'd always liked blared from the radio.

Jackson slid in on his side and slammed the door. "Let the adventure begin." He leaned toward her, his right hand outstretched, fingers callused from the guitar strings. "Now that you're here."

"Jackson—"

"Hush." He tugged her bag from her lap. "This is all you could bring,

I guess. Don't worry, we'll get you some new duds in Branson. You can't dress like that for your auditions."

Her heart did a two-step. Auditions.

She reached for the bag. He swung it beyond her reach and stuffed it into the extended cab beside Captain. On the other side set a small Styrofoam cooler, a duffel bag, and three guitar cases stacked on top of each other. Three guitars. What a wealth of music. Captain flopped down and laid his head on his paws. Adah settled against her seat, somehow comforted by the sight. Jackson meant what he said about playing music and Captain looked at peace.

"Look, I know this is hard." Jackson leaned toward her again. She inhaled his scent, held captive by it. He smelled good. Like spicy cologne, but not overpowering like some of the Englisch men. "It's hard for me too. I know my mom will be upset and Dad will yell. But sometimes a man's gotta do what a man's gotta do."

He squeezed her hand hard but let go before she could protest his touch. "So does a woman. I figure God gave us these gifts so no one should argue against us using them. Right?"

She opened her mouth and closed it. He had a point. Jackson had all his arguments lined up. He'd spent some time honing them. He wanted her to come with him that bad. Because of the music or because of the kiss. She couldn't be sure and she couldn't see her way to ask.

"Right." Jackson grinned. "I knew you'd see it my way. It'll be fine, I promise. You're gonna love Branson and you'll be way too busy to be homesick."

Homesickness didn't worry her. Abandoning her way of life and her family—that worried her. "God gave us family too."

"Everyone grows up and leaves home sometime."

Not where she came from. And not by sneaking out. Adah measured the distance to the door. She could slide out and run away. Music wafted from the radio. A beautiful song by Martina McBride.

Adah didn't move.

"Put your seatbelt on." Jackson must've seen something in her face. He put the truck in gear, backed away from the curb, and pointed the truck south. "We're leaving this town in our rearview mirror."

Doing as she was told, she gazed out the window, memorizing the view so she could hold it in her heart. Would she be homesick? She'd never gone anywhere without family. She'd only lived in New Hope three years, but it had become her home. Her home was wherever her family lived.

Mudder and Daed. Hiram, Daniel, Melinda, Abram, Joanna, and little Jonathan.

The knot in her throat grew. She heaved a breath, trying to calm the beating of her heart.

"Exciting, isn't it?"

"Jah. I mean yes." No more *Deutsch*. "It's exciting, yes."

Jackson turned on to the road that led to the edge of town and the highway. A buggy came toward them at a quick clip. Adah's hand tightened around her seatbelt. She swallowed against bitter bile that burned the back of her throat.

The buggy came closer. She could see the driver now.

Matthew.

His head turned as the truck roared by. She couldn't be sure if he saw her. She hazarded a glance back. The buggy had stopped.

He'd seen her.

Jackson didn't slow down. He didn't stop. He kept right on going, toward his dream.

And hers.

Leaving Matthew behind.

Chapter 26

Matthew snapped the reins and forced the buggy into a wide turn in the middle of the highway. Ignoring the belligerent honking of a minivan that roared past him after he made the turn, he snapped the reins harder and urged Cookie forward. He had to stop Adah from making whatever new mistake she seemed bent on making. Dust billowed in his face, coating his skin. He tasted dirt as his teeth ground the grit in his mouth. The smell of diesel fuel burned his nose. "Haw, haw, come on, Cookie, come on."

Whinnying in protest, Cookie strained to do as instructed. Wheels creaking and groaning, the swaying buggy picked up pace. Still the silver truck drew away, leaving him farther and farther behind.

"Adah!"

The ridiculous futility of his shout only served to infuriate Matthew more. He drew back on the reins until the horse slowed. No sense in endangering the animal or his family's buggy with a race he couldn't win. His heart revved as if it hadn't received the message or had received it and refused to heed. It galloped after Adah and Jackson Hart and that beast of a truck that would take her someplace a good Plain girl shouldn't go.

"Adah." He whispered her name this time. Visions of her at the pond with this man crowded him. "Come back."

She wouldn't. She'd climbed into that truck willingly, no doubt.

"Adah, what are you thinking?" Again aloud. Heat stained his face even though no one sat in the buggy with him to hear. "Stop blathering to yourself like an idiot."

Make a plan, instead. Be a man.

Tonight he had to be at home for Grandma Frannie's birthday. He would go to Adah's house tomorrow night. Talk to her. Try to make her see the error of her ways. She couldn't be riding around in a pickup truck in broad daylight with this Englisch boy. Her father would find out. The whole community would know. The truck didn't only take her far from him, it took her far from her family and her faith. It might take her so far she couldn't find her way back.

He practiced breathing at a normal, steady pace. His heart slowed. Calm stole over him. God willing, he'd talk to her tomorrow night. After Daed and Mudder went to bed. After the Gringriches followed. Especially Elizabeth. No more chatting with Elizabeth on the porch. No more leading her to believe something was possible. The look on her face the previous night had said it all. She had expectations. She'd heard his conversation with Adah. She knew that Adah had kissed another. Such private, personal information she had no right to know or repeat. Whether she would tell remained to be seen. She'd turned away and rushed up the stairs before he could ask her.

Matthew had no way to meet Elizabeth's expectations. No way he could do what Daed wanted him to do. Land or no land, he couldn't walk away from Adah. The feelings he had for her came with him. They had burrowed into his heart and sewn themselves into the fabric of his being. Daed hadn't said anything more about Adah or the land, but Matthew had felt his stern gaze contemplating him at the supper table, in the fields, everywhere. Watching. Waiting to see what Matthew would do.

Enoch seemed to be doing the same thing. Watching and waiting. As did Elizabeth.

It seemed the whole world watched and waited. Everyone but Adah.

He wiped sweat that burned his eyes from his face. The brilliant afternoon sun blinded him for a second as he turned onto the dirt road that led to his home. The horse whinnied and the buggy jolted forward. He tightened his grip on the reins. "Easy, girl, easy."

A second later he saw what Cookie had seen. "Groossdaadi?"

Headed away from home, his grandfather trotted alongside the road, his skinny legs pumping with the enthusiasm of a much younger man. He didn't look up at the sound of Matthew's voice.

"Groossdaadi!"

Nothing. Matthew halted the buggy in the middle of the road and climbed down. "Joseph! Wait. It's me. Matthew." Groossdaadi looked up, his expression startled. His stride slowed and finally, he stopped. Matthew edged closer, not sure how good his hearing was. "Do you need a ride somewhere?"

Groossdaadi shook his head, his long, thin, silver beard swaying a bit. "Nee. I'm fine, but thanks for the offer."

"It's me, Matthew, your grandson."

Groossdaadi's bushy eyebrows, darker than his beard, made like caterpillars above pale blue eyes clouded with confusion. His nose wrinkled and his full lips twisted as he studied Matthew's face. Matthew had a sudden, clear vision of what Daed would look like in a few years. What he himself would look like in many years, Gott willing.

Except Groossdaadi's clothes hung on a wasted frame that held nary a pinch of fat. His legs and arms were sticks compared to Daed's, thick as stumps from hard work.

"Let me give you a lift." Matthew tried again. "It's on my way."

"What's on your way?" His mind might be cloudy, but his tone was crisp and sharp, as always. "Boy, you don't know where I'm going."

"Aren't you looking for Frannie?"

The confusion cleared and his frown lifted. "Frannie. You know where I can find Frannie? It's her birthday and I got her a surprise."

"Groossmammi went with Mudder—Mary—to the quilting frolic. They're finishing some pieces for the store in town. Remember? They'll be back any minute, I reckon. Molly and Elizabeth and the girls are getting supper. They're fixing her favorite—ham, mashed potatoes and gravy, and corn on the cob. Molly's making her a carrot cake with spicy cream cheese frosting. You know Frannie, she can't abide by sitting around, so she'll jump into the thick of it when she gets back."

Groossdaadi stared at some distant point on the far horizon. He seemed to be studying Matthew's words. After a bit he nodded, his beard bobbing. "Nee, she can't. Makes her downright skittish."

"You too, huh, Groossdaadi? You can't abide by sitting around either, can you?"

Groossdaadi eyed Matthew. His gaze narrowed as he lifted one hand to his straw hat and tugged it down to shade his eyes from the sun. "Who did you say you were?"

"Matthew. It's me, Matthew."

"You're the spitting image of my son, Aaron."

"That's what they tell me. Can't rightly see it myself."

"I reckon I could use a ride, Matthew."

Matthew jerked his head toward the buggy. "Climb in."

Groossdaadi grabbed the edge of the buggy and attempted to heave himself up and in. He couldn't quite muster enough strength. Matthew offered the older man his hand. His groossdaadi looked up at him, uncertain, offended, and then sheepish.

"Matthew. Give your groossdaadi a hand up, will you?"

Matthew obliged.

Groossdaadi grunted and hoisted himself into the seat. "Where have you been? I've worked out a powerful thirst out here, walking around."

"Been to town...I intended to go into the harness shop, but something came up."

"Didn't Aaron want you to check on a halter he left for repair?"

Groossdaadi was back. A hard knot in Matthew's chest dissolved. "He did, but it'll wait until tomorrow."

"What came up?"

"What?"

"You said something came up."

"I saw something...I remembered something I needed to do back here."

"Could it have something to do with Enoch's girl? What's her name...the oldest?"

"Elizabeth?" Matthew shifted in his seat. "What about her?"

"She's been mooning around all day, grinding on my nerves." Groossdaadi sniffed. "She's got her eye on you, no doubt about it. In my day, we didn't go around wearing our feelings on our sleeves for everyone to see."

"Nee, she's homesick, that's all, I reckon. And tired of being squeezed into someone else's house with all her brothers and sisters like a litter of puppies in a cardboard box."

"I know the feeling." Groossdaadi sniffed again, a disdainful sound. "I don't know what your aunt was thinking, sending Frannie and me out here like we were wayward teenagers who needed a good talking-to by your daed. I'm their daed, not the other way around."

"We wanted a visit with you. It was our turn. Why should Aenti get you all to herself?"

"You do talk a good line of hooey, son."

Matthew peeked sideways, wanting to make sure Groossdaadi hadn't disappeared again. His grandfather settled back in the seat, one hand gripping the edge of the buggy as if he feared falling out. The hand was covered with ropy veins that bulged against his wrinkled, age-spotted skin. He stared ahead, an almost vacant expression on his weathered face. Old age sat hard on Groossdaadi and that fact rubbed raw spots on Matthew's heart. "It's not hooey. It's good to have you here."

"So tell me about the girl."

"What?"

"One of the strange blessings of this old age is that I remember the things that happened when I was young better than today. I remember when I met Frannie and I took her for rides in the two-seater and sat on the rocks by the creek and gabbed half the night."

The image sounded so familiar. How many nights had Matthew done that exact same thing with Adah? Too many or not enough, he didn't know which. He'd done everything he could to make her see how he felt. He'd told her flat out, and still she rode around New Hope in a truck with an Englisch man. He cleared his throat. "I imagine Groossmammi was quite the talker."

"Still is. I liked listening to the sound of her voice, even if I didn't always listen to what she said. That's our little secret." He chuckled and sniffed again, then wiped his nose on his sleeve like a little boy. "She wouldn't cotton to the idea that I don't hang on her every word. When every word usually has something to do with how dirty I get my pants and how I don't like new shirts. Too stiff. Anyways, I may not listen to what she says, but I never get tired of listening to her talk. That's what it feels like."

The memory of Adah's voice singing a lullaby to baby John wafted through Matthew's mind. She had such a voice. It whispered in his ear late at night and early in the morning, soft and high, singing a song only he could hear. "It what?"

"What you're looking for." His grandfather slapped gnarled fingers with swollen joints on Matthew's knee and squeezed, real quick, then let go. "Don't let anyone tell you different. If you're planning to spend the next fifty years with a woman, it best be someone whose voice you could listen to every day for the rest of your life. Think on that, son."

"I have been." A woman whose voice lifted in song sounded like no other he'd ever heard. "Sometimes I can't think about anything else."

"It's that girl, Adah, the one everyone's talking about."

"Everyone?"

"Leastways, your folks, Luke, Thomas. Everyone who counts."

"It's no one's business."

Groossdaadi snorted. "That's what everyone likes to say, but you know better. In a district this size? Everyone's looking. Everyone's watching. Not out of malice. They want you to make the right choices. To be right with God. They care about your eternal salvation. That kind of caring keeps the district strong."

"And they're nosey too."

"Yep. That too."

"She's…wayward."

"I figured as much."

"Daed thinks I'm wasting my time."

"Your daed has a short memory."

"What do you mean?"

"Wasn't so long ago that people were whispering and talking about him and your mudder."

They seemed made for each other. They rarely exchanged a cross word and Mudder still looked at Daed like he hung the moon. "You didn't think he should marry Mudder?"

"Frannie had her doubts. So did I, truth be told."

"Why?"

"She was all hands and feet and the clumsiest girl I'd ever met. Terrible cook. Can't say that about too many Plain girls, but your mudder managed to burn bread."

Irene Troyer a bad cook. It couldn't be. Maybe Groossdaadi was confused. "Mudder is a good cook. She makes great bread."

"Now. I reckon the problem was just nerves. She wanted to be a good fraa so bad she got the jitters. Especially around Frannie."

"Daed thinks I'm daft for picking Adah."

"Your heart, your next fifty years. He done got his girl."

"I think Adah may have chosen another."

"You think? You're not sure?"

"Nee."

"You best find out, son."

Matthew tugged on the reins and halted the buggy near the front steps. "Danki."

Groossdaadi hopped from the buggy, looking spry all of a sudden. He turned and stared up at Matthew. "This ain't my house."

"Groossdaadi—"

A smile spread across his face. "Just joshing you!" He turned and sped up the steps. "I hope there's carrot cake with that cream cheese frosting. That's Frannie's favorite. I got me a hankering for cake."

Matthew watched him disappear through the screen door. If only a piece of carrot cake could make things right in his world. Groossdaadi was right. He had to find out. He had to make Adah see. He wanted his next fifty years to be with her.

Kelly Irvin

Even if it meant winning her away from a man who drove a silver beast and lured her away with a guitar. He couldn't leave the house tonight, not with the frolic planned for Groossmammi's seventieth birthday. Half the district would be there. Maybe Adah would come with her folks.

Maybe Jackson Hart had dropped her off by now.

It seemed like an awful lot of maybes.

Chapter 27

Jackson's voice burrowed its way into Adah's dreams. He was singing. A beautiful song. A hymn. She dragged herself from a dreamravaged sleep that involved Matthew, a buggy, and a raging river. She drove the buggy on one side. Matthew ran along the river on the other. His mouth moved, but she couldn't hear what he said. Every time she drifted off, lulled by the rumble of the truck's engine and the tires on Highway 65, the dream came back. She wanted to wake up. She didn't like this dream. She forced open gritty eyes, squinting against the fading sun. Jackson glanced down at her. "There you are, sleeping beauty. You're missing the scenery."

Still groggy, she struggled to pull herself from the depths of her dream. Her head lolled against Jackson's shoulder. The realization hit her like cold water sprayed from a hose. She jolted upright. "Where are we?"

"Still on Highway 65."

The sound of those tires humming against the pavement sang to her, drowning Jackson's voice. The road sang an unfamiliar song with a new melody and words that hadn't been written yet. A song that took her away from home. She'd never been away from home before. She scrubbed her eyes with the back of her hands and inhaled. The smell of greasy burgers, onions, and cold fries made her stomach contract.

Her disorientation had nothing to do with geography. "Are we almost there?"

"Getting close." He lifted one index finger from the steering wheel and pointed. "See the billboards?"

How could she miss them? All along the highway enormous billboards blocked her view of the rock jutting from the earth, protruding as if trying to reclaim its territory. She saw a billboard with the words WANT FUNNY? Then another: WE GOT FUNNY. Followed by a third. PIERCE ARROW. What did that mean?

PRESLEY COUNTRY JUBILEE. SILVER DOLLAR CITY. THE OAK RIDGE BOYS. DOLLY PARTON. YAKOV SMIRNOFF. Other billboards sang the praises of a museum, zip lines, hotels, golf courses, and a steamboat. It seemed one could do just about anything in Branson, Missouri.

"Pretty impressive, huh?"

Adah glanced at Jackson. He didn't look tired. He looked pumped up. She waited for some of his energy to wash over her. "What will we do first?"

"Sing. Are you nervous?"

She glanced at the next billboard. BALDKNOBBERS. Whatever that was. "A little."

"A little. You're cute when you try to be brave."

"Jackson. You promised."

He gave her his usual hangdog grin. "That doesn't mean I can't admire the scenery."

Englischers had such a strange way of talking sometimes. "No calling me cute or baby or honey."

"Just Amish girl, huh?"

No. Definitely not. By getting in this truck she'd set aside the right to be called Amish girl. "My name would be fine."

He was silent for a few seconds, the squeak of the Styrofoam chest in the backseat half-drowned by the rumble of the engine. Captain whined in his sleep. A song floated from the radio.

"*Adah*, first we get settled at the lake house. Then I call Mac and tell him we're in town. Then we get you some clothes. And we practice. We practice a lot." He turned up the radio. "Come on, sing along with me. Get your voice warmed up and then we'll sing our song."

"What do you mean, get me some clothes?"

"You can't perform dressed like that. You need to get your bling on, girl."

Her bling. A sick feeling churned in the pit of her stomach, Adah scooted closer to her door. "I don't do *bling*."

"Don't worry about it right now. Right now, let's just sing."

That was Jackson, barging ahead, sure she would follow.

So far, she had. Why, she couldn't say. *Gott, what am I doing?*

Jackson's baritone filled the cabin, sweet and sure, calling to her. She shook her head, determined not to get drawn in by his charm.

"Come on, baby—I mean Adah." He sang along with a new Blake Shelton song for a few lines, then poked her with one long finger. "Come on, you know you want to."

She did want to sing. Gott forgive her, she couldn't help herself. Jackson knew the one way to get her to acquiesce. Every time. Her voice mingled nicely with his. They sang louder and louder until she couldn't hear the naysayers in her head or the wind rushing by outside the cocoon in which they rode. Even Captain sat up and added a howl now and again.

The song ended. Commercials started. "Change the station; find us another song." Jackson pounded a fist on the wheel. "We sound great together. We're ready to rock 'n' roll."

"I thought we were country singers." She flipped the knob. Nothing but commercials or static. "I'm not doing rock."

"It's a figure of speech."

She turned the volume down. They still had to have a talk, whether he liked it or not. Some things had to be settled before they reached this cabin on the lake. "I brought my savings. I can pay for my room and board with that until I get a job."

"You're not paying rent and you don't need a job." The wheedling humor gone from his voice, Jackson swerved to avoid a dead animal in the road. "You'll be my guest."

"First of all, I'll not have you support me. It wouldn't be right." He liked to make these sweeping statements as if she would do as she was told. Maybe in her old world, but not in this one and not with an Englisch man. "Secondly, how will you afford it? Surely your parents won't pay your bills now."

"Remember I told you about my Gramps?"

"He gave you your first guitar."

"Yep. He also left me and my sister and brother money for college and I have the money from my 4-H steers. I sold a grand champion my senior year. Good money." Jackson tapped the wheel in a beat that matched the song on the radio. "I'm still studying music, just not on a college campus. Gramps would understand that."

"Even if your parents don't?"

"Sometimes these things skip generations."

"But we'll be staying in your parents' house. That doesn't seem right."

"They won't mind. They'll be glad I'm all right. They're like that."

Jackson might be overestimating his mother's goodwill. He saw what he wanted to see. Just as he did with her. The thought made Adah scoot still closer to the door. What had she started? It didn't matter. There was no going back now. She'd chosen her path. God forgive her if it were the wrong one.

Her parents would see this as a terrible sign that Adah had abandoned her faith and her community. She loved them both, more than ever, but she had to do this. She didn't know why. Why would God give her this desire, this calling, if He didn't intend for her to use it? "I can't let you pay my way."

"Look." He nodded toward the windshield. She followed his gaze. Trees lined both sides of the highway now. "Busiek State Forest."

"It's pretty."

"I'm glad you like it."

As if he'd created the forest especially for her. Then they were in it. The thick walls of trees on either side deep, green, and inviting. The truck's engine strained to carry them up the hill. Then the scenery opened up again and they whooshed down the hill, the drop taking her stomach with it.

"It's like a roller coaster." Jackson grinned like a little boy. "Does it tickle your stomach?"

She nodded, knowing she had the same silly grin on her own face. The hills and valleys made her stomach drop the way it did whenever she thought about their destination and her new life.

"Good." He flipped on the turn signal and steered toward the exit. "We're almost there."

He'd managed to highjack the conversation and take it away from the issue of her paying for herself. Something else Jackson did a lot. He pushed away subjects he didn't want to talk about. Until later. Later didn't come. This she wouldn't let go. He wouldn't pay her way. It wouldn't be right.

She turned and pulled her bag from the backseat so she could hold it in her lap. As if this had been some sort of invitation, Captain hopped over the seat and sat between her and Jackson, a grin on his face. No one spoke. The air hung heavy in the truck's cab, filled with something she couldn't quite identify.

Anticipation. That was it. Unbearable anticipation.

"There it is. See it?" Jackson's grin stretched from ear to ear, reminding her of that first day she'd met him in the corral. The things Jackson loved, he loved with all his heart, a fierce, abiding happiness filling him. Like a child who hasn't learned about the disappointment that follows unrealistic expectations. "That's where we'll make music. We could've gone around the town, but I'm taking you down the main drag before we go out to the lake so you can see what it's like."

Neon signs greeted her on all sides, bright and intense against the deepening dusk. They flashed and blinked their messages. PRESLEY'S COUNTRY JUBILEE. TONIGHT. 8 P.M.

One building looked like an enormous ship. A huge, fake gorilla towered over another building. "A gorilla?"

"That's the Hollywood Wax Museum."

A wax museum. "And the ship?"

"That's a museum. Cool, right?"

Surely. The truck barely moved, stuck in a sea of cars that clogged the streets, back to back, spewing exhaust, honking, but mostly not moving. They lined the street, bumper to bumper, rolling a few feet, then stopping, rolling, then stopping.

"Why is it so crowded?" A horn blared and she jumped. "Where is everyone going?"

"To shows, honey. They come from near and far to hear music. And we're here to make music for them."

She needed to break him of calling her those names. *Honey. Baby.* But not now. Now she feasted her gaze on the hordes of people who came to this town to hear music.

Just like her. They loved music.

"Are we going to a show now?"

"You're so cute when you're excited!" Jackson chuckled, sounding a lot like her onkel handing her a present on her birthday. "All the time, actually. We probably ought to unpack first and get settled in. Tomorrow's plenty soon enough to get started."

"I need to practice." Adah could already feel the guitar strings under her fingers, biting into the skin of her fingertips. "You really think we can make music here? That people will listen to us sing at these shows?"

"You bet your bottom dollar, girl."

Plain folks didn't bet.

They didn't go to Branson to be songwriters, either.

He turned the truck off the crowded main road and sped up, moving away from the long lines of traffic. She craned her neck, looking back at the flashing neon lights that lit up the sky. So much light. Flashing like a beacon. Calling her.

"Are you sure?"

"Honey, the only things sure in this life are death and taxes." He chuckled again as they pulled onto another highway. A sign read something about Silver Dollar City. What a name. She'd never seen a silver dollar. "But sure as shootin', we have a better chance than if we'd stayed at home in New Hope and done nothing."

She couldn't argue with that reasoning. She leaned against the door and stared at the bobbing lights of oncoming traffic. It seemed like a dream, a dream from which she couldn't wake.

Fifteen minutes later, they pulled into a long tree-lined drive and slowed. Jackson punched a button and their windows rolled down. Tepid air that smelled of mud, trees, and grass wafted through the truck, replacing the stale odor of food and sweat. To their left stretched a beautiful expanse of water. The sunset bounced off the shimmering water a few hundred yards from the road. A boat bobbed off a nearby dock. The lake. Jackson hadn't mentioned how beautiful it was. Almost as pretty as Stockton Lake where the New Hope Plain folks sometimes went camping and fishing. "That's our place over there." Jackson pointed to their right. "Do you like it?"

He sounded like a little boy, hoping for praise. He eased onto the long paved drive that looped in front of the house. The place he'd described as a lake cabin turned out to be twice the size of the house Adah shared with her entire family. It did have that brown, rustic log cabin look, but it had two stories with a second floor balcony featuring fancy outdoor furniture and an overhang with a ceiling fan. "Yes, I like it." She managed to shut her mouth after a second or two. "It's very pretty."

"Uh-oh." The truck jolted to a stop in the middle of the paved driveway. Jackson shoved the gear in park and leaned back in the seat. He didn't look so happy now. "That's my pop's truck."

A green truck much like the one Jackson drove sat in the driveway, parked crooked and blocking the way out.

The screen door swung open and Mr. Hart strode out to meet them, letting it slam hard behind him.

From the look on his face under his black cowboy hat, he wasn't the welcoming committee.

Chapter 28

Adah sat still, her hand slick with sweat on the truck door handle. She waited for Jackson to move first. He stared out the dirty, bug-splattered windshield, his hands gripping the wheel so tightly his knuckles turned white. Mr. Hart stood, boot-clad feet wide apart, hands on his hips, glaring right back from under the brim of his big cowboy hat. It was a stand-off between the Hart men. Adah felt like a rabbit caught between two coyotes in an open meadow. Nowhere to run. Nowhere to hide.

This was silly. "He's your father. Aren't you going to greet him?" She wiped her hand on her apron and pulled the door open. "We can't sit here all night."

"You're right. Guess I better see what he wants. It's not like he bites and I'm too big for him to haul me off to the woodshed."

Jackson jerked the key from the ignition and let the chain jingle from his fingers for a minute. Finally, he shoved open his door and got out. Captain hopped out after him and raced toward Mr. Hart. The older man squatted and patted the dog's head. He couldn't be all that bad, could he? Captain liked him.

Jackson looked back at Adah through the open window. "You're pretty small, though, he might could put you over his knee." He grinned, that same old cocky grin. Nothing could keep this man down.

"He's a pro with a switch. He practiced on me and RaeAnne plenty. Jeff, not so much. He's too much of a brown-noser."

Adah wasn't a child and she wasn't Mr. Hart's daughter to be punishing.

"I'll take my chances."

Jackson would be enough to provoke any person, Adah was sure of that. She slid from the seat but stayed close to the truck, letting Jackson go forward first. Mr. Hart would want to talk with his son. To him, she would be baggage, nothing more. As if feeling her uncertainty, Captain raced back, circled once, and flopped at her feet, panting, waiting.

"Pop, what's up?" Jackson tilted his hat back at a smart angle, his voice jovial. "What are you doing here? Mom didn't say anything about you taking a fishing trip this weekend."

"Don't give me that innocent act." Mr. Hart's tone had an acid quality that burned Adah's ears. "Did you think we wouldn't figure it out in two seconds? You tell your sister you're leaving town and you think we don't know where you're going? I hopped in the truck and did eighty all the way. I've already had a glass of ice tea and a visit with your Aunt Charlene."

A woman, Aunt Charlene, Adah presumed, appeared at the screen door as if she'd heard her name. She had the same fair skin and dark hair as Mr. Hart and Jackson. She wore a long, flowing skirt of ruffles and a flowered, sleeveless blouse. If it weren't for the ribbons of gray in her hair, caught back in a braid that reached her waist, Adah would've thought her a teenager.

"Hey, Aunt Charlene." Jackson tipped his hat at her. "What's shaking?"

"I was about to ask you the same thing." She had a bit of a drawl as if she might have lived down South a while. "Besides your profound desire to irritate your daddy."

The attention shifted back to Mr. Hart, whose face darkened at their light banter.

"He has no call to complain about my driving, if what he just said was true. Who's the immature one?" Jackson leaned against the hood of the truck, his slouch saying *no worries*. "Why run down here? I won't mess up your place. I just need a base of operation."

"Why? You're dropping out of school to chase some crazy pipe dream." Mr. Hart threw up both his hands in the air as if surrendering. "You're throwing your life away."

"Whoa, that's kind of dramatic isn't it?" For some reason, Jackson's voice slowed to a drawl. Or maybe it seemed that way because Mr. Hart spoke so fast and furious. "If it doesn't work out, it's not the end of the world. I can always go back to school."

"You're wasting your time." Mr. Hart's gaze bounced to Adah and back to Jackson. "In more ways than one, if RaeAnne's telling the truth."

"RaeAnne needs to mind her own business. I only told her so she'd stop pestering me about Dani Jo."

"RaeAnne's worried about you. She has the good sense to know you belong in college, not running around trying to be some kind of music star."

"She does not. And she's not worried about me. She's jealous. She just can't stand it that I might get a life of my own." Jackson glanced at Adah as if to say *come on out*. Adah stayed where she was, not wanting to draw attention to herself. She would fight her own battles with her own parents. This one belonged to Jackson. He scowled at her, then at his dad. "I'm twenty-one. I'm old enough to know what I want to do with my life. And who I want to spend it with."

Nee, don't go there, don't go there. Adah held her breath, waiting to see which statement Mr. Hart would attack first.

"If you're so grownup, then fine, stay here." Mr. Hart waved a hand toward the house. "But this is my house. I own it. I'll expect you to pay rent and your share of the utilities. First month up front. Buy your own groceries. And stay out of the liquor cabinet."

She let her breath out. She'd been right. His parents wouldn't pay his bills if he didn't live under their roof and follow their rules. It was the way of all parents, it seemed, Plain or Englisch. It made sense. No one should expect a free ride.

"That's fine." Jackson sounded so sure of himself. He could pay his bills with his grandpa's money, but not hers. She'd pay her own way. Maybe they had a bakery in Branson that needed someone handy with bread dough and pie crust. Jackson straightened and shrugged. "Will you take a check? You know it's good."

Mr. Hart laughed, a hard, brittle sound. "Your steer money is your money. I talked to the lawyers about your trust fund. Nothing I can do about that, either. It became yours when you turned twenty-one." A strange sadness wafted across the older man's face. "Your granddaddy wanted you to get an education with that money. I hope you'll at least try not to waste it on this craziness."

"It's not craziness. Gramps was the one who gave me my first guitar. He knew about music. He knew I had something special. If you ever listened to my music, you'd know." Jackson's voice roughened with emotion. Sadness. They were both sad about something more than Jackson's refusal to go back to school. "You'd know I'm good. Good enough to make it."

Mr. Hart snorted. "You were always so full of yourself. I can't believe Dad encouraged you."

"At least he believed in me. You sure don't."

"All your mom and I want is for you to be realistic. Get an education. Be able to support yourself."

"I can support myself. I'm a grown man."

"I can tell by the way you snuck off to stay at my house and take advantage of the hospitality of my sister who takes care of it."

"It just made sense. I'm looking for work as a musician in Branson. We have a family home in Branson. Aunt Charlene doesn't mind, do you?"

Charlene pushed through the screen door and sashayed onto the porch. Her feet were bare, her toenails painted a bright red. "This is between you and your daddy. I suggest y'all work it out like two grown men." She smiled at Adah. "You must be Jackson's friend. Why don't you come into the house? I'll get you some iced tea while these two duke it out. It's too hot for this."

Duke it out? Adah tightened her grip on her bag. Would they really come to blows?

"I was speaking figuratively." Charlene's smile widened. "They're big boys. They'll figure it out."

"She doesn't go in the house. Not until Jackson and I reach an agreement." Mr. Hart gave his sister a hard look. "I may still decide to make them find their own place."

"That's crazy. This is a family home. I'm part of the family," Jackson blustered. "You'd turn me out of a house where we've spent our vacations almost every year since I was six?"

"It's exactly that sense of entitlement I can't understand." Mr. Hart's expression dissolved into weariness. "I tried to give you and your sister and your brother a good life. Now you don't appreciate it."

"I do appreciate it. I'm grateful." Jackson's tone softened. "I just want a chance to find out if I can make it. Is that too much to ask?"

Shaking his head, Mr. Hart sat suddenly on the top porch step as if his legs wouldn't hold him anymore. "I'll make you a deal, son. I'll give you six months. You don't have a paying gig as a musician in six months, you come home. You go back to college and this time, you actually go to class. You get your degree. Then you can do whatever you want with it. What do you think?"

It seemed a fair deal. Adah's parents would never make such an offer. The Englisch were so different. Breaking the rules, it seemed, could be rewarded. Or at least tolerated.

Jackson kicked at the gravel with his boot. Dust rose and settled on it, dimming the shine. He raised his head and nodded, his expression somber. "It's a deal."

"Deal."

His dad rose and held out his hand. Jackson straightened and took it. The shake lasted a mere split second. They didn't look at each other. The air seemed to shimmer with all the words they hadn't said. So many words spoken, but none of them the right ones. Adah had experience with those kinds of conversations. She had them with her own daed all the time.

Mr. Hart's gaze swung to Adah over his son's shoulder. She worked to hold herself tall under his glare. It quickly shifted back to Jackson. "So you'll support your girlfriend too?"

"She's not my girlfriend, I mean…" For the first time, Jackson stammered. He swiveled and met Adah's gaze. His face turned radish red. "Adah's my partner. She's a singer and a songwriter."

"I'll bet she is. Your mother told me about the conversation she had with your partner about doing her work and minding her own business." Mr. Hart sidestepped Jackson and planted himself near the bumper of the truck. His gaze raked over Adah, head to toe. "Do your parents know where you are?"

An unbearable shiver ran through her. She ignored it. She'd entered the Englisch world, a world where she would have to talk to Englisch men and stand up for herself. No more hiding behind Plain dress and shrinking from notice. "I left them a note saying I was leaving to be a singer. I didn't tell them where I was going or who was taking me."

"Tell me you're of age, at least."

"Eighteen."

"If you were my daughter, I'd bend you over my knee and give you a whopping with a switch." Adah's daed had been known to do that too, but it had been a long while. "They'll be worried sick about you. At least call them."

"They don't have a phone." His tone made her chin come up and her back straighten. "I'll write them as soon as I get settled."

"They got that phone shack."

True, but she could only imagine leaving that message and having Luke listen to it tomorrow or the next day when he finally got around to checking the answering machine. "They do, but we mostly write letters. It's our way."

"Give them a break; let them know you're all right. That you have a decent place to stay with decent folks." His gaze swiveled back to Jackson. "I raised my son right. At least, I thought I did."

"I am decent." Jackson's hands fisted. "I'm a gentleman. Tell him, Adah."

"I'll write them a letter." Adah tried to summon a smile to soften the firmness of her response. "Your son is giving me a chance at something I want real bad. I'm beholden to him for that."

"Don't let him talk you into doing something you don't want to do just because he gave you a ride and a place to stay."

"Monroe, that's enough." Charlene slapped a hand on her brother's arm. "Give them a break. They're just kids."

"What do you know?" Mr. Hart shook off her touch, his face a grimace. "How many kids did you raise?"

A sudden intake of air from Jackson told Adah a blow had been struck. From Charlene's expression, an ugly blow. She plopped onto the porch step.

Mr. Hart glanced back at his sister. "Sorry, Char, I didn't mean that."

"Sure you did."

"I'm just mad, that's all. In my generation, a man turned twenty-one, he was a man and he was expected to start acting like one."

"Give Jackson a chance to prove it, then."

"Like you said, Mr. Hart, you raised your son right." Adah took a step forward so she stood next to Jackson. "We'll be fine, both of us."

"Then I wash my hands of the whole thing."

Mr. Hart jerked open his truck door, slid in, and slammed it shut. He leaned out the window as he started the engine. "Remember, we have a deal. Six months. And help your aunt with the groceries. Don't be mooching off her."

He drove off, gravel spitting at them in his wake.

"Woo-hoo!"

Jackson tossed his hat in the air, grabbed Adah around the waist, and twirled her around until her stomach rocked.

Charlene laughed and got to her feet. "You're one crazy man, nephew of mine. You tangled with big Monroe and lived to tell about it. You should celebrate. Y'all come in and get cleaned up. I'll fix you something to eat as soon as I show Adah her room. Which, Jack, will be on the second floor far, far from your room on the first floor. I won't put up with any hanky panky under my roof. Do you hear me?"

"Hanky panky? How old are you? A hundred?" His face reddening, Jackson dropped Adah onto her feet. "And what is it with you people, always thinking the worst of me?"

"Not you, sweet cakes. Guys your age in general. We were young once too."

"I don't believe that." Jackson took off when Charlene came after him, hand out to give him a swat. "You still move pretty fast for an old lady."

"Who're you calling old?"

Charlene chased him up the steps and into the house. Still dizzy with relief, Adah followed more slowly.

Jackson held the screen door open. "Come on, sweet cakes. We just got a get-out-of-jail-free pass from my own dad. Time to celebrate."

She squeezed past him into a foyer that opened into a mammoth living room filled with floor-to-ceiling bookshelves and complete with an enormous stone fireplace that had the head of a deer hanging over it. The deer seemed to stare at her, its eyes stony. She sighed.

"Don't look at me like that, Amish girl." Jackson let the door slam behind her. "My dad just gave me six months to figure this thing out. We're home free, girl."

Except for the job part and the music part and the part where she gave up her family and her entire life to be here.

Except for that part.

Chapter 29

Matthew craned his neck from side to side, trying to work out a kink that had his shoulders aching. The August sun beat down on him, the air so hot it scorched his lungs every time he inhaled. He couldn't complain. As long as the sun shone, they could get the last of the corn harvested. He swiped at his forehead with his sleeve and went back to work tightening the wheel. Gott willing, they'd finish this field of corn and then he could go home, eat, and wait for dark so he could go talk to Adah. He forced himself to focus on the task at hand. The weariness that resulted from not sleeping a wink the previous night didn't help. Every time he closed his eyes he saw that monstrous silver pile of engine and tires driving away, Adah looking like a little doll propped up in the cabin.

She looked scared. Why, he couldn't imagine. Apparently it wasn't the first time she'd gone for a ride in Jackson Hart's truck. It didn't seem likely that the kiss had happened around the house. Nee, they'd gone somewhere together. For another kiss.

Why he kept torturing himself with that image, he couldn't imagine. He'd thought she really would try to do better. She would try to follow the Ordnung. She'd finish the classes. He'd been sure of that.

Until yesterday.

The clip-clop of hooves in the distance sounded loud in the afternoon quiet. He tipped his hat back for a better view.

"Looks like Daniel is paying us a visit," Rueben called from his vantage point in front of the wagon. "Wonder what he wants."

"What makes you think he wants something?" Matthew regretted his curt tone. He sounded like Daed. None of this was Rueben's fault. "Maybe he has good news."

Good news would be much appreciated. Rueben cackled and hopped from his seat. "Maybe he's coming to invite you to supper and Adah will be there. How would that be for good news?"

"You just hush and untangle the reins."

Rueben began to sing some silly song he'd picked up from the other boys when they went fishing. The singing reminded Matthew of Adah, which only made him grumpier.

"Hey." Daniel pulled his buggy alongside the wagon. "There you are."

"Here I am." Matthew stalked around to the buggy. "How come you're not working your fields? Knocked off early today?"

"Nee." Daniel climbed down from the buggy and stood next to Matthew. His features were so like Adah's. They could be twins, were he a few years younger. He took off his hat, fanned his sweaty, tanned face with it, and slapped it back on his head. "I thought...well, I just thought."

"Spit it out." Matthew had known Daniel since they were knee-high to daed's britches, but he'd never been close to him. Daniel was a little older and a lot more prone to talking out of turn. "Why are you here in the middle of the day?"

Daniel studied the ground as if looking for a lost dollar. "Didn't know if you'd heard?"

"Heard what?"

"Adah's done run off."

Matthew's stomach did a strange double dip. His lungs flattened and didn't bother to refill. His vision darkened around the edges. Purple spots danced in the middle.

"Matthew? Did you hear me? Adah didn't come home last night."

"She didn't come home?" He cleared his throat and forced himself to take a long breath. *Breathe in. Breathe out.* "How do you know she ran off? Maybe something happened to her."

Maybe Jackson Hart happened to her.

"She left a note."

"A note."

"She said she was leaving because of the music. She wants to make music. Don't that beat all?"

Matthew straightened and dropped the wrench into the back of the wagon. "Figures."

"Figures?" Daniel drew the word into two long syllables. "I thought you…I mean…it seemed…well, weren't you…"

"We were." Not since this very moment. "Not anymore."

A snort from the front of the wagon reminded Matthew his little brother had big ears.

"Since when?"

"Since she started…" At the last second he reminded himself that he spoke to Adah's brother, a man who cared for his sister and who deserved respect despite what she had done to Matthew's heart. "We've had some differences lately."

"Did she have another special friend?"

Matthew looked at Daniel square-on. "It's not my place—"

"My mudder is beside herself. Both my parents are. They already lost one daughter. They want this one back, but we don't know where to start looking."

"I'd start with the Harts."

"She stopped working there weeks ago."

"Did your mudder tell you why?"

"Nee. She just said it would be best if she worked with our kind."

"Ask her what made her say that."

"You know. You tell me."

"Not my place."

Daniel drew a long breath. "I'm asking you to do me the favor of helping me find my *schweschder*."

"I know." Matthew dug the heel of his boot—he felt like a heel himself—into the dirt and dragged it back, making a line. He stepped over it, then cocked his head toward the road. Daniel followed him as they walked away from the wagon, out of Rueben's earshot. "I don't know where Adah is, but I did see her yesterday."

"Where?"

"In Jackson Hart's truck. Headed south out of town."

Daniel plowed to a stop. His face blanched under a deep tan. "Nee. Jackson Hart?"

"Jah."

"And you didn't try to stop her?"

"She looked content."

"What's that supposed to mean?"

"What did you want me to do, chase after his truck in my buggy?"

"Maybe if you had, we wouldn't have to go after her now."

"You want to go after her, go after her. I can't do it." And risk being rejected by her again. She'd made her choice. "I have work here."

"My sister is somewhere out there." Daniel jabbed toward the south, his face red with heat and anger. "Whether you care about her as a future fraa or not, you're supposed to care about her eternal salvation."

Daniel was right. Matthew swallowed. His heart wanted to go. His head insisted he would only get hurt again. Why keep doing that?

Daniel whirled and strode toward his buggy. "I'm going to see the Harts."

"Wait." He couldn't help himself. Matthew double-timed after Adah's brother. "I'll go with you."

Not much later they pulled up in front of the Hart house, an oversized home with a wraparound porch that featured ceiling fans. Daniel hopped from the buggy and tied the reins to a porch post.

"Wait." Matthew climbed down with more decorum. "Let me do the talking."

"Why?"

"You know Luke won't want us to rile up our Englisch neighbors. We need to be calm. You're angry and you're jumping to conclusions."

"You saw them riding out of town together."

"Maybe they went for a ride, nothing more." He knew better than that. He had the memory of that voice on the cell phone burned into his brain. *I'm sorry I kissed you.* "Maybe she left after that, by herself. You don't know until you hear their side of the story."

"She's your girl and you're not even a little peeved?" Daniel stalked up the steps. "I guess she wasn't the one for you."

"She was—she is." Matthew slipped past Daniel and knocked. "There seemed to be a question in her mind as to whether I'm the one."

"Sorry." Daniel had the good grace to look embarrassed. "I didn't know. I guess I should have figured if she was in a truck with Jackson Hart."

"Jah." Matthew couldn't keep the tartness from his voice. "She made her choice."

The door opened and Liz Hart peered out at them. She stood nearly as tall as Daniel, a few inches shorter than Matthew. Her red eyes matched her tousled hair. "What is it?"

Daniel introduced himself and Matthew, his tone more civil than it had been in the buggy. "My sister Adah worked for you."

"Not anymore." Mrs. Hart opened the door a little wider and craned her head as if looking to see if Adah stood there. "She up and quit for no reason a few weeks ago. Left me stranded with no one to clean the house. She won't get a reference from me, even less now."

Anger mingled with something else—sadness—stained her words.

"She's left town." Daniel shifted from foot to foot. He cleared his throat. "Matthew says he saw her with your son Jackson last night."

"And?"

"Is Jackson here?" Matthew didn't ask the question he wanted to ask. What did Jackson want with a Plain girl like Adah? He must've gotten her all mixed up. She would never do this on her own. Or maybe that was what Matthew wanted to believe. "We thought maybe he knows where she went."

"He knows." Mrs. Hart pulled the door wider, but instead of inviting them in, squeezed between them, forcing them to step back and let her through. Fancy gold earrings jingling, she sauntered over to the porch railing and leaned against it, her arms looking like scrawny sticks in her sleeveless shiny blue blouse. "My husband saw them together too."

"Where?"

She sniffed, disdain written all over her face. "She's in Branson with my son. The fools think they're going to be music stars. She's got him convinced he can do anything. She's a schemer, that one."

Branson.

Daniel scoffed and shook his head. Matthew couldn't move. She'd chosen music. Not only music, but Jackson. She'd chosen music and an Englisch man over her faith and her family.

Over him.

"My sister is no schemer." Daniel stalked across the porch and stood next to Mrs. Hart, arms crossed over his dirty, sweat-stained shirt. "She's a good girl."

"She spent some time in this house. She knows what's in it. She knows everything about us. The farm, the house in town, the lake house in Branson. She worked some magic on my son, knowing how much she had to gain."

"Adah doesn't care about houses or money." Matthew waved a hand at the house. "She doesn't care about things. It's the music."

"The music and my son."

Maybe.

Jackson's voice reverberated in his ears again. Apologizing for that kiss. She'd rebuffed him at least once. Jackson had pursued her. "She loves music. So does your son. That's what they have in common."

Nothing else. *Please, Gott, nothing else.*

"She seems pretty set on staying with my son, music or not."

He didn't believe that. He tried not to believe it. "Your husband saw them in Branson. Did he try to make them come home?"

"He did."

"But they wouldn't."

Mrs. Hart took her time lighting a cigarette with a silver lighter that glinted in the sun. The smoke curled around her head and drifted away like fog. "They wouldn't. They're set on their silly dream." She glanced back at Matthew. "No point in running after her. She's made her choice."

Indeed, she had.

"Are they getting married?" Daniel's voice skated over the last word as if it were dangerous, thin ice. "Where is she living?"

"Jackson swore to my husband that it wasn't like that, but Monroe knows the look Jackson gets. He's a lady's man, my son. She might not be his girlfriend yet, but she will be."

She sucked on the cigarette and blew out smoke with an exaggerated sigh. "Don't worry. My sister-in-law lives at the house. She's our caretaker. She'll make sure your sister's virtue is safe."

Daniel's face deepened to an almost purple shade of red. "I'll go fetch her home where she belongs."

"Good luck with that."

Mrs. Hart was right about that. If Adah didn't want to return home, there was no point in making the trip. Matthew knew Adah well enough to know she had not made the decision to leave her community lightly. It would've been a heartbreaking, difficult decision. Only for something she wanted terribly. That might include Jackson, but it didn't end there.

It all revolved around the music.

Matthew couldn't compete with the music. Moreover, he didn't want to compete.

"Let's go."

"What? No!" Daniel shook Matthew's hand from his shoulder. "I'd like directions. What's the address?"

"There's no point in it." Mrs. Hart's voice cracked. "She's made her move. And dragged my son into it. They'll come home eventually, when his trust fund runs out and they find out they're just two more would-be second-rate singers in a town full of second-rate singers."

The sound of Adah's high, sweet soprano floating on the air as she sang a simple lullaby to baby John echoed in Matthew's head. He didn't know a thing about Branson or country music, but Adah would never be a second-rate singer. Not only did she sing like a songbird, but she wrote songs. A special combination of talents. Even he knew that. If only she were second-rate. She would be forced to come home sooner. Was that a selfish thought? He tried to examine it, turn it over in his mind. No. He wanted her home, first because she needed her faith and her family, second because he needed her.

A little selfish. If he went after her, it would be for himself. And it might have repercussions for his own walk in faith. As a single man, not her husband, he had no right to go gallivanting across the country searching for her. It wouldn't be right. "Let's go." Matthew started down the steps. "We need to talk to your daed and to Luke."

"We have to go get her before...we have to bring her home while we still can."

"That may be your place. Yours and your daed's. But first you need to talk to Luke, Thomas, and Silas. Let them decide if anyone should go for her. She's not been baptized. This is more rumspringa. They may think she needs to come home on her own."

The bluster went out of Daniel. His shoulders sagged. "It'll break Mudder's heart."

"Your mudder is strong."

"She's already lost one daughter."

Matthew glanced at Mrs. Hart. Tears brightened her blue eyes. She dabbed at them with the back of her bony hand. The Harts must also feel they were losing a son, but Jackson wasn't leaving his faith or his way of life. He'd taken up residence in his family's home in Branson with his aunt to keep house for him. He lost nothing in this move. His had been simply a choice of occupation and geography. "Let's go talk to them. Maybe we can convince them to let us go get her."

If not, Daniel and her family would have to live with God's plan.

So would Matthew. Somehow.

Chapter 30

Her eyes red, face puffy, Irene ushered Matthew and the other men into the Knepp house with barely a greeting. Matthew tried to catch her gaze, but it remained fixed on the wooden floor as she led them to the sitting area by the fireplace mantel where Ben stood, stony faced, staring at the dark empty space where flames would leap and catch on wood during the cold winter months. They both looked as if they hadn't slept in weeks. They looked like Matthew felt. Overcome by despair. Resigned. Confused.

He slowed and held back, letting the older men take the straight-back chairs Irene had arranged around a pine rocking chair. Luke sat first and Thomas and Silas followed. Finally, Ben sank into the rocking chair. It groaned under his weight. Daniel hovered in the space between the living room and the kitchen as if he expected to be sent away. The soft, high-pitched murmurs wafting from the kitchen told Matthew his friend's wife and sisters still washed dishes and cleaned after the day's final meal, which, from the aroma lingering in the air, had included tuna casserole.

Luke began. "We've come to talk about Adah." A bit of emotion colored the words spoken in a gentle tone—rare from a man such as Luke. Sadness maybe. Regret. What did Luke regret? Having this conversation with Adah's parents or not doing more to make sure Adah didn't stray? They'd all done what they could. "Have you heard from her?"

"Only the note." Ben cleared his voice. He leaned forward, elbows on his knees, his big hands gripped tightly in front of him. "Nothing since. No point in jawing about it. What's done is done. She's made her choice."

From the post she'd taken behind Ben, her hands resting on the back of his chair, Irene made a small noise, a tiny cry of pain as if she'd bitten her tongue. Ben didn't look back at her, but his knuckles whitened.

"Daniel and Matthew came to us." Luke motioned to Silas and Thomas, who nodded in tandem. "They thought it worth considering that a few of us go to Branson and talk with her. Try to persuade her to return before she becomes too tied up in the ways of the world."

"She made her choice."

"Ben—"

"Hush, fraa." Ben's hands become unknotted and he flipped one up, thick fingers splayed in the air. He stood. "I have chores to do."

"Your daughter's eternal salvation is at stake here." Luke also rose as he spoke, the words clipped and sharp. "Think on that, Ben, before you let your pride get in the way of doing everything you possibly can to bring her back into the fold."

"Pride?" Ben's voice fell to a raspy whisper. "Pride? All I feel is shame."

"And love." Irene slapped her hand to her mouth and swallowed as if she could force back the sob that had escaped. "And fear. You won't admit it, but I know you feel it. We're afraid for her and we want her back."

"You're angry at her as I would be." Luke directed his words to Ben as if he hadn't heard Irene's outburst. "You're thinking about what your family and friends will think. No one thinks less of you or Irene. We've all had sons, daughters, brothers, sisters, who've strayed. Gott knows I have. Remember Josiah? Remember Catherine? It's not a matter for shame, but for prayer."

"I have prayed. Long and hard. She's still out there doing who knows what with that Englisch boy." Ben stomped toward the door, his boots thudding on the floor. "The chores won't do themselves. Are you here to visit with the women, Daniel, or do you have a hankering to help?"

Daniel hustled after his father. He threw an entreating glance at Matthew as he reached the door.

"Daniel and I could go." Matthew's voice sounded lame in his ears. He shifted from one foot to the other, aware of six pairs of eyes staring at him, waiting. "Daniel's her brother and I'm...I'm...I'm concerned for her well-being. This Jackson Hart may think he means well but he's leading her down a path—"

"She's chosen to go down that path. By now, who knows what she's done with that Englischer?" Ben's voice thundered now, no longer sad or bewildered. Anger broke free. "She'll not come back here and bring her Englisch ways, her fanciful ways with her songwriting and her Englisch music and poison the rest of my children."

"Mrs. Hart said her sister-in-law is there, at the house, and she'll not let anything untoward happen." Matthew refused to be cowed by the older man. Ben deserved respect and his anger and hurt were understandable. Matthew felt them himself. But Luke was right. They couldn't give up on Adah. "What if she's gotten herself into something she can't get out of? What if she regrets it? What if she needs us to come get her?"

"Then she'll write to her parents, I reckon." Thomas spoke for the first time. "We need to give her time to realize she's made a mistake. Let her feel the consequences of that mistake."

"What if she doesn't? What if she only gets mired deeper into the pit she's digging for herself?" Matthew tried to corral his emotions. Luke and the other men had treated him as an equal when he came to them with the proposition that he and Daniel go to Branson. He wanted their continued respect. "Shouldn't we at least try to set her straight? Daniel has experience. He brought back Michael last year. This is his sister. She'll listen to him."

"We're all brothers and sisters in Christ," Luke said, his dark eyes thoughtful. "This is different, though. Michael didn't run away with an Englisch girl."

"She's my sister." Daniel seemed to take strength from Matthew's willingness to speak up. "She'll listen to me."

"That might be true." Thomas looked to Luke. The other man

nodded. "But let's wait a bit. I've spent enough time talking with Adah during the course of the baptism classes to know she grasps the seriousness of her actions. She's torn. She has to choose. She has to make the choice herself. That's what rumspringa is about."

Matthew clamped his mouth shut to keep from arguing. This wasn't the answer he wanted.

Ben shoved through the screen door and let it slam behind him. Daniel stalked after his father, letting the door close more softly.

"I'm sorry for your troubles, Irene." Luke headed toward the door. Thomas and Silas followed suit. "I've had a few myself so I know how it feels. Pray. We all will pray for Gott's will to be done in this."

"I know." Irene's struggle to hold on to her composure played out in her face. Adah's face. They looked so much alike, except Irene had weathered tragedy and the lines around her mouth and eyes reflected it. Her sculpted features had been honed by pain. What was Adah thinking, adding to those lines? "I will pray."

They moved toward the door. Irene followed, her fingers working the material of her apron, bunching and unbunching it. Matthew waited for the older men to pass through first. To his surprise, Irene touched his shoulder with one fingertip. He paused. Her gaze beseeched him. He glanced at the other men. They'd already started down the steps to their buggies. "What is it?"

"Don't wait too long," she whispered. "Adah needs you. I can feel it."

"But Luke and Thomas said...I can't just..."

"I know." She held open the screen door and Matthew passed through. On the other side, he stopped and glanced back at her. Tears streamed down her face as if the men's departure had opened the floodgates. "We need to bring my dochder back. For her sake. Don't wait too long. Bring her back."

The screen door closed and she disappeared into the recesses of the house.

How long was too long?

Chapter 31

Adah polished off the last bite of scalloped potatoes and speared a small piece of ham she'd missed on the pretty flowered plate. On their second night in Branson, Charlene had been convinced to let her set the table while she cooked up a storm in the kitchen. Charlene wanted to treat her as a guest, but Adah wasn't having it. They ate at the smaller round table in the alcove adjacent to the kitchen rather than the massive pine table that seated twelve in the dining room. Adah couldn't get over how lovely and delicate the place settings were alongside ornate silverware that weighed heavy in her hands.

It all looked so pretty on the lacy white tablecloth, now marred by Jackson's sloppy eating habits. If stuffing his mouth with gusto was any indication, he enjoyed the food. Charlene cooked a good meal. Sure, the bread was store-bought and the green beans came out of a can, but a hungry person didn't nitpick the details. Adah needed to speak with Charlene after dinner about their arrangements—how much would she pay for room and board. She wanted to pay a fair price. She wasn't a guest here. In the meantime, she could help earn her keep by cleaning up.

Spurred by the thought, she stood, barely avoiding Captain's tail as it whopped on the floor, his face expectant as he waited patiently and hopefully for a piece of ham to fall from the table. As if the dog didn't have a full bowl of food in the kitchen. Adah stacked her silverware on her plate and picked it up. Jackson burped, excused himself, and then shoved his plate away from him. Adah reached for it.

"What are you doing, girl?" Charlene shook a thin finger dressed in a silver ring of entwined hearts at Adah. "Don't you be picking up his plate."

"What do you mean?" She held a plate in each hand, surprised by Charlene's sharp tone. "I'm clearing the table. You cooked, I wash the dishes. It's only fair."

"Yeah, it's only fair. She's clearing the table." Jackson leaned back and shook a round jar until a toothpick slid from the holes in the lid. He applied it to his side teeth, his lips bared like a dog worrying a bone. "You got a problem with that?"

"Yeah, I got a problem." Charlene dropped her fork on her plate with a sharp *plink*. "She set the table. You clear the table. She's not your maid, anymore."

His smile gone, Jackson tossed the toothpick on the table. "I never said she was."

"Don't let him treat you like hired help." Charlene shook her head so hard her huge silver earrings banged against her neck. "You're not his maid, you're not his girlfriend, as far as I can tell, and you're sure not his wife."

"No, but I *am* a woman."

"You're telling me this is women's work?" Charlene waved a hand toward the dirty plates and the bowls of food. "Honey, this is a new day for you and it'll take some getting used to. You need to lay down some ground rules. If you two are friends, he won't want to take advantage of that friendship."

Adah studied Jackson. He shifted in his seat. She waited. He crossed his arms. She waited some more. He cleared his throat and stood. "Let me help you with these dishes." He took the plates from her hands. "Wouldn't want you to strain yourself."

"You like to wash or dry?" She couldn't believe those words came from her mouth. "I kind of prefer washing, especially since I don't know where your aunt keeps things in the cabinets."

"We have a dishwasher, so there's no need for washing or drying."

"Where I come from, I am the dish washer."

Jackson stacked Charlene's plate on top of the other two and swiped her dirty silverware from the table. "Here we just scrape them off, run a little water on them, and stack them in the dishwasher."

She trailed after him into the kitchen. "If you're going to all that trouble, why not finish the job and wash them?"

"Good question. I don't know." He stacked the plates in the sink and turned on the water. "Just the way we do things, I guess."

So she was learning.

"Hey guys, my friend Brenda is picking me up. It's movie night." Charlene stuck her head through the door. "I assume I can trust you two to clean up and behave yourselves while I'm gone."

"Yes, ma'am." Jackson's respectful tone didn't match the small grin spreading across his face. "I'm planning to watch a baseball game. The Cardinals are playing."

"And I have some letters to write." Adah could stay in her room and stay out of any trouble that silly grin might imply. As much as she dreaded the thought, she needed to try to explain her actions to her parents and to Matthew. "Don't worry, we'll get everything spotless first."

Charlene blew a kiss at Jackson as she headed for the back door. "I won't be late. Unless Brenda wants to get a bite to eat after. She always wants coffee and pie even though we get popcorn and root beer at the movie. The woman has a hollow leg."

With that, the door slammed behind her and Adah stood alone in the kitchen with Jackson. He began to whistle as he rinsed the plates and stuck them in the dishwasher. The notes were familiar. An old Alan Jackson song. She hummed along.

After a few moments of companionable work side by side, Jackson shut the dishwasher and began drying his hands. "You go on. I'll wipe down the table and finish up in here."

"You sure?" It seemed so strange to have a man cleaning in the kitchen. She'd never seen such a thing in all her life. Like everything else right now, it seemed like a dream she couldn't shake. "I can do it."

"Nope, Charlene's right. Go write those letters. The game doesn't start for another fifteen minutes. I've got this."

Would wonders never cease? Feeling guilty for something—she wasn't exactly sure what—she trudged up the stairs to the large bedroom at the end of the hallway. It had surely been RaeAnne's room at one time. The décor was Western but with a girly touch. A four-poster bed with a pink-checked canopy. Pictures of horses, mostly Palominos, and posters of country music singers, young, handsome men with cowboy hats and guitars. Definitely RaeAnne's taste. A bookshelf along one wall showed the girl's progression in reading skill and life—Dr. Seuss picture books, June B. Jones, Nancy Drew, classics she'd read for school, even some adult novels. Running her fingers over the spines, Adah considered pulling one from the shelf. No, she would not procrastinate another night. Letters first, then a novel.

She climbed onto the bed and sat cross-legged, her notebook in her lap. Time to get this over with. At first she doodled. Then she made lists of rhyming words. Then words became sentences. Not letters to her parents. A song.

Always a song.

Stop it. Stop it, Adah. She could hear her mudder's voice. How often had she said those words in the first eighteen years of Adah's life? More than she could possibly count. The thought forced Adah back to her original task. Write the letter. Mudder deserved that. She'd suffered the loss of one daughter to fire; now another to something even Adah couldn't define. Wanderlust? Discontent? Seeking. Seeking what?

Stop it.

So she wrote. And wrote. And wrote some more. She told Mudder all about Jackson and the songs and the concert at the rodeo and the time down by the creek. She told her everything. How else could Mudder understand? Or Matthew. How could he understand?

Daed would never understand so it didn't matter what she said. He'd stop reading after the second or third paragraph. Still, she wrote on, hoping at the end she'd understand too.

Finally, she stopped. Her wrist and fingers ached from gripping the pencil. Her neck and shoulders throbbed and her legs were numb. She sighed. Time for a break. She still needed to write to Daniel and Molly. But first she needed a drink of water and a long stretch.

For the first time, she became aware of the noise emanating from beyond her door. What was that? The TV? Jackson had spent most of the day watching television. He didn't seem in any hurry to make the big entrance into the Branson music scene while she practiced the guitar for endless hours, her wrists and fingers burning. When she asked, he told her to be patient, that he'd been making calls and doing something he called "networking." He assured her this "networking" took time. He tried to interest Adah in TV, but she didn't see the point. If she wanted make believe she'd read a good book. She opened her door and strode to the top of the stairs.

Raucous laughter and deep voices—several of them—floated up the stairs. Riffs of guitar music came and went. Somebody—more than one somebody—played music in Charlene's living room. Sure didn't sound like a baseball game. Smoothing her kapp, Adah tiptoed—why she didn't know—down the stairs and peeked around the corner into the living room.

Jackson sat on the couch, his guitar balanced on his knee. As always, Captain lay at his feet, head lolling, tongue half out of his mouth. He didn't seem to mind the volume of the music. It made Adah's ears hurt. A look of fierce concentration on his face, Jackson picked a tune she'd never heard before. Loud and fast, the lyrics had what Matthew called a honkytonk tone to them. He never let her sing along to those songs at the concerts and when their friends went to the little bar in New Hope, he never let her join them. His line in the sand.

"Adah!" Jackson saw her and lifted his hand, pick clutched between thumb and forefinger. "We're jammin'. Join us. These are my buddies Rick, Sam, and Derek. Guys, this is the girl I was telling you about, the one with a voice like an angel."

"I thought you were watching the ballgame." She nodded to the buddies, who mostly stared, the same odd expression she saw on the faces of people who'd never met a Plain person before. "You didn't say anything about having company."

"The ballgame's on. The Cardinals are losing three to one." He slapped his hand on the guitar. "I can multitask. I couldn't wait to get started with the songwriting so I made some calls. We need to get our A-stuff ready."

"Ready for what?"

"The call came in. From Mac McMillan. He's scheduled some time for us tomorrow."

"Tomorrow?"

"Yeah, tomorrow. Pull up a chair. We need to get ourselves ready."

Tomorrow was way too soon. She needed more practice. Trying to ignore the sudden appearance of a horde of butterflies flying upside down in her stomach, Adah took in the liquor bottle sitting open on the huge oak coffee table. Four glasses with ice melting in them sat on the table, condensation making puddles around them. A cigarette burned in an ashtray, its spiral of smoke hanging in the air. A bag of tortilla chips had been torn open next to a bowl of soupy-looking cheese dip. Droplets of cheese and chunks of tomato and chili pepper spotted the table. Apparently they hadn't heard of napkins. Charlene wouldn't be happy about that. "Your dad said to stay out of the liquor cabinet."

"That was a metaphor for staying out of his house and his life. For not bothering him." Strumming again, Jackson sang the words. "Stay out of my house, son. Stay out of my life, boy."

He stopped playing long enough to turn over a piece of paper lying on the table. "Hey, what do you think of this bridge?" He strummed several chords. "Sharp, right?"

"I don't know. What do you mean by *bridge*?"

Sam snorted. "I thought you said she wrote songs. You sure you got the right girl? She looks a little naïve."

The way he said it reflected what he really meant: *She seems a little stupid.*

"She does write songs. She just doesn't speak the lingo. I forget that. She's an Amish girl."

Sam looked her over again, his gaze meandering from her face to her toes, his lips curled in a smirk. "You know how to quilt, girl? Cuz my mom really likes those Amish quilts. She goes up to Webster County to get them all the time."

"Yes, I quilt." Adah began to edge toward the hallway. Her tightly entwined fingers felt damp. Captain growled low in his throat and got to his feet. "I sew."

"But you don't bridge." Sam laughed and slapped his hand on the gaping holes in the knees of his jeans as if this were the funniest thing he'd ever said. "How about pre-chorus? Do you do that?"

"Yes. I don't know."

More snickering. "Honey, why don't you get us some more ice?" Derek held up his empty glass. "And pull that bottle of Pepsi from the refrigerator and bring it on out here."

Adah glanced at Jackson, waiting for him to set these guys straight. She was his friend, not the maid. Jackson had his head down, his eyes closed, as he mumbled words and strummed unfamiliar chords.

Feeling dismissed, she swiveled and hurried into the kitchen. To her surprise, Captain hobbled along with her, his snout pierced with his usual grin. She didn't plan to get ice, but to clean up the mess. Charlene would be home soon and Adah didn't want to make more work for her or take advantage of her hospitality. Jackson might be used to doing that, but she wasn't.

She grabbed a washcloth and sopped up spilled soda on the counter. "Sticky mess," she muttered under her breath as she turned on the faucet and let water run over the cloth. "Pigs."

Captain woofed as if in agreement, then plopped down on the linoleum under the table in what Charlene liked to call the breakfast nook. "Some help you are." Adah felt foolish complaining to a dog, but right now, Captain seemed the most intelligent male in the house.

Captain cocked his head, woofed again, and sprawled out as if ready for a nap.

"Like I said, you're no help at all."

"You talking about us?" Sam stopped in the doorway and propped his long, lean body against the frame, one arm over his head, a lazy, half-amused expression on his acne-scarred face. He shoved thick hair from his eyes with fingers that had nails on the long side for a man. "It's not nice to talk to people behind their backs, even if it is to a dog."

"It's not nice to leave a mess in someone else's house." She surprised herself with her tart response. She could stand up to these Englisch guys. It was time to start. "Did you need something?"

He shifted and moved toward her. "Just information."

"I'm new in town. I don't have a lot of information."

He leaned against the counter next to where she stood at the sink. She could smell his aftershave and see the sweat ring forming under the arms of his dingy white T-shirt. "Are you and Jackson a thing?"

"A thing?" Trying not to show sudden nerves, she squirted dish soap in a dirty glass and held it under the running water. "I don't know what you mean."

"Sure you do." He touched her kapp with one long finger. Heat rushed up her neck. She jerked back. He grinned, revealing crooked teeth with a gap in the middle. A piece of food had lodged itself there. "You're cute. Something about the dress and the apron. I just don't want to step on Jackson's toes."

She scooted back, out of his reach. Captain scrambled to his feet. A low growl made him sound a lot more fierce than he looked. "Jackson's my friend."

Sam straightened and took a long step, cutting the space between them to a mere few inches. His breath stank of alcohol and cigarettes. "Just friends? That's good. Then he won't mind if I ask you out."

Captain began to bark. He abandoned his spot under the table, his toenails clacking on the floor as he shoved himself into the space between Sam and Adah, his teeth bared in a menacing scowl Adah hadn't seen before, but welcomed in this moment.

"I'm not interested." She kept her tone firm, not wanting him to see that his closeness scared her. "I don't even know you—"

"Sure you do. Any friend of Jackson's is a friend of yours, right?" Sam gave Captain a vicious shove with the point of his cowboy boot. The dog rolled back and smacked against the cabinets. His agitated barking filled the kitchen. Sam seemed oblivious to it. He tilted his head forward, his lips so close to her ear she could feel his stinking breath on her cheek. "My truck's parked out front. I can fire her up and take you down by the lake. We can be alone."

She pushed back as hard as she could. "Get off me."

"Hey, what's Captain barking about?" Jackson barged into the kitchen. He covered the distance from the door to Adah in fast forward. He shoved Sam back with such force that the other man banged up against the cabinets much the same way Captain had done a few seconds before. "What is wrong with you?"

"Don't get all worked up, buddy." Sam rubbed his shoulder, his expression as innocent as a kid caught stealing a pie from a windowsill. "She said you was just friends."

Captain continued his frenzied barking, his mouth inches from Sam's ankle. "Call off your dog, man. I didn't do nothing. I was just being friendly!"

"Captain, stop, stop!" Jackson grabbed the dog's collar and yanked him back. "Good boy, good boy, good job."

For a second no one spoke or moved, the only sound their breathing and Captain's agitated panting.

"I was just being friendly—"

"Get out." Jackson jabbed a finger at the back door. "Don't let the door hit you on the way out."

Still grinning, Sam rubbed his arm. "Come on, it was just a misunderstanding. I didn't mean anything by it. Tell him, Adah."

Adah shook her head. "Maybe you were confused, but I wasn't."

Jackson wedged himself between Adah and the other man. She backed toward the hallway, relief so intense she wasn't sure her legs would hold her long enough to get up the stairs. Jackson glanced at her, one hand hovering near her shoulder. "You okay?"

She nodded, sure her voice would betray her fear if she spoke.

"You sure?"

His hand landed on her shoulder and squeezed. "Did he hurt you?"

"No."

He let go and turned back to Sam. "I said get out."

"Oh, come on, don't be that way."

"Get out."

"You're never going to make points in this town if you don't have a sense of humor." Despite his words, Sam eased toward the back door. "You need people like me."

"No. I don't." Jackson got in the other man's face. "Out."

Sam shrugged, his long hair bouncing on his shoulders, and strolled out the back door, his smirk still firmly in place.

Relief made Adah lightheaded. She slipped out of the kitchen and started toward the stairs, hoping the shaking muscles in her legs wouldn't let her down.

"Adah, wait." Jackson followed. He slapped one hand on the banister and blocked the way. "Come on, wait. I'm sorry about that. I'm so sorry. I would never have invited him if I knew he was like that. You gotta believe me."

Captain in the lead, she dodged him and started up the stairs.

"Adah! Forget about him. Come on, come sing with us. We need to practice."

"If those are the kind of musicians you know, I'll pass." She didn't look back, but she could hear his boots thudding on the steps behind her. "You'd better clean up that mess before Charlene gets home. She'll be madder than a hornet."

"They're not my friends. They're just guys who know guys. That's how you get into the shows here—by knowing someone. I'm sorry, really I am."

"Your apology is accepted." She hated the trembling in her voice, but she couldn't help it. Sam had scared her, much as she would never admit it. "I'm going to my room now. I'm tired."

"Come down. Sing with us. Have a drink. It'll calm your nerves." Jackson stopped at the top of the stairs. "Rick and Derek are good guys. I promise."

"That shows how much you know about me. I don't drink." Adah turned to face him. This was as far as she dared let him go. It wouldn't be proper for them to talk in her room. "You shouldn't either."

His gaze flickered from the floor to her, confronting her head-on. It was full of something she couldn't quite identify. Beseeching. Uncertain. Longing. "So I had a few. What's going on here is enough to drive any man to drink."

"What's going on? What exactly is going on here?"

"You know."

"I don't know. I only know I came here to write songs and play music."

"With me. You came with me, Adah."

"We made rules—"

"I know about the rules. I'm abiding by the rules. But I'm hoping you'll feel like bending the rules one of these days."

The hoarse emotion in those words warmed Adah's face and neck. She swallowed against the feelings that welled in her, so caught was she by the longing in his gaze and her own terrible sense of loneliness. She was alone except for Jackson and he had been there for her. He'd brought her to a place where she could have her dream. Because he cared about her.

His hand, fingers warm, came out and touched hers. "Please."

She shook her head but didn't move her hand. "I can't."

"Why?"

"You move too fast."

"I'll slow down." He withdrew his hand, but the touch of his fingers lingered on hers. "I promise. Just come make music with me. That would make me happy."

His happiness depended on her. The burden felt like a wagon of bricks balanced across her shoulders. "I will, but not tonight."

Disappointment pinched the skin around his eyes and mouth. "Tomorrow or the next day?"

"The music, yes."

"Thanks for the crumbs."

"I told you, this isn't how we do this. I'm sorry."

"Okay. Come on, Cap, let's go." His hair hung in his eyes, making him look like a little boy who needed a haircut and a hug. "Let's go, boy."

Captain flopped down at Adah's feet, laid his head on his paws, and let out a woof of a sigh.

"You stole my dog."

"I did not." She liked Cap's company. It wasn't her fault the feeling was mutual. "His choice."

"Nothing's ever your fault, is it?" Jackson's tone softened to almost a whisper as he pivoted and moved away. The distance between them grew and she had the sudden urge to grab the back of his belt and hang on. The merest shred of dignity held her back. He ducked his head, still muttering. "Man's best friend, yeah, right!"

What did he mean by that? She rushed into her room, nearly running, and shut the door without posing the question aloud. She leaned against it, her throat aching with each breath. What was she doing here? What had she done? She felt like the Israelites stumbling around in the wilderness. She couldn't bear forty years like this. She missed Mudder and the kinner. She missed Matthew.

The thought stung like an arrow that found its mark right below her collarbone. Right by her heart.

Gott, I don't know what I'm doing. I'm sorry. I'm lost.

"Adah, come on. I didn't mean it. Come sing with me!"

The sound of Jackson's voice, rough yet tender, hoarse with emotion, wound its way under the door and touched her cheeks and her neck. Shivering, she whirled and turned the old-fashioned key stuck in the door knob. She hadn't felt the need to use it.

Until now. She couldn't be sure if she were locking him out or herself in.

Chapter 32

Matthew rolled over and stared at his bedroom ceiling. After a few seconds he rolled to his side again, letting one bare foot hang over the side of the narrow bunk bed. Despite the open window within reach, the night air hung heavy, the humidity nearly choking him. No breeze ruffled the curtains. His nightshirt stuck to his chest, sodden with sweat. The sheets under him seemed hot to the touch.

The heat had never bothered him before. He preferred the deep warmth of the sun to the bitter cold that made his fingers feel brittle and numb even in the warmest of gloves. So why couldn't he sleep now? He'd spent all day harvesting milo from sunrise to sunset with barely a break for the noon meal and supper. He should be weary to the bone. He was.

Just not sleepy. A song Adah used to sing while they drove into town popped into his head, the words whirling around in a circle. He wanted to capture them and throw them away. He wriggled until he lay on his back again. The darkness above him revealed nothing new.

"Go to sleep already." Rueben's voice floated from the big bed he occupied with Abram and Alexander on the other side of the room. "It's bad enough we're all packed in this room like sardines. All that tossing and turning isn't helping."

Rueben hadn't complained before about sharing the room and the bed. Probably because he liked having Elizabeth's little sister Loretta around the house. "Then sleep."

"I'd like to. Your wiggling around like a hog in a gunny sack and your bed squeaking ain't helping."

"Talking doesn't help. You'll wake the twins."

"They could sleep through a tornado." Rueben's whisper grew louder. "Whatever's eating you, leave it until morning."

"What do you know about anything?" His brother had barely started going to the singings. As far as Matthew knew he didn't even have a girl yet. "Your biggest worry is someone beating you to the last piece of bacon at breakfast."

"With all these folks at the table, a guy could starve to death." The hiss in Reuben's voice softened. The boy did love to eat. Just the thought of food made him happy. "I may be younger than you, but I know better than to worry something to death the way you're doing."

Matthew knew better too. He simply couldn't figure out how to stop it. The Bible said not to worry. Luke and Silas said not to worry. How did a man turn it off? Like a lantern knob? "Hush up and go to sleep."

"If it's about Adah, go get her back already so we can all get some sleep."

Matthew sat up, the bed frame protesting. Rueben groaned and threw a pillow over his head.

Matthew ignored him as he leaned against the window and stuck his head out, trying to get a breath of fresh air, feeling as if he would never breathe right again. His chest would hurt until the day he died. Rueben was right about the worrying. Matthew had said his prayers for Adah before he laid down to a sleep that wouldn't come. He should've received the peace that passed understanding. Gott's will. Gott's timing. His worry reflected a lack of faith he found troublesome. Gott might bring Adah back. He might not. Whatever happened, Matthew needed to learn to live with it.

Maybe God intended for him to go to Branson and bring her home. To return the lamb to the fold. Maybe God was waiting for him to strike out in faith and convince Adah her eternal salvation rested in returning to her community and her faith.

Luke and Thomas said to wait.

Daed and Mudder said to move on.

Groossdaadi said to follow his heart and not his head.

Even his little bruder had cast a vote.

Too many voices talking in his head. He couldn't hear himself think. No wonder he couldn't sleep. He needed a drink of water. He needed to cool his throat and his face. He jerked on his pants and padded barefoot from the room, across the hallway, and down the stairs. Halfway down, he heard a noise in the kitchen. A pot or a pan banged. Something like silverware clattered.

He paused, one foot on the next step down.

A thief stealing pots and pans. Didn't seem likely. Thieves didn't take time to cook and he could definitely smell the aroma of beef stroganoff wafting through the air.

They never even locked their doors at night. If someone wanted something, they were welcome to it provided they moved along without bothering anyone. However, he might draw the line at Molly's beef stroganoff. It was mighty fine.

More likely someone else couldn't sleep. It had to be at least ten-thirty or eleven. Who would be up at this hour?

He hesitated. Best to make sure it wasn't Groossdaadi trying to cook for himself. He would start a fire and burn down the house if left on his own.

Suddenly feeling more urgency, Matthew sped down the remaining stairs and across the front room. He popped through the kitchen door, not giving the cook a chance to run out. Molly stood with a pot in one hand, her startled expression illuminated by the kerosene lantern hanging from its hook over the sink. "What are you doing up?"

Matthew followed her gaze to the person sitting at the kitchen prep table. Richard Bontrager.

"I…" He managed to close his mouth as he searched for the thing to say. He had no idea. None. He'd been—he could admit it—jealous when he'd seen Adah talking to Richard. "I was thirsty. I didn't know anyone was up."

"Evening." Richard stretched his long legs under the table and planted both elbows on the pine. "It's fiercely hot, isn't it?"

"It is." Matthew hesitated in the doorway. "I'll just get a glass…"

"I'm heating up some of my beef stroganoff. Richard said he was a little hungry." Molly stepped toward the counter, the pot still held high. "You want some?"

"Nee." Matthew grabbed the first glass on the shelf and picked up the pitcher. His hands didn't want to cooperate but he managed to fill the glass without spilling all over himself. "I'll get out of your way."

"No need to rush off." Something in Richard's tone said he was enjoying this strange little encounter. "Have a seat."

Courting late at night was meant to be between two people. Three definitely became a crowd. "Nee. Got a lot of work tomorrow."

"True. I'm still working with Peter Daugherty. At least two more days before I head to Tobias's."

Matthew edged toward the door. "Don't look like rain anytime soon. We should be done with the milo by the end of the week."

"Gott willing."

"Gott willing."

Matthew strode through the front room. Molly had a special friend. How could he have missed that? Did Mudder and Daed know?

"Matthew!"

Molly's loud whisper forced him to stop at the bottom of the stairs. He turned. His sister smiled at him, her eyes bright in the lantern's light. "Don't say anything."

"Courting is private."

She nodded, her smile spreading. He'd never seen his sister look so happy. "It's Adah's doing, you know?"

Adah's doing. "What do you mean?"

"She did a little matchmaking." Molly's expression turned wistful. "I was wrong about her. I wish I could thank her."

She whirled and disappeared into the kitchen.

Adah the matchmaker. She'd done something nice for Molly before leaving and shattering the lives of her parents. Before shattering his life.

In all of this, Adah remained a mystery he couldn't solve.

Chapter 33

"You need some different clothes."

Surprised at Jackson's tone, Adah looked up from the notebook she gripped between two sweaty hands. Her stomach did cartwheels, making it hard to sit still on the plush sofa. The waiting room with its tangerine walls hurt her eyes. The waiting room that led to where Mac McMillan was meeting them. She searched for a wastebasket and found one in the corner, all the while hoping she wouldn't need to vomit it in. "What's wrong with my clothes?"

"You can't dress like a Puritan and expect people to notice you. Not for the right reasons, anyway." Jackson shifted his guitar case on his knees. Despite being clean shaven this morning, he looked bleary eyed and groggy. He'd been silent and morose the entire drive into town. There had been no mention of the previous evening. Whatever heated emotion flowed between them only hours earlier now ebbed, leaving a cool expanse of empty space. "This town is all about the sparkle and shine."

"I thought it was about the music." She smoothed her apron, dropped the notebook, and leaned over to pick it up. It slipped from her damp fingers a second time. "I don't want people to notice me. Only my music."

"It's a package deal. You gotta market yourself."

"Market myself? I only want to write songs…and sometimes play them." Without being bothered by drunken cowboys. She kept that part to herself. "I don't need to draw attention to myself with a bunch of shiny stuff."

"We've been over this. With your voice, you could do so much more." Jackson squirmed on his seat and pressed a hand to his forehead, massaging with two fingers the spot between his eyes. "You don't have to be so contrary. Or talk so loud."

"I'm not talking loud." She raised the volume a little and took childish pleasure in his wince. "People who drink too much can expect to feel bad the next day."

From what she'd heard. She'd found him sprawled on the couch, head back, mouth open, snoring so loudly the furniture seemed to shake. Even Captain had forsaken his owner and taken refuge in a corner in the kitchen. She'd given him an extra dog biscuit and a good scratch around his ears in thanks for his brave defense of her the previous evening. From the surly look on Charlene's face at the breakfast table, she'd been the one to clean up the mess. Adah regretted that. Had the circumstances been different, she would've done it. The thought of Sam's putrid breath on her face made her stomach rock again.

"I thought you guys were into forgiveness." Jackson reminded her of her little brother whining about not getting to go hunting with the men. The thought wedged between her shoulders like the blade of an ax. *Don't think about Abram. Or the rest of the family.* Jackson cleared his throat so loudly she jumped. "Are you even listening to me?"

"I'm trying not to, but your whining is coming through loud and clear."

"Are you two fighting?" A tall, gaunt man wearing a gray cowboy hat clumped down the hall toward them in what looked like rattlesnake skin boots. He had an accent straight out of Texas. "No need. You're both right."

"Mr. McMillan." Jackson stood. Adah followed suit. "Thanks for seeing us."

"Call me Mac." Mac looked Adah over through round rimless glasses that perched halfway down his bent nose. "I don't usually do this, but Clayton has a good ear for talent. I listened to your song and it wasn't half bad."

Was that a compliment? From the look on Jackson's face it surely was. "Thanks. I—we appreciate that." Jackson had developed a stutter. "Does that mean you'll represent us?"

"Whoa, hold your horses. Let's not get ahead of ourselves." Mac turned to Adah. "Turn around."

"What?"

"Turn around. I want to see all of you."

Feeling like a horse at the auction house, she did as she was told. Jackson struck a pose next to Mac. The two of them looking her over made Adah want to run for the wastebasket. Matthew had been right about the ogling.

"I'm thinking an electric blue cowgirl shirt, fringe on the sleeves, a matching skirt, more fringe, white cowboy boots. Hair loose down her back." Jackson spoke to Mac as if Adah had left the room. "What are you thinking?"

"A little Dale Evans?" Mac shook his head. "Been done. You got yourself something different here. A novelty. A little singing Amish girl. A pretty one. Clayton was right about that."

Jackson pursed his lips, his eyebrows drawn up on his forehead. "You think folks will go for that? I was thinking bling was the thing."

"We got a lot of family shows here in Branson. The Amish thing is a different twist, a novelty. I could see one of the traditional shows letting her sing a song or two."

"I thought we would be a duet." Jackson's smile had faded into the woodwork. "I'd play and we'd both sing."

Mac cocked his head, his gaze still on Adah. She wanted him to look somewhere else. Badly. "We'll see. She'll need to let her hair down, but the little hat thing stays. And she'll need makeup. Not a lot, but some. Otherwise the stage lights will wash out that pretty face something fierce. Right now I want to get you into the studio to record a demo song. I lined up some musicians to back you up."

"We don't have money for that—"

"This one's on me. If I decide to manage you, I need something more professional to work with. Let's go. Follow me."

"Now?"

"Now."

Jackson couldn't move fast enough. Adah, on the other hand, found she couldn't move. After a few seconds, he looked around. "Adah?"

"We have to sing now?" she whispered, not wanting to hurt his chances.

"Now. Come on, girl, this is our chance."

She shambled after him on legs that seemed to have turned to wet hay.

The studio was small and surprisingly cool. Air rushed from overhead vents, making goose bumps prickle on her arms. A man with an electric guitar stood to one side, a drummer in the middle, and a bass guitarist on the other. What would Jackson play? His hangdog expression suggested he was thinking the same thing.

"Okay, missy, take a seat on the stool there in the middle and adjust that microphone so it's close, but not too close, if you know what I mean."

"What about Jackson?" The words came out in a stutter. "Where's he going to stand?"

"Right there next to you. Come on, Jackson, the lady's waiting."

Finally, Jackson's nerves had shown up. His face looked pale in the studio lights. He nodded to the other musicians. They nodded and everyone shook hands all around. No one seemed to notice Adah's agitation. The oatmeal she ate for breakfast threatened to reappear.

"Okay, let's get a sound level. Adah, your name's Adah, right?" A man wearing earphones behind the glass waved at her. "Adah?"

"Yes...yes, it's Adah."

"Sing a few notes for us so we can adjust the sound levels."

"Sing? Me?" Warm blood rushed Adah's face. Her lungs stopped working. A noose tightened around her throat. She cleared her throat, the sound like a frog. "Now?"

"That's why you're in the studio, honey. To sing. Jackson, you gonna strum that guitar, or what? We ain't got all day."

"Sure. Absolutely." Jackson fumbled with the clasps on the guitar case. "Right, Adah, we can do that new song we've been working on."

"I gave the boys here your original song. They know it." Mac sank onto a chair behind the glass. "Let's start with that. Come on, girl, you'll sound even better with a real band and good sound equipment."

Her mouth so dry her tongue stuck to the roof, Adah tried to swallow. Her throat constricted.

Jackson strummed his guitar. The other musicians joined in. The familiar music rolled over Adah. She searched her brain. Not one word of the song materialized. *Come on, come on.* Nothing.

"She does speak, doesn't she?" His irritation apparent despite his attempts to smooth it away, Mac moved restlessly. He pointed to a gold watch on his wrist. "I have another band lined up for studio time."

"Sure, she does. Come on, Adah." Jackson strummed again. "You can do it, girl."

"She looks like she's gonna hurl." Mac opened the door and slipped inside the tiny studio. Now they truly had a crowd. "She has performed in public before, right?"

"Well, not exactly, but you heard the recording."

"I need to know she can get up on a stage and sing in front of thousands."

Thousands. Lightheaded, Adah closed her eyes. That made the swaying of the room worse. She opened them before she fell off the stool.

"Adah, come on, Adah." Jackson's hand gripped her elbow. "Pretend we're in the back of my truck down by the pond. We're singing, just the two of us."

"Okay." A squeak in her voice made more heat rush to her face. Her ears were on fire. "You start."

He plucked a few notes and began to sing. The band ran with it. She listened to his voice, so familiar now, and tried to find hers. The first verse came and went. "Now, Adah, come on."

She opened her mouth and sang the chorus with him. Breathy, soft, barely noticeable against his rich baritone. She stumbled twice over the words, which seemed to play a game of hide and seek in her brain.

Jackson stopped playing. The other instruments petered out. Everyone looked at her. "Come on, Adah." Jackson sounded desperate now. He glanced at the big window. "You can do this. You can do it! Come on!"

Adah opened her mouth. A squeaky little note came out. Like someone squeezed a stuffed animal too hard.

"Well." Mac wrinkled his nose, making his glasses bump up and down. He glanced at his watch again. "That's gonna have to be it for today. I'm backing up folks to squeeze you in."

"She can do better. She's just nervous. She'll get her stage legs, give her a chance."

Why was Jackson trying so hard to persuade the man? She obviously did not have what it took. If she couldn't sing in front of a few strangers, how could she do it in front of hundreds or thousands? Mac's expression said he was thinking something along the same lines. Still, he held out his hand to her. "Nice to meet you, Miss Adah."

She forced herself to take it. Her hand was enveloped in one three times its size. "I'm sorry."

"Don't be sorry, little lady. Performing ain't for everyone. You might be more suited as a songwriter. Nothing wrong with that."

"But the plan is for us to perform together." Jackson insisted as he slipped the guitar strap over his head and laid his guitar in its case. "A voice like hers shouldn't go to waste."

Mac shook with him as well. "I got plenty of little girls with big voices wanting my attention. Stage fright is a big bump in the road from where I sit. If she can't sing for me, how's she going to sing in public?"

"She'll get over it."

"Best do it quick."

Mac thanked the other musicians, who were already leaving the studio, their instruments packed away. How often did they get called out to do this? Did it matter to them if she sang or not? Most likely they received their payment, regardless.

As the big man strolled away, Adah let out her breath. "Why were you so stubborn, like an old mule?" She hadn't realized how angry she was with Jackson until that moment. It rushed out of her in giant, hot, crashing waves. "Why did you put me on the spot like that?"

"Put *you* on the spot?" he sputtered. "Put *you* on the spot? This is why we came here. Do you realize that you just blew the biggest chance we had to make it here? You didn't just blow it for you. You blew for me."

He snapped the clasps shut on the guitar case, jerked it from the stool, and shoved through the door, leaving Adah standing alone in the studio. The sound technician, a chunky man in a too small T-shirt featuring a picture of Johnny Cash, smiled and gave her a thumbs-up on the other side of the glass. "Why don't you practice without an audience?"

Because her lungs refused to accept oxygen. Because little pinpoints of black danced in front of her eyes. Because her mouth was so dry, her tongue might crumble. "I don't know."

"Honey, I've done this a lot of times. You get used to it. Give it time, you'll fly." His enormous handlebar mustache wiggled when he talked in a voice that seemed too high for such a big man. He grinned and pointed to his earphones. "I promise not to listen. I'll do some paperwork. Promise."

How sweet of him. Why not? What would it prove? Nothing. No one would hear except the nice man behind the window. And what did he care? He got paid, either way. Adah hesitated, then grabbed the microphone so it swung a little closer. She opened her mouth and sang. Just her voice with no instruments.

The entire song. No hitches.

And no audience.

Chapter 34

By the time Adah made it to where Jackson had parked the truck, he was gone. He'd left a note under a windshield wiper. *I went to get something to eat at the restaurant on the corner. J.* Adah put a hand to her forehead to shade her eyes from the noonday sun. The neon sign said BAR AND GRILL. So had Jackson gone there to eat or to drink? She'd never been in a bar. Could it possibly be more grill than bar? It was noon. Surely people were eating lunch rather than drinking. It didn't matter, anyway. She'd let Jackson down, and she had to march in there and apologize. She owed him that. Ignoring the sweat that trickled down her neck and dampened her dress, she trudged to the corner. She opened the door and a gust of AC-cooled air brushed her face. Inside, the smell of old grease and French fries greeted her. A big screen TV featuring men in what looked like swimming suits punching at each other blared, competing with rock music with too much bass emanating from some unseen source.

The noise made her wince and rub the aching spot on her temple. A headache pulsed between her eyes. At least hers wasn't brought on by drink. Her stomach rumbled. She'd been too nervous to eat much of that oatmeal. A server brushed past her, muscles rigid in her thick arms as she balanced heavy china plates of huge hamburgers and thick-cut French fries in both hands. "Help yourself to a seat, honey. The hostess called in sick and her replacement won't be here until two."

"I'm looking for…"

She saw him then. Jackson hadn't taken a table. He sat alone at the long, slick bar, shot glasses, two empty, three full, arranged in a row in front of him. His reflection in the long mirror that covered the wall behind the bar was dark, pensive. He lifted a glass to his lips, opened his mouth, and tossed back the amber liquid in one quick flick of his wrist.

His gaze caught hers. He smirked, a painful twist of his lips, and swiveled to face her, disappointment etched in the way he held his body stiff and upright. "Hey, Amish girl. Join me." He patted the seat next to him. "A little hair of the dog, so to speak. I'm practicing my technique."

"Isn't it a little early in the day for drinking?" She didn't have much experience with it, but mostly the Englisch boys drank at parties at night, after dark, when they could hide it from their parents. "Maybe we should get something to eat."

"Where are my manners?" He stood. "A man always stands when a lady comes into the room. That's what my momma says. Sit, sit!"

"I can't sit here."

"Sure you can." He doffed his hat and slapped it on the bar. "I'll order you a glass of milk, how about that?"

"You're making fun of me, aren't you?"

"I would never do that." He laughed, a half snort. "I would never make fun of the girl I love—"

"Stop saying that."

"Why? It's true. And why would I make fun of the Amish girl who wants to be a singer but can't sing a decent note in front of anyone but me?"

"I never said I wanted to be a singer." Adah shut her mouth and looked around. The other patrons were busy with their food, chewing and talking, living their own lives. They didn't care about her drama. Or Jackson's. "I wanted to write songs. All this stuff…this is your dream."

"So why'd you come with me?"

The memory of that one kiss still hung suspended between them. It couldn't go any further than that one kiss. She knew it and so did he. Yet here she stood. "I don't know."

"Nice." He grabbed another shot glass and tilted it to his mouth, draining it just as efficiently as he had the previous shot. "Ahhh, nice. Smooth." He smacked the glass on the bar and wiped his mouth with the back of his sleeve. "Nice. You know what, Amish girl, that's fine. I can make my own way. I don't need you to make my dreams come true."

He staggered past her, brushing so close she smelled his sweat and his longing, and stomped toward the door.

"Jackson!"

The door opened, letting sunlight flood into the dark recesses of the bar. It blinded her for a second. She put her hand to her forehead to shade her eyes. By the time they adjusted, he was gone.

Jackson was right. Why had she come if not to sing? To sing with him and to find out where this road would take them. Both of them. *Gott, forgive me. I'm lost. I don't know what I'm doing.*

What now? *Gott, what now?*

Any attempt to hear His response would be futile in the midst of the blaring music and strident sound of an announcer shouting the play-by-play involving two men beating each other to a bloody pulp.

Here she stood in the middle of a bar. How did she get home?

To the house at the lake? Or to New Hope? Her real home.

She couldn't go home. Daed wouldn't understand. Matthew had already moved on. The life she'd had in New Hope no longer existed. She slapped her hand to her mouth to hold back the sobs. The only thing worse than a rebellious, stubborn soul was a whiny one.

"Do you want to order something?" The same waitress passed by, this time with plates of steaming chicken fried steak and gravy in both hands. The aroma made Adah's mouth water and her stomach rumble. "Have a seat. I'll get you a menu."

"No, no thank you." Adah patted her denim bag, aware that it held exactly five dollars and six cents. She'd given her nest egg to Charlene to cover room and board. "I changed my mind."

The waitress shrugged, making the beads in her multitude of tiny braids bounce on her head. "Better hurry or that man of yours will leave you standing on the curb."

"He's not my man…"

"That's a shame. He's cute as can be, honey. You'd be crazy to let him get away."

"He's a friend…"

The waitress had already moved on.

Would Jackson still be her friend if he thought she couldn't help him reach his dream or rush into being what he would call a girlfriend? If she couldn't sing and perform in public or let him get closer to her, would he have any use for her?

Jackson might leave her stranded, but she could still do what she needed to survive in this strange new world. She would get a job.

Chapter 35

Wiping his face and neck with a bandana, Matthew stomped his feet outside the door to the kitchen, trying to shake the worst of the dirt from his boots, and then opened the screen door. The heat billowed inside just as it did outside. From the smell of it, supper involved fried pork chops and fried potatoes and onions. His stomach growled at the thought. It had been a long time since the noonday meal of navy beans, ham, and cornbread. He hoped his nose was right. It rarely failed him. Ella looked up from her spot next to the prep table where she dropped rolls into a basket big enough to hold a load of laundry.

"Ouch, yikes, hot, hot!" she yelped as she tossed in another one. "Wow, those are hot."

"As is to be expected when you take them out of the oven, little sister." Matthew ruffled the top of her head, shoving her kapp a little to one side. "Ever hear of oven mitts?"

Grinning, she ducked away from his touch. "Didn't have time. Daed's chomping at the bit to eat. You're late."

"I wanted to get the last of the alfalfa cut so it has time to dry. We may get some rain later in the week."

"They keep saying that, but it never comes." At eight years old, Ella sounded like an old hand at this farming business. "We're more likely to get a dust storm than a rainstorm."

Matthew stuck his hands in a tub of water in the sink and washed them. "Mostly they're just guessing, I reckon."

"You got a letter."

He turned to look at Ella, a young miniature of his mudder, all bony and angular, who grinned at him, obviously delighting in being the bearer of such surprising news. "I got a letter?"

He didn't ever remember getting his own letter. Not even after they moved to New Hope from Bliss Creek. All his closest friends came with him. Family sent letters to Mudder and Daed who passed them around after they finished reading them.

"So did Molly. She ran off to her room to read it."

"Molly got a letter? From the same person?"

"I don't know. She didn't say. She just got all excited like she does and hightailed it out of here."

Smart girl. She wanted to savor the moment before everyone clamored for her to share her news. Letters were big. "Where's mine?"

"Mudder put it on Daed's desk in the front room. Better get in there or all the pork chops and taters will be gone before you get a bite."

Ella was right about that, but he was more worried about keeping Daed waiting than the food. "I'll read it afterward."

He followed her out to the dining room, where Molly was pouring water into the glasses set at each plate. She seemed intent on the task, her face placid. They hadn't spoken of the other night when he'd found her visiting with Richard in the kitchen. It wasn't his business, but he was glad for her. Richard seemed like a decent man. If God's plan was for her to be his fraa, then they would both be blessed. He tried to ignore the thought that he would never have such a chance himself. Whatever God's plan, he couldn't see it. Maybe he wore blinders. Maybe God had set an opportunity in front of him and he'd missed it somehow. He gritted his teeth and strode across the room. Molly looked up. Her cheeks turned a deep pink.

"Did you hear? Did Ella tell you I got a letter?" She poured water so fast it sloshed from her glass in her hand and dripped on the floor. "Whoops! Did you get yours?"

"She did and not yet." He handed her the nearest napkin. "I'll do it after supper. Where's Daed?"

"He said something about getting a Band-Aid and went upstairs. He'll be right back."

"The letter will wait until after we eat."

"You have to read it." Molly's face turned from pink to red and she leaned in close. She smelled like bleach and fresh soap. He could always tell when it was laundry day—aside from the rows of wet clothes drying on the lines outside. "Mine's from Adah."

Matthew's lungs forgot what to do. He let his hands fall to the back of a chair in front of him, his fingers gripping the familiar knotted pine. The room spun until it became a white blur.

"Go get the letter!" Molly dropped her voice to a whisper as if someone lurked nearby. "Hurry before Daed gets back."

Matthew's body obeyed even as his thoughts cartwheeled back and forth through his mind. Did Adah want to come home? Did she want him to come get her? Was she sorry? Was she saying goodbye forever?

The questions whirled around him. Supper or no supper, he needed answers. He'd waited long enough.

He headed toward the front room. Daed, who smoothed a Band-Aid over his thumb, met him halfway. "We're about to sit down to eat." Daed's raised eyebrows said it all. "Your groossmammi and groossdaadi are waiting."

"Let the boy take care of business." Groossdaadi rose from the rocking chair parked in front of an empty fireplace. "Didn't you hear? He got a letter from his special friend."

Groossdaadi's hearing was mighty good for an old man. Daed's gaze darkened. "We're about to eat. You want to read a letter, do it. But we're not waiting. Food's getting cold."

Matthew glanced back at Molly. She gave him the *go-you-won't-regret-it* look.

"I'll make it quick."

"See that you do."

It wasn't about the letter. Daed didn't want him thinking about

Adah. Or worse, trying to convince her to come back. Daed had forgotten what this felt like. Matthew made a beeline for the old, scarred pine desk and the mail Mudder had stacked on top of it. The *Budget*. A seed catalogue. A letter from Aenti Hazel. A flier about a horse auction. There it was. Small, rectangular, and blue. Adah's familiar loopy cursive on the front. A stamp of the U.S. flag in one corner. The inked postmark and return address read *Branson, MO*.

His legs went weak. He inhaled and sank into Daed's straight-back chair. At first he intended to open the envelope slowly, to preserve it. His fingers shook. *Get a grip.* It was just a letter from a girl who walked away from her family and her faith and her future with him. Better to rip it off fast, like a bandage stuck to his wounded skin. He unfolded the blue and purple stationery. Monarch butterflies fluttered in one corner. The handwriting wavered before his eyes.

He breathed and began to read.

> *Dear Matthew,*
>
> *I can only start with I'm sorry. That's the first thing. There are so many things I want to tell you. I'm okay. I wouldn't say fine, but okay. I hope you weren't worried. I know I don't have a right to expect you to worry about me. But I know you. You wouldn't be able to help yourself because you are a kind, decent man.*

Matthew gritted his teeth against the desire to say something uncharitable. Heaping compliments on him did nothing to help her case. He was like every Plain man he knew. He worked hard and tried to conform to God's will. She need not ply him with sweet words intended to soothe, like a mother with a child.

> *I am sorry if I hurt you, but I suspect your heart is already headed in another direction. I came to talk to you that night before I left. I thought if I could talk to you, I might feel differently about staying in New Hope. I might be able to see my way clear to a future that didn't include music. You were on the front porch courting Elizabeth and I realized I waited too*

long. I'd dabbled in things you couldn't understand. I let things happen that should never happen to a Plain girl like me—not if I wanted you for my special friend. So I did what I thought was best for us both. I came here to start a new life.

I don't know what will happen, but I can only move forward with my dream of making music. My dream of being your fraa is gone. I look back at the past few months and I can't figure out how I got to this place in my life. I feel like a cat chasing her own tail. I can never quite catch up. I can't catch my breath because it hurts so much. My throat aches with it, like a permanent cold. I've only been here a small time and I figure I'll get used to it. There's no going back now. I know you won't have me. So I'll try to make the best of it and sleep in the bed I made for myself, as my daed would say. I just wanted to say how sorry I am. I hope you are happy with Elizabeth. She will make a good fraa and mudder. Much better than me. Of that I am sure. God bless you.

Adah

Matthew stared at the words, reading them over and over again. He could still feel the heat of the sun on his face that night on the porch and taste the ice cream and the apple pie. He remembered the smell of the honeysuckle on the lattice. He remembered the look on her face. She never gave him a chance to explain. Typical Adah. Running full tilt, never taking the time to get all the information before making a decision. That was his Adah. Was.

Now she made a new life in Branson.

He trudged along here in New Hope, trying to figure out how to do the same. They both wondered how they'd managed to get to this place. She felt like a cat chasing her own tail. He felt like a caged mountain lion, prowling in circles, banging against the walls, wanting out, wanting to find the only woman who mattered to him.

"What did she say?"

He looked up to find Molly standing in the doorway. "She's fine."

"She doesn't sound fine in my letter."

"What did she say?"

Molly held it out. "Read it."

"It's not private?" He hesitated, wanting to read it, but not wanting to feel more blows raining down on his head. "Are you sure?"

"She says she's sorry she didn't finish what she started."

"What she started?" He stared at the envelope as if it were a rabid dog about to lunge at him. It sounded like a familiar theme. She hadn't finished her business with him either. "What did she start with you?"

"Richard, silly. She doesn't know that we're..." Molly's cheeks grew an even brighter pink. She ducked her head. "You know."

"I'd rather not know."

"Well, that's water under the bridge, isn't it?" Molly sounded so much like Mudder in that moment, Matthew could imagine her with a baby on one hip and a plate of cookies in her hand, herding her flock to Sunday prayer service. "What I'm saying is she doesn't realize what she did for me. How she helped make my life so much sweeter."

"At least she did one good thing before she left."

"Adah is a kind, sweet girl who's lost. She needs us to help bring her back into the fold." Molly shook the letter at Matthew. "This proves it. She thinks she's done nothing but bad, but it's not true. She's done good things. Good things for me. I want her to know that. I want to help her."

"Molly..." Matthew pushed the letter back at her. "She made her choices. She has to recognize the error of her way and return here of her own accord. That's what Luke and Thomas think. And Silas. And Daed."

Molly took a step closer. "They're old men. They've forgotten what it's like to be our age." Her voice dropped to a whisper. "They're wrong. I know that sounds prideful coming from a girl like me, but Luke went after Josiah when he went to Wichita and got mixed up with that Mennonite girl."

"This is different."

"How?"

"Josiah needed to come home because his parents had died. Emma and Luke and the rest of the kinner needed him home."

"I'm talking about the second time."

"He almost died. They had to bring him home to take care of him."

"Adah might not be dying physically, but she's dying spiritually. Her spirit is dying."

"You're a fanciful girl. It must be all that book reading."

"Don't you feel like you're dying inside? If Richard left, I don't know what—"

"Don't." He held up a hand. "I don't want to talk about my own sister's courting."

"Fine. Let's talk about your courting then."

"Nee—"

"You need Adah home." Molly was like the wind that whipped the bushes around and turned them into tumbleweed. She couldn't be stopped. "And she needs to come home before she loses faith. She probably thinks it's too late. But it's never too late to come back to God."

She was right. Adah needed to come home—if not for him, then for her community of faith. "Thomas says we have to wait until she's ready to come home. She has to decide for herself. She has to want this life."

"Maybe she needs a nudge." Molly stuck her hands on her hips, looking just like Mudder when she had a bone to pick with Daed. "What are you waiting for?"

"The right time."

"See that you don't wait too long." She turned and marched away.

Her words echoed those of Irene Knepp. How long was too long? Matthew waited until Molly disappeared into the dining room. He ran a finger over the blue envelope. It was wrinkled from his grip. He smoothed it. *Gott, please. I need to know what to do. Your plan. Your timing. Your will. But I need to know what to do.*

Having no pockets, he did the next best thing and tucked Adah's letter inside his shirt. Close to his heart.

Chapter 36

Adah shoved the mop and broom into the closet next to the empty bucket and closed the door. She brushed her hands together and looked around. The coffeehouse looked spiffy. It had that rich, mouth-watering aroma of coffee beans and freshly brewed coffee. No amount of bleach and glass cleaner and dish soap would take that away. The café was full of round tables that seated no more than four, mostly two, and was small compared to the houses she used to clean. People came here to sip coffee, chat, and use the free wi-fi. She wasn't totally clear on what that was, but it didn't matter as long as they bought the cookies and muffins she made. She could do this job with one hand tied behind her back. For the amount they paid her, she felt she should do it twice as often. Jolene had left her to finish mopping the floors and wiping down the counters, but the assistant manager had taken care of the coffee urns and running the dishwasher. Adah appreciated that. She still had a lingering sense of unease when she dealt with electrical appliances.

Fingering the check in the pocket of the red café apron Jolene insisted she wear, Adah peered out the rain-splattered window. Jackson's truck sat idling in front of the café. Good. She was pleased to be able to tell him she had another paycheck. Tomorrow, he could take her to the bank to cash it. In the month that had passed since Jolene hired her on the spot and took the HELP WANTED sign out of the window,

Adah had gone back and forth a hundred times on what to do next. The more she practiced the guitar, the more she liked it. She had written a dozen songs. They flowed from her with the help of the musical accompaniment. She could write. She simply couldn't perform in public. She loved playing with Jackson down by the lake. When he was sober and had a guitar in his hands, the music flowed between them so freely she couldn't imagine being anywhere else. Certainly not in a studio or on a stage. Jackson refused to accept this as her fate, but he hadn't pushed her into auditioning again.

The uneasy truce between them had held, but she often saw him watching her, the waiting and the wanting clearly written on his face. No matter how quickly she looked away or how quickly he wiped the feelings from his face, leaving sadness and bewilderment, they both knew the unanswered questions would never leave of their own accord.

Today, the sadness had left the premises—at least for a short time. He thought he was about to land a job on the Sullivan Keats Show. But he'd been saying some variation of that claim every day since they arrived. He worked hard for his dream and he believed. She prayed today would be the day it came true for him. Even if it meant leaving her behind. Especially if it meant leaving her behind.

She shoved through the door, pulled it closed behind her, and locked it with the key Jolene had given her. The traffic had cleared for the night and the streets were almost quiet. Streetlights shimmered on puddles that dotted the sidewalk. A gust of warm, moist wind sent trash and leaves scuttling along the sidewalk around her. Fine mist settled on her cheeks, cooling her after the heat of the café. It was a welcome preview to the fall weather that surely couldn't be far behind. Her pillow would feel good under her head tonight. Something akin to contentment stole over her. Something she hadn't felt in a long while. She welcomed it back like an old friend.

"Hey, baby. There you are. I was just coming in for you." Jackson leaned through the open window, waving wildly. "I could use a cup of coffee."

His words slurred. Cup of coffee came out *cuffofee*.

Adah halted halfway between the building and the street. "Are you all right?"

"Couldn't be better." He laughed so loudly a couple walking on the other side of the street looked over at them, ducked their heads, and sped up. "I been hanging with my pal Clay and the band. Jammin'. We been writing songs."

She'd heard that line before, many times since their arrival in Branson. It was getting old, like a song played on the radio too many times. "Jamming and drinking?"

"A little. To grease the wheels, make the song come faster."

She'd never needed alcohol to write a song. "I don't think you're supposed to drink and drive." Even she, who didn't drive, knew that. "Maybe we should go inside and I'll make you some coffee."

Coffee and alcohol. Did one cancel out the other? It didn't seem likely, but at least it would give the alcohol time to wear off. Exactly how long did that take?

"I brought you some." He held up a metal flask that sparkled in the streetlight. "Clayton gave it to me. One for the road. He knew I was feeling down and he wanted to give me a pick-me-up."

"A pick-me-up. He knew you were driving?" The meaning of his words hit her. "Why were you feeling down?"

"Sullivan hired someone else to sing backup and play guitar. Not me. Said I was a little too green. To come back after I had a little more pickin' and grinnin' under my belt." He burped, then slapped his hand over his mouth. After a second or two, he removed it, a sheepish grin still plastered across his face. "How am I supposed to get more experience if no one will hire me?"

She didn't know the answer to that question. "I'm sorry. You need to keep practicing and getting better. That's all."

"In this town it ain't about getting better. It's about who you know."

"What about Clayton?"

"Clayton's going to Nashville. He's got an offer to sign with a label. He's gonna cut a record and then he's gonna tour with a couple of other bands, big names."

"Good for him."

"I asked him for a job too."

If Jackson went with Clayton to Nashville, what would she do? Work at the café? Find another place to live? Go home? She shied away from the thought. She couldn't go home and watch Matthew court another woman. "And he said no?"

"He said he didn't need any more musicians and he doesn't need a female singer." Singer came out *shinger*. "He was real apologetic about it. If he had an opening he would take us both in a heartbeat, but he can't pay no more folks than he already has. Not until his record starts selling."

"You asked for me?"

"'Course I did. I told him we were a package deal."

Jackson had such a good heart. She did love that about him. Loved that. But the rest of it…the restlessness, the inability to go slow, the impulsiveness…it reminded her of herself. Put the two of them together and they were bound to explode. She closed her eyes against another gust of wind that knocked her back a step. Two flash fires roaring across a dry field, meeting in the middle, creating an inferno, were bound to leave destruction in their wake.

It would never work. She needed slow and steady. She needed Matthew.

Too late.

"Why are you standing there looking like you just swallowed a porcupine, girl? Come on, get in." He slapped the side of the truck. "They're jammin' over at the Lariat. Pete and Josh and Cody, they're all there. Let's go play some music."

And all drunk, she had no doubt. This tape on rewind was getting mighty old. "I can't get in the truck with you."

"Why not?"

"You're drunk."

"No, I ain't." Jackson banged the flask on the door. It dropped to the ground. "Oh, man." He shoved open his door and slid out, his boot connecting with the flask, sending it spinning across the sidewalk. He staggered, took a swipe at it, and missed. "It's a slippery little *shucker*, isn't it?"

He straightened and whooped with laughter.

Adah picked it up for him. It reeked of whiskey. "Let's go inside."

"No, no, no. We need to get to our pickin' and grinnin'. We need to practice. Only way we can get good enough." He grabbed her arm and leaned close. His breath reeked worse than the flask. "Come on, get in on my side and scoot over—or don't. You can sit real close if you want. I won't mind. We gotta play. The boys are waiting."

"I can't." She tried to tug free. His grip tightened.

"Come on, baby."

"Don't call me that." She tugged harder and jerked away. "Stop it. Right now."

He stepped back, both hands lifted as if in surrender. The hazy alcohol-induced happiness ebbed away. His shoulders dropped and his blue eyes begged her for something she couldn't give him. "I'm still waiting, you know."

"Waiting for what?"

"See, it's not even that important to you." He took a swig from the flask and tossed it into the street. "I'm still waiting for you to give me permission."

"We've talked about this. You know I can't."

"I told you I wouldn't do it again until you gave me permission." He tossed his hat through the truck's window and faced her, bareheaded in the rain. "How long will I have to wait?"

"We don't do that."

"You don't kiss?"

"Not unless we're serious about getting married."

"So marry me."

He really was drunk. Or crazy.

"I'm sorry. I can't."

"You don't want me either, do you?" He clamored into the truck. The tip of his boot caught on the foot guard, causing him to tumble into the seat. He cursed. "No one wants me."

"I'm so sorry." She shut his door and leaned in the window, searching for a way to offer him comfort without encouraging something that couldn't be. "It's not that I don't like you. I like you, I care about what happens to you, but I can't marry you. You've been good to me. I appreciate what you've done for me, giving me a chance to write songs and learn music."

"Like me? You're killing me, Amish girl." He started the truck and revved the engine. "You think I like you? I love you. Don't you get that? I love you."

"No, you don't. You like the idea of me, the singing Amish girl." She wanted to wipe the rain from his face and smooth back the hair that hung in his eyes, but he would see it as something more than it was. "We're partners, remember? Songwriters and singers."

"You don't love me because you love that other guy—the one you were dreaming about."

"What are you talking about?"

The rain made his hair curl in damp ringlets on his forehead, the streetlights giving his eyes a sad shine. "The one whose name you said when you were sleeping on the ride down here in July. Matthew."

Her skin went hot despite the cool rain that slid like tears down her cheeks. She raised her hands to her face, trying to hide the heat that blossomed there. She'd called Matthew's name in her sleep that first day. And many nights since, if her dreams were any indication. "I'm sorry."

"Yeah. Me too."

He took off, gears grinding, tires screeching, zigzagging as the truck sought traction on the wet pavement. A horn blared. He responded with the repeated strident honking of his own horn and sped up.

She stood there breathing the exhaust fumes until the noise of the truck disappeared into the night. The rain soaked her dress and chilled her skin. Shivering, she stared at the space where the truck had been. She never meant to hurt Jackson. Just like she'd never meant to hurt Matthew. Her selfish desire to run to her dreams had left two men's feelings trampled. She'd put herself first. Not them and surely not God.

Bowing her head against a wet wind that picked up the rain and pelted her, Adah prayed. For forgiveness. For understanding. For peace. For courage. For direction. She needed God to tell her what to do next.

Nothing.

No voice spoke to her. The wind whistled in the hollow silence of her head.

She raised her face and let the rain wash away the filth and grime that no one but God could see. Her mudder's favorite saying played in her head: *JOY: Jesus, Others, You.* Adah had gotten them backward and look what happened.

A cluster of folks hooted and hollered down the block a piece. An intense shiver scurried up her spine and shook her body. Standing here on a dark street wasn't wise. Branson wasn't New Hope. It was a strange new world. She groped for the café key and unlocked the door with shaking fingers. Inside, she flipped on the lights, leaned against the heavy wood for a second, and then turned and re-locked the door. Just to be safe.

Now what?

Her head ached and her eyes burned. *Gott, I'm so sorry. So sorry. I've been so selfish and so foolish.*

She closed her eyes and waited, listening. The tick-tock of Jolene's favorite kitty-cat clock with its long tail swishing back and forth filled the room, mixing with the sound of rain. It picked up in a sudden gust of wind and slammed against the windows. No loving voice of reason. Had God forsaken her? No. According to Luke, He would never do that. Maybe He was waiting for her to do the right thing.

First step, figure out how to get back to the Hart cabin. Grownup women dealt with situations like this. One step at a time. Sucking in air, she marched to the back of the café to the small work area that contained Jolene's desk, her computer, a calculator, and a smattering of office supplies. And a phone. Jolene rarely used it, what with her cell phone being practically stuck to her ear like a favorite accessory.

Charlene answered on the fourth ring, sounding sleepy and more than a little peeved. "Who's this? Do you know what time it is?"

"It's me."

"Adah? What's wrong?" She sounded wide awake now. "Why aren't you home yet?"

"I'm sorry to bother you so late."

"Where's Jackson? Didn't he pick you up?"

"He started to, but then he didn't."

"Drinking, was he?"

"Yes."

"I'm on my way."

Adah started to say she was sorry again, but it was too late. Charlene had already disconnected.

Twenty minutes later Charlene's tiny red car—the one she called Ladybug—pulled up to the curb with a screech. Adah locked up and dashed through a now steady downpour and slid in on the passenger's side.

"Girl, you're a mess," Charlene observed as she pulled from the curb. "Ever heard of an umbrella?"

"It's just water and it cools a person off."

"True. Maybe we should cool Jackson off with a hose when he comes home tonight."

"I plan to be asleep when he comes home." Adah instantly regretted her tart tone. "Sorry. I know you're his aunt and all."

"That don't mean I don't see what he's doing to you."

"He's not doing anything to me. It's my fault."

"He took you away from your home and your family. You think I can't see how miserable you are?"

"I shouldn't have come, but I did, willingly. He can't be blamed for my mistake. I came here with a dream, same as he did."

"Or Jackson fed you a load of bull and made you think this was your dream."

"I love writing songs."

"Which you can do anywhere. It doesn't have to be here. You don't like to perform and people here have to perform."

Charlene was a smart woman. Adah gazed at the streaks left by the windshield wipers. The *whop-whop* sound as they flashed back and forth against the glass lulled her. She was so tired. Daed would say she had made her bed and she'd better be prepared to lie in it. She missed Daed with all his gruffness and his silly sayings and his certainty that theirs was the right way, the best way.

She wasn't certain of much. Only that God had a plan for her and she'd taken matters into her own hands and gone off with her own plan. How could God forgive that? Her audacity. Her arrogance. "I don't know what to do." A shiver ran through Adah. She clutched her arms to her chest, trying to warm them. "I don't want to hurt your nephew. He's a good friend and he's right about us having the same dream. It's just not a dream I should have."

"I came to Branson twenty years ago with my husband, Joe. I met him at a concert he played in Texas. I was a first grade teacher barely out of college. I'd gone down there following a guy in the Air Force stationed in San Antonio, who then dumped me when he got his orders. Joe eventually talked me into coming back to Missouri with him." Charlene hunched over the steering wheel, her gaze glued to the road. The brake lights of the car in front of them served as beacons that helped keep them in their lane in the blinding sheets of rain. "He wanted to be a big time star of stage and screen too."

"Stage and screen?"

"It's an expression, honey. He had big aspirations." Charlene leaned forward as if it would help her to see. "And a little more than average talent."

"He made it?"

"He might have." She shook her head as if disagreeing with her own statement. A bolt of lightning lit the sky directly overhead, followed by a crack of thunder that nearly drowned out her voice. "I don't know. We'll never know, because he drank himself to death before he had a chance to prove himself."

"To death?"

"Some people can drink now and again. Or have one or two drinks and then stop. Joe wasn't like that. Once he started, he drank like there was no tomorrow. Until there was no tomorrow."

"I'm sorry." How did a person know when it became a problem? It seemed Jackson did a lot of drinking these days. "Very sorry."

"It was a long time ago. I guess this situation with you and Jackson reminded me of how I felt. It's hard to be in love with someone who's crazy in love with something he can't wrap his arms around, something that's always just beyond his reach. This town digs its claws into a kid like Jackson and never lets go. The music will always come first. If he's like his daddy, the drinking will ease up as he gets a little older. He's just sowing wild oats because he's twenty-one and he can. But the hunger for the music—that will never let up."

"I'm not in love with Jackson."

"I figured as much. If you loved him like I loved my Joe, you wouldn't be here with me now. You'd be with him."

"I don't understand the feelings I have for him, but I know they're not love. Not the kind that lasts."

"Jackson is a good-looking, charming, sweet-talking, sweetheart of a young man. Attention from him is bound to make a girl's heart flutter and get her all flustered so she doesn't know what to think. So she'd walk off a cliff for him."

That was Adah's situation summed up all neat and tidy. "We're too much alike. If we go on like this, we'll walk off that cliff together."

"You're a smart girl."

"A smart girl would've figured it out sooner."

"This love stuff isn't easy." Charlene maneuvered around a slow-moving truck, her fingernails tapping out her impatience on the wheel. "I loved Joe so much, I gave up everything for him. I moved to this town, put up with his running around and his drinking and his never-ending certainty that his big hit was just around the corner. I put up with it right up until the moment I found him lying on the bathroom floor one morning, dead, choked on his own vomit."

The ugly image made bitter bile rise in Adah's throat. The ham and cheese sandwich she'd eaten for supper at the coffeehouse roiled in her stomach. She breathed and let the sound of the rain on the windshield soothe her. The memory of Charlene's expression when Jackson's father asked her if she had experience raising children rose up in Adah's mind. "You never had children?"

"No. We lost two babies before they were born."

"I'm sorry."

"Again, a long time ago. After Joe died, I went back to teaching school. I have my little ones I teach to read every year. I love them." Charlene flipped the windshield wiper lever. They sped up, but didn't do much good in the driving rain. "But I still wonder if things would've been different if our babies had lived. Maybe Joe wouldn't have felt the need to drink so much. His heart was broken."

"He had you, didn't he?"

"Sometimes a person isn't enough."

Adah was learning that lesson. She didn't like it. "But you never left Branson after your husband died."

"I was too old to run home to New Hope. I didn't have any place else to go." Charlene pulled into the drive in front of the house and killed the engine. She left the headlights on, letting them spotlight the dancing branches of the trees bending and lashing out in the wind. "You do."

Adah wasn't so sure of that. No one waited for her at home. As the weeks had gone by, she'd given up hope of getting an answer to her letters. She'd written two more to Mudder and another one to Molly, but no more to Matthew. His silence after the first one had been his answer. "It's not that simple."

"People tend to make it harder than it is." Charlene patted Adah's shoulder. "You'll go home when you're ready. And when you do, your folks will thank God and throw you a big party. Like the prodigal daughter."

But Plain folks didn't throw parties—not for wayward daughters who broke all the rules.

Chapter 37

Matthew could almost feel the gazes boring into his back. Many people had come to watch him do the most important thing he'd ever do in his life. He tried to focus on Luke's words. His breathing sounded loud in the silence of everyone watching, everyone waiting. A baby whimpered; a woman hushed him. Someone coughed, then quieted. The old barn creaked in a gusty wind that blew hay from the rafters and sent it showering down on him and the others who stood in front. Dust dried his throat and made it ache. Or more likely it ached because Adah didn't stand on the other side, next to Elizabeth. He had always known he would be baptized, come what may. The fact that Adah wasn't with him hurt. Scratch that, it agonized him.

One thing at a time. He would do this. Then he would go get her and bring her home. Her baptism would come in the spring. He'd waited and he'd prayed, doing exactly what Luke and Thomas had insisted he do. Ignore the letter. Wait. Let her learn.

He'd waited and he'd prayed and now, he'd made up his mind.

Luke fixed Matthew with a stern stare that surely saw his anger and his doubt as well as his bedrock certainty that this was where he belonged. "Do you renounce the devil?"

"Jah."

"Do you renounce the world?"

"Jah."

293

"Do you accept the Ordnung?"

"I do."

The questions from the bishop came one by one, slow, deliberate, careful. Each time Matthew had the opportunity to step back, to say no, to wait. But he didn't. This commitment to God and his community would carry him through. Just as it would Adah, when her time came.

The minutes picked up speed until they zoomed by. The questions were repeated to the others who stood, like him, legs trembling, hands slick with sweat.

Finally, the water from the tin cup soaked his hair and trickled down his forehead, his cheeks, and his neck. He raised his head and looked up at Luke. Now?

Luke nodded and smiled. "Welcome to God's family."

Matthew rose and accepted the traditional kiss on the cheek. He turned to face his community of faith. Some of the women had tears in their eyes. The men's faces bore broad smiles. His family of faith. He had been born into a Plain community. Now, he had chosen to be Amish of his own free will. So would Adah. He would see to it.

It took a good half hour, but Matthew finally managed to tear himself away from Mudder, Daed, and the rest of the family, Groossmammi being the hardest. She kept squeezing his arm and making him lean over so she could give him one more peck on the cheek. Her own cheeks were wet with tears she kept swiping at with the back of a sleeve until it was soaked.

"I have to go." He liked having his grandparents close on this important day. He liked that Groossdaadi's mind seemed to be clear as a bell today. For this day. "But I'll be back in a bit so we can eat together."

"Let the boy go." Groossdaadi patted his fraa's arm. "He has rounds to make. People to see. Things to do."

"Nee, this is a day for family." Groossmammi tilted her head, eyes still bright with tears. "And girls, I reckon. Go on. But come back before all the food gets eaten."

She tugged on his arm, he leaned down, and she planted one more peck on his cheek. He strode across Thomas's yard and around the house, filled with yakking women preparing to serve the food. Sure enough, Thomas, Silas, and Luke sat at a picnic table under a poplar tree in the backyard. Ben, Hiram, and Daniel sat across from them. He didn't wait for them to speak. "Now. The time is now."

Luke smoothed his beard. "If you're talking about Adah, we were just discussing that situation."

"Adah isn't a situation—"

"Easy, Matthew." Thomas held up his hand, long, callused fingers spread. "You're a man now, a voting member of this district, but that brings with it responsibility to the entire community. It also doesn't release you from showing respect."

"I meant no disrespect. It's time for her to come home." He let his gaze fall to Ben, Hiram, and Daniel. The men of Adah's family. Their agreement was critical in this. "It's time for me to go talk to her and set her straight."

"If anyone goes, it should be me and Hiram," Daniel interrupted. "We're her brothers."

"I think she'll listen to me."

"Why?" Luke's tone was abrupt but his expression kind. "What will you say to her?"

"Daniel and Hiram see Adah as their little sister, someone to be protected. Ben wants to protect her, but he also wants to teach her and punish her and make her do the right thing." Matthew paced as he grappled for the right words. He had to make them understand without offending them. "What I have with Adah, at least what I had, is different. It's more…equal."

As Plain men they might not understand that word. Not when it came to speaking of women, but Matthew knew in his heart that each of the married men at the table loved his fraa and valued her opinion. They wanted to please their fraas, even if they would never, ever say it aloud. A man might be the head of the household, but his fraa was the heart. Neither could exist without the other. "I understand why she left. I know what she hungers for. I know why she struggles."

"What makes you think she'll listen to you?" Ben drummed his fingers on the table in an impatient rhythm. "She left you as much as she left her family."

The words sliced through Matthew, sharp as any scythe. He couldn't say the words that pulsed in his head. It wasn't done. *She loves me and I love her.* "She'll come."

Ben didn't look convinced. "She left you much as she left us."

"She's Adah."

"That we can agree on." Ben cleared his throat. "Her…everything is riding on this."

"I'll bring her home."

"Branson is a crowded place." Daniel scratched at his chin as if he still hadn't gotten used to the beard he'd started growing after his marriage the previous year. "When I went to fetch Michael, I had a hard time finding him in Jefferson City. How will you find her in a place like Branson?"

"Daniel's right. I talked with Mrs. Hart on Friday. She said to leave them alone. She called Adah and Jackson both lost causes." Ben's voice broke and his face reddened. "She wouldn't give me the address."

The fact that Ben had gone to the Harts nearly knocked Matthew to the ground in surprise. Ben had put aside his hurt pride and gone to the Englischers. He tried to cover his broken heart with a thorny exterior, but he must miss his daughter something fierce to go talk to Mrs. Hart.

"I'll find a way." Matthew had to bring her home, not just for himself but for Ben and Irene. "There's always a way. If I have to visit every house in the town, I'll find her." He locked gazes with Ben. "That's the plan."

"*Gut.*"

Matthew nodded at the other men and left them sitting there, already moving on to the topic of the weather in the coming week. He strode to the table where his own father sat a few feet from the boys, his expression morose as he devoured a plate of what looked like taco casserole. Matthew sat on the bench across from him and waited. Finally, Daed looked up. He finished chewing and wiped his beard with a napkin. "You're going after her, aren't you?"

"I am."

Daed tossed the napkin on his plate. "You're a man now. You make your own decisions."

"Luke, Silas, and Thomas agree that we have to at least try."

"Why you?"

"Because she might listen to me."

"Even if she does come back, there's no guarantee she won't run off again."

"I know."

"You have a girl right under your nose who would make a fine fraa."

"Did you marry Mudder for her cooking?"

Daed's jaw worked. "You may be a member of the church now, but that doesn't give you the right to disrespect me."

"I don't mean to be disrespectful." Matthew put his elbows on the table and leaned forward. He sought to keep his voice low. "A man doesn't choose a wife with his head."

"You've been talking to your groossdaadi."

"He's been talking to me. He told me not everyone thought you should marry Mudder."

Daed's face went a dark purple. "Your mudder is a fine woman."

"I know. She's my mudder."

"We married young. We had a lot to learn, but we learned. Me as much as your mudder."

"Which is what I'm trying to get at."

"I know what you're getting at." Daed cleared his throat. He glanced at the twins, who were demolishing plates heaped with ham, potato salad, coleslaw, and three rolls apiece. He pushed his plate aside and leaned closer. "Today you made the most important decision you'll ever make. Taking a fraa is the second. You done good today. I just want you to stay on the right road."

A veritable speech for a man like Daed. "Trust my judgment. You raised me right." Matthew rose. "The decision, in the end is mine."

Daed rose as well. "Remember, Gott's will, not yours."

Matthew never forgot that fact. "They say God helps those who help themselves."

"Then go, help yourself. But guard your heart."

Guarding his heart had gotten him to this place. Time to let go and trust. Time to bring Adah home.

Chapter 38

Adah plucked a few long pieces of grass and began to braid them together. The sun hung low over the lake, giving it a glassy sheen. No wind rustled the leaves in the branches of the sycamore tree that gave her small spot of shade. She closed her eyes and inhaled the steamy air. It smelled like dirt and lake and peace. The sound of the lapping water soothed her to the core. So did Captain's snoring, silly as that sounded. The dog could sleep anywhere. Another minute or two and she might lay her head on his back and snore right along with him. The dog had taken to meeting her at the door when she arrived home from work and following her about the house like her faithful companion. Another fact among many that irritated Jackson.

Since their discussion in the rain on the street, he'd been polite and distant. The easy give and take had disappeared, leaving behind awkward silences and sudden exits from rooms. She wanted to fix it, but that wasn't possible. More and more, she knew that. She had to find a way to tell him. What he was waiting for would never come.

She let the thought drift off on the lapping water. The anxiety of the songs she couldn't write in that house—or anywhere close to Jackson these days—dissipated in the light airiness of a Sunday summer evening. Her inability to sing in front of an audience no longer seemed a monumental failure. At least as long as she could smell peace and hear the blue jays bickering on their perch overhead. *Thank You Gott, for this.*

"Adah! Adah, where are you?"

She sighed and opened her eyes. The sun dipped beyond the horizon, its absence resulting in a drab, gray-black dusk somewhere between night and day.

"Adah, come on. I've got news. Mac called."

She tossed the miniature grass braid into the water and stood. Captain stirred, yawned until his jaw should've cracked, and rose next to her, his smiling face quizzical. The cool grass tickled her bare feet. She forced a smile and stepped out from behind the tree. "Here I am. What is it?"

Clad in a swim suit and wrinkled T-shirt stained with pizza sauce, Jackson stomped down the path toward her looking like an Englisch teenager on a camping trip. "I just got the wildest phone call from Mac. You won't believe it. Or maybe you will."

Something in his voice told Adah Jackson didn't quite believe it. This might be good news for someone, but not for him. "What did he say?"

"They want you. Country Notes want you."

Earlier in the summer, Jackson had taken her to see their show with its patriotic theme and gospel songs and three generations of singers from one family. She'd been awestruck by the music, but not as excited about the strange comedy acts and the volume. Everything boomed. The bright lights made their clothes glitter and sparkle. She didn't know where to look first. A confetti canon in the first act had sent her diving under her seat. By the end, she didn't know whether to clap her hands over her ears or her eyes.

Jackson assured her over and over on the ride home that she'd get used to it. At the time she'd kept the thought to herself that she hoped she would never have to do that.

"How do they know about me?"

Jackson stopped a few feet away. His gaze, filled with something she couldn't decipher, lifted to the lake beyond her shoulder. "You know the answer to that question better than I do."

"I have no idea what you're talk about."

"You suddenly have amnesia?"

"Amnesia?"

His gaze dropped like a stone into the water. "You recorded a song at the studio the day we met Mac there and you don't remember doing it? Were you sleepwalking at the time? Or drunk? Oh, no, I forgot, you don't drink. You're too perfect for that."

"I'm not perfect." Her throat tight with unshed tears, she choked on the words. God and her parents knew how far from perfect their daughter was. She was so filled with shame, she could barely lift her voice to pray or sing. "I'm not."

"No, you're sure not. Not when it comes to being a partner...or a friend."

"What song are you talking about?"

"You really don't remember recording a song at the studio the day we went over there back in July, the day you freaked out and couldn't sing a decent note?" He smoothed the black whiskers on his chin that had been allowed to grow beyond the five o'clock shadow he usually sported. "After I left, suddenly you got it together, apparently, and sang like a pro for the sound tech."

The truth of his words flooded her. Singing alone, without the band, and without Jackson. "I didn't know he was recording."

"It's a recording studio. What did you think he was doing?"

"He said to practice so I practiced, that's all. Trying to get over my stage fright."

"Apparently you practiced real good. Ralph Dillon wants to meet you tomorrow morning. He wants you to sing with his daughters."

"I can't." And she shouldn't. "This isn't for me."

"This is your big break. You gave up everything for this—at least that's what you keep telling me."

Harping on that surely hurt Jackson more than he let on. "You've seen what happens to me in public."

"Get over it." He whirled and trudged up the path. "I'll drive you. Ain't got nothing better to do."

Maybe she could still make it up to him. If he sang, they would see how good he was and she could leave him to his dream. "Will you sing with me?"

He turned back to face her. "Don't work that way. They ain't asking for me."

"I won't do it without you."

"Don't be an idiot."

The force of his words hit her like the switch Daed used to whack on her backside. She flinched but stood her ground. "I'm not singing unless you sing too. That was the deal."

"Look." He blew out air and began to trace a pattern in the dirt with his bare toe, his gaze averted. "I appreciate that. Really I do. But that's not the way things work in this town. You get a chance, you take it. It won't come around again."

"I don't care."

"I do. You get your foot in the door. Maybe you get a chance to throw some of that luck my way."

"You think that's possible?"

"I'm sure." He smiled at her for the first time, not that blinding smile that nearly knocked her from her sneakers that first day at the corral on the farm, but an older, sadder smile that made him look like his father. "You should be practicing instead of standing around talking to me. You're singing with the Dillon sisters tomorrow."

She wanted to stay here by the lake in the fading sun with Jackson, playing guitars and singing for the frogs and crickets the way they used to do at the pond on his parents' farm, but she would try to do this for him. Once he had a foot in the door, she would go home. And face the music of another kind. "I'll try. I'll do my best, but you know I'm not cut out for this."

"Come on, Amish girl, pony up." Still smiling, he cocked his head toward the house. "Don't chicken out. I'll help you."

She wasn't a chicken. "I'm sorry about the recording."

"I'm sorry I called you an idiot."

"Apology accepted."

He stomped up the path, not looking back to see if she and Captain followed.

Adah gazed at the lake one last time. It had lost its shimmer in the prevailing dark of night. Captain whimpered. "It's okay, boy, he's just hurt. We all are."

The words of a hymn she'd grown up singing at prayer service washed over her. She began to sing the familiar words, softly at first, barely a whisper. Then louder as the last wisp of light faded away.

With joy I sing. The first line reverberated around her again and again.

With joy I sing.

How long had it been since she sang with joy?

Chapter 39

Matthew sat in the buggy, waiting. The sun beat down on its black roof, sucking in the heat. No breeze wafted through the small, square windows. He felt as if he were baking in an oven. If he got out, he'd endure the stares of every child and every teenager who had spent the last several hours cooling off at New Hope's only public swimming pool. He was used to the stares, but today he wasn't in the mood. The clean smell of the chlorine wafted through the metal fence that surrounded the swimming pool. It mixed with the aroma of hotdogs steaming at the concession stand. The sound of whoops and hollers built to a crescendo as some child he couldn't see got up the nerve to hop from the top diving board or do a belly flop from the side.

It would be worth the wait as soon as RaeAnne Hart strolled from the stone building that had served as the bath house for the pool since it opened in the seventies. Or so said the plaque on the front next to the open doors. He'd read it forty times while waiting for her. Maybe she'd taken the day off from her lifeguarding job. Her first job, according to Molly, who heard everything while shelving books at the library. According to some girl who chattered with a friend in the magazine section, RaeAnne's parents made her do it to keep her out of trouble until her senior year at New Hope High. They didn't want her to end up like her big brother Jackson, down in Branson on some wild goose chase. Too much information as far as Matthew was concerned. Englisch kids working to pass the time.

He didn't have time for this. He had actual work to do. He had soybeans and milo to harvest and fryers to butcher. And a fence that needed mending. And a horse with a lame leg. He picked up the reins. Then put them down again. He'd promised Ben he would bring Adah home and that was what he intended to do. Even if his own father didn't approve.

If Daed remembered at all how he felt about Mudder when they courted, he would understand. A man might be able to change his mind about a woman, but not his heart. A heart did what it wanted to do.

Gott, help me.

RaeAnne strolled through the door on the girls' side, a pink and white striped bag slung over one bare shoulder. She'd pulled her long, wet hair back in a ponytail. Her tanned face glistened with sweat under a sprinkling of freckles. She tugged at a red bathing suit top that covered little, but didn't seem concerned about cut-off jean shorts determined to ride low on her hips. "Bye, Kyle, see you tomorrow," she called over her shoulder to some unseen person. "Unless I find something better to do."

Keeping his gaze on rubber flip-flops that matched her fire-engine-red toenail polish, Matthew slid from the buggy and stepped into her path. "Can I talk to you a minute?"

"I don't know." She snapped her gum with a loud *pop-pop*. "You gonna look me in the eye or do you have a foot fetish?"

He forced his gaze to her face. She looked as if she'd be happier to see a wild hog barreling toward her. "What do you want?"

"I'm a friend of Adah Knepp's."

"So I assumed." Frowning, she shifted her bag to her other shoulder. "What do you want?"

"I need to find out where she is." A gaggle of girls rushed from the building, all skinny arms and legs, chattering and giggling over a lone boy who marched ahead of them, head bent as if ignoring them, the red of his face announcing that he wasn't succeeding. Matthew shifted toward the buggy. RaeAnne followed. "I mean, I know she's in Branson. I want directions to your house there."

RaeAnne climbed into the buggy without an invitation and planted herself on the seat. "I've been on my feet in the blazing sun for the last six hours." She patted the seat. "I won't bite. Sit."

As if she could tell him what to do in his own buggy. Still, he climbed in and sat a careful distance away. Up close she smelled of flowery shampoo, recently applied deodorant, and bubblegum. "Can you give me directions to your family's home there in Branson?"

"You're going after her?"

"Yes."

Chomping on a wad of gum so big her cheek bulged, RaeAnne undid the clasp holding her hair back and began to comb her fingers through it. Droplets of water flung themselves at Matthew, tiny spots darkening the blue of his work shirt. "How are you getting there?"

"What do you mean?"

She waved fingers with nails painted the same shade of red as her toes. "You're not driving this thing all the way to Branson, are you?"

"I'll hire a driver."

"Just you going?"

Why the twenty questions? He curbed his impatience. He wanted something from her. Apparently to get it, he would have to answer her questions. "No. Adah's brother Daniel and my sister Molly want to go with me. The bishop and her parents have given us permission to go talk to her."

"Are you her boyfriend?"

Matthew studied his hands. He could've done a better job of washing them before making this trip into town. He concentrated on scrapping dirt from under his fingernails, but the question still burrowed under his skin. "I don't know."

"Then why are you going after her?"

"For her own good. She needs to come back to her community. To her faith." He looked at RaeAnne head-on. "She needs to be with her own kind."

"You're so full of it." RaeAnne hooted. "What a crock."

"Excuse me?"

"You're going after her because you have a thing for her."

"That's private."

Wrinkling her freckled nose, RaeAnne blew a bubble and then popped it with her thumb and forefinger. "You really think she'll want you after being with Jackson?"

"What do you mean?"

"Jackson is a force of a nature when it comes to girls."

Dread knotted in his stomach. Her words only fueled his unspoken fears. *Steady. Steady.* "Adah's not a girl."

"Not like me, you mean."

"I don't know anything about you. I just know Adah."

"Okay." RaeAnne wrapped her hair in a knot and secured it with a scrunchie. "Hire me."

"What?"

"To drive you. It'll be easier for me to show you where the house is. It's on the lake. It's not in Branson exactly and traffic is terrible."

Matthew couldn't believe he would even contemplate the possibility. With her wet hair, scrawny frame, and wad of bubble gum bulging in one cheek, she looked about twelve. "Do you even have a driver's license?"

"I'm eighteen. Of course I have a driver's license." Her lower lip puffed out in a pout. "And access to a car."

"You want to go to Branson?"

"I miss my brother." Emotions flitted across her face. A sadness Matthew found surprising. Something like longing. Despite all her bluster, the girl was lonely. "And I don't want him to make a big mistake."

"A big mistake?"

"Getting all tied up in knots over an Amish girl is a big mistake. Even I know that. You all don't usually mix with our kind." She picked at a hangnail on her thumb. "And I'm tired of listening to my parents fight about it. They're gonna end up divorced and it'll be Jack's fault. He couldn't live with that."

RaeAnne Hart was smarter than she looked. Not book-learning smarts, but the kind that came from living. His judgment of her as shallow based on her looks and her kin convicted him. He owed her an apology she wouldn't even understand. "Okay."

"You'll let me take you? I'm gonna be like one of those Amish drivers." Now she sounded like a little girl again. "When do we go?"

"Today?" He wanted to go now. Right now. "Can you ask your parents today?"

"Who said anything about asking my parents?" She hopped from the buggy and turned to look up at him. "I'll be at your place in two hours. Be ready to go."

"Hey, you need to ask—"

"Let me take care of my parents. Two hours. Be ready."

Chapter 40

Adah hesitated at the Country Notes dressing room door. The array of clothes and boots and hats and doodads she didn't recognize made the long, deep room seem small. Two pink sofas faced each other in one corner and a long dining room table with six chairs took up another corner. In front of her, a counter stretched from one side to the other completely covered with jars, tubes, fingernail polish, lotions, and perfumes. The Dillon sisters had a lot of stuff.

In between the furniture stretched racks filled with dresses, blouses, jackets, and pants in every color. Reds, blues, purples, shimmering greens, sunshine yellow, tangerine orange, and creamy pink. Rhinestones glittered and sparkled in the bright overhead lights that hung low from the ceiling. She'd never seen so much clothing anyplace besides a department store.

Instinct screamed at Adah to run. She put her hand on the doorframe to steady herself. On the drive over she told herself over and over again, *You can do this. You can do this. Last chance. Last chance. Do it. Do it. It's now or never. Do it for Jackson.*

I can do this.

But should she? That was a different question. She shivered against the icy air blasting from overhead vents. She had to do this for Jackson. She owed him that much.

Maisie Dillon grabbed her arm, her long red nails digging into

Adah's wrist. "It's okay, I promise. Mac said you were a little skittish, but that's okay. We don't bite. Ain't that right, Dottie?"

Shiny red hair cascaded down Dottie Dillon's back, matching the deep red hue of her suede jacket. When she moved the long fringe that decorated the shoulders and the back of the sleeves rippled. "Bless your heart! Aren't you just the sweetest thing ever." She pursed lips painted a matching shade of red and tilted her head to one side, making her long silver and gold earrings jingle. "The audience will love you, especially the boys!"

"I'm not—"

"You have gorgeous skin." Maisie Dillon chimed in as if she didn't hear Adah's feeble attempt to deny any desire to be loved by an audience—especially the boys. She stalked around Adah, the heels of her red and blue cowboy boots making a *tap tap* sound on the burnished wood floor. "And your hair is like spun gold—what I can see under that little cap doohickey. Anyone ever tell you that, honey?"

No one had. Or ever would. Not back home, leastways. Where Adah desperately wanted to be at this very moment.

"A little lipstick, some mascara, we'll make those baby blues pop." Maisie's eyes narrowed. She wore enough mascara and eyeliner for a horde of Englisch women. She followed her sister in the same tight circle around Adah. Her jacket was black but had the same long red fringe as Dottie's. "Daddy told us to fix you up right nice and that's what we aim to do."

"You haven't heard me sing yet." They needed to stop circling. They were making her dizzy. She hadn't eaten breakfast or lunch. "You shouldn't go to any trouble for a girl who might get cold feet."

"Don't you worry yourself none. You'll give yourself wrinkles." Dottie waved a hand as if to wave away Adah's concerns. "Daddy heard your demo. He loved it. He said you sing real pretty. Once we get you fixed up you'll be so gorgeous you'll be chomping at the bit to get on the stage and show off your good looks and that sweet voice."

The knot in Adah's stomach ballooned. *Be not conformed to this world.* How many times had she heard Luke and Silas say that? Now she truly knew what they meant. "I don't think I—"

"Come on, girl, you look like you're about to lose your lunch." Maisie patted a padded red stool situated in front of the enormous mirror that ran the length of the counter under an equally long row of oversized lightbulbs. "Take a load off. We'll do the rest."

Adah's pale, sweaty face stared back at her, her blue eyes huge against her pasty white skin. "I'd rather not—"

"Daddy says he doesn't want to change up your clothes too much." Dottie bustled across the room and took a long blue dress wrapped in a plastic bag from the rack. "But this color would be so good on you."

"I brought an outfit Jackson got for me." Adah remembered with a start the bag clutched to her midsection. "A Western shirt and pants with sparkling things on them."

How could she wear pants in front of a bunch of people? Her heart pounded. Her palms were so slick the paper sack was dark and damp. For Jackson. To give him his chance. She would do this.

"No, no, Daddy wants you to look like the sweet, innocent Amish girl you are. Cowgirls are a dime a dozen around here." Maisie held the dress up, her gaze going from the garment to Adah and back. "We can have it sized for you. You can use the same apron, I suppose—gives you that innocent homegrown look."

She ripped off the plastic and dropped it on the floor. "See, it's perfect."

Adah fingered the gauzy material. It felt silky under her chapped, dry hands. "It's so fancy."

"Fancy!" Dottie chortled. Maisie joined in. "It doesn't have a single rhinestone and it's all one color. It's as plain as we get around here. It's perfect. It'll make the color of your eyes pop!"

Maisie picked up a tube and unscrewed the lid. "Close those eyes now, sweetie."

The two women took turns painting and brushing and fluffing until Adah didn't recognize herself in the mirror. The pain in her stomach blossomed until it became entwined with the throbbing in her head. Everything felt wrong. Her joints ached with a pain the likes of which she'd never experienced before. Her jaw clenched and her hands balled in fists. Did God recognize her? *Do you really want to strut around on a stage with goop all over your face in front of a bunch of strangers ogling you?* The memory of Matthew's scornful face as he uttered that question smacked her across burning cheeks.

Did she? Was it worth it?

She opened her mouth, but no words escaped. Her tongue felt swollen, her throat closed.

"Honey, you need to relax." Dottie leaned back, arms crossed, surveying her handiwork. "You're wound up tighter than a jack-in-the-box. How about a cup of tea with a dollop of cream and a shot of whiskey?"

Adah shook her head. Pain shot through her neck and ran down her spine.

"Then it's time to put on the dress so we can see how much to take it in."

"No. Thank you, but no."

"Okay, sweetie. For now." Maisie tucked one arm through Adah's. "It's so fun having a sweetie like you to gussy up. Like having a little sister."

"Oh, she's a lot nicer than a little sister." Dottie took the other arm. "Up you go. Time for rehearsal."

Adah's legs were planks of wood. They refused to bend. "Now?"

"No better time than the present." Maisie beamed.

Together, Maisie and Dottie propelled Adah out the door and down the long corridor that seemed to stretch farther and farther, filled with people talking and talking and rushing to and fro, back and forth, but not seeming to get anywhere.

"There you are." A man cut in front of them, forcing the sisters to slow and leaving Adah teetering on legs that seemed to belong to someone else.

"Not now." Dottie waved him away. "Can't you see we're helping the new girl get ready to rehearse?"

Dottie edged Adah onto the expanse of a stage so massive she couldn't see the other side. Stars sparked behind her eyes. The lights were so bright overhead, so intense, she couldn't see. She stood on the edge of the world and stared out at a void so deep and so dark, it seemed to have no end. Half a dozen men who looked enough alike to be brothers stood in clusters toward the middle of the shiny wooden floor. One held a guitar, another a bass, and then a fiddle and a banjo. A man sat behind a pile of drums, tossing sticks into the air and catching them like a juggler. A band.

Her band?

Waiting for her? The desire to sink to the floor in a puddle that would seep through the planks and disappear into the earth overwhelmed her. *Please, Gott. What am I doing here?*

Indeed, what are you doing here?

"Somebody bring up the house lights," Dottie commanded.

Lights burst from the ceiling. Seats appeared and with them, Mac, Roy, and Jackson. Jackson slouched in the front row, his arms crossed over his chest, his face stony. He lifted one hand and gave her a half wave.

"I thought Jackson was going to sing with me." Her voice sounded odd in her ears, disengaged, floating around her head. "He said he would ask to sing with me."

"Not today, honey. Roy wants to try something a little bit different." Dottie patted her shoulder. "My brothers and my cousins have been practicing your song. They're ready for you."

She tugged Adah forward to the center of the stage. "This here is my brother Jason and my other brother Mark and my cousin Bobby and my other cousin Larry. Boys, this is Adah, the Amish girl."

They nodded a greeting. "We're ready when you are." Jason plinked a string on his guitar. "Have at it, Adah."

"They'll introduce you as Adah, the singing Amish girl. You'll walk out onto the stage to this spot and pick up the microphone from the stool, sit down, and sing. That's all there is to it."

Dottie handed Adah the microphone. It felt heavy in her hand. She wrapped her fingers around it. Still too heavy. She gripped her other hand around it.

Still too heavy.

"One, two, three…"

The music began. It no longer sounded beautiful to her. It screeched and tore at her ears. She wanted to slap her hands over them, protect them, but she couldn't. The microphone was too heavy. She needed both hands to hold it.

The drums pounded against her temples, beating in a painful staccato. *It's wrong. It's wrong. This is wrong. Wrong. Wrong. Wrong. Wrong for you, wrong, Adah, wrong.*

The words she knew so well were gone, swallowed up in the certain knowledge that she did not belong here on this stage.

Gott, forgive me. Please forgive me.

She dropped the microphone on the stool, whirled, and fled, followed by the reverberating screech as it rolled, fell to the floor, and rolled some more.

"Adah, Adah, stop!"

Jackson's shouts mingled with the music as it chased her off the stage, down the long hallway, and out into the street. She couldn't stop. Not for him. Not for anyone. Long after the notes died away, they nipped at her heels and threatened to trip her up. As she ran, she wiped at her face with her sleeve, trying desperately to remove the slick lipstick and the powder and the goop. The stuff that hid her face but couldn't hide the real her. The one who knew she didn't belong on a stage, showing off as if her talent, whatever talent she possessed, was her doing. It wasn't; it never had been. God gave her the voice. He gave her the words. They belonged to Him. Not to a world that needed bangles and rhinestones to see and amps and speakers to hear.

All He needed from her was a quiet voice that said, *Lord, Your will, not mine. In Your time, not mine.*

The songs belonged to Him.

Finally, she couldn't run anymore. She slowed, her legs shaking. Gasping for air, she bent over, hands on heaving chest. "Gott, forgive me. Forgive me."

She sank to her knees on the hard cement, ignoring the strangers who passed by, eyes averted, faces advertising their embarrassment at having seen this public display. "I'm so sorry. Forgive me."

A hand touched her shoulder. She couldn't bear to look up.

"Come on. I'll take you home."

"I'm sorry. I'm so sorry." She wrapped her arms around her waist, still gasping for air. "I didn't mean to disappoint you. I didn't mean to hurt you."

"I know." Jackson knelt and gathered her into his arms. She had no strength left to protest or hold back. Her head landed against his hard chest. He felt like the boulders that jutted from the side of the hills. Rock-hard and safe. She knotted her hands together to keep from holding on to him. He patted her back as if he soothed a baby. "It's okay. It's all right."

Not okay. "I wanted to do this for you. I wanted to give you your dream."

"I know, and I love you even more for trying."

"You can't love me."

"But I do."

"You can't."

His grip tightened until she couldn't breathe. He touched her chin with one finger, gently forcing her to raise her face to him. His gaze held such a knowing, such a disappointment, such an understanding. Her heart broke for him. "I know. Let's go home."

He helped her to her feet and together they started toward the truck.

"Tomorrow's another day."

He sounded so hopeful.

It would be another day. But it wouldn't change a thing.

This wasn't Adah's home and it never would be.

Chapter 41

RaeAnne was as good as her word. Matthew barely had time to pick up Daniel and get back to the house, where he told Molly what had happened while she packed a bag and prepared food to take with them. No one took a trip anywhere without proper provisions. Molly's number-one rule to live by. Repeated, incessant honking drew them out to the porch exactly two hours after RaeAnne walked away from the buggy at the pool.

Their transportation to Branson turned out to be a dust-covered rusty station wagon of an indeterminate color and no hubcaps. Rae-Anne rolled the window down with much contorting of her face. "Get in. I'd like to be there before dark."

"Will it make it to Branson and back?" Daniel held back while Matthew opened the door for Molly to slide in. "The engine sounds rough. It's kind of old, isn't it?"

"So are you." RaeAnne looked Daniel over. "You sit up front with me."

"I'm not old." Red blossomed and spread over his face. "I don't think I should—"

"I'll sit up front." Matthew hiked around the car and jerked open the passenger door. "Let's go."

After the introductions, conversation drifted away. RaeAnne concentrated on the road and Matthew concentrated on praying he would

319

have the words to convince Adah to come home. For a teenage girl, RaeAnne seemed pretty capable of keeping her mouth shut and her gaze on the road. Again a surprise. Maybe because she didn't know any of them. Or maybe because she didn't have that much experience driving on the highway. Not a comforting thought. He added getting to Branson safely to his prayers.

And back.

With Adah in the car with them.

The scenery whooshed by in a whir that left him a little dizzy, as did the smell of RaeAnne's perfume with its fake flowery scent. The only other noise was the crackle of a radio that didn't seem to be able to find a station and Molly's gentle snore as she slumbered, head propped against her window. True to form, his sister could sleep anywhere, anytime.

"Do you know what you'll say?" RaeAnne broke the silence for the first time in more than an hour. "To your girlfriend."

"What did your parents say about you driving to Branson?" Matthew didn't see any reason to share those thoughts with this girl. "You did talk to them, didn't you?"

"I left a note."

Matthew snorted and concentrated on scenery that gave way to limestone rock walls and billboards of musicians he'd never heard of. "Like Adah did to her parents."

"I'm coming back."

"So's Adah."

"She hasn't yet."

"Maybe she doesn't have a way."

"Haven't you ever heard of the bus?" RaeAnne drilled him with a quick frown and returned her gaze to the road. "You really think my brother would leave her stranded?"

"I don't know. I don't know your brother."

"He may be a lady's man, but he's a gentleman, if you know what I mean."

"I don't."

"He's one of the good guys."

"He's Englisch."

"What?"

Matthew searched for the right words. "Like you said it would be a mistake for your brother to get tangled up with an Amish girl, the same is true for Adah. It's a mistake to get tangled up with a—"

"Guys like my brother."

"Any Englisch man. Like you said, we believe in sticking to our own kind."

"Apparently Adah didn't get that message."

Apparently not.

"Sorry, I'm not usually so mean."

"It's okay. You're right." Matthew rummaged in the cooler wedged between them and brought out a root beer. "Would you like one?"

"No thanks. I don't want to have to stop for a bathroom."

Embarrassment heating his neck and face, Matthew turned back to the window.

"You guys are really old fashioned, aren't you?"

"If that means we stand by our traditions, then yes, I guess."

"Why?"

"Why what?"

"Why do you dress like that and drive buggies and give up electricity?"

"We didn't give up electricity. We never had it." Matthew took a sip of his pop, searching for words. "We hold ourselves apart from the world so we won't be like it."

"The world's so bad?"

"If it keeps us from focusing on God and His plan for us, yes."

"So Adah singing in Branson is bad."

"If it takes her further from God, yes."

"Wow."

She had no idea.

"What if she doesn't want to come back?"

"We'll convince her."

"Why's it so important to you? Why would you chase after a girl who dumped you for some sweet-talking guy with a guitar?" RaeAnne snapped her gum as if to punctuate her disbelief. "Don't you have any pride? You're never gonna be able to beat a guy with a band. She's like a groupie by now."

"It's not about me." Matthew tried to ignore the way her words hit him like stones battering his face and chest. "Or my pride."

"Then what is it?"

"It's about Adah's life." Would this Englisch girl understand about eternal life and salvation? He had no idea what her family believed. "It's about choosing God over things that aren't important."

RaeAnne beat her hand against the steering wheel in time to the scratchy, static-filled song on the radio. "So Adah needs to pick God instead of Jackson."

"Something like that."

"But she can pick you and still be right with God."

Matthew swallowed. God's will. God's plan. "I hope so."

"Lucky for you."

He didn't believe in luck, but he hoped she was right. "I don't expect you to understand."

"Good, because I don't." RaeAnne wiggled in her seat and leaned forward as if she were having trouble seeing. "But it doesn't matter, as long as we both get what we want."

Not what he wanted. What God wanted. Matthew had to keep reminding himself of that important fact. *I'm sorry, Gott. Help me get this right. Your will, not mine.*

"Are we almost there?" Daniel piped up from the backseat. Matthew thought he'd been sleeping too.

"No, go back to sleep." RaeAnne sounded like his mother. She nodded at Matthew and returned her gaze to the road. "You too. You don't have to stay awake on my account."

"I'd rather stay awake." He settled against the seat, determined to help her to stay alert. He wouldn't sleep until Adah was safe. "For however long it takes."

Chapter 42

Adah smoothed the folds of the apron and laid it in the tattered duffle bag. It only took her a few minutes to pack her things. She hadn't accumulated much in the few months she'd been in Branson. She regretted not being able to return her work apron to the coffee shop before she left. The experience with the Dillon sisters, those revealing moments on the sidewalk, told her she couldn't wait. She and Jackson hadn't attempted to speak on the trip back to the house. He hadn't even turned on the radio. The silence had vibrated with words already spoken, feelings bared, emotions poured out. Everything had been said. More than said.

She had to go home. Today. Now. Staying here would only be a constant reminder to Jackson that she wasn't the girl he wanted her to be. Adah smoothed the silky material of the pink Western shirt with its white piping around the pockets and the sparkling pink and white rhinestones and shiny snaps. Maybe Jackson could return it to the store and get his money. She fingered the denim jeans. She'd never even tried them on. Sighing, she laid them aside and zipped up the half-empty bag.

Captain, who hadn't left her side since she hopped from the truck and ran into the house, lifted his head and whined, his expression troubled.

"You should be downstairs." She patted his head and scratched behind his ears, eliciting another soft whine in the back of the dog's throat. It sounded like she felt. "Jackson needs you more than I do. Come on."

He got to his feet and hobbled to the door, then stopped and looked back, his ears lifted, nose up. She hoisted her bag to her shoulder. "I'm coming."

She took one last look around. RaeAnne wouldn't be able to tell anyone had used her room. Everything remained exactly as Adah had found it. The posters of horses, the Nancy Drew mysteries on the bookshelves, the checkered bedspread on the four-poster canopy bed. The only changes were to herself. She knew this wasn't her world. She missed her family and her home and her life with an ache so big her entire body hurt. Uncertainty magnified the ache. Would they take her back?

They would. Mudder and Daed would forgive her and take her back. That was what Plain families did. They would want her back for her sake, no matter how much pain she'd caused them. They would want her to be baptized and become a full-fledged member of the district.

Matthew, on the other hand, would forgive her, but whether he would take her back...well, that remained to be seen.

She drew a deep breath and exhaled. Time to find out. She shut the door and marched down the stairs, aware of the thud of her sneakers against the carpet and her damp hand as it slid down the smooth, varnished banister. Captain led the way, occasionally looking back as if to say *Come on, get it over with.*

Time to go.

Time to face the consequences.

Time to say goodbye to Jackson.

The pain of that thought made her want to run back up the stairs. Saying goodbye would cause him pain and she'd never wanted to do that. Best to do it quick.

The sound of music blaring from the living room stopped her midway down the stairs. Captain paused at the bottom and swiveled his head to look back. Her hand tightened on the banister. Jackson had wasted no time mourning what had happened earlier in the day. His friends were back. Another jam session. She didn't want to do this in front of his newfound friends or jamming buddies. She listened, her heart jabbering away in her chest, telling her to run back up the stairs, not to do this, not to him, not now. Let him enjoy the music. It sounded so good. Really good.

He could do this without her. Easy. He was good. He'd chained himself to a girl who would never make it in this world. He needed to go on without her.

No turning back now.

She breathed, clomped down the remaining stairs, and marched into the living room. Jackson sat in his usual place on the couch, his guitar on his knees, a cigarette dangling from his lip. Two men and a woman she didn't recognize occupied the rest of the chairs in the room. The woman tucked a fiddle under her chin and leaned forward, her elbow held high, her eyes closed, expression rapturous, as she plied the bow up and down, back and forth in a vigorous, gorgeous outpouring of high, tight notes that sounded like a woman crying—first deep sobbing, then high-pitched wailing. A sad, sad song.

Next to her, one man played a bass guitar, the other a mandolin. Their picking sped up, then eased off, up and down, back and forth in perfect harmony.

Adah stopped, transfixed as each note danced across her skin, raising goose bumps in its wake. No one sang. No lyrics? She could already hear words in her head, attaching themselves to the notes.

Jackson looked up at her, his expression oblique. His strumming came to an abrupt halt. He took the cigarette from his lip, took a long drag, and let the smoke stream from his nostrils. The others stopped. They seemed to come awake as if startled from a dream. The room became utterly silent.

Jackson picked up a beer bottle from a coffee table dotted with bottles and overflowing ashtrays, took a long swallow, and slapped the bottle down with a crack against the wood.

He plucked a note as if he would continue to play with her standing there, knowing she had something to say. Maybe the only way they could communicate was through the music. What did that last song say? It said *I hurt*. It said *The pain is too much*. It said *Don't go*.

She had to go or more pain would follow. "Can I talk to you for a second?"

He stubbed his cigarette in the closest ashtray. Ashes and butts spilled onto the polished oak. "What's with the duffel bag?"

She glanced at the other folks. The woman smiled and waved the bow in the air. Her poufy white-blond curls bounced. "I'm Darla."

"Adah." She nodded at the men who grinned in unison, but didn't speak. They were twins with teeth so bleached white they couldn't possibly be real. She focused on Jackson. "I really need to talk to you outside. On the porch."

He leaned the guitar against the couch. "Sorry, guys, I'm done for the day. I hear a fishing rod calling my name. Let's give it a shot again tomorrow, okay?"

The two men stood without speaking. Darla shrugged and laid her fiddle in a carrying case at her feet. "Whenever, babe, just let us know. You're on to something with that last riff."

Babe?

Jackson shrugged. "Yeah, we'll see."

"We'll let ourselves out the front. You go make up with your girlfriend."

"She's not my girlfriend." Jackson's voice dropped on the last word. His Adam's apple bobbed. "She's a guest."

Darla turned away, but not before Adah saw the delighted smile spread across her face. She had red lipstick on her teeth.

Ignoring the pinprick of something like jealousy—jealousy she had no right to feel—Adah headed to the back door, Captain padding behind her. She hoped Jackson did the same. On the porch she gazed at the lake, absorbing the view one last time. Such beauty in the midst of such disharmony.

"What's going on?" Jackson stuffed his hands into the pockets of his jean shorts. "What's with the bag?"

She faced him. "I'm going home. I've saved enough money for my bus fare, but I need a ride to the station." The words came out in a rush and picked up speed as his expression darkened. "I thought you might do me the favor."

"No, no." He shook his head. One hand jerked from his pocket and he slammed his palm against the porch column with a force that made her stumble back two steps. "You can't go. You had a bad day. It'll get better. We're just getting started."

"You're just getting started. It's obvious this isn't for me." Adah sought words to explain. "I belong with my family, with my folks."

"Your church, you mean."

"I mean performing isn't for me. This dream isn't as important as my faith or my family. You'll do better without me." She waved a hand toward the house. "You already are."

"Faith and performing are not mutually exclusive."

"They are for me."

He moved into her space. The anger and bluster disappeared, replaced with an expression that reminded Adah of her little brother when he didn't get the hunting rifle he so hoped would be his for Christmas. "Don't go."

"I can't stay here. I don't belong."

"You're not trying." His voice rose again, the anger overtaking him. "You don't practice. You stopped writing lyrics."

"The words are gone. Completely gone. My joy is gone." Adah paused a beat, determined to still the trembling in her voice. "I can't. I can't play or sing or dress for you."

"Because if you did change for me, you would have to admit you love me."

"You shouldn't have to change yourself for a person." Adah chewed on her lip until she could force the tears back. She breathed in and out. "I'm sorry, but I don't love you."

"You do too. I can see it on your face."

"What you see is a kindred spirit. We have something in common. It has to do with the words we hear in our heads." She gripped her hands in front of her, trying to calm the shaking that spread to her whole body. "That's not the same as love."

"The feeling that goes with those words is love." His voice cracked on the last word. "Deny it all you want, but it's love."

"I'm sorry. I can't." She picked up the duffel bag. She'd been wrong to ask him for a ride. It poured salt in his open wound. "I'm going. It's better if we say goodbye here."

"You think you can quit. You can't. Songwriting is an addiction for you. Just like it is for me. We're addicted."

"That's silly."

"Is it?" He gripped the porch railing so hard the blood vessels stood out on his forearms. "You tried to quit and couldn't. That's why you got in that truck and came to Branson with me. You couldn't quit. That's the definition of addiction."

"I'm quitting now. For good."

"You're running away like a scared chicken."

"I'm running home to face the people I love and ask their forgiveness for hurting them more than I can bear to think of. There's nothing chicken about that."

His lips twisted in a bitter smile. "Fine. Fine. I'll give you a ride."

"I shouldn't have asked you. I'm sorry. Go back to your jam session. I'll get there on my own."

"You can't walk to the bus station. I'll take you."

"No. You'll spend the whole time trying to convince me to stay."

He turned his back on her. His shoulders heaved. "Go on, then. Go."

"Jackson, I want you to know I do care for you. I hope you get your dream. I hope you get everything you're working toward." He didn't turn around. Somehow that made it easier for Adah to say the words. "Thank you for trying. Thank you for believing in me and giving me a chance to have my dream."

"Just go." His voice broke. "Please."

He threw open the screen door so hard it smacked against the wall. Adah jumped. He stomped through it, and let it slam behind him. Captain barked once, a loud objection. Adah jumped again.

"Jackson." She swallowed tears that burned and ached in her throat. "Goodbye."

She ran down the steps, driven by thoughts that whirled round and round in her head. She hadn't expected it to hurt so much. *I'm sorry. I'm sorry. I'm sorry.*

After a few yards, she realized Captain followed. She stopped. "No, no, you have to go back. You have to stay." Captain halted, panting as hard as she was. "Stay!"

The dog woofed, his expression puzzled. He looked a lot like his owner in that moment.

"Stay." She fought to make her voice deeper, more commanding. "You can't go."

Her voice broke. Squatting, she dropped her bag, threw her arms around the dog, and buried her head in his thick, soft fur. "I'm sorry. You can't go. I can't stay and you can't go."

Wiping at her face with the back of her hand, she stood and gave him a gentle push. "Go on, Jackson needs you. Go on. Go home. Go to Jackson."

Captain cocked his head, snorted, turned in that painful, awkward way he had, and hobbled home.

"Good boy," she whispered. "Good boy."

Time to go home for everyone. *Gott, forgive me. Please forgive me.*

The words of contrition rushed from every pore as she trudged down the dirt road, dust billowing under her sneakers, turning them gray. If it weren't for the need to get to the bus station and get started on the journey home as quickly as possible, she would've dropped to her knees and bowed her head. If it weren't for the burden of her bag, she would've thrown her arms up, begging for mercy. The words in her head took on a melody and began to sing of their own accord in her head. Singing for mercy. Singing for grace. Singing for her very life. The only life she truly wanted or needed.

Forgive me. Forgive me. Forgive me.

The more the words repeated, the less she saw Jackson's face. The jut of his jaw as he tried to control his emotions. The liquid blue of his eyes under that dark hair. The way he looked at her when he said *I love you.*

She loved him too, but not the way he wanted.

For him, she was truly sorry. For the hurt she caused him, she begged forgiveness. Over and over again.

By the time she hit the road to Branson, the bag bit into her shoulder, the bodice of her dress was soaked in sweat, and her head ached from the blinding light of the sun. And her emotions. She continued to pick up one foot and then the other. A mile. Then another. Sweat ran down her forehead and burned her eyes. Her feet ached and her mouth grew so parched her tongue stuck to the roof of her mouth.

Frightening as the idea seemed, she stuck her thumb out, hoping someone nice would stop.

Would she be able to tell if they were nice? Did only nice people drive minivans?

A brazen honk shook her from her reverie. She lifted her hand to her forehead to shield her eyes from the sun. Charlene's VW bug rolled to a stop several yards beyond her and began to back up.

"Are you crazy, girl?" Charlene ground the gears and brought the bug to a halt as she yelled through the window. "Didn't your parents teach you right? I'd paddle any child of mine who hitchhiked."

"I was tired of walking."

"Ever hear of a taxi?"

"Taxis cost money. I have just enough for my bus ticket home."

Charlene sighed, an exaggerated loud sigh. "Because you gave me next month's rent yesterday. If you were leaving, why pay for the rent?"

"Because I didn't know yesterday."

Charlene jerked her head toward the interior. "Get in."

Adah did as she was told, fighting tears as she sank into the seat and felt the delicious chill of the air conditioned interior on her face.

"That nephew of mine is no gentleman."

"He would've given me a ride, but I didn't want him to." She might not have been able to leave had he come with her. "I didn't want him to have to do it, knowing how much he wanted me to stay. It seemed cruel."

"So you decided to walk fifteen miles instead." Charlene wheeled the car around and headed to Branson. "Don't you worry. Stick with Aunt Charlene and you'll be home in no time."

Adah didn't know if that was a good or a bad thing, but it was time she found out.

Chapter 43

When the Hart house came into view on the edge of a lake that shivered in the sun now hanging low in the west, Matthew straightened in his seat, simultaneously relieved they'd made it despite RaeAnne's driving and shot through with adrenaline at what came next. After months, he would finally be face to face with Adah. What the rest of his life would look like hung in the balance, shifting one way and then the other as he chose the words he hoped would convince her to come home.

Molly and Daniel stirred in the backseat. Molly leaned forward. "This is it? It's very pretty. I like lakes."

"Molly, we're not here to talk about the lake. We need…"

The sentence died in his throat. A figure sauntered across the grass in the distance, carrying a fishing pole and a line heavy with freshly caught fish. Jackson Hart. His chest and feet were bare. A pair of jean shorts rode down on his hips. From the looks of him, he'd been spending his time lounging in the sun getting a tan. Half-naked.

Jackson strolled a few more feet and slowed. He'd seen the car. After a minute, he veered in their direction.

So this was the man with whom Adah had been spending all her time. The one who had kissed her. Had he kissed her again? No wonder she had only written Matthew one letter. Matthew gripped the door handle and tried to lasso his anger to the ground. Even as he did, he recognized the overpowering emotion boiling inside him was not anger. Hurt joined together with jealousy in a bitter brew that burned his throat.

I'm sorry, God.

A bigger man would not let jealousy stand in the way of what was right and good.

"It's Jackson." RaeAnne shoved open her door. "Jackson!"

Jackson's somber expression disappeared, swallowed by a grin. "Hey, sis. You're a sight for sore eyes. What are you doing here?"

Matthew swiveled toward the backseat. "Molly, stay in the car."

"But I want to—"

"Stay in the car."

He opened his door and stood, the muscles in his legs cramped and weak. From the long ride. Not emotion. For the first time, he was aware of his sweaty shirt stuck to his back and the faded material of work pants that had seen better days. He pulled his straw hat down on his forehead and shut the door with a gentle shove.

Daniel had his door open. They exchanged glances over the roof of the car. Daniel bent down again and spoke to Molly through the open back window. "Let Matthew talk to him first. If Adah's here, you can talk to her inside."

Inside away from Jackson Hart with his bare chest for all the world to see. Conceit? Or indifference to what the world thought?

RaeAnne shot across the yard and threw her arms around Jackson. He staggered back a step. The dog raced around the two of them, barking wildly. "Hush up, Cap, hush! Hey, hey, you'll make me drop the fish." His gaze connected with Matthew's and the smile disappeared as it wandered to Daniel. He disentangled himself from his sister's arms. "What are they doing here with you?"

"They hired me to drive them up here."

"You? They really are crazy. Don't they know you flunked your driver's test? Do Mom and Dad know?"

"They came for Adah." RaeAnne ignored the questions. "Where is she? Is she in the house? Shall I go get her? She's gonna freak when she sees them. This is Matthew, her—"

"Shut up." Jackson handed the fish to his sister and tossed the rod in the grass. "I know who he is."

"And I'm her brother." Daniel stepped up so he stood next to Matthew. "I came for my sister."

A blank expression stole all emotion from Jackson's face. He crossed the yard so he stood directly in front of Matthew as if Daniel's presence meant nothing to him. "She's not here."

Of all the things Matthew had expected him to say, this wasn't one of them.

"Your mother said she came here with you," Daniel pressed. "She said your dad—"

"I said she's not here."

Matthew put a hand on Daniel's arm. He jerked away, his face the color of beets. "Where is she?"

"I'm Molly, Matthew's sister. Adah's a friend of mine. She needs her family." To Matthew's chagrin, Molly had slipped from the car. She walked right past him and into Jackson's path. "She needs her faith. She can't be baptized in her faith if she doesn't come home. Do you want that for her?"

Conflicting emotions shot across Jackson's face. Matthew recognized the same emotions he'd been feeling all summer long. Frustration. Longing. Anger. Hurt. Jackson licked lips cracked and dry from the sun. He knelt and wrapped an arm around the dog, who kept yipping and attacking his owner's face with a long, pink tongue. "Like I said, she's not here." He rubbed between the dog's ears. "Truth be told she left. You just missed her."

Molly reached down and gave the dog a pet. "That must be awful hard for you."

Jackson stood and tucked his thumbs in the belt loops of his shorts. His dark, whiskered chin came up. "You don't know nothing about me."

"Like I said, I know Adah." Molly's voice was soft and sweet. Matthew felt his own anger drain away. All the pent-up emotion of the long summer receded. Molly had a way about her. Richard Bontrager was a lucky man. "If she came here with you it was because she trusted you and she thought you were a good person."

The bravado drained from the man's face. For the first time, the dark circles around his eyes and the strain around his mouth registered. Jackson hadn't slept in a while. He looked like Matthew felt. "I also know some things about Adah."

He'd known Adah one summer. Matthew had known her all his life. "What's that?"

"She's a songbird. You can put a songbird in a cage, but you can't keep her from singing."

"The question is whether Branson is the cage or New Hope."

"I know."

"You know?"

"Why do you think I let her go?" The question hung between them for a few seconds. "If you're gonna catch her, you better hurry."

"Catch her?"

"She went to the bus station. RaeAnne knows how to get there."

"Thank you." Matthew touched the brim of his hat, wishing he knew what to say to this man. The pain carved on his face looked so familiar. "Sorry."

"The best man won."

"It wasn't a game. No one wins."

"I know." Jackson slid his hand in his pocket and pulled out a folded piece of paper, white against the dark tan of his fingers. "Do me a favor. Give this to her."

His voice cracked. He flung it at Matthew and brushed past him without looking back.

Matthew grasped the paper, feeling as if he held a sharp sword. "What is it?"

"One last song." Jackson kept walking, the dog following along after him. "For her."

Matthew let his fingers close around it, tightening until the paper crumpled.

Adah had all the songs she needed.

Chapter 44

Adah smoothed the bus ticket. If she kept crumpling it with her sweaty hands the driver wouldn't be able to read it. The incessant hum of people talking and the periodic burst of singsong words over the loudspeaker made her head ache. The air in the bus station was rank with the stale smell of people and dust and old food. She wiggled on the hard plastic seat, wishing Charlene would go home. She'd been sitting by her side for over an hour. Everything had been said already. Charlene could go back to her house and give some comfort to her nephew.

"Stop fidgeting, girl, you're making me crazy." Charlene crossed her arms over her ample chest. "It'll be all right."

"Of course it won't." Adah immediately regretted her tart tone and surly words. "I know you're trying to make me feel better, but it'll take a lot more than words to make this right."

"You already took the first steps. Saying goodbye to Jackson and buying that ticket—you're already back on track."

She didn't know Daed. Or Matthew. Would either of them take her back? If Matthew wanted her back, why hadn't he come for her? Maybe Luke had told him not to. In all likelihood she would have to meet with Luke and Thomas and make amends for her behavior, even though she was still in her rumspringa. She would do it, do anything necessary to sit on the bench on Sunday morning and to sing those familiar hymns with her family and her community. To have joy in her song again.

"You're right. I'm just a little nervous." She managed a weak smile. "You really don't have to stay. I'll be fine."

"You said that three times already. That nephew of mine may be a stubborn fool, but I'm not the type of person who lets a young woman like you wait at the bus station by herself."

"I'll be fine."

"I know you will. You got guts, girl."

"If I had guts I would stay and sing with the Dillon sisters."

"No. No, it takes way more guts to go home and admit you were wrong and ask your family to forgive you."

"My family will forgive me." Adah swallowed the tears this statement wrung from her. "That's what we do. We forgive. God calls us to forgive."

"Then why are you so worried about your young man?"

"He's not my young man anymore." She clutched her bag to her chest as if it could warm the cold loneliness of this truth. "He might forgive, but that doesn't mean he'll risk being hurt again."

"I don't know about that. He looks prepared to forgive to me."

"What do you mean?"

"There aren't a whole lot of Amish men running around Branson, especially handsome ones like this particular young man." Charlene cocked her head. "I can see why you're smitten. Jackson really didn't have a chance."

Adah swiveled. In that moment, her breath ran away from her. She couldn't swallow. Her hands fluttered as if going somewhere. She tried to corral them. She stood, but sat down again when she realized her legs wouldn't hold her.

"I take it I'm right. So that's Matthew."

Adah nodded and remembered to close her mouth, finally.

Charlene stood and held out a hand. "Matthew, I'm Charlene. Pleased to meet you." They shook. She relinquished his hand and patted Adah's shoulder. "I reckon I can leave you now. You'll get home for sure, one way or the other."

She bent and kissed Adah's forehead. "It was a pleasure knowing you, Adah Knepp. Take care."

"Take care," Adah whispered, but Charlene had already turned away. Adah would've given anything to get her to stay for a minute or two longer. Until she found her words and her voice.

Matthew seemed to have the same dilemma. He stared at his boots for a few seconds and then raised his head to meet her gaze. His jaw worked. "I didn't imagine having this talk here." He glanced around. "With so many people around."

She nodded. Her fingers ached from gripping them together. She tried to loosen them. Nothing happened. "I wanted to talk to you too." The words came out in a hoarse garble. "I meant to talk to you first thing."

"First thing?"

"When I got home." She held up her ticket. "My bus comes in a few minutes."

A voice burst forth over the loud speakers, announcing her bus had begun boarding.

"It's here, I mean, now."

The words came out in a stutter and her voice trailed away as if she had no control over it.

"You need to get a refund."

"I do?"

He nodded.

She waited.

He shoved his hat back and stared at the floor.

"What are you doing here?"

"Jackson said you were coming here. How come he didn't bring you?"

He'd talked to Jackson. Adah squashed the selfish thought that she was glad she hadn't been there for that talk. "I didn't want to put him out any more than I already had."

She didn't want to give him any more time to try to convince her to stay. Any more time to stare at her with mournful, accusing eyes. Any more time to make her feel horribly guilty for doing what was right, even at the cost of his heart. "I figure I can make my own way."

"That's obvious."

The curtness of his tone jerked her from reliving the painful farewell with Jackson.

"Where's Elizabeth?"

"The Gringriches have moved onto their own farm."

"That's not what I meant."

"Elizabeth's not for me." Matthew's jaw pulsed as he gritted his teeth. "You jumped ahead like you always do."

"So I have no one to blame but myself for this mess." She'd seen them together and ran away without giving him a chance to explain. All this heartache and it was her fault. "Why did you come?"

He raised his head and met her gaze. "I can't. Not here. Too many people."

She stood. This time her legs held. "Is someone waiting for you?"

"Molly and Daniel are in the car with RaeAnne."

"RaeAnne." For the first time she saw a glimmer of humor in the situation. "How did she get here?"

Matthew must've seen the same glimmer. His expression eased. "She drove us. In a very old, very beat-up station wagon. Apparently without a driver's license."

"Will they wait while we take a walk?"

"They'll wait."

She threaded her way between an elderly couple pulling suitcases on wheels and a family with crying, rosy-cheeked twins in a double stroller. "It's not much for pretty scenery like we have back home, but at least the air is fresher."

Not speaking, he held the door for her. The bright sunlight blinded her at first. She stumbled on the sidewalk. Matthew's hand steadied her, his grip almost bruising.

"Danki."

His hand dropped. They walked half a block before he spoke. "Did you find what you're looking for here?"

"Nee."

Tires screeched and horns dueled. Matthew's pace picked up. Adah tried to match his stride. After a half a block, she gave up, slowed, and waited for him to notice. He glanced back and stopped. "Did you learn anything?"

She covered the ground between them, searching for and gathering up the words she needed like flower petals that had been flung about by the wind. "I found out that a strong and steady flame is better than a flash fire that can't be controlled."

"I don't know what that means."

"I know, but I do."

"I can't write you songs."

The hollowness of his voice told her how much he regretted not being able to give her what he thought she most wanted. "I don't need songs from you."

"I came here to say my piece."

"Sorry."

"I hope you'll forgive me."

Forgive him? "For what?"

"For not fighting harder for you. Groossdaadi says a man has to pick a fraa who has a voice he can listen to for fifty years. I could listen to yours for a hundred years and not get tired of it."

"Matthew—"

"You can always sing for me. I hope that will be enough for you." He cleared his throat. "God's song is the only one that counts. He writes a song for each one of us. If we don't choose His song, our lives are empty of His music."

"I know."

He stopped walking. "You know?"

"That's what I was coming home to tell you. I was coming home to tell you that you were right. I was wrong. I didn't expect you to take me back, but I wanted to tell you that."

"You were wrong?"

"I'm not saying there's anything wrong with the music Jackson and I make—made." Adah faced Matthew in the middle of a sidewalk steaming with heat, the rumble of car engines threatening to drown out their words. "Music is fine unless you set it up on a pedestal and worship it instead of God. That's what I've done. I couldn't figure out why I couldn't sing in front of all those folks."

She paused, hoping he would see and understand and believe her. His expression said he was trying. "Then I realized God had taken my joy. He took it because I no longer deserved it. I made an idol of my music. I wanted it more than I wanted God. I was willing to give up everything for it. My family. My faith. You."

"And now?"

"Now, I see. It's as if the blinders have been ripped off. It's all wrong. This is wrong." She swept her hand through the air in a wide flourish toward the crowded Branson street. "For me, it's wrong. I'm not judging anyone else. I love to hear this music. But I won't let it stand in the way of God's plan for me."

"I'm glad."

"You don't seem to be." Maybe he came because they made him. Not because he wanted to bring her back to his side. "You look disappointed."

"More discombobulated. I came here to convince you to come back. And I find I don't have to do that." His dark eyes glowed in the sunlight. His Adam's apple bobbed. "I'm happy about that."

"Happy for me or happy for you?"

He took a step closer. "Both."

Adah edged closer yet. "You'll still have me?" She whispered, afraid her words would break the connection that held them together like a thin, fragile thread. "After all this?"

"I don't know how to be without you."

"You don't?"

He shook his head. "Nee."

"Me neither."

"What about Jackson Hart?"

She held perfectly still, waiting for the words to come that would make Matthew understand. "We're too much alike. We both run ahead of ourselves. There's no balance. We'll topple each other over. There's a woman out there somewhere who's right for him. One who can help him with his dreams. It can't be me."

"What about songwriting?"

"I think I'll always write songs. That's how I figure out how I feel and what I want to say to God."

"To me songs and music are mostly noise."

"I know."

"I reckon there's music in the silence too."

"I know, but in my head, I put words to the silence."

"So you can't stop?"

She listened in her heart and in her head. The words that always milled about inside her were still there. But they no longer pushed and shoved, all sharp edges and pinpricks. "I told Jackson I could, but now I realize I don't want to quit singing or writing songs. I look forward to singing to my kinner someday. I want to sing praises to my Lord and Savior. Only music that pleases Him."

Matthew heaved a sigh so great he sounded as if he'd just run a race. He grabbed her hand, his grip so tight it hurt. "Matthew!"

The grip loosened, but he didn't let go. "I've already been baptized."

"I figured."

"New classes start in January."

"I hope to be there, Gott willing."

He ducked his head.

"Is there something else?"

"Jackson gave me something to give to you." He held out a wrinkled, folded piece of paper. "I considered throwing it away, but that seemed cowardly."

She plucked the paper from the palm of his hand, held it against her chest for a second, and stuck it in her bag.

"Aren't you going to read it?"

"No. I know what it is."

"How can you know?"

"Jackson is Jackson. It's a song. That's how we talk to each other best. Sometimes the only way we can tell each other what we mean."

"You don't want to know what he's saying?"

"I expect someday I'll walk into the Five and Dime and hear him singing it on the radio. I'll remember back to this summer and the songs we wrote and we sang and it'll make me smile. I hope."

"That's all, smile? You won't regret it?"

"Maybe some."

Matthew was silent for several long seconds. Her words must have cut him to the bone. Adah rushed to assure him. "That doesn't mean—"

"Are you sure you want to give it up?"

"I'm sure. The songs aren't enough. They're not what makes a bond between a woman and a man. It takes more—like family and faith and wanting the same things in life."

"You won't miss it—him?"

"Nee. Not like I miss home. Not like I miss Mudder and Daed—jah, even him—and the kinner. Not like I miss you."

Matthew stared down at her. His emotions flitted across his face, one by one, until something like hope remained. She waited, letting him make the decision. *Please, Gott.*

He bent his head and leaned into her. She stretched on her tiptoes, reaching for him. His lips touched hers. His long, thin fingers brushed her cheeks and trailed down her neck in a touch so soft she shivered. The kiss lasted only a few seconds, but the emotions it sparked were like stars that flung themselves across the sky, burning away the memory of another day and another kiss that came too soon and left only regret as a memory.

This was their dream. Hers and Matthews. Their Plain love song. A song they would sing together for the rest of their lives.

Epilogue

Unable to gather much forward momentum, such was her girth, Adah waddled across the sidewalk to the restaurant door. She slowed, giggled, and rubbed her swollen belly with both hands. "She's kicking."

"You keep saying *she*." Matthew opened the door to Tom's Steakhouse and held it for Adah to pass through first. "How do you know it's not a boy? It's a fifty-fifty chance."

"Feels like a girl to me." Inhaling the mouthwatering scent of frying chicken and hamburgers, Adah waved to Eve, the restaurant hostess, who strolled toward them, a stack of oversized menus covered in plastic nestled in the crook of her arm. "We'll know soon enough, I expect."

"The sooner the better." Matthew's hand came up toward Adah's elbow, but he didn't touch her. Not in a crowded restaurant. "I mean, Gott willing."

Adah hoped so too. On God's time, but her aching back couldn't take much more of this. Nor her longing to hold this baby in her arms. To see if she had Matthew's eyes or her chin. To count her fingers and toes and hold her close so she could get a whiff of her baby smell. She might tease Matthew about it being a girl, but she really didn't care. Girl or boy, all she wanted was a healthy baby.

"Hey, you two, follow me." Eve pivoted and pointed to an empty table near the front windows. "No way you're fitting into a booth.

Better have a table. You can push the chair out. That baby looks like it was due yesterday."

Adah felt heat creep up her neck and spread to her cheeks. Plain folks didn't discuss such things outside the family, but Eve was right. No way could she squeeze into a booth. Any day now this baby would make an appearance. She couldn't wait. Their little house would be perfect with the addition of a baby's squalls and smells. She followed Eve to the table and plopped down across from Matthew, who opened a menu, even though he would order what he always did on these rare occasions when they splurged on supper out. He'd surprised her with the suggestion, saying it would be the last time in a long time. Once the baby came, they wouldn't be coming to town together—not for a long while.

"A T-bone sounds good." He closed the menu. "I could eat a whole cow."

Adah smiled to herself behind her menu. "I suppose you'll have a salad with green goddess dressing and extra croutons and a baked potato with all the trimmings."

"What's so funny? So what if I will?"

"What do you need a menu for?"

They both laughed and then lapsed into a silence Adah found comfortable. She never had to rummage for conversation with Matthew. She loved that about him. He was comfortable with silence. They sat together in the evenings, she with her sewing, he with his crossword puzzles or his newspaper. Sometimes she'd look up to see him looking at her. He'd smile and go back to his newspaper without uttering a word, but looking so content it made her heart flutter with the unexpected enormity of her love for him.

At that moment, he smiled as if he knew what she was thinking. She smiled back and hid her face behind her menu again. Not that she wouldn't have her usual. Chicken fried steak with mashed potatoes and gravy and a side of corn and peach cobbler for dessert. Maybe a scoop of vanilla ice cream with it.

Music wafted through a speaker perched on a shelf over Adah's head. A familiar yet almost forgotten voice filled the air over the murmur of the other customers and the clink of silverware against thick white china plates. She paused, caught by the timbre that gave her goose bumps.

The other shoe dropped tonight
And I didn't even hear it hit the floor.
I was too busy writing a song
You couldn't hear,
Making up lyrics as I went along,
Thinking you'd be singing the same song.

The other shoe dropped tonight
And I didn't even hear it hit the floor.
It was lost in the sound of the slamming door
And the riot of two hearts that don't beat together anymore.

Adah's hand gripped the menu so hard it seemed the bones in her fingers might break. She inhaled a hiccup of air, thinking her lungs might stop working. She couldn't make herself look up.

"That's him, isn't it?" Matthew's voice rasped as if he'd suddenly come down with a cold. "That's Jackson singing the song he wrote for you, isn't it?"

She forced her gaze from the menu to his face. He didn't look mad. He cocked his head, his eyebrows raised, his expression bemused.

"It is."

As if in silent acquiescence, Matthew's mouth closed and he leaned back in his chair, hands resting in his lap. Adah breathed a sigh of relief. She wanted to hear it. God forgive her, she needed to hear it. She knew the words, but had sometimes wondered, as she worked in the garden, weeding, how it would sound. She had made up the tune in her head in those quiet times when she hung laundry on the line or kneaded bread for supper. Jackson had chosen riffs of a steel guitar, bass, fiddle, and drums, giving the song a dark, somber feel. She could almost see him sitting there in the banks of the lake, guitar in hand, head bent, fingers strumming as he wrote the song in his head.

I had this dream of two pairs of shoes
Lined up beside a bed covered
With a lilac quilt.
The color of your eyes
And the Missouri sky.
The shoes were black sneakers and cowboy boots.
Yours looking small next to mine.

I thought later maybe there'd be more,
Smaller sneakers and little pink cowboy boots with fringe
That shakes when she takes her first steps.

You told me you couldn't stay.
You told me you're going away.
Back to the place where things are easier,
Back to the place where no one
Looks at you strange.

Where you make bread and sew your dresses
On that treadle machine,
Your black sneakers
Pumping in time to the song in your head.

I was too busy writing a song you couldn't hear
Making up lyrics as I went along,
Thinking you'd be singing the same song.

The other shoe dropped tonight
And I didn't even hear it hit the floor.
It was lost in the sound of the slamming door.
And a heart not beating anymore.

Adah watched emotions flit across Matthew's face, knowing he did the same with her. He turned his fork over and over on the tablecloth, but his gaze never left hers. When the music died away, he sat back in his chair. "You read the piece of paper I gave you after all."

"I did. But not until later. After I was baptized. Not long before the wedding."

"Why then?"

"I wanted to make sure."

"Sure you didn't want to go back to him?"

"Not to him." She traced the pattern of flowers on the tablecloth, trying to find the words to explain something she couldn't even explain to herself. "To the songs."

"And?"

She smiled and relaxed into the chair. "What do you think, Matthew Troyer? I'm sitting here, aren't I?"

"No regrets?"

"No regrets."

He unfolded his napkin and laid it in his lap, his gaze still locked with hers. "I didn't tell you I saw RaeAnne Hart on the street the other day."

"Nee." She could only imagine why he hadn't brought up that subject. "I hope she's doing well."

"She's home from college on spring break. She informed me—without me asking—that her brother is living in Nashville and now he has a record deal and he's touring. Opening for some guy named Clayton Star."

"*Wunderbarr.*" She had no regrets and it helped that her leaving Branson had not changed the course of God's plan for Jackson. "I'm glad for him."

Matthew's somber gaze traced her features. He knew her so well. He would know she spoke only the truth. She chose to say no more, knowing he would read her thoughts on her face. Matthew straightened the fork and knife. "She says his first single is in the top forty on the country music charts. Whatever that means."

"It means he did good." Adah pointed to the speaker. "They're playing his song on the radio."

"A song he wrote about you."

She shrugged. "Having your heart broken gives you something to write about and people can relate to it."

"You broke his heart?"

"I think I may have. But I know I was right to leave. He proved to me over and over again that we were from two different worlds. He saw something between us that didn't exist. I belong here. He belongs in Nashville."

"What about the hymns I hear you singing when you're hanging laundry or pulling weeds in the garden? They don't come from the Ausbund."

"They're praises for Gott. I don't need for anyone else to hear them. Gott hears. Gott knows what's in my heart when I sing them."

"You're sure? No regrets?"

A pain radiated through her belly and back. She gasped. "Nee, not about that." Panting, she dropped her napkin on her plate and eased from her chair. The pain made it hard to straighten. "My only regret is I'll not have time to eat my chicken fried steak."

Matthew shot from his chair, knocking it into the table behind him. "Why? What's the matter?"

"Time to go." One hand on her back, she waddled toward the door. "We're having a baby."

He grabbed her elbow and gripped it hard. "We're having a baby." The words were like a joyful song written on Adah's heart.

Her joyful song had returned. As Matthew wrapped his arm around her shoulders and threw open the door, letting in the brilliant sun, Adah knew for certain. She'd never lose that joyful song again.

Discussion Questions

1. Adah recalls that her father told her the Amish in her community don't play instruments because it draws attention to the individual, saying "look at me, I'm special," instead of focusing on God. Many of us are taught from a young age to be competitive, to strive to be the best, to win, to stand out in a crowd, to use our God-given talents. What are the pros and cons of both attitudes? Can they coexist?

2. Jackson Hart finds it difficult to understand Adah's community's prohibition against musical instruments. Can you think of instances where an activity you participate in— while innocent in and of itself—leads you to do something you know you shouldn't have? Something that takes you farther from God?

3. We often admire people with special talents, such as musicians, actors, and professional athletes. Do you think there are times that this admiration amounts to adulation or even idolatry? Why do you think professional athletes make so much more money than teachers or firefighters or police officers or soldiers?

4. In the world's eyes, Adah's choice to leave her family and her home to pursue her dreams with Jackson in Branson might be seen as brave or adventuresome. We're often told as we grow up that we should pursue our dreams relentlessly. How do you think Adah's choice affected her family? Matthew? Her faith? Should she have told Matthew what she was doing and why before she left town? Why do you think she didn't?

5. Although idols and idolatry are often spoken of in the Bible, we don't talk about this sin much in modern society. What examples of idols (aside from people) do we often see? Is there something in your life that you feel is becoming too important? How is that manifested? How do we find a balance between what we want and what's good for us and what gives the glory to God?

6. What concrete ways do you use to make sure God is at the center of your life? What does the statement "Thy will be done" mean to you?

7. After she gets to Branson, Adah discovers she can't perform in public. She can't see herself wearing flashy clothes and makeup. She freezes in front of the microphone. To make her dream a reality, she would have to make herself into something she isn't. Did you ever have a dream only to realize you're not really cut out for becoming a professional basketball player or an opera singer? How did you deal with it?

8. Most of us may find the prohibition against performing in public and playing musical instruments hard to understand. Can you see how not participating in those activities knits Amish communities closer together? Do you see a danger in letting individuals shine at the expense of the group? Or would you argue, as Adah did, that a God-given talent is meant to be used for His glory? Can a quiet song for God's

ears only be the one performance Adah needs to give? Is a middle ground possible?

9. Adah decides she and Jackson are too much alike to ever be happy together. Is that a surprising conclusion, given her background as an Amish girl brought up in a conservative community and Jackson's wild ways as a musician? Do you think it's an astute assessment of her own willfulness? Could you imagine them living "happily ever after"?

10. Why (or why not) do you think Adah made the right choice when she returned to Matthew? Do you think they are more alike or different? In successful relationships, which is more important, in your estimation?

Check out an alternate ending to
*Adah's story at **www.kellyirvin.com**!*

Kelly Irvin is a Kansas native and has been writing professionally for 30 years. She and her husband, Tim, make their home in Texas. They have two children, three cats, and a tankful of fish. A public relations professional, Kelly is also the author of two romantic suspense novels and writes short stories in her spare time. To learn more about her work, visit www.kellyirvin.com.

To learn more about books by Kelly Irvin or
to read sample chapters, log on to our website:

www.harvesthousepublishers.com